# The Big Book of
# Dolls

**Mabs Tyler**

*Photographs by Gina Harris*
*Line drawings by Janine Kirwan*

The Dial Press    New York 1976

Library of Congress Cataloging in Publication Data

Tyler, Mabs.
    The big book of dolls

    1. Dollmaking.    1. Title
TT175.T9 1976 745. 59'22                    75-23222

    ISBN 0-8037-0580-8

First printing 1976

Printed in The Netherlands by Smeets Offset ◯ Weert

# Contents

# Introduction

All dolls in this book are very uncomplicated, easy-to-make ones. All kinds of fabrics and other materials can be used — most of them are inexpensive and many of them, like wire, card, cord, cartons, tubes etc., can be found at home along with remnants of fabric and trimmings for dressing the dolls. Instructions are included for soft, cuddly, conventional types made from fabrics such as felt and stockinette with a choice of clothes for the different sizes and for different occasions. You will also find puppets, comical clowns, dolls made from household materials, favourite nursery rhyme and fairy tale characters like Miss Muffet and her spider, and Jack and the Giant, and dolls for a Nativity scene. All the faces are simple — features are indicated by embroidery or appliqué-felt or are painted on with pens or crayons.

## HINTS FOR MAKING

### Grid System

The pattern for each toy is overlaid by a blue grid. Each square on this grid represents 1 in. To transfer the pattern, draw a grid of 1 in. squares. On this grid mark with dots where the lines of the drawing cross the lines of the blue grid. Join up the dots to get your pattern at full size.

There are two sizes of grid used in the book: ¼ in. and ½ in. Each is the equivalent of 1 in. on the final pattern, so that the ¼ in. grid has to be enlarged four times, and the ½ in. grid enlarged twice. You can, of course, make the toys larger than their intended size by drawing out your own grid of, say, 1½ or 2 in. squares.

### Hair

Here are some suggestions for creating different styles.

### Wool

**1.** Cut in short strands and sew across the forehead as a fringe. Fold other longer strands in half and sew in layers round the back of the head from side to side. Trim to the required length.

**2.** Lay longer strands across the head and sew down from forehead to nape. Trim to length and catch down in several places, stitching through the strands to hide the stitches.

**3.** As **2**, tied in bunches with a bow at each side of the face.

**4.** As **2**, plaited on each side of the face.

**5.** As **2**, drawn to the back and tied, or coiled in a chignon at the back of the head.

**6.** Sew in loops from top of head all round forehead, the loops sloping down the face at each side and round the back of the head.

**7.** Sew loops in twos or threes close together along the hair line and over the rest of the head.

**8.** Sew in single loops all over the head, and leave as loops or trim.

**9.** For a boy, sew alternate long and short stitches at each side of a parting, and fill in with straight stitches over the rest of the head.

### Felt

**10.** For a boy, shape to the head and cut in notches to resemble strands over the forehead and back of head.

**11.** Cut a narrow strip of felt in a fringe and sew along the forehead. Fringe some wider strips and sew in one or two layers round the head from cheek to cheek.

**12.** Sew coarse string (binder twine) across the head from shoulder to shoulder and knot the ends.

**13.** For an older doll, coil shiny string or cord round the head on the hair line in decreasing circles to cover the head, then form a 'bun'.

**14.** Cut fur or fur fabric to shape then seam.

**15.** Cut circles of felt in spirals and sew on by one end round the head to form curls.

**16.** Coil ricrac braid round and sew in

waves, or lay pieces across the head and finish at the nape.

17.     Cut the knitted fine welt of an old sock in a fringe, sew round the head on the hair line and trim.

18.     Use wire wool for a witch's hair.

### Features

1.     Embroider with coloured embroidery silks.

2.     Cut felt to shape and stick or sew on.

3.     Combine felt with embroidery.

4.     Draw on to suitable fabrics with felt tip pens or coloured crayons. Do not use this method on felt, and always test first on a spare piece of the fabric for smudging or running.

### Fabrics and other materials

Here are the characteristics and uses of some of the materials you will come across in this book.

**Felt**—compressed fibres, with no right or wrong side. Does not fray when cut.

**Fluffy pile fabric**—thick jersey weave.

**Interlining**—compressed fibres, in various thicknesses. Does not fray when cut and will take paint successfully.

**Fusible interlining**—irons on as a backing, stiffens and prevents fabrics from fraying.

**Wadding**—compressed fibres, flattened and enclosed in a thin skin. Used for padding.

**Kapok**—loose fluffy short fibres. Used for stuffing.

**Calico**—firm strong natural colour or white cotton, like sheeting.

**Crash**—coarse strongly woven unbleached linen type fabric.

**Poplin**—firm woven finer cotton with a smooth surface.

**Stockinette**—woven jersey fabric in wide tubular length.

**Cambric**—finely woven, soft, thin cotton fabric in white, natural and colours.

**Gingham**—firmly woven in plain, check, striped, or plaid patterns.

**Finger bandage**—tubular natural jersey weave in various narrow widths.

**Ricrac braid**—firmly woven cotton or silk braid with a wavy outline.

**Felt tip pens**—marker pens in many colours — thin fibre tips or thicker felt tips.

**Dowel rod**—thin, round, hard wooden rods, in various thicknesses and lengths.

**Pipe cleaners**—short lengths of thin wire covered with a short cotton pile.

**Pipe cleaner chenille**—obtainable in lengths of 10 ft. Pliable wire, covered in a thick fluffy pile, in white and colours.

**Lurex thread**—fine flat metal thread on spools, in gold, silver and colours.

**Bias binding**—narrow cross-cut tape with narrow turnings on each side.

## Stitches

### Joining stitches

**Running stitch**—small stitches taken through two thicknesses of fabric. Put the needle in and out in one motion, keeping the spaces the same length as the stitches.

**Stab stitch**—similar to running, but each stitch is made in two movements. Put needle in at front at right angles and then from back to front at right angles. Use to join thick fabrics like felt.

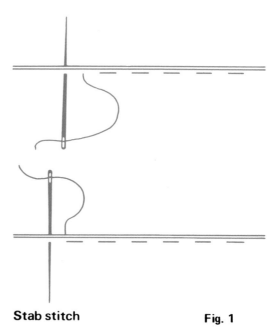

**Stab stitch**                      **Fig. 1**

**Oversewing**—insert the needle from back to front through the two edges of the fabric for every stitch.

**Double oversewing**—as oversewing but take two stitches into each place to give a zigzag effect on the seam, locking the stitch.

**Crossed oversewing**—work one row of oversewing each way from right to left and then from left to right, putting the needle into the same place.

**Ladder stitch**—lay the two pieces to be joined with the edges butted together and take stitches parallel to the edges first on one piece and then on the other. Pull them firmly to draw the edges together.

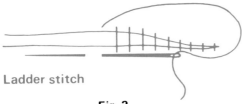

Ladder stitch

**Fig. 2**

**Back stitch**—bring the thread out to the front of the seam, and make a running stitch. Put the needle into the end of the stitch and bring it out a stitch's length to the left. Each new stitch will fill the space left by the previous stitch, making a continuous line.

Back stitch

**Fig. 3**

### Decorative stitches
**Double running**—can be done in two separate rows of running stitch but with contrasting thread, the second row of stitches filling the spaces in the first row.

Double running

**Fig. 4**

**Whipped running**—do a row of running stitch. The second row has the needle threaded in the same direction through each stitch.
**Threaded running**—the second row here is threaded up and down through alternate stitches.
**Double whipped and double threaded**—the second row in each case is followed by a third row in the opposite direction.

**Chain stitch**—bring thread out to the front. Hold the thread under the left thumb, put the needle back into the same hole, bringing it out lower down and over the held thread. This stitch can be whipped and threaded for a more solid colour. It can also be worked as single stitches, when it is called lazy daisy or detached chain.

A

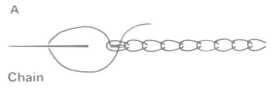

Chain

B

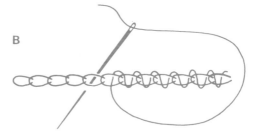

Whipped chain – can also be threaded

**Fig. 5**

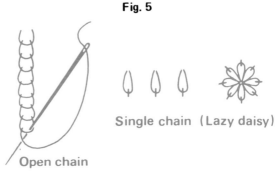

Single chain (Lazy daisy)

Open chain

**Fly stitch**—bring the thread out to the front. Hold the thread under the thumb, insert needle to the right, bringing it out lower down in the centre and over the held thread. Pull firm and insert the needle under the loop, bringing it out in position for the next stitch.
**Stem stitch**—work from left to right. Bring thread out to front. Insert needle to the right and bring out half way along and touching the last stitch to give a corded effect.
**Couching**—threads or cord are held down under left thumb and sewn down with vertical stitches over the cord. Bring the needle out close under the cord and push it through close to the top of the cord.

**Herringbone stitch**—as well as being decorative this is a good stitch for sewing down a raw edged hem turning. Work from left to right. Bring the thread out in front and take a small stitch above and to the right. Take the second stitch down close to the first stitch, crossing the thread. Continue so, keeping the lines of stitches parallel.

**Shell stitch**—make two hemming stitches, over-sewing into the same hole, followed by another two hemming stitches, oversewing again, and so on all along the edge. Pull the oversewing stitches quite tight and they will form small scallop shapes on the hem.

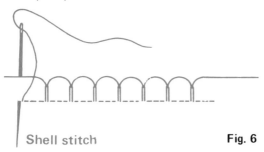

Shell stitch                          **Fig. 6**

## Cutting out

Patterns made in thin card are easier to trace round and can be re-used many times. Write on each piece of template any directions for cutting out, placing etc., and any sewing instructions and keep together all the templates for each doll or dress, preferably on a tag.

Before you begin cutting out, place all the pattern pieces in position on the fabric, starting with the biggest ones. Reverse the template when tracing the second piece of the same shape (e.g. front and back of doll, hands, feet, etc.) so that any slight variation in the template will match up.

Keep all tracing or other pencil marks on the wrong side. Cut just inside or just outside the pencil tracings on felt to avoid grubby looking seams, but cut ¼-½ in. outside the traced lines if using any other fabric to allow for joins. Use a sharply pointed pencil for tracing on felt, but mark places for features, buttons etc., with tacking thread not pencil. Always trace on the wrong side and use the pencil lines as sewing guides.

Cut off all surplus fabric on seams on the wrong side and snip V's out of curves and corners to make the seams lie flat.

## Tools

Sharp cutting out scissors for fabrics
Scissors for paper or thin card
Small sharp-pointed scissors
Sharp knife for cutting card
Pinking shears
Selection of needles
Pins
Knitting needles
Crochet hook
Tape measure
Ruler
Wire nippers and fret saw
Sticks of varying thickness for stuffing — from blunted skewers to orange sticks
Sharp pointed pencils — black and white
Felt tip pens — red, black, blue, brown, pink
Upholstery adhesive
Thin card for templates
Cutting out paper
Compasses
Protractor
Selection of remnants of various fabrics — also lace, fur or fur fabric, ribbon, old nylons, sequins, beads etc.

# 1. Soft Dolls

The dolls described in this chapter are all soft, cuddly dolls, very suitable as presents for small children. None of them is sophisticated but all are easy to make as basic dolls. Dressing them can be either a simple or a very elaborate process, depending on your preference and the style of dressing, whilst some, like the Kewpie dolls, need no further dressing at all. Others can illustrate stories (see chapter 4), or represent historical characters or may be dressed in national or period costume.

The fabrics and trimmings used in making the dolls are inexpensive and easily obtainable. You could make them from used fabrics, though of course these must be in good condition. The good parts of linen, cotton or nylon sheets for instance, or of old wool stockinette type vests or jerseys are suitable. Take care to discard any thin, worn places for these will soon wear out in use and a lot of work will be wasted.

Most types of fabric can be used, except very thick or heavy types such as tweed or hessian, or thin, flimsy fabrics which fray easily or have a shiny surface and so are difficult to hold in place. Felt is very easy to work with, especially for children to sew, and poplin, calico and unbleached calico, linen or linen type fabrics, crash (which is a heavier type linen), cotton prints, stockinette and similar fabrics are also suitable.

Most of these dolls in the fabrics mentioned have been experimented with successfully for many years with children in primary schools, as well as with handicapped children and adults.

The dolls range in size from 20 in. to 7 in., some of the smaller ones being adaptations of the larger templates. You can vary the styles, if you wish, in any of the following ways:

**Arms**—stretched out, arms at sides, separate arms.

**Hands**—with and without thumbs.

**Bodies and legs**—fatter, thinner bodies and longer legs.

**Heads**—rounder with an inserted gusset, wider, fatter faces, etc.

A basic pattern of the right proportions can be adapted at will, using any of the above variations, but in general, when enlarging a pattern, allow ¼ in. extra width for every 1 in. extra height.

The larger dolls are on the whole, easier to handle when making, so the templates for the basic dolls in this chapter have been numbered from the largest to the smallest, with the exception of templates 2 and 3 which, though smaller, are easy to make because of their shape:

Dolls 15—20 in. are templates 1, 2, 4, 5, 6, 7.

Dolls 9—11 in. are templates 3, 8, 9, 12, 15.

Dolls 7 in. or less are templates 10, 11, 13, 13A.

## Methods of making

Always trace round the template shape with a sharp pencil on the wrong side of all fabric or felt. The traced side is treated as the wrong side when making the doll too, so that any pencil marks will be on the inside when it is sewn up.

The pieces can be joined together in the following ways.

## Machine stitched

Whether using felt or fabric, this must be done on the wrong side. Trace round the template once on to half the fabric. Pin this piece, pencilled side uppermost, to the second piece so right sides will be inside, and tack them together. Machine stitch them together on the pencilled outline as a guide. Begin the stitching under one arm, round the top of the doll, and finish at the top of the second leg leaving the rest of that side open for stuffing. Trim off the surplus material close to the stitching. Snip V's out of all the curves on head, hands and feet, and snip into the corners of shoulders, under arms and between legs, as close as possible to the stitching. This will allow the

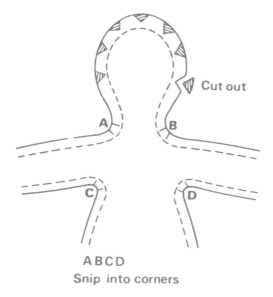

ABCD
Snip into corners

**Fig. 7**

seams to lie flat. Turn inside out, press the
seams flat, and stuff.

### Hand sewn by backstitch

This is done on the wrong side. Trace and tack
the two pieces of fabric together as above. Sew
along the pencil lines as a guide, using a close
backstitch and leaving an opening for stuffing.
Finish as machine stitched doll.

### Oversewing on the wrong side

Felt and non-fraying materials can be sewn
together by this method. Trace round the template on to both pieces of felt, reversing the
template to draw the second one. Cut out the
shapes, cutting just inside or just outside the
pencil lines to avoid grubby seams. Tack them
together with the right sides inside and oversew
all the edges together, leaving an opening at one
side for stuffing. Turn inside out and finish as
machine stitched doll.

### Oversewing on the right side

Trace round the template on to both pieces and
cut them out as above. Tack the pieces together
with right sides outside and oversew the edges
leaving one side open for stuffing. Stuff and
sew up the opening.

### Stab stitch

This gives a seam finish similar to a hand
stitched glove. Trace on to the two pieces, cut
out and tack together with right sides outside.
Stab stitch together as ordinary running stitch

would stretch one side of the pieces and would
give a puckered finish.

Felt and non-fray fabrics can be sewn in all
the above ways, but other fabrics should be
sewn only on the wrong side. The 7 in. and
smaller dolls made in felt should be sewn on the
right side only, for they are too small and the
felt too thick for them to be turned inside out
successfully when sewn.

A rounder, fatter head can be obtained by
sewing a gusset into the head and in most cases
the gusset should be sewn on to each side of the
head first, and then the rest of the shape sewn
together.

### Cutting a head gusset

Measure the head from one side of the neck to
the other and draw a straight line of this length.
Through the middle of this line at right
angles, draw another about 1 in. long. Draw
curves from one end to the other of the long
line on each side, touching each end of the
shorter line and meeting at a point at each end.

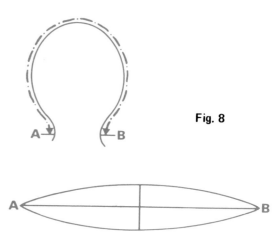

**Fig. 8**

### Inserting the gusset

Mark the middle points of each side of the
gusset, and pin them to the middle points at the
top of each head piece. Pin the rest of the gusset
round the head to the neck on either side, and
sew in place. The width of the gusset can range
from ½ in. to 1¼ in. according to the size of the
doll.

### Features

These can be cut from small scraps of coloured
felt and either stuck or sewn in place, or they
can be sewn on in coloured embroidery silks
using a variety of stitches. Or you could com-

10

bine felt and embroidery. For very small dolls use coloured sewing thread, as embroidery silks are too thick. Coloured felt tip pens can be used on certain types of smooth fabrics, but test on a piece of the fabric first to check for running or smudging. They are not successful on hairy surfaces like felt.

Embroidery can be used very effectively with felt tip pens. Cut a face shape in paper and experiment with the placing of features etc., before sticking or sewing them on to the doll. Place the nose in position first, or, if there is no nose, start with the mouth. Do not place features too high on the face; if you are making

a baby doll, all the features should be in the bottom half.

Use pins and needles carefully with felt, as it retains marks very stubbornly. Stick pins as close to the edge as possible, and do not leave work with a needle stuck in a prominent place like the middle of the face.

## MAKING DOLLS FROM THE VARIOUS TEMPLATES

Paper patterns can be used for cutting out the dolls, but card templates are easier to use and,

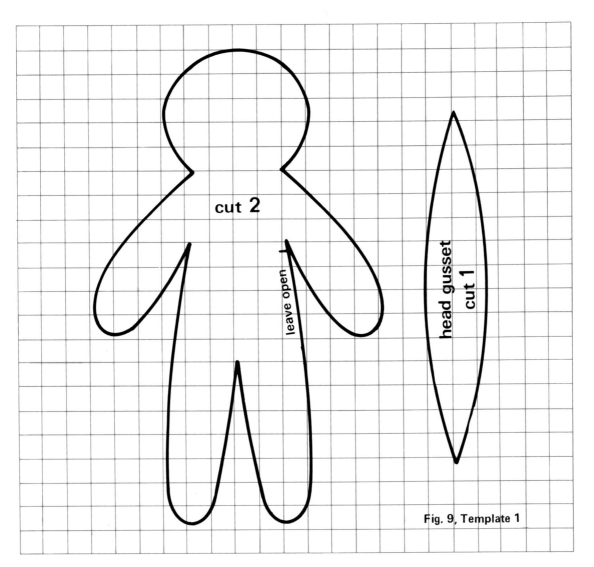

cut 2

leave open

head gusset
cut 1

Fig. 9, Template 1

if several dolls are to be cut from it, last much longer.

## Template 1

This first basic doll is 20 in. when finished and is made in two pieces, back and front alike. It can have a head gusset inserted (this is optional and a gusset pattern is provided). The arms are cut in one with the body and are close to the sides. This one is made in pale pink poplin, so turnings must be allowed for when cutting out the pieces.

*You will need:*
    poplin *for body:* two pieces, 21¼ x 13¼ in.
    poplin *for gusset (optional):* 15¼ x 3 in.
     OR
    felt *for body:* two pieces, 20¼ x 12¼ in.
    felt *for gusset (optional):* 14¼ x 2 in.
    red felt *for mouth:* 1½ x 1 in.
    white felt *for eyes:* two pieces, 1¼ x ½ in.
    blue felt *for eyes:* two ½ in. circles
    two blue sequins *for eyes*
    kapok (or similar stuffing material)
    black embroidery silk
    thick brown wool
    narrow blue or white ribbon
    matching sewing thread

Trace round the template on to one piece of poplin. Pin the two pieces of poplin together with the pencil line uppermost and tack them together outside the line. Machine stitch or backstitch by hand all round the pencilled out-line starting under one arm, round the top of the body to the top of the second leg, leaving the rest of that side open for stuffing.

Cut away all surplus fabric leaving a ½ in. turning at the opening. Cut V's out of all the curves of head, hands and feet and snip into the corners of neck, under arms and between legs. Turn inside out and press the seams flat. Stuff the head with small pieces of stuffing, and keep it smooth and not too hard. Push stuffing in gently to the seams so that they do not pucker. Stuff the arms and legs similarly, and then the rest of the body. Sew up the side seam with ladder stitch drawing the two edges together.

## Features

**Mouth**    Round off the two lower corners of the red felt rectangle to make a curve. Mark the middle point of the opposite side, cut a very

*The basic dolls 1–13A*

small crescent from the middle and a longer crescent from each side (see Fig. 10). Stick or sew this in place near the bottom of the face.

**Eyes**    From white felt or interlining cut two leaf shapes by rounding off all four corners, and cut two ½ in. circles in blue felt. Sew a blue sequin to each blue circle and sew the circles to the middle of each leaf shape. Stick or sew them in place. With black embroidery silk sew an arc in stem stitch above each eye, and a few straight stitches immediately above each eye for lashes.

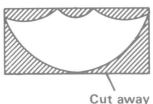

Cut away

**Fig. 10**

## Hair

Cut about 18 to 24 strands of wool 3 in. long. Fold each strand in half and sew across the hair line on the forehead for a fringe. Trim the ends level. Cut the remaining wool into 16 in. long strands. Lay these across the head from shoulder to shoulder and sew down the centre of the head for a parting, using backstitch. Draw them to each side of the face and fasten in bunches with ribbon bows. Alternatively, they could be plaited.

## Making up with a gusset in the head (for a felt doll)

The gusset stretches over the head from one side of the neck to the other. Mark the centre of one edge of the gusset and the top centre of the front head and pin these two points to-gether with the right sides outside. Pin the rest of the gusset round the head from one side of the neck to the other. Oversew the edges to-gether. Pin the back of the head to the gusset in the same way, but do not sew it.

Pin the rest of the body pieces together with the right sides outside and oversew the edges together starting under one arm and sewing round the arm to the shoulder. Stuff this sewn arm with small pieces of kapok or similar stuff-ing, because small pieces will give a smooth finish without being lumpy. Sew together the head and second side of the gusset and stuff the head. Continue in this way, stuffing arms and legs when each one has been sewn, and stuffing

13

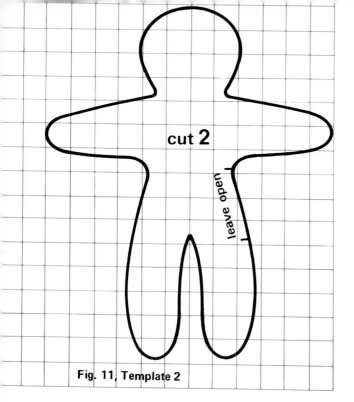

cut 2

leave open

Fig. 11, Template 2

the body last of all. Complete the sewing up.

Stuffing in sections in this way, when sewing up on the right side, does not strain stitches as would be the case if the limbs were stuffed through the side opening.

## Template 2

This doll, 15 in. tall, is cut in two pieces, back and front alike, with its arms stretched out at each side. Arms and legs can be made flexible by stuffing thinly at the top of the limbs and stitching across the top of shoulders and legs.

*You will need:*

unbleached calico *for body:* two pieces, 16 x 12 in.
kapok or other stuffing
white sewing thread
red, blue, brown or black felt tip pens

Trace round the template on to one piece of the calico. Pin the two pieces together with the right sides inside and machine stitch or backstitch by hand round the pencilled outline leaving one side open for stuffing.

Trim off all the surplus material close to the stitching. Snip V's out of all the curves on head, hands and feet and snip in close to the stitching at neck, under arms and between legs. Turn

14

inside out and press the seams flat. Stuff smoothly and firmly and sew up the opening.

### Features

These can be drawn on the face with coloured felt tip pens, as calico has a smooth enough surface.

## Template 3

A Kewpie doll, about 11 in. when sewn.

Kewpie dolls are made in two pieces for back and front with arms outstretched and fat little hands which have a suggestion of a thumb sticking up. They are softly rounded little dolls and the gusset inserted in the girl doll's head gives her a much more rounded shape. Both boy and girl dolls are made in flesh coloured felt.

### Kewpie Girl

*You will need:*

flesh coloured felt *for body:* two pieces, 11 x 9 in.
flesh coloured felt *for gusset:* 6¼ x 1 in.
kapok
red felt *for mouth:* 1 x $\frac{2}{5}$ in.
white felt *for eyes:* two pieces, $\frac{9}{10}$ x $\frac{2}{5}$ in.
blue felt *for eyes:* two pieces, ¼ x $\frac{1}{5}$ in.
black embroidery silk
wool
flesh coloured sewing thread

The girl doll is oversewn on the right side.

Trace round the template on to both pieces of felt and cut out the pieces inside the pencil lines. Trace round the gusset and cut out in the same way. Pin the centre points of gusset sides to the top of the head pieces with the right sides outside and oversew the edges.

Pin the rest of the doll pieces together, pinning right on the edges to avoid leaving pin marks, and oversew the edges all round leaving one side open for stuffing. Press out the head seams as flat as possible and stuff carefully with small pieces of stuffing, but not too hard. Press out other seams and stuff arms, then legs and body. Sew up the opening.

**Mouth**    Trim off the two lower corners of the red felt rectangle in a curve. Cut a crescent shape from the other side and sew in place low down on the face.

**Fig. 12**

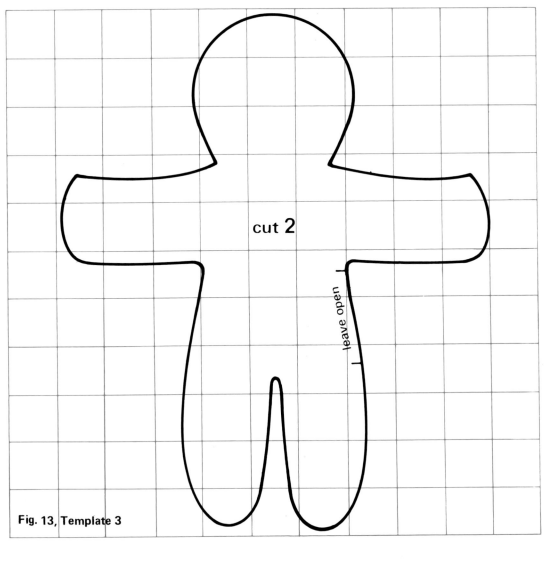

cut 2

leave open

Fig. 13, Template 3

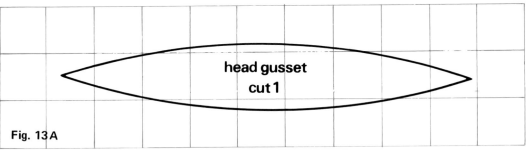

head gusset
cut 1

Fig. 13 A

15

**Eyes** Cut each white rectangle to shape (Fig. 14). Cut the blue felt pieces in semicircles and stick each in place on the white felt shapes with the straight edges together. Stick or sew them in place above the mouth and sew straight stitches in black embroidery silk radiating out from the top curve for eye lashes. Using the same silk, sew two arcs in stem stitch above the eyes for brows.

**Fig. 14**

## Hair
Cut the wool into 9 in. strands. Lay them across the head from shoulder to shoulder and sew them in place down the centre with back stitch. Catch them down at each side of the face, gather the strands together and plait at each side.

### Kewpie Boy
*You will need:*
   natural felt *for body:* two pieces, 11 x 9 in.
   kapok
   red felt *for mouth:* 1 x 1½ in.
   black felt *for eyes:* two ½ in. circles
   pink felt *for cheeks:* two ½ in. circles
   yellow felt *for hair front:* 3½ x 3½ in.
   yellow felt *for hair back:* 3½ x 2 in.
   black embroidery silk
   natural sewing thread

The boy doll is machine stitched on the wrong side.
   Trace round the template on to one piece of felt. Pin it to the second piece with the pencil outline uppermost. Tack them together round the outside of the outline. Machine stitch (or backstitch by hand) using the pencil line as a guide, leaving one side open. Cut away the surplus felt as close as possible to the stitching, turn it inside out and press the seams as flat as possible. Stuff smoothly and firmly and sew up the opening with ladder stitch (see page 7).

## Features
Cut red felt into a deep crescent shape and stick or sew in place. Cut circles for eyes and cheeks and fix in place. Sew an arc of stem stitch above each eye in black embroidery silk.

16

## Hair
Trace round the top of the head curve on to yellow felt, reversing the template when tracing for the back piece. Mark the wrong sides with tacking thread near the top curve. Cut the lower edge of the wide piece for the back in a deep notched curve and sew it in place round the top edge of the head. Cut the front piece in a narrow notched arc nearly 1 in. deep over the forehead and tapering to the sides. Pin in place and oversew to the back hair curve. Catch down in the V's with small stitches.

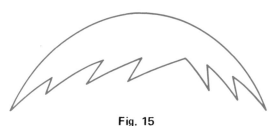

**Fig. 15**

### Templates 4 and 5
These make 16 in. dolls.
The two templates are very similar, the legs on 4 being more curved and with a small thumb on the hands. No. 5 is a sturdier looking shape with straight legs. The making up is the same for each. This one is made in flesh pink poplin, machine stitched on the wrong·side.

*You will need:*
   poplin or other firm cotton *for body:* two pieces, 18 x 7½ in.
   kapok or similar stuffing
   red felt *for mouth:* 1¼ x ½ in.
   brown felt *for eyes:* two ½ in. circles
   brown embroidery silk
   blond wool
   pipe cleaner
   pink sewing thread

Trace round the template on to one piece of fabric and pin the two pieces together with pencil outline uppermost, so the right sides will be inside. Either machine stitch them together or backstitch by hand, using the pencil line as a guide. Leave one side open for stuffing.
   Trim off all the surplus fabric, snip V's out of all the curves of head, hands and feet and snip into the corners at neck, under arms and between legs. Turn inside out and press all the seams flat. Stuff the top of the head. Fold the pipe cleaner in half, twist it together, wind some stuffing round it and insert it in the doll so that half of it is in the head and half in the body. Stuff kapok all round it, filling the head

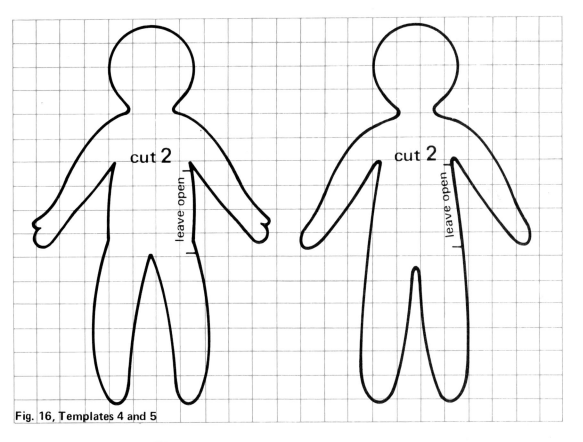

Fig. 16, Templates 4 and 5

In the figure: cut 2, leave open (left template); cut 2, leave open (right template)

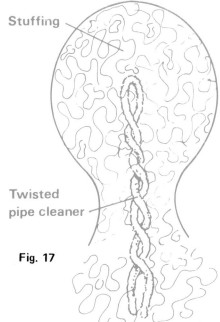

Stuffing

Twisted
pipe cleaner

Fig. 17

smoothly and keeping the pipe cleaner twist in the middle of the neck to give support to the head.

The arms are slender, and so only very small pieces of stuffing should be used at a time, pushing it in place gently with a blunt pencil or knitting needle. Stuff the remainder of the doll. Sew up the side seam.

## Features

Cut a crescent shape from the rectangle of red felt and stick or sew in place for a mouth. Stick two brown circles in place for eyes with straight stitches in brown embroidery silk above them for lashes, and arcs of brown stem stitch above for brows.

## Hair

Cut the wool into 11 in. strands and lay them across the head from shoulder to shoulder. Backstitch them to one side for a side parting. Catch them in two or three places down each side of the face sewing through the middle of

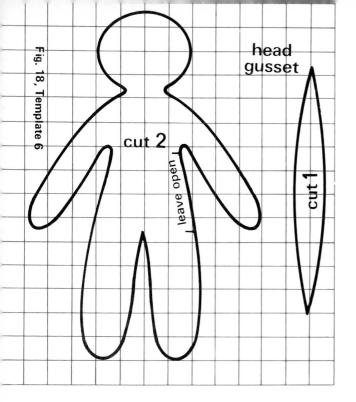

head
gusset

cut 2

leave open

cut 1

the strands to hide the stitches, and leave the ends to hang loose.

## Template 6

This makes a sturdy 15 in. doll, whose head is a little wider, and this can of course be made rounder by inserting a gusset in it. The arms point down to the sides and a little way out from the body so that it is easy to dress. It can be made in a variety of fabrics, but this one is of felt, and is oversewn on the wrong side.

*You will need:*
    flesh coloured felt *for body:* two pieces, 15½ x 10½ in.
    flesh coloured felt *for gusset:* 10 x 1¼ in.
    kapok
    matching sewing thread
    red felt *for mouth:* 1¼ x ½ in.
    blue felt *for eyes:* two ½ in. circles
    black embroidery silk
    wool *for hair*

Trace round the template on to the two pieces of felt, and round the gusset pattern. Cut out all the pieces. Sew the gusset on to the head curves as in template 1. Pin the two bodies together with right sides inside, and tack them. Oversew the edges together leaving one side

open for stuffing. Turn inside out and press all the seams flat. Stuff it firmly and smoothly with small pieces of stuffing. Sew up the opening with ladder stitch (see page 7).

### Features
Cut one long side of the red felt rectangle in a curve and from the other side cut out two small crescents. Sew in place. Sew the two blue circles in place for eyes. Embroider some straight stitches in black silk radiating from the circles for eye lashes, and arcs of black stem stitch for brows.

### Hair
Cut the wool in 10 in. strands and lay them across the head from shoulder to shoulder. Backstitch them in place down the middle. Catch in place at eye level on each side, sewing through the strands to hide the stitches, and catch in bunches at the neck. Trim the ends.

## Template 7
A 16 in. doll very similar to templates 4 and 5, the body being the same shape but having separate arms. This one is made up in poplin, machine stitched and with a head gusset.

*You will need:*
    poplin *for body:* two pieces, 18 x 4½ in.
    poplin *for arms:* four pieces, 7 x 1½ in.
    poplin *for gusset:* 10½ x 2½ in.
    kapok
    pipe cleaner
    red felt *for mouth:* 1 x ½ in.
    white felt *for eyes:* two pieces, 1 x ½ in.
    blue felt *for eyes:* two ½ in. circles
    black embroidery silk
    wool *for hair*

Trace round the template of body, arms and gusset on to the appropriate pieces of poplin. Pin the gusset to the head curves on the wrong side, pinning through the pencil lines on head and gusset. Tack them together and machine stitch.

Make up the body in the same way as for templates 4 and 5. Stitch the arms together in twos, trim the seams, snip curves etc., turn right side out, press, stuff them and sew on to the shoulders.

### Features
Cut red felt as shown in Fig. 20 and stick in place. Cut two leaf shapes from the white felt, stick a blue felt circle on each one and stick or

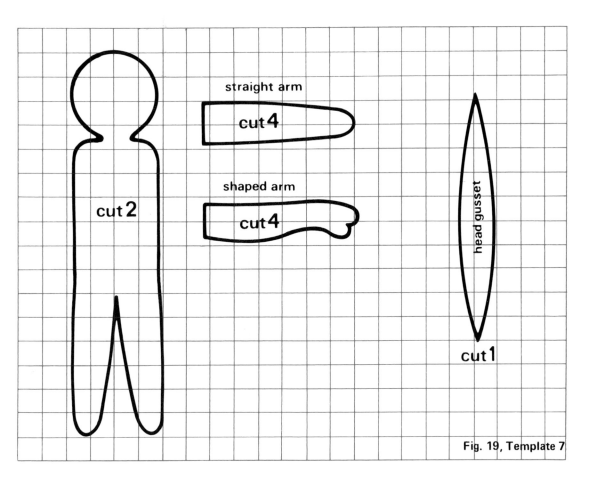

straight arm

cut 4

shaped arm

cut 4

cut 2

head gusset

cut 1

Fig. 19, Template 7

sew them on to the face. Embroider eye lashes and brows with black embroidery silk.

Fig. 20

## Hair

Cut and sew the wool as in template 6, catching it down in waves in three or four places round the face and taking the ends round to the back of the head to sew in a coil on the neck.

## Template 8

An 11 in. doll in felt oversewn on the right side.

The template is adapted from the Kewpie doll (page 14), but the body has more shape and both the body and arms are slimmer.

*You will need:*
   flesh coloured felt *for body:* two pieces 11¼ x 9 in.
   flesh coloured felt *for gusset:* 8 x 1 in.
   kapok
   red felt *for mouth:* 1 x ½ in.
   white felt *for eyes:* two ½ in. circles
   blue felt *for eyes:* two $\frac{2}{5}$ in. circles
   black embroidery silk
   yellow wool *for hair*
   flesh coloured sewing thread

Trace the template on to both pieces of felt, and the gusset on to the strip of felt and cut them out inside the pencil lines. Pin and sew the gusset to the head on the right side. Pin and oversew the rest of the body, leaving a side

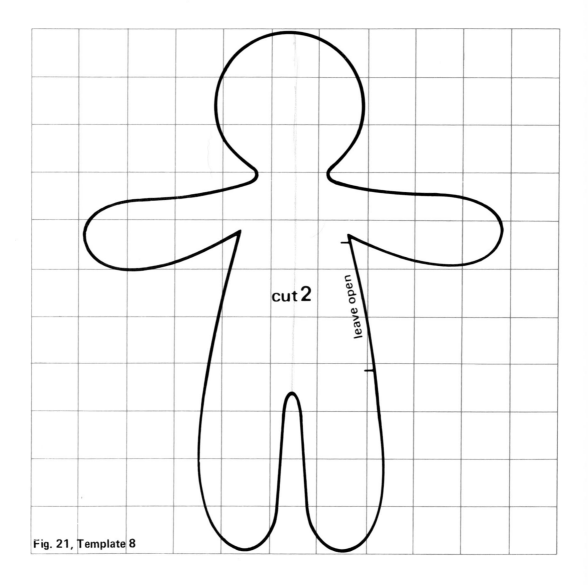

cut 2

leave open

Fig. 21, Template 8

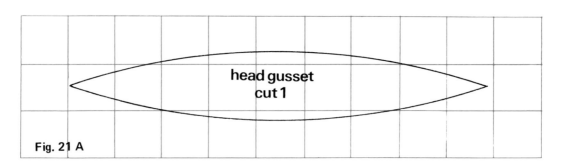

head gusset
cut 1

Fig. 21 A

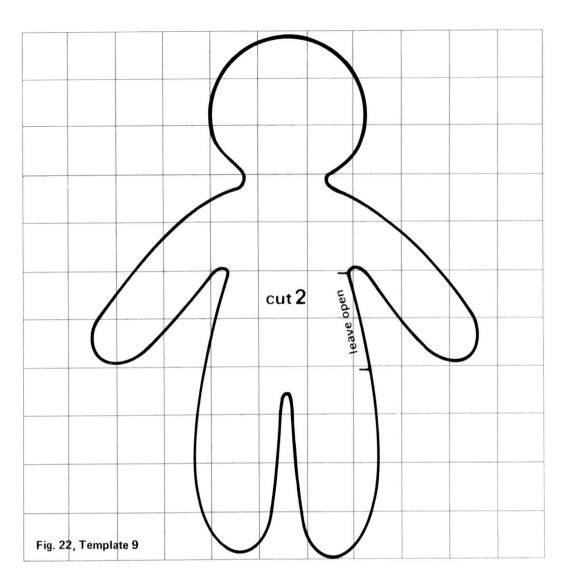

cut 2

leave open

Fig. 22, Template 9

open. Press seams flat, stuff firmly, but not hard, and oversew the opening.

## Features

Cut a crescent shape from the red felt for a mouth and sew in place. Sew blue circles at the bottom edge of the white circles and sew on for eyes. Embroider four or five straight stitches in black embroidery silk for lashes and two fly stitches almost on top of each other for each brow.

## Hair

Sew loops of yellow wool from the crown of the head to the hair line along the forehead. Extend them in longer loops down the side of the face and round the back of the head.

Template 9
An 11 in. stockinette doll, machine stitched.

*You will need:*
pink stockinette or vest material *for body:* two pieces, 11¼ x 9½ in.
red felt *for mouth:* 1½ x ½ in.
white felt *for eyes:* two ½ in. circles

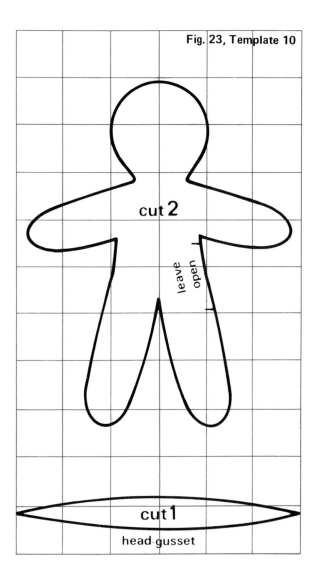

**Fig. 23, Template 10**

cut 2

leave open

cut 1

head gusset

Tack the two pieces together with the pencilled outline on top. Sew the two pieces together using the lines as guides and leaving one side open. It can be machine stitched or hand sewn using backstitch for firmness. Trim off surplus material about ¼ in. outside the stitching. Snip into curves and corners, turn inside out and press seams flat.

Stuff the top of the head, pad the twisted pipe cleaner with stuffing and insert in the neck. Pad firmly all round it (see page 16, template 4). Complete the stuffing and sew up the opening.

## Features
Cut a long thin crescent in red felt and sew in place for a mouth. Stick the brown circles at the bottom of the white circles, cut a small piece off straight across the bottom of each and sew in place. Embroider the brows.

## Hair
Trace round the curve of the head on to the brown felt, for front and back. Cut the bottom of the back piece in a curve and sew on to the back of the head. Cut the front piece into a notched arc and oversew on to the back hair.

## Template 10
This makes a 7 in. boy or girl doll.

Both are smaller versions of template 2, with outstretched arms. The boy is oversewn on the right side and has a gussetted head, and the girl is sewn on the right side with stab stitch.

*You will need for each doll:*
    flesh coloured felt *for body:* two pieces, 7¼ x 5½ in.
    kapok
    brown wool *for hair*
    red, blue and brown embroidery silks OR red felt *for mouth:* ¾ x ¼ in.
    blue felt *for eyes:* two ¼ in. circles
*For the boy, you will need in addition:*
    flesh coloured felt *for gusset:* 5½ x ¾ in.

## Girl
Trace and cut out the body pieces, inside the pencil lines. For the girl, pin the pieces together and stab stitch all round leaving one side open (see page 6). Stuff and sew up opening.

For the mouth, embroider fly stitches in red and two satin stitch circles for eyes with a fly stitch in black above each for brows.

Cut wool in 4½ in. strands, lay them across the

brown felt *for eyes:* two $\frac{2}{5}$ in. circles
kapok
pipe cleaner
black embroidery silk
brown felt *for hair back:* 2½ x 3½ in.
brown felt *for hair front:* 1½ x 3½ in.
pink sewing thread

Trace the template on to one piece of stockinette. Use a very sharply pointed pencil and press down firmly on the very edge of the template to prevent the material from stretching under the pencil and so spoiling the shape.

22

head, sew down the middle and catch in bunches at each side.

### Boy

To make the boy trace and cut out the pieces inside the pencil lines. Oversew the gusset to both head pieces on the right side pinning the middle first of all to the top of each head piece. Pin the rest of the body pieces together all round on the right side and finish off by oversewing all round and then stuffing.

Cut a crescent of red felt for a mouth and blue felt circles for eyes with straight stitches above them in black.

With brown wool embroider long and short stitches alternately each side of a parting and then over the rest of the head.

### Template 11

A 7 in. doll. It can be made in natural muslin, and backstitched (method 1), or alternatively in felt and oversewn (method 2). It is a sturdy, compact little doll with rounded shoulders and arms at its sides.

### Method 1

*You will need:*
   natural muslin *for body:* 7½ in. square
   kapok
   natural sewing thread
   red, blue and brown felt tip pens
   wool *for hair*

Trace round the template on to half the square. Fold it in half with the pencil outline on top and tack together. Sew round the pencil line with a small close backstitch, leaving one side open. Trim off all surplus material, turn inside out, press, stuff and sew up opening.

### Method 2

*You will need:*
   felt *for body:* two pieces, 7¼ x 3½ in.
   scraps of felt *for features*
   flesh coloured sewing thread
   kapok
   wool *for hair*

Trace round template on to both pieces of felt and cut out just outside the pencil lines. Pin together with pencil lines inside and oversew the edges leaving one side open. With a small doll it is easier to sew and stuff as you go, thus avoiding unnecessary pull on stitches.

Stick or sew on felt features. Sew loops of

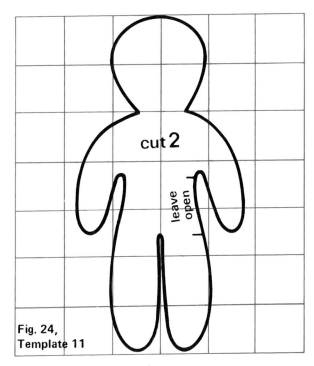

**cut 2**

**leave open**

Fig. 24,
Template 11

wool round hair line from cheek to cheek and then over the rest of the head.

### Template 12

A 9 in. felt doll machine stitched on the wrong side. It has outstretched arms and is similar to template 8 but with straighter arms and a slightly flattened head.

*You will need:*
   flesh coloured felt *for body:* two pieces, 9¼ x 7¼ in.
   kapok
   flesh coloured sewing thread
   scraps of red and blue felt *for features*
   brown felt *for hair back:* 2 x 3 in.
   brown felt *for hair front:* 1½ x 3 in.
   brown embroidery silk

Trace outline on to one piece of felt, pin on to second piece of felt with pencil outline on top and machine stitch together or backstitch by hand, leaving one side open. Complete the doll as described for template 9.

### Template 13

A 7 in. felt doll which is a slimmer version of template 11.

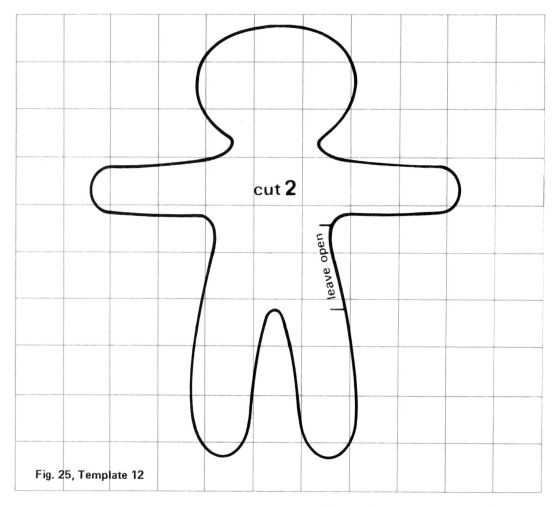

cut **2**

leave open

**Fig. 25, Template 12**

*You will need:*
> flesh coloured felt *for body:* two pieces, 7¼ x 2¼ in.
> scraps of red and blue felt *for features*
> brown felt *for hair front and back:* two pieces, 1½ x 1¾ in.

Cut out and make up as template 10 but with no head gusset. Make the hair out of felt as for template 12.

## Template 13A

A 6½ in. doll in stockinette or vest material with separate arms.

*You will need:*
> stockinette *for body:* two pieces, 7 x 2 in.

stockinette *for arms:* two pieces, 2½ x 1½ in.
red and brown embroidery silk
brown sewing thread

Trace and make up body as template 9. Fold the arm piece in half, and sew together round the hand and side seam leaving top open. Cut away surplus material and turn inside out. Stuff body and arms and sew arms on at shoulder.

## Features

Sew an arc of red stem stitch for the mouth, eyes in brown stem stitch, lashes in brown straight stitch, brows in brown sewing thread chain stitch.

## Hair

Sew on strands of brown embroidery silk and finish as template 6.

24

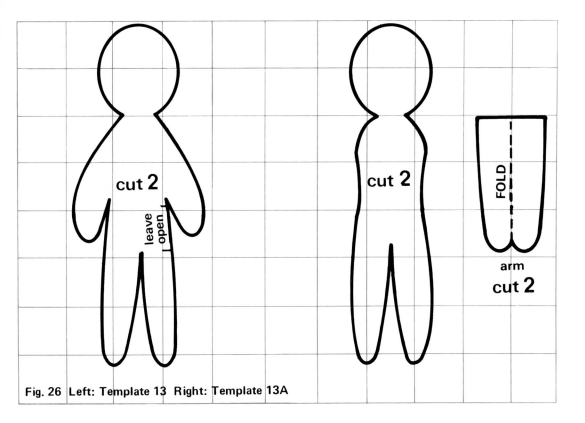

Fig. 26 Left: Template 13 Right: Template 13A

cut 2

leave open

cut 2

FOLD

arm
cut 2

## VARIATIONS

These are the basic shapes used for most of the dolls and of course any of them can be adapted to individual taste, bearing in mind the requirements of particular materials or methods of making up.

The following dolls are dressed versions of some of the basic dolls.

### Kewpie dolls with inset faces

These two Kewpies are made up in fabric, one in a sprigged cotton, and the other in a striped piqué type rayon mixture in a close weave which does not fray. Both are made up from template 3A in the same way, so the materials and directions given apply to both dolls.

*You will need:*
  fabric (see above) *for body:* two pieces, 11 x 10 in.
  kapok
  interlining or plain white fabric *for face:* 4 in. square

white sewing thread
red and black felt tip pens
card circle: 2 in. diameter

Tack the piece of plain white fabric in the middle of one of the shorter sides of the body piece, on the wrong side and with edges together (see Fig. 27). Place the template on top so

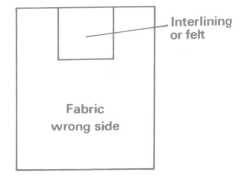

Interlining or felt

Fabric wrong side

Fig. 28, Template 3A, adapted from Template 3

25

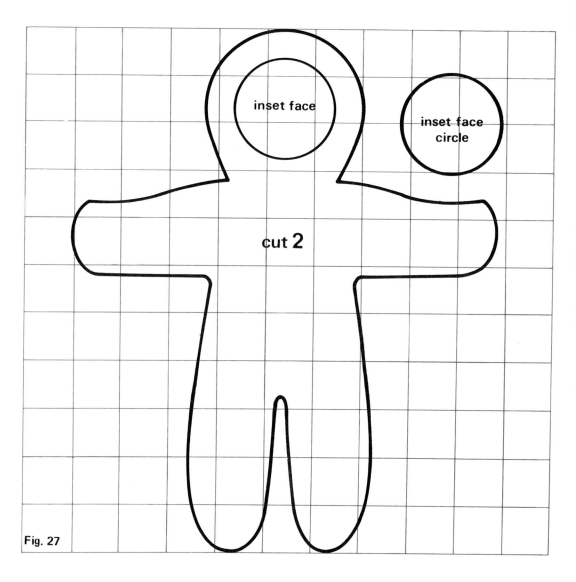

inset face

inset face circle

cut 2

Fig. 27

that the head fits into the white fabric (see Fig. 29). Trace round the template. Tack round

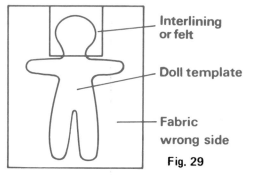

Interlining or felt

Doll template

Fabric wrong side

Fig. 29

the pencilled head line with a contrasting cotton. Turn over to the right side, and place the card circle for the face in the middle of the tacked outline, and lightly trace round it. Cut out the fabric circle so exposing the white fabric underneath. Take care to cut only the body fabric and not the white face fabric underneath it.

Snip all round the outside edge of the fabric face (not the inserted white one), turn the edge under and hem to the white face under it. Place the second piece of print on top, with the right sides inside, tack them together and machine stitch or backstitch by hand on the pencilled outline, leaving one side open for stuffing. Trim

26

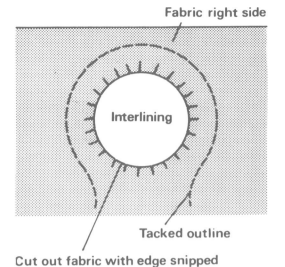

Fabric right side

Interlining

Tacked outline

Cut out fabric with edge snipped

**Fig. 30**

off the surplus fabric close to the stitching, and snip V's into the curves of head, hands and feet, and into the corners of neck, under arms and between legs. Turn inside out, press the seams flat and stuff smoothly but not too hard. Sew up the opening.

## Features
Draw features on the white face with felt tip pens.

### A Kewpie girl
This Kewpie girl doll in her green felt dress is made from template 3B, which has been adapted from the basic Kewpie pattern, template 3. It has been cut into five pieces — head, hand, foot, leg and dress.

*You will need:*
    flesh coloured felt *for head:* two pieces, 3¾ x 3¾ in.
    flesh coloured felt *for hands:* four pieces, 1½ x 2 in.
    flesh coloured felt *for legs:* four pieces, 2 x 2 in.
    green felt *for dress:* two pieces, 6 x 7 in.
    white felt *for feet:* four pieces, 1¼ x 1½ in.
    white felt *for buttons:* six 1¼ in. circles
    orange felt *for trim:* one piece, 4 x ½ in. and one piece, 5½ x ¼ in.
    orange felt *for collar:* 2¾ x ½ in.
    kapok

matching thread
narrow orange ribbon: 12 in.
red felt *for mouth:* 1 x $\frac{2}{5}$ in.
blue felt *for eyes:* two $\frac{2}{5}$ in. circles
black embroidery silk
yellow wool *for hair*

The body part of the pattern has been widened down each side to make the dress shape. The back and front of the doll when made up must match exactly, and parts for the front must not be mixed up with those for the back. Mark one side of each piece of pattern with a cross and trace all pieces for the front of the doll with the cross uppermost. Trace the front pieces first and pin them together as follows:
    on flesh felt trace one head, two hands, two legs,
    on green felt trace one dress,
    on white felt trace two feet.

Cut out all these pieces, the head first, then the dress, hands, legs and feet and pin them together as soon as they are cut. Check hands to ensure that both thumbs point upwards. The traced side will be the wrong side. Trace the pieces for the back in the same way but reversing all the patterns so that the cross on them is underneath. Pin all the back pieces together in the same way. Oversew all the seams.

## Trimming
Stick or sew the narrow orange felt strip down one side of the dress and the wider orange strip across the waist for a belt. Sew three white felt buttons above and below the belt to simulate a fastening. Cut the orange felt for a collar in a crescent shape, by trimming it off towards the shoulders and leaving it wider in the centre.

Pin the back and front together with the right sides inside, matching all the joins of colour. Oversew all round leaving open the second side of the dress. Turn inside out and press all the seams flat. Stuff the doll smoothly and not too hard and sew up the opening with ladder stitch (see page 7).

## Features
Round off the two lower corners of the red felt rectangle to make a curve, mark the middle point of the opposite side and cut out a small crescent shape each side of it. Sew mouth and eyes in place. With black silk embroider four straight stitches radiating from each eye for lashes and a fly stitch above each for a brow.

## Hair
Cut wool in 8 in. strands and lay them across

27

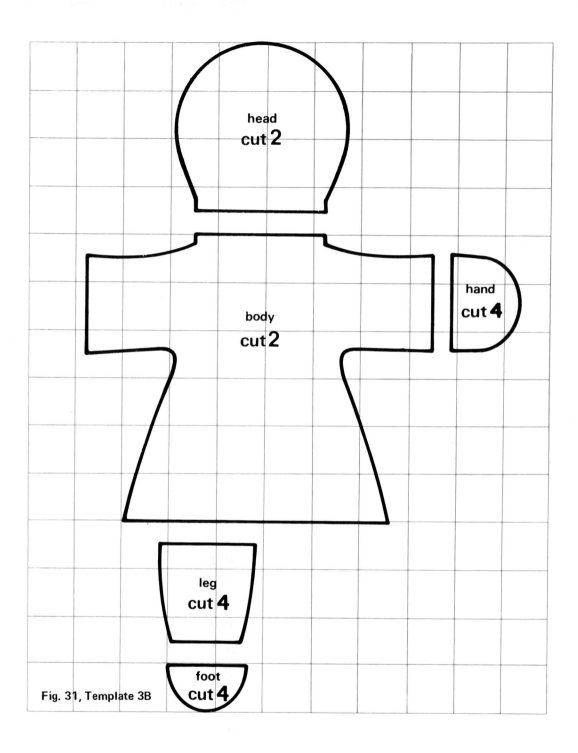

head
cut 2

hand
cut 4

body
cut 2

leg
cut 4

foot
cut 4

Fig. 31, Template 3B

the head from side to side. Sew them down the middle of the head with backstitch. Catch them in bunches each side of the face and tie with a ribbon.

28

## Kewpie boy

Template 3C is used for the body and this again is the basic template 3 cut into six pieces — head, hands, jersey, trousers, legs and shoes. The whole doll is made in felt.

*You will need:*
  flesh coloured felt *for head:* two pieces, 3¼ x 3½ in.
  flesh coloured felt *for hands:* four pieces, 1¼ x 1¾ in.
  flesh coloured felt *for legs:* four pieces, 1⅗ x 1¾ in.
  yellow felt *for jersey:* two pieces, 3½ x 7 in.
  green felt *for trousers:* two pieces, 2½ x 3½ in.
  black felt *for shoes:* four pieces, 1 x 1½ in.
  kapok
  matching thread
  red, blue and brown felt tip pens
  orange embroidery silk

Trace, cut out, pin and sew front pieces then back pieces as for Kewpie girl. Features can be drawn with felt tip pens in appropriate colours or worked with embroidery silks, using crescents of red stem stitch for mouth and nose and circles of blue satin stitch for eyes with circles of brown stem stitch worked round them and arcs of stem stitch above. Hair can be straight stitches in brown. Sew and finish as for the Kewpie girl.

## Kewpie footballer

Template 3D used for him is developed from the basic template 3 cut into seven pieces — head, hands, jersey, shorts, legs, stockings, shoes. He is made in cotton fabric.

*You will need:*
  pink poplin *for head:* two pieces, 4 in. square
  pink poplin *for arms:* four pieces, 3 x 2½ in.
  pink poplin *for legs:* four pieces, 1¾ x 2½ in.
  striped fabric *for jersey:* two pieces, 4 x 6 in.
  white fabric *for shorts:* two pieces, 2½ x 4 in.
  red fabric *for socks:* four pieces, 2¼ x 2½ in.
  black fabric *for shoes:* four pieces, 1¾ x 2 in.
  kapok

---

*Right above: kewpie dolls with inset faces, kewpie footballer, and kewpie rabbit.*

*Right below: kewpie boy and girl*

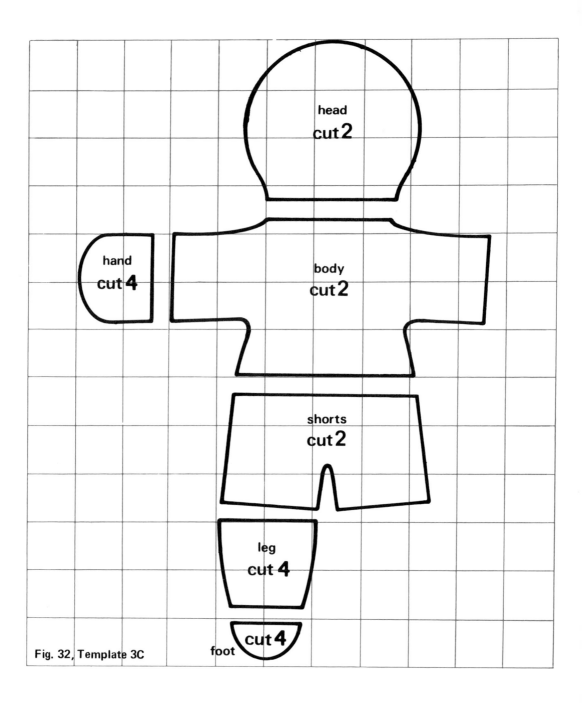

head
cut 2

hand
cut 4

body
cut 2

shorts
cut 2

leg
cut 4

foot cut 4

Fig. 32, Template 3C

matching thread
red, blue and brown felt tip pens
orange embroidery silk

Trace pieces on to wrong sides of fabric and cut ½ in. outside the pencil lines to allow for seams.

Cut, pin and tack front pieces and then back pieces together with right sides inside. Machine stitch or backstitch by hand ½ in. inside the cut edges. Trim off all surplus material to less than ¼ in. Cut V's from all curved edges and snip

30

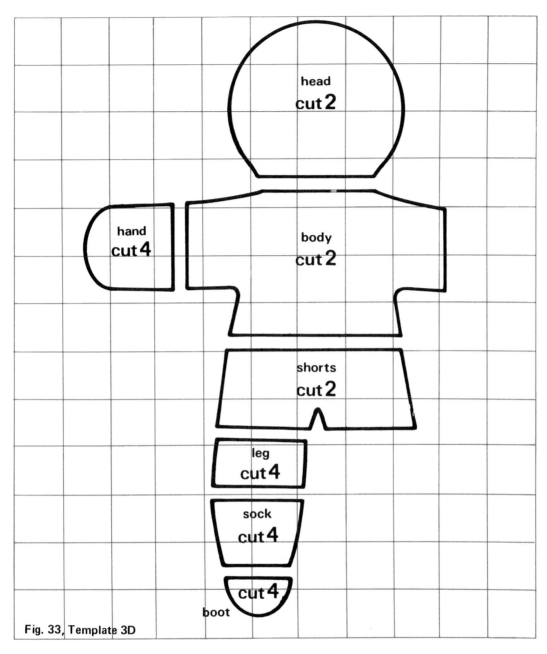

head
cut 2

hand
cut 4

body
cut 2

shorts
cut 2

leg
cut 4

sock
cut 4

cut 4
boot

**Fig. 33, Template 3D**

into all corners to make the seams lie flat. Press all the seams. Either draw features with coloured felt tip pens or embroider them. Finish the making up as for the boy.

**Kewpie rabbit**

Template 3E is used. The sides of the head in template 3 have been straightened slightly to give a shape which is more oval than round, and a pattern for the ears is given in addition.

*You will need:*
white fluffy pile fabric *for body:* two pieces 11 x 10 in.
white fluffy pile fabric *for ears:* four pieces, 2¾ x 1¾ in.

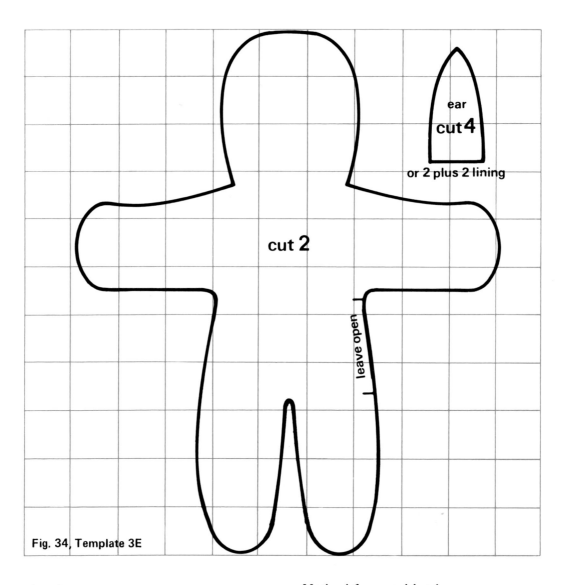

Fig. 34, Template 3E

ear
cut 4
or 2 plus 2 lining

cut 2

leave open

kapok
fluffy white nylon or wool *for tail*
white sewing thread
black and pink embroidery silks

Trace round the template on to the wrong side
of one piece of fluffy fabric, using a very sharp
pencil, and pressing very firmly on to the edge
of the template and material beneath to prevent
it moving, as this type of fabric stretches easily
and this could spoil the shape. Trace the ears on
two pieces of the material leaving the other two
plain. The pieces can be machine stitched together or sewn by hand in two ways as
described below.

## Method 1 — machined

Do not cut out the pieces. Pin a traced ear to an
uncut ear piece with right sides inside and
machine stitch together on the pencil lines,
leaving the short side open. Trim off the surplus
material close to the stitching and turn inside
out. Make up the second ear. Press the seams
flat. The ears are not stuffed. Make pleats in the
middle of the unsewn edges and sew them.

Pin the ears in place on the right side of the
traced rabbit head with the pleated edges projecting over the stitching line (the pencil line on
the wrong side) and the ears pointing down to
the body (see Fig. 35). Place the plain piece
of fluffy fabric on top with the right side to the

ears, and pin firmly together. Machine stitch together on the pencil line, starting under one arm, round the top of the body and leaving the last side open. Trim off all surplus material, turn inside out and press seams flat. Stuff head first (the ears will now stand up straight), then the rest of the body. Sew up opening.

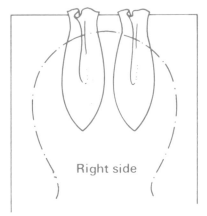

Fig. 35

## Method 2 – backstitched by hand
Pin the pieces together in exactly the same way as for machine stitching and tack together firmly. Backstitch all round the pencil lines, leaving the last side open. Trim off surplus material and turn inside out.

## Method 2 – oversewn by hand
The stitch used is double oversewing (see page 6). Tack the pieces together firmly just inside the pencil lines. Trim off all the surplus material leaving about $\frac{1}{8}$ in. outside the pencil lines. Oversew and complete as for the back-stitched version.

## Features
Embroider the features, with pink embroidery silk. Sew a single lazy daisy (detached chain stitch) vertically in the middle of the face and a horizontal one to either side of it at both ends. With black embroidery silk mark two downward curves in running stitch for closed eyes and work over them in chain stitch, with straight stitches sewn along each each curve for lashes. Sew three or four straight stitches at either side of the nose for whiskers.

Fig. 36

## Tail
Cut a 6 in. length from the white wool. Lay this strand along a finger and wind the wool round both finger and strand of wool about 20 times. Pull the loops from the finger and tie round tightly with the strand. Sew this firmly to the rabbit's back. Cut the loops and trim into a ball, fluffing out the ends.

Other Kewpies can be made into cats, bears, mice, lions, etc., by changing the shape of the ears, the features, and the colour.

## Towelling dolls
Made of towelling and padded with towelling or washable nylon. These soft dolls can quite happily go into the bath with their young owners, and are quickly dried off. They are made in two parts like the Kewpie dolls.

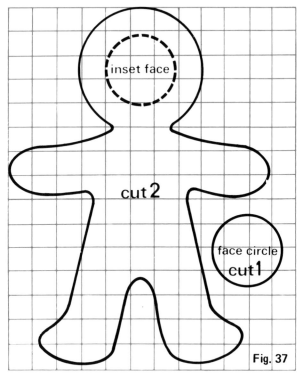

inset face

cut 2

face circle
cut 1

Fig. 37

*You will need*

    towelling *for body:* two pieces, 17 x 12 in.
    nylon wadding or old towelling: three pieces,
      16 x 11 in.
    white nylon felt or interlining *for face:* 5 x
      5½ in.
    red nylon wool
    matching thread
    red and black embroidery silks

Trace round the template on to the wrong side of one piece of towelling, and tack round the outline of the head with a contrasting coloured thread. Trace the head of the template on to the piece of white face fabric and cut it out; tack this on to the wrong side of the towelling head. Sew all round it with herringbone stitch taking small stitches through to the right side.

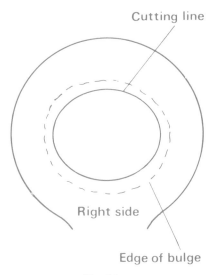

Fig. 38

On the right side the outline of the white face will show as a slight bulge. Mark an oval with tacking stitches ¾ in. inside this bulge and cut out the resulting oval of towelling to expose the white face. Make a narrow single turning on the towelling and hem it to the face. Cut out the template shape in padding and trim it so that it is smaller than the towelling by ¼ to ½ in. Tack it to the back piece of the doll and then sew it with herringbone stitch, taking only small stitches in the towelling so that they will not show.

    Place the two towelling shapes together with

*Left: towelling doll and wee bather*

right sides inside and tack them together on the outline. Machine stitch or backstitch them together all round the outline, leaving the top of the head open. Turn inside out, and pull out the seams as flat as possible. Tack narrow single turnings on the back and front of the head opening.

## Features

Cut about twenty-four 2 in. lengths of red wool, fold them in half and tack the folded ends to the front of the head opening. Oversew the back and front of the head opening together, stitching in the wool folds with the seam.

    Stitch across the neck, arms and legs. Embroider the features, or cut out a crescent in washable nylon felt for the mouth and black circles for the eyes and sew them in place.

### The wee bather

This doll is made from its own template, Fig. 39, quickly and easily. Old nylon tights or slips will stuff her quite well.

*You will need:*

    orange towelling *for body:* two pieces, 6 x
      4 in.
    nylon padding
    matching thread
    black and red embroidery silk
    white fluffy wool

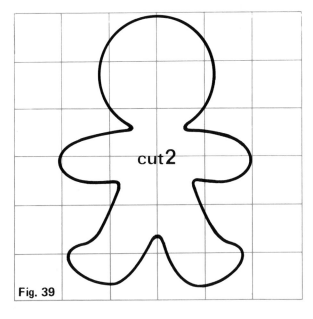

Fig. 39

Fig. 40

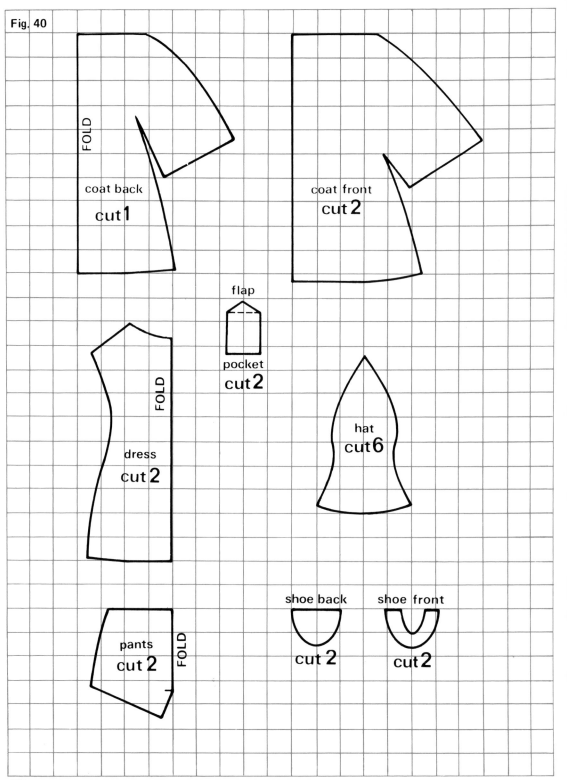

coat back
cut 1

coat front
cut 2

flap

pocket
cut 2

dress
cut 2

hat
cut 6

pants
cut 2

shoe back

shoe front

cut 2

cut 2

FOLD

FOLD

FOLD

Cut out two doll shapes from the pattern and sew them together all round with backstitch, leaving the top of the head open. Turn inside out and press the seams flat. Stuff sparingly to make a soft flattish doll. Sew up the opening.

## Features
Sew the white wool in loops round the top of the head, or cut it in twelve strands about 6 in. long, fasten it in a bunch at the top of the head and tie in bunches at each side of the face. Embroider the features and tie a narrow nylon ribbon round the neck.

## The big dressed doll
This doll is a dressed version of template 1. She has a blue nylon or silk dress with pants to match and over it she wears a fitted darker blue felt coat with a half belt at the back and two big patch pockets in the front.

*You will need:*
blue felt *for coat back:* 10 x 13 in.
blue felt *for coat front:* two pieces, 10 x 7½ in.
blue felt *for collar:* 8 x 1 in.
blue felt *for cuffs:* two pieces, 6½ x $\frac{5}{8}$ in.
blue felt *for pockets:* two pieces, 1½ x 2 in.
blue felt *for belt:* 5½ x $\frac{5}{8}$ in.
five small pearl or silver buttons
felt *for hat:* one piece, 18 x 7 in. or six pieces, 6 x 6½ in.
blue silk *for dress:* two pieces, 9½ x 7 in.
blue silk *for pants:* two pieces, 6 x 4 in.
round elastic: 4 in.
four press studs
matching sewing threads
black felt *for shoes:* four pieces, 1½ x 2 in.
narrow blue ribbon
thick brown wool
black embroidery silk

Cut out all the clothes from the patterns. (See also page 52.)

## Pants
Join side seams and inner leg seams using either machine stitch or running stitch by hand. Make narrow hems at waist and legs. Thread round elastic through the waist. Legs can be hemmed with shell stitch (see page 8) or have narrow lace added.

## Dress
Join the side seams. Make a narrow hem on the bottom and round the sleeves and neck and sew

them. The pictured doll's dress is of pleated nylon. Cut the neckline straight across, and turn over the frilling on to the right side to make a collar. Plain fabrics can be finished off with binding round the neck, shoulders and sleeves then decorated with ric-rac braid, embroidery, beads or lace as desired. Fasten at the shoulders with press studs.

## Coat
This particular coat has been cut from a thick felt which needs no turnings. Pin the belt to the back just below the sleeves. Oversew side and shoulder seams on the wrong side, including the belt in the side seams. Press the seams flat. Pin the cuffs on to the wrong side of the sleeves, oversew together, press the seam flat and turn back the cuffs on to the right side. Turn down the pocket flaps and sew on small buttons to hold them down. Pin the pockets in place about ½ in. from the side seam and sew them in place with back stitch. Find the middle of the shorter of the collar's two long sides and pin it to the middle of the neck at the back on the wrong side. Pin the rest of the collar in place round the neck to within ½ in. of each front edge. Oversew and press the seam flat. Fit the coat on to the doll and mark the position of the three buttons, placing the bottom one level with the top of the pocket, on the left side. Cut three small buttonholes to fit them on the right side.

## Hat
Pin two sections of the hat together on the wrong side and oversew from the point at the top to the part where it curves in, then take the sewing thread through to the other side and finish the oversewing on the right side to the edge. Repeat this with the other pieces until all are sewn. Press the seams very flat. Turn back the brim and fit it on to the head.

Thread through to other side

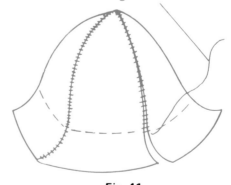

**Fig. 41**

## Shoes

Oversew the curved edges together in pairs. Fit them on to the feet and sew to the leg round the top of the shoe. With thick black embroidery silk sew from the front bottom edge of the cut-out curve, leaving a long end, from one side to the other along the top edge of the shoe. Leave the end. Re-thread the needle with the long end which was left and sew from side to side to cross over the first lot of stitches. Tie in a bow at the top.

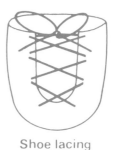

Shoe lacing

**Fig. 42**

## Doll in a kaftan

This doll is made in natural coloured muslin from template 5 (see page 17).

She is dressed in a kaftan — a long, straight dress, trimmed with decorative braid, with long sleeves and a short opening at the neck in front. The fabric used is a soft, figured brushed nylon.

*You will need:*
  felt tip pens
  artificial hair: 6 in. length
  brushed nylon *for dress:* two pieces, 12½ x 12 in.
  braid, ½ in. wide: 1 yd.
  matching thread
  one or two press studs

---

*Left above: big dressed doll, shown with flared dress and pants and playsuit.*

*Left below: doll in a kaftan and doll in a long frilled evening skirt and velvet blouse.*

*Right: template 4 dolls wearing the beach outfit, and a small sister in her beach suit*

## Features

These are drawn on with felt tip pens. Spread the hair across the head from side to side, then sew along the hair line and back of the head with small stitches hidden in the wavy strands.

## The kaftan

Back and front are alike when cut out. Fold each piece of fabric in half so that it measures 12½ x 6 in. Pin the pattern on to it with the long straight edge to the fold of the material

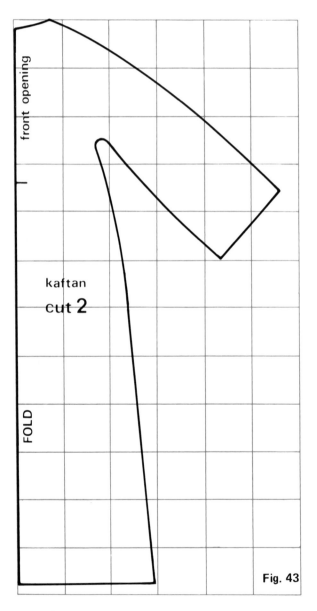

front opening

kaftan

cut 2

FOLD

Fig. 43

and cut out one from each piece allowing an extra ½ in. on each edge for the seams. Cut one of the pieces down the centre from the neck for about 3 in. for a front opening. Make narrow turnings on the neck opening and hem them. Pin braid down the centre of the dress from neck to hem covering the front opening. Sew it down on one side of the opening and down both sides to the hem.

Pin the pieces together with the right sides inside and machine stitch or hand sew the side and shoulder seams. Turn inside out and press the seams flat. Make a narrow turning at the hem on the right side, pin the braid all along the edge and sew, then sew it in place along the top edge also.

Pin the braid to the edges of the sleeves, with half the width on the right side and half on the wrong side so that the raw edge is enclosed. Sew it on both sides of the sleeves. Measure the braid for the neck from the edge of the front braid, then add a further ½ in. Make a single ¼in. turning at each end and pin and sew to the neck edge as for the sleeves. Fasten at the neck with one or two press studs.

## The doll in a beach outfit

She is made in flesh coloured felt from template 5, but templates 4, 6 or 7 could be used to give the same sized doll.

Her holiday beach outfit is made in printed towelling and consists of a bikini, a covering tabard, a short skirt, a bolero jacket and a head scarf. The skirt and jacket are lined and are reversible so that she can have a different outfit. Patterns are given for all of them. Amounts needed are given for each piece separately, so that they can be made singly if wished. Allow an extra ½ in. on each edge for seams.

*You will need:*
  red, black and brown embroidery silks
  thick brown wool
  printed towelling *for bikini bottom:* 8 x 3¼ in.
  printed towelling *for bikini top:* 7¾ x 1¾ in.
  printed towelling *for tabard:* two pieces, 6¼ x 4½ in.
  printed towelling *for skirt:* 11½ x 5¾ in.
  printed towelling *for bolero:* 4½ x 8¾ in.
  towelling *for headscarf:* 11 in. square
  lining *for tabard:* two pieces, 6¼ x 4½ in.
  lining *for skirt:* 11½ x 5¾ in.
  lining *for bolero:* 4½ x 8¾ in.
  matching sewing thread

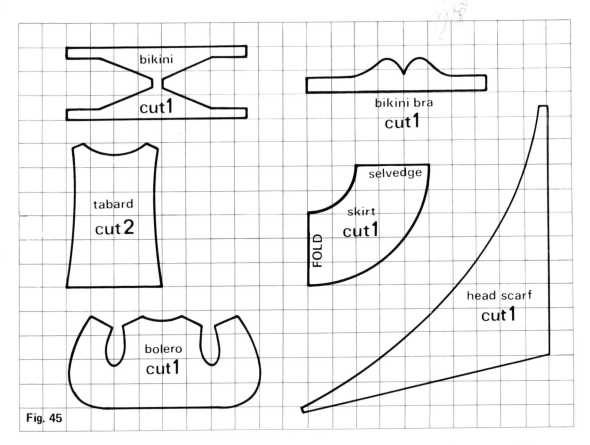

bikini
cut 1

bikini bra
cut 1

tabard
cut 2

selvedge

FOLD
skirt
cut 1

head scarf
cut 1

bolero
cut 1

Fig. 45

two press studs
narrow ribbon or cord: 6 in.

## Features

Embroider the mouth using one long fly stitch in red with two smaller graduated ones above and below. The eyes are two open triangles in black with five straight stitches above each for lashes and two arcs in stem stitch for eyebrows. For hair, cut the wool into 10 in. lengths, tease out into single strands and lay across the head from side to side. Catch in place with small stitches. Gather the ends at each side of the face and plait.

Fig. 44

## The beach outfit

Towelling is not easy to trace on in pencil, so trace the templates on to thin paper and pin this on to the towelling. Allow an extra ½ in. on all edges for seam allowances. Traced pencil lines on the lining should be used as guide lines for stitching.

## Bikini bottom

Cut out in one piece. Snip into the V's of legs. Make single turnings on leg edges and then on the long sides and machine stitch with a zig-zag stitch or hand sew with herringbone stitch (see page 6 ). Oversew the ends and tie on each hip.

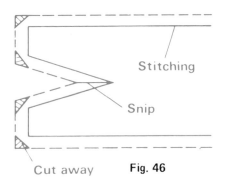

Stitching

Snip

Cut away       Fig. 46

## Bikini top

Cut out in one piece. It is easier to sew if the bottom straight edge can be placed on the selvedge when cutting out and then no hem is needed. Snip into the front edge. Make single turnings on all edges and hand sew or machine with zig-zag stitch. Fasten at the back with a press stud. Sew on ribbon or cord for a halter neck, fastening at the back.

Cut

**Fig. 47**

## Tabard (unlined)

Cut two allowing an extra ½ in. for seams and hems. Join the shoulder seams with a flat seam. Make narrow single turnings down each side and machine or sew as for the bikini. Make hems on the bottom edges and sew them. Make narrow single turnings on the neck edges and machine with zig-zag stitch. Join the sides with buttonhole bars.

## Tabard (lined)

Cut two pieces in towelling and two in lining. Join the shoulder seams of both towelling and lining with flat seams. Pin them together all round the edges with right sides inside. Machine together with straight stitch or hand sew all round leaving a small opening about 2 in. at one side.

Trim off corners and all surplus fabric to about ¼ in. from the stitching and turn inside out. Press all seams flat. Turn in the raw edges of the opening and sew. Make narrow turnings round the neckline of each piece and slip stitch the edges together. Fasten at the sides with buttonhole bars.

## Skirt

The pattern is for half the skirt. Fold the material in half and place one straight edge of the pattern on the fold. Allow extra for turnings when cutting out.

This one is lined but if necessary it can be made up singly, making hems on all the edges. Care should be taken with the hem on the bottom edge because most of it is on the cross and is very easily stretched out of shape.

Cut one skirt each from the folded towelling and folded lining and pin them together with the right sides inside and stitch together round

all the edges leaving a 1½ in. opening on one front edge.

Trim off all surplus material and corners, cut small V's at intervals round the curved bottom edge and waist and turn inside out. Press seams flat. Make narrow single turnings on the open piece and slip stitch together. Sew on a press stud for fastening.

## Bolero

This also can be made up without a lining, and again care should be taken not to stretch the curved edge when sewing.

Cut out one each from towelling and lining and pin them together with the right sides inside. Machine stitch or hand sew round all the edges leaving about 1½ in. open at the back of the neck. Trim off all surplus fabric, cut out V's from curves, and turn inside out. Press the seams flat. Make narrow single turnings at the back of the neck and sew the two edges together. The bolero has no fastening.

## Head scarf

This is triangular and unlined. It can, of course, be lined if wished, in which case make it up in the same way as the skirt. Make single turnings on all edges and machine with a zig-zag stitch or hand sew. The two narrow ends tie under the chin.

## Small sister in her beach suit

The small doll is made up from template 10 in flesh coloured felt and with a head gusset, all seams oversewn on the right side.

*You will need:*
   red, blue and black embroidery silks
   yellow wool
   towelling *for playsuit:* two pieces, 5 x 3½ in.
   felt *for spade:* two pieces, $\frac{4}{5}$ x $\frac{3}{5}$ in.
   felt *for pail:* 2¼ x 1 in.
   felt *for pail base:* $\frac{2}{5}$ in. circle
   narrow ribbon or cord: 1½ in.
   pipe cleaner to match felt
   matching sewing thread

## Features

Embroider three fly stitches, in red, close to and touching each other for a mouth. Her eyes are two circles in blue satin stitch with fly stitches in black for brows.

For hair, cut the wool in 5 in. long strands. Lay them across the head and backstitch them from forehead to back of neck. Gather some strands in to each side of the face and sew the rest across the head at the back, sewing through the strands. Trim the ends level in a bob cut.

## The playsuit

Cut out the pieces to the above sizes allowing ½ in. extra for turnings. Snip into the corners of the bib as at A in Fig. **48**. Make a single turning across the front and sew. Snip at B on bib and C at waist. Make single turnings on each side of the strap, sewing one turning on top of the other. Complete the other side to match. Pin the two pieces together with right sides inside and sew the side seams and the inner leg seams.

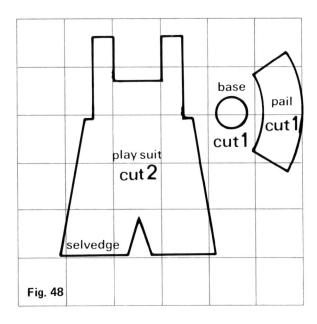

Fig. 48

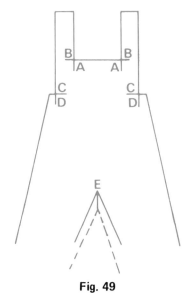

Fig. 49

Snip under the arm at D, make a single turning on each side of the waist and sew. Snip into the corners between the legs at E. Make single turnings on the leg hems and sew. Turn it inside out, press out the seams and fit on to the doll.

## Spade

Fold the pipe cleaner in half and twist it together leaving a small loop at the top for a handle. Oversew together three edges of the felt for the spade leaving one short side open. Insert the twisted ends of the pipe cleaner, and sew up the seam, sewing in the pipe cleaner too.

## Pail

Oversew the circle to the smaller curve of the pail and sew together the two straight edges. Sew the handle on from side to side. Sew the handles of spade and pail to the doll's hands.

## Doll in a long frilled evening skirt and velvet blouse

She is also made from template 4, but could be made in the same size from templates 5, 6 or 7. She is in flesh coloured felt, machine stitched on the wrong side.

The skirt and blouse patterns are each in two parts; for back and front. The skirt can be made in any soft material so that it hangs in folds — this one is in brushed nylon. The blouse is in black velvet which ties round the waist, but it could be made in silk or a lurex fabric.

*You will need:*
   red, blue and black embroidery silks
   artificial dolls' hair
   brushed nylon *for skirt back and front:* 24 x 8 in.
   black silk *for frill:* 96 x 1 in. (a piece measuring 24 x 4 in. can be cut into four and joined)
   black velvet *for blouse front:* two pieces, 5½ x 12 in.
   black velvet *for blouse back:* 5¼ x 11½ in.
   black sewing thread
   one press stud

## Features

For her mouth, embroider a crescent shape in red stem stitch and over the top a double arc to make a shaped top lip. Above the mouth make a small half circle in red stem stitch for a nose.

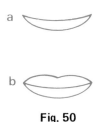

a

b

**Fig. 50**

Her eyes are ½ in. circles of buttonhole stitch wheels in blue. Starting from the edge of the circle, bring the silk out from the back. Hold the thread under the left thumb, insert the needle in the centre of the circle and bring out on the edge slightly to the right and over the held thread. Pull the stitch tight. Repeat this all round, always inserting the needle in the same hole in the centre and bringing it out on the edge a little to the right of the last stitch. Sew a curve of stem stitch above each eye and some straight stitches for lashes. The hair is sewn on like that for the kaftan dressed doll and finished off in a soft coil on the neck.

## The clothes

Cut the patterns in paper and pin on the fabric.

## Skirt

The pattern is in two pieces for back and front. Fold the material in half and place the pattern so that one straight edge of the back is on the fold of the material and the front pattern reversed is beside it. Allow an extra ¼ in. on the edges for turnings. Sew the side seams and press. Make a single turning all round the curved front and back edges and tack. Make a hem on the waist and sew.

With pinking shears cut the black silk into four lengths 1 in. wide and join them in a continuous strip. Gather along one edge into a frill. Mark the quarters on the whole of the hem from the waist on one side to the other. Pin the joins in the frill to these marks, and ease out the gathers evenly to fit. Pin all round and then tack in place. Machine stitch the frill on to the skirt. If sewing by hand use backstitch for strength. The pinked edges of the frill will prevent fraying. Fasten at the waist with a press stud.

## Blouse

Fold the blouse material for the back in half to measure 5¼ x 5¾ in. Place the straight edge of the centre back of the pattern to the fold and cut out allowing ½ in. extra for turnings. Pin the two

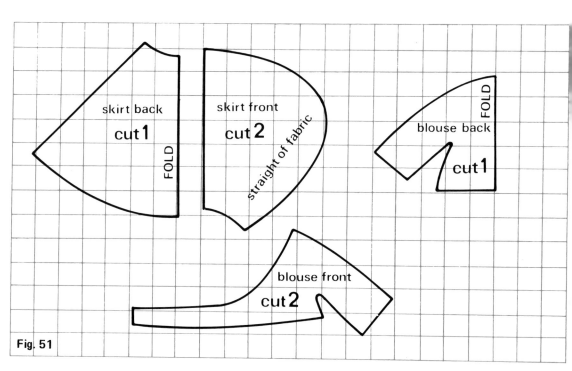

skirt back cut 1  FOLD

skirt front cut 2  straight of fabric

blouse back cut 1  FOLD

blouse front cut 2

**Fig. 51**

pieces of material for the fronts together with right sides inside and pin the pattern on to it with the straight of the material from shoulder to hem. Cut it out. Sew up the side, under arm and top arm seams. Make narrow hems on the sleeves, round the neck and front, including the ties, and along the bottom of the blouse and ties. Sew them all. A single turning sewn in herringbone stitch is very successful.

No fastenings are required. The back of the blouse is slightly longer than the front to enable it to be tucked into the skirt, while the fronts come over the top of the skirt, cross over and tie at the back. Fit the blouse on to the doll and fasten the skirt round the waist covering the blouse edge at the back. Cross over the blouse fronts and tie at the back.

## Doll in a pram suit
This small boy in his cosy red knitted pram suit is also made from template 4 (or 5, 6, or 7).

*You will need:*
dark pink, black and blue embroidery silks
brown wool *for hair*
4 ply wool *for pram suit:* 2 ounces
pair No. 10 knitting needles
two safety pins
two or three press studs

## Features
Embroider a curve in pink stem stitch for a smiling mouth and two seed stitches above for a nose. His eyes are two circles in black or brown stem stitch with a straight edge at the bottom, and two satin stitch circles in blue on the straight edge.

## Hair
Thread a large eyed needle with brown wool, wind the end of it round a finger three or four times, slip the loops off and sew on to the hair line on the cheek. Continue sewing loops all round the hair line to the other cheek, and then over the rest of the head.

## The pram suit
**Casting on method to give a firm edge**    Cast on 2 stitches. Put the right hand needle in between the 2 stitches and cast on the third stitch. Continue so, always putting the needle in between the last 2 stitches on the left hand needle to cast on the next stitch. There is no need to work into the back of stitches on the first knit row.

**Back of coat**    With 4 ply wool and No. 10 needles cast on 42 stitches.
\*\*Work 4 rows in garter stitch (every row plain).
Work 5 rows in stocking stitch (one row plain and one row purl) ending on a plain row which is the right side.
**Next row**    Knit.
**Next row**    K1 \* wool round needle, K2 together\*.
Repeat from \* to \* to last stitch, k 1.
**Next row**    Knit\*\*.
Continue work repeating from \*\* to \*\* till the work measures 2¾ in. from the beginning.
**Next row** \* K 1, k 2 tog.\* Repeat from \* to \* to end.
**Next row** Purl.
Knit 4 rows of stocking stitch.
Cast off 3 stitches at the beginning of the next 2 rows, for the armholes.
Continue in stocking stitch for 2 in. Cast off.
**Right front**    Cast on 26 stitches, and work 4 rows of garter stitch.
Work 5 rows of stocking stitch keeping a border of 3 garter stitches by knitting plain the last 3 stitches of every purl row. Continue in pattern as the back till the work measures 2¾ in. finishing on a purl row.
**Next row**    K 3, \*k 2 tog., k 1 \*. Knit from \* to \* to the end of the row (18 sts).
Knit 4 rows in stocking stitch beginning with a purl row and ending with a knit row.
**Next row**    Cast off 3 sts for armholes, p to the last 3, k 3.
Continue in stocking stitch till the armhole measures 1½ in. finishing at the neck edge and keeping front border of 3 garter sts.
**Next row**    Cast off 5 for neck decreasing, knit to end. Decrease 1 stitch in every row at the neck edge till 4 stitches are left. Cast off.
**Left front**    Cast on 26 sts and knit as for the right side as far as the waist decreasing, and keeping the border of 3 garter sts at the beginning of the purl row.
**Next row**    Purl.
**Next row**    Knit.
**Next row**    Purl.
**Next row**    Cast off 3 sts at the beginning of the next row for the armhole decreasing.
Finish as for the right front.
**Sleeves**    Cast on 25 sts and work 3 rows in garter stitch.
**Next row**    \*\*Knit.
**Next row**    K 1 \*wool round needle, k 2 tog.\*
Repeat from \* to \* to end of row.

**Next row** Knit.
**Next row** Purl.
**Next row** Knit.** Repeat ** to ** till sleeve measures 3½ in. Cast off 3 sts at the beginning of the next 2 rows. Decrease 1 stitch at the beginning of the next 7 rows. Cast off.
Press all pieces lightly. Join the shoulder seams.
**Collar** With right side of work facing, pick up 34 sts round the neck missing the first and last sts.
*K one row.
**Next row** K3, p to last 3, k 3.*
Repeat from * to * 3 times. Work 5 rows, cast off.
Sew in the sleeves, join sleeve and side seams. Sew 2 or 3 press studs on the front edge.
**Leggings** Cast on 28 sts for the waist and work in rib of k 1, p 1 for 4 rows.
Work in stocking stitch till work measures 3½ in. from the beginning.
Cast on 3 sts at the beginning of the next 2 rows.
Work 4 rows in stocking stitch.
**Next row** Decrease 1 stitch at each end of the row. Continue decreasing 1 stitch at each end of every following fifth row till 22 sts remain.
Work 5 rows finishing on a purl row.
**Shaping foot** Knit 15 sts, turn, put 7 sts on a safety pin.
P 8, turn, put 7 sts on the second safety pin.
Work 6 rows in stocking stitch on these 8 sts.
**Next row** K 8, pick up and k 4 sts down the side of the top of the foot. K the 7 sts left on the pin.
**Next row** P 19, pick up and p 4 sts on the other side of the top of the foot, p 7 from the second safety pin (30 sts).
**Next row** K 1, k 2 tog., k 7, k 2 tog., k 6, k 2 tog., k 7, k 2 tog., k 1.
**Next row** Purl.
**Next row** K 1, k 2 tog., k 6, k 2 tog., k 4, k 2 tog., k 6, k 2 tog., k 1.
**Next row** Purl.
**Next row** K 1, k 2 tog., k 5, k 2 tog., k 2, k 2 tog., k 5, k 2 tog., k 1. Cast off.
Knit a second leg reversing the shapings.
**Hood** Cast on 48 sts and work 4 rows in garter stitch.
Continue working in stocking stitch keeping a border each side of 3 sts in garter stitch, for 2¼ in. Cast off. Fold the piece in half and sew together the cast off stitches.
**Ties** Pick up 3 sts on the face edge at the corner and on them work a strip 4 in. long. Repeat this on the other corner. Make a small tassel by winding wool round a finger and a

strand of wool, about 20 times. Push the loops off and tie the strand tightly round the loops. Cut the loops and sew the tassel to the point of the hood.

### Doll in a blue knitted dress and panties

The doll shown in the picture was made in pale pink poplin from template No. 5, but her clothes will fit any doll made from templates 4 to 7.

*You will need:*
felt tip pens
brown wool *for hair*
3 ply wool *for clothes:* 2 ounces
pair No. 10 knitting needles
three small pearl buttons
crochet hook
round elastic: 6 in.

With a red pen draw a small O for a nose and a bigger O for a mouth. Draw two circles in blue for eyes and round them embroider a three-quarter circle on a straight line in brown silk stem stitch with three straight stitches radiating from the top of each.

**Fig. 52**

For hair, cut the wool in 10 in. lengths, lay them across the head and sew down the centre of the head with backstitch. Sew them down also each side of the face, sewing through the strands to hide the stitches.

### Dress and panties
**Dress back** Cast on 72 sts and work 4 rows of garter stitch.
Work 4 rows of stocking stitch ending with a purl row.
**Next row** **K1 *, wool forward, k 2 tog.*
Repeat from * to * to the last stitch, k 1.

**Next row**      Knit.
Work 6 rows of stocking stitch.**
Repeat these 8 rows of pattern from** to ** 3 more times.
**Next row**      Knit.
**Next row**      P 2 tog. 12 times, p 3 tog. 8 times, p 2 tog. 12 times (32 sts).
Work 10 rows in k 1 p 1 rib.
Cast on 7 sts at the beginning of the next 2 rows for sleeves. (46 sts)
**Next row**      Knit.
**Next row**      K 3, p to last 3 sts, k 3.
Continue in stocking stitch for another 2 in. keeping a border of 3 sts in garter stitch at the edge of each sleeve. Cast off.
**Dress front**      Cast on 72 sts and work as for the back until the sleeve sts have been cast on.
**Next row**      K 23, turn, put the last 23 sts on a safety pin.
**Next row**      K 3, p to the last 3 sts, k 3.
Continue working for 1½ in. keeping the garter stitch border of 3 sts at each end and finishing at the neck end.
**Next row**      Cast off 8 sts, p to the last 3, k 3.
**Next row**      Knit.
**Next row**      P to the last 3 sts, k 3.
Repeat the last 2 rows once. Cast off.
Take the stitches off the pin on to a needle and join on the wool at the back opening.
Work the second side to match the first but cast off the neck sts at the beginning of the row.
Join the side and shoulder seams on the wrong side and press them flat.

   With the right side of the work facing, join the wool at the neck edge and work two rows of double crochet round the neck (put the crochet hook through the cast off stitch, loop the wool round the hook, and pull the loop through; put the wool round the hook again and pull the loop through both stitches.)

   Continue down the opening of the dress making loops of four chain at the top, middle and bottom of the opening.

   Fasten off.

*Right above: girl dolls wearing the blue knitted dress and pants and the pram suit, and a boy doll in jersey and shorts.*

*Right below: a party doll and a doll in a red and white knitted dress*

Sew three small buttons on the side of the opening opposite the loops.

**Panties**     Cast on 30 sts and work 2 rows of k 1, p 1.

**Next row**     K 1, *wool round needle, k 2 tog*. Repeat from * to * to last stitch, k 1.

**Next row**     K 1, p 1 to end.

Continue in stocking stitch for 2¼ in.

**Next row**     K 2 tog., at each end of every row till 6 stitches are left.

Work 6 rows of stocking stitch.

**Next row**     Increase 1 stitch at each end of every row till 30 sts are on the needle.

Work in stocking stitch for 2¼ in.

**Next row**     K 1 p 1.

**Next row**     K 1 * wool round needle, k 2 tog*.

Repeat from * to * to last stitch, k 1.

K 1 p 1 for 2 rows. Cast off.

Join the side seams on the wrong side and press seams. Thread round elastic through the holes at the waist.

### A party girl

She wears a long, sleeveless knitted blue and silver dress; she is made from template 5 in natural colour cotton muslin. Her dress is knitted in a silky cotton and lurex thread, with sequins sewn on at the neck and a silver cord tied in a bow at the waist. Under it she wears a slim white silk slip.

*You will need:*
   red, blue and brown felt tip pens
   blond artifical doll's hair: about 5 in. un-
      stretched
   white silk *for slip:* 10¾ x 13 in.
   white narrow ribbon: 6 in.
   white sewing thread
   silky yarn *for dress:* 1 skein
   pair No. 11 and No. 13 knitting needles
   spool Lurex thread
   about 24 silver sequins
   silver cord: 27 in.

### Features

For a mouth, draw a crescent shape with the red pen and on top of it draw a bow shape to make a smiling mouth. Draw a small half circle curve for a nose. The eyes are solid blue circles with the centres left uncoloured. Above and below draw arcs in brown with straight stitches above them for lashes.

### Hair

Spread the wavy doll's hair across the head from one side of the neck to the other and catch it in place round the face with invisible stitches. Spread the hair out over the back of the head and catch down with small stitches here and there.

### Slip

Fold the silk in half to measure 10¾ x 6½ in. Lay on the pattern and cut out the pieces, back and front alike. Sew the sides together in narrow french seams, or sew single seams and oversew the raw edges to prevent fraying. Make a hem at top and bottom and sew. Sew ribbon on the top for shoulder straps.

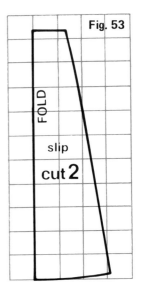

Fig. 53

FOLD

slip

cut 2

### Dress

With No. 11 needles cast on 36 sts.

Work 8 rows of garter stitch.

Join in the Lurex thread and knit in with the silky yarn. Work 2 rows of garter stitch. Leave the Lurex and work * 8 rows of garter stitch with silk only.

Knit 2 rows with Lurex and silk. Leave Lurex and work 2 rows of stocking stitch. With Lurex and silk work 2 rows of garter stitch *.

Repeat from * to * 4 times. Break off the Lurex.

Work 8 rows of stocking stitch.

Change to No. 13 needles.

Work 10 rows of k 1 p 1 rib.

Change to No. 11 needles.

**Next row**     K 3, *k 2 tog., k 2*. Repeat from * to * to last 5 sts. K 2 tog., k 3 (28 sts).

Continue in stocking stitch for 1 in. finishing on a purl row.

Cast off 3 sts at the beginning of the next 2 rows.

**Next row**    Knit.

**Next row**    K 2, p to the last 2, k 2.

**Next row**    K 11, turn, k 2, p 7, k 2.

Continue on these 11 sts in stocking stitch with a border of 2 sts of garter stitch at each end. Decrease at the neck edge on every plain row till 1 stitch is left. Cast off.

Join the thread to the neck edge of the other stitches and complete the right side to match the left. Work the back of the dress to match the front. Sew silver sequins round the front V and tie a silver cord round the waist.

## Doll in a red and white knitted dress

She has matching pants and a poncho top and red socks to match. She is made from template 6 in natural linen-type fabric and has a head gusset inserted.

*You will need:*

  red, blue and brown felt tip pens

  yellow or blond wool *for hair*

  white 3 ply wool *for dress and pants:* 2 ounces

  red 3 ply wool *for poncho, dress stripes and socks:* 1 ounce

  round elastic, 6 in.

  pair No. 9 and No. 11 knitting needles

  two buttons

## Features

These are similar to those of the doll in the knitted evening dress (see page **47**). The hair is curly. Twist the wool three or four times round a finger and sew the loops to the side of the head. Continue forming loops and sewing them round the face on the hair line and over the rest of the head.

## Dress

With No. 11 needles cast on 98 sts in white wool.

K 2 rows. Join on red wool. Change to No. 9 needles.

**1st row**    K 1*, wool round needle, k 2 tog*. Repeat * to * to end of row.

**2nd row**    P to end. Break off red wool.

Work 4 rows in white wool. Join on red wool. Repeat the above 6 rows once more and then the 1st and 2nd rows above to give three red stripes. Break off red wool.

Continue working in white wool in garter stitch till the work measures 3½ in. finishing on the wrong side.

**Next row**    K 2 tog. 14 times.

(K 1, k 2 tog.) 14 times then k 2 tog. 14 times (56 sts).

K 1 row. Divide for the 2 backs.

**Next row**    K 11, cast off 6 sts, k 22 sts including the stitch left on the needle after casting off, cast off 6 sts, k 11.

On the last 11 sts knit for 2¾ in. finishing at the neck edge. Cast off 6 sts.

K 3 rows on the remaining 5 sts. Cast off.

Join wool to the front sts and work in garter stitch on these 22 sts for 2½ in.

**Next row**    K 5, cast off 12, k 4, plus the stitch on the needle.

On the last 5 sts k 4 rows. Cast off.

Join wool to the remaining 5 sts and knit for 4 rows.

Cast off.

Join wool to the armhole edge of the remaining 11 sts.

Complete as for the other side of back, reversing where necessary.

**Sleeves**    With No. 11 needles cast on 24 sts and k 2 rows. Join on red wool.

Change to No. 9 needles.

K 1*, wool round needle, k 2 tog. Repeat * to * end of row.

P to end. Break off red wool.

**Next row**    Increase in every stitch (48 sts).

Work in garter stitch for 1 in. Cast off.

Work a second sleeve to match.

**Making up**    Join the back seam of the skirt up to the waist line. Join shoulder and sleeve seams. Sew in the sleeves. Work a row of double crochet up the opening from the waist making two loops of five chain stitches for buttonholes at equal distances apart. Continue working double crochet round the neck.

Sew on the buttons. Press the seams.

With double red wool work a crochet chain about 20 in. long.

Make two small tassels for the ends and tie around waist.

## Panties

With No. 11 needles cast on 28 sts in white wool. K 1 p 1 for 4 rows.

Work in garter stitch for 2 in.

K 2 tog. at each end of every row till 4 sts are left.

Knit 6 rows on these 4 sts.

Increase 1 stitch at each end of every row till 28 sts are on the needle.

K 1 p 1 for 4 rows. Cast off.

**Frill**    With red wool pick up 24 sts on the leg.

**Next row**    K 1 p 1 in every stitch.

**Next row**    Knit. Cast off. Repeat on other leg.

Join side seams. If needed thread round elastic through the top ribbing.

## Poncho

**Front**    With red wool and No. 11 needles cast on 75 sts.

Knit 2 rows. Mark the centre stitch.

**Next row**    K 34, k 3 tog., k 1, k 3 tog., k 34.

**Next row**    Knit.

Continue as these 2 rows, knitting 3 tog. each side of the centre stitch on alternate rows till 27 sts remain.

K 1 p 1 for 6 rows. Cast off.

Work a second piece to match for the back.

Press lightly. Join the side seams. Wind wool round a flat ruler and cut it into strands 2 in. long. Knot them in twos into alternate loops of the cast on stitches, working from the wrong side, to form a fringe. Trim ends level.

## Socks

With No. 11 needles cast on 20 sts in red wool.

K 2 rows. Join on white wool.

**Next row**    K 1*, wool round needle, k 2 tog.* Repeat * to * to last stitch, k 1.

**Next row**    Purl. Break off white wool.

Continue in garter stitch for 1 in.

**Next row**    K 4, k 2 tog., k 8, k 2 tog., k 4.

**Next row**    Knit.

**Next row**    K 3, k 2 tog., k 8, k 2 tog., k 3.

**Next row**    Knit.

**Next row**    K 3, k 2 tog., k 6, k 2 tog., k 3.

**Next row**    Knit.

**Next row**    K 2, k 2 tog., k 6, k 2 tog., k 2.

**Next row**    Knit.

**Next row**    K 2, k 2 tog., k 4, k 2 tog., k 2.

**Next row**    Knit. Cast off.

Knit another to match. Join the back seams and toe seam. Press lightly.

## A boy doll

He is warmly dressed in a knitted jersey and shorts, and is made from template 6 in flesh coloured felt.

*You will need:*

    red, blue and black embroidery silks
    brown felt *for hair back:* 3 x 4½ in.
    brown felt *for hair front:* 1 x 4½ in.
    3 ply wool *for jersey and shorts:* 1 ounce
    pair No. 12 and No. 10 knitting needles
    safety pin

    press stud
    round elastic: 6 in.

## Features

For his mouth, sew a crescent of red stem stitch with a shorter line across the middle. Above this make a small red circle in backstitch for a nose. The eyes are outlined in black stem stitch and are circles, with a segment cut out at the bottom. Work a blue circle of satin stitch in each right corner. Make arcs of black chain stitch above the eyes for brows.

**Fig. 54**

## Hair

Trace the head curve from the template on to both pieces of brown felt. On the larger piece cut the bottom edge into a notched curve and sew it to the back of the head. Cut the front piece in notches making it narrower at each side. Oversew it to the back hair, and catch down the notches in a few places.

## Blue jersey

**Back**    With No. 12 needles cast on 36 sts.

\*\*Work 6 rows of garter stitch.

Change to No. 10 needles and knit 4 rows of stocking stitch.

**11th row**    K 1, *wool round needle, k 2 tog*. Repeat from * to * to last stitch, k 1.

**12th row**    Purl.

**13th row**    K 2, * wool round needle, k 2 tog*. Repeat to end of row.

**14th row**    Purl.

**15th row**    K 1, * wool round needle, k 2 tog*. Repeat to last stitch, k 1.

**16th row**    Purl.

Work in stocking stitch for 2 in.

Cast off 4 sts at beginning of next 2 rows\*\*.

Work ¾ in. finishing on a purl row.

K 14, turn, put other 14 sts on a safety pin.

K 3, p to end.

Work for 1 in. keeping a border of 3 garter sts at the neck edge. Cast off.

Join on wool to the centre and cast on 3 sts.

Complete as for the first side.

**Front**    Cast on 36 sts on No. 12 needles.

Work as for the back from \*\* to \*\*.

Work 1 in. finishing on a purl row.

K 8 sts, put the rest on to a safety pin, turn and purl back.
K 2 tog. at the end of the next and alternate 2 rows.

**Next row**      Purl.
**Next row**      Knit.
**Next row**      Purl. Cast off.

Leave 12 sts on the safety pin and join the wool to the next stitch. Complete this side to match the other reversing the decreasings.

**Sleeves**      With No. 12 needles cast on 20 sts.
Work 4 rows of garter stitch. Change to No. 10 needles.
Work 2 rows of stocking stitch.
Work 4 pattern rows as back of jersey.
Continue in stocking stitch increasing at each end of every fourth row till 32 sts remain. Work 4 rows.
Cast off 3 sts at the beginning of the next 2 rows.
Work 2 rows. Cast off.
Knit a second sleeve to match.
Press the pieces lightly under a damp cloth.
Join side, shoulder and sleeve seams. Sew in sleeves.
Join the wool to the neck opening. Pick up and knit 14 sts from the opening and round the side of neck, knit 12 sts off the pin, pick up and knit 14 sts on rest of neck (40 sts). Work 4 rows of garter stitch.
Cast off. Sew press studs on the back opening.

## Shorts

With No. 12 needles cast on 30 sts.
Work in rib of k 1 p 1 for 4 rows.
Change to No. 10 needles.
Work in stocking stitch for 1¾ in.
Decrease 1 stitch at each end of every row till 6 sts remain. Work 8 rows.
Increase 1 stitch at each end of every row till 30 sts are on the needle.
Work in stocking stitch for 1¾ in.
Change to No. 12 needles.
Knit 4 rows of k 1 p 1 rib. Cast off.
With No. 12 needles and right side of work facing, pick up and knit 36 sts along the leg.
Work 4 rows of garter stitch. Cast off.
Repeat for other leg.
Press lightly and sew up side seams.
If necessary thread round elastic through the top.

## EXTRA CLOTHES

The patterns for these extra clothes are de-
signed to fit dolls made from the basic templates 1, 2, 4 – 7, 8, 9, 10 – 13A.

Seams used are generally flat seams, edges can be pinked, or oversewn, but do not use french seams as they are too thick for these small articles. Thicker fabrics such as jersey can be oversewn using a double oversewing stitch which has a locking effect on the edges (see page 6). Shell edging is a simple and effective finish on thin cotton or silk dresses etc. (see page 8).

## Flared dress and pants for template 1

The dress is cut in three pieces, two for the back because it has a back fastening, and the front.

*You will need:*
    cotton fabric *for dress back:* two pieces, 9½ x 6¼ in.
    cotton fabric *for dress front:* 9½ x 10½ in.
    cotton fabric *for pants:* 8 x 6¼ in.
    cotton bias binding: 45 in.
    matching sewing thread
    embroidery silk
    three 000 size press studs
    three small pearl buttons

### Dress

Place the fabric pieces for the back together with right sides outside, placing straight edge of pattern if possible on the selvedge, and cut them out. Fold the facing strip on the pattern underneath. Fold fabric for the front in half to measure 9½ x 5¼ in. and place pattern on it with the straight edge to the fold, and cut it out. Allow an extra ½ in. on all turnings when cutting out.

Sew the side and shoulder seams and press. Cut off one of the turnings all along the binding to make it narrower. Sew this cut edge to the wrong side of the neck, armholes and hem. Turn it over to the right side and sew down with even running stitches in matching or contrasting embroidery silk to look like saddle stitching. Sew press studs down the back opening with buttons over them. As an alternative, the back can be seamed to within 2 in. of the neck to make it into a dress instead of a pinafore style.

### Pants

Fold the fabric in half with right sides inside. Place narrow straight edge between the legs on the fold and cut out allowing for small turnings. Sew the side seams. Sew a hem at the top and if

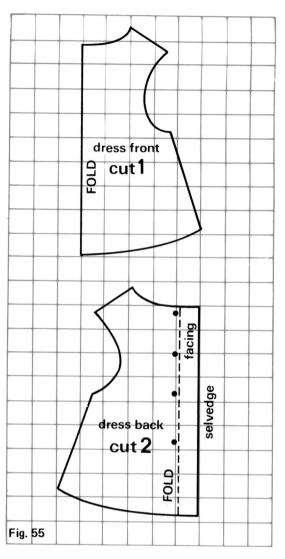

**dress front**
**cut 1**
FOLD

**dress back**
**cut 2**
facing
selvedge
FOLD

Fig. 55

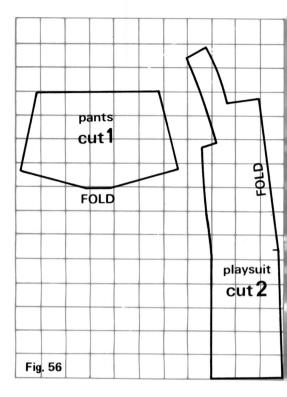

**pants**
**cut 1**
FOLD

FOLD
**playsuit**
**cut 2**

Fig. 56

Cut out the two pieces. Oversew together the side, shoulder and inner leg seams. Turn inside out and press out seams. Sew the braid across the front bib. Sew braid across each strap from the waist at the front to waist at the back, make narrow turnings at each end. If wished, the braid can be sewn round the ends of the legs, in which case an extra 12 in. will be needed.

If using fabric sew seams. Snip into the straps at waist and bib, make hems and sew. Hem the leg ends.

### Coat for template 4 — 7
The pattern is made with the sleeve cut in one.

*You will need:*
  pink jersey fabric *for back:* 8 x 6¼ in.
  pink jersey fabric *for front:* two pieces, 8 x 3¾ in.
  pink jersey fabric *for collar:* 9 x ¾ in.
  matching thread
  one press stud
  five very small buttons

Cut 1 back and 2 fronts allowing an extra ¼ in. for turnings. Sew up side and under sleeve

necessary run a round elastic through it. Make narrow single turnings on the wrong sides of the legs and sew with shell stitch. Press the seams.

### Playsuit for template 1 (See also page 38.)
This one is made in green felt with a bright braid trimming. If fabric is used allow an extra ½ in. all round for turnings.

*You will need:*
  felt *for back and front:* two pieces, 14 x 7 in.
  decorative braid, ½ in. wide 20 in.
  matching sewing thread

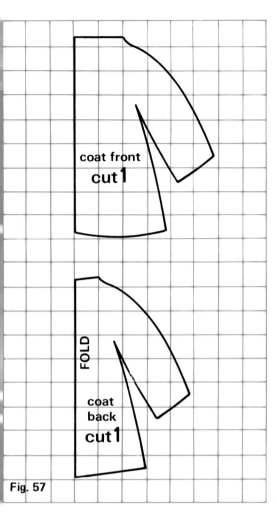

coat front
cut **1**

FOLD

coat
back
cut **1**

**Fig. 57**

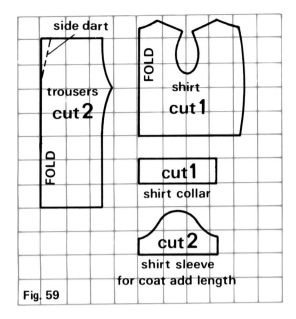

side dart

FOLD

trousers
cut **2**

shirt
cut **1**

FOLD

cut **1**

shirt collar

cut **2**

shirt sleeve
for coat add length

**Fig. 59**

seams on the wrong side with double over-sewing which is a locking stitch (see page **6**). Make narrow single turnings on sleeve ends and bottom edge and sew with herringbone stitch. Oversew the top seams of sleeves. Fold the collar piece in half and cut one end in an arrow shape. Oversew the ends and turn inside out. Pin it to the neck edge on the wrong side and sew with backstitch. Turn over to the right side and catch down along the edge. Sew a press stud under the arrow shaped end.

**Fig. 58**

Cut away

Cut 2 small buttonholes on the right edge of coat 1½ in. from the top and 1½ in. apart. Sew buttons to match on the left side and two more opposite them on the right side.

### Trousers for template 4 – 7

*You will need:*
   cotton fabric: two pieces, 8 x 6 in.
   sewing thread
   elastic

Cut two from the pattern allowing ½ in. extra all round for turnings and hems. Sew each leg seam on the wrong side. Sew small side seams over the hips, tapering them off to nothing. Pin the two legs together at the seams, then pin front seams and back seams together. Sew the seams, and press them. Make ½ in. hems on the legs and a smaller hem at the waist. If necessary thread round elastic through the waist.

### Shirt for templates 4 – 7
This could also serve as a jacket.

*You will need:*
   cotton fabric *for back and front:* 5¼ x 8 in.
   cotton fabric *for sleeves:* two pieces, 2¼ x 3¾ in.
   cotton fabric *for collar:* 1 x 3½ in.

matching thread
press studs
small buttons

Cut out as above allowing extra for turnings and hems. Sew shoulder seams. Pin sleeves into armhole and sew in on the wrong side with backstitch. Sew side and sleeve seams. Sew narrow hems on the two fronts and along the bottom. Make narrow hems ¾ in. long at each end of the neck. Fold the collar in half lengthwise and sew the two short seams together. Turn inside out and press seams flat. Mark the middle of the long edge of collar and the middle of the back neck and pin them together with right sides outside. Pin the rest of the collar round the neck and sew. Make a narrow single turning on the other edge of collar and pin over the collar stitching on the right side of shirt. Sew, making sure that no stitches show. Sew on press studs with buttons sewn on top of them.

## Mini dress and pants for templates 4 — 7

One piece of pattern because back and front are alike.

*You will need:*
  cotton check *for dress:* two pieces, 7¾ x 6 in.
  cotton check *for pants:* 7 x 4¾ in.
  matching thread
  four 000 size press studs

Cut out the pieces allowing extra for turnings. Sew the side seams of the dress. Make single turnings on the hem and sew in place with shell stitch. Make single turnings in a continuous line round neck, shoulders and armholes and sew down with shell stitch. Sew two press studs on each shoulder. Fold the pants in half and sew

*Left: the template 7 doll with the clothes described on pages 52–56 — the coat, trousers, shirt, mini dress and pants, bolero, and kilt. Also shown is the circular skating skirt for the template 9 doll.*

*Right above: the playsuit, flared dress and pants for the template 9 doll*

*Right below: mini dress and pants, coat, and full skirted dress for templates 10–13*

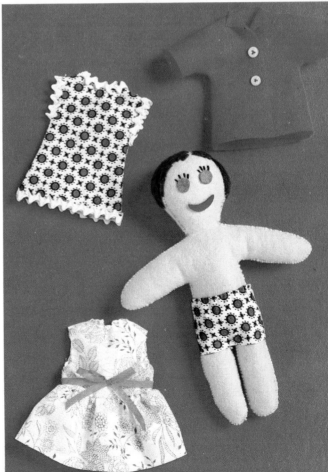

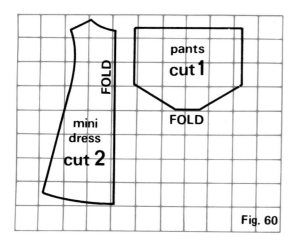

**Fig. 60**

ing an opening at the back of the neck. Trim off surplus fabric and snip curves and into corners, turn inside out and press seams flat. Make narrow turnings at the neck and slip stitch together. Make narrow single turnings on each armhole matching the lining with the outside and slip stitch together.

## Kilt

*You will need:*
    cotton plaid fabric 28 x 4¼ in.
    bias or plaid strip 9 x ¾ in.
    matching thread
    size 000 press stud
    small safety pin

Make a single turning on one long side of the plaid strip and sew with small stitches — these must not show on the right side. Pink the short edges. Pleat the kilt to follow the pattern of the plaid and tack the pleats at hem and waist. Turn in the short edges and sew. Pin bias binding along the waist on the right side and sew. Turn binding over to the wrong side making a double fold to reduce the width of the binding and sew to the wrong side of the pleats. Press with a hot iron and a damp cloth. Lap one front over the other and fasten at waist with press stud. Pin near the bottom edge with safety pin.

## Playsuit for template 9

*You will need:*
    linen or cotton fabric: two pieces, 7½ x 4½ in.
    matching thread

Front and back are alike. Cut two. Snip ¼ in. down the side of the bib AA (see Fig. 62), make a single turning on the wrong side and sew down with herringbone stitch. Make similar snips across the strap BB and on the strap at waist CC. Make single turnings on each side of the strap, overlapping them from point BB and sewing with herringbone stitch.

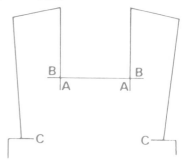

**Fig. 62**

the side seams. Make a narrow hem at the waist and sew and if necessary insert round elastic. Make single narrow turnings on the wrong side of each leg and sew with shell stitch.

## Bolero or waistcoat and kilt for templates 4 — 7

### Bolero

*You will need:*
    red felt *for back:* 4¼ x 5 in.
    red felt *for front:* two pieces, 4¼ x 2¼ in.
    matching sewing thread

Cut one back and two fronts as above. Oversew side and shoulder seams and press them flat, and the bolero is ready to wear. If using fabric cut the pieces larger to allow for turnings and cut a second set for linings. Make up each as above. Pin together round the outside edges with right sides inside and stitch together leav-

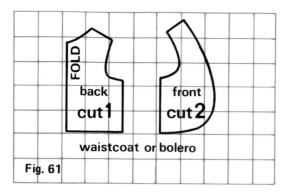

**Fig. 61**

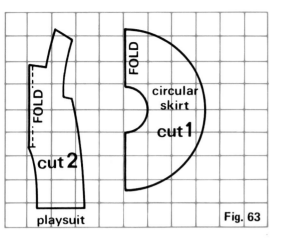

playsuit       Fig. 63

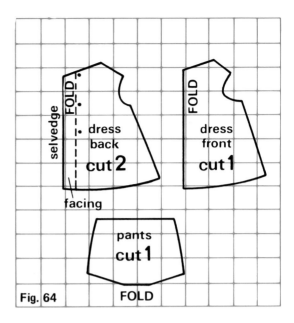

Fig. 64      FOLD

Repeat all this on the back piece of the suit. Pin both pieces together with right sides inside and sew the inside leg seams. Make small hems on the leg ends and sew them. Turn the right sides inside again and sew the side seams and the shoulder seams. Make single turnings at the waist and sew. Turn inside out and press the seams and hems.

### Circular skating skirt for template 9
*You will need:*
    soft silk *for skirt:* 7½ in. square
    soft silk *for tie:* 10 x ¾ in.
    matching thread

Fold the silk in four to form a square and place the straight edges of the pattern on each folded edge of silk. Cut out the top arc (waist) but cut the bottom edge with pinking shears. Cut down from the waist 1 in. on the straight of the material for an opening. Make small hems on each edge of the opening and sew. Place the middle of the tie to the middle of the waist opposite the opening and pin it round the rest of the waist on the right side. Sew in place. Fold the bind over on to the wrong side, make a narrow turning and sew down on the wrong side. Hem the ties. The skirt ties on to the doll with a bow at the back.

### Flared dress and pants for template 9
*You will need:*
    flowered print cotton *for dress front:* 5½ x 7 in.
    flowered print cotton *for dress back:* two pieces, 5½ x 4 in.

flowered print cotton *for pants:* 5 x 4 in.
matching cotton
size 000 press stud

Cut out the pieces as above. This set is a smaller version of the one for template 1 and is made up in the same way. Instead of binding for the hems, a single turning is made on the wrong side and sewn down with shell stitch. Sew up the back seam to 1½ in. from the neck and fasten with a press stud. The pants are made up in the same way as those for template 1.

### Mini dress and pants for template 10 — 13
*You will need:*
    cotton print *for dress:* two pieces, 4 in. square
    cotton print *for pants:* two pieces, 1½ x 2½ in.
    matching thread
    size 000 press stud
    narrow ric-rac braid: about 15 in.

### Dress
Cut the pieces out as above. The back and front of the dress are alike. Pin the pieces together with the right sides inside and sew the shoulder seams. Press out flat. Make a single turning on to the right side of the armholes. Sew ric-rac braid on top of the turning.
    Cut a centre opening 1 in. long down the

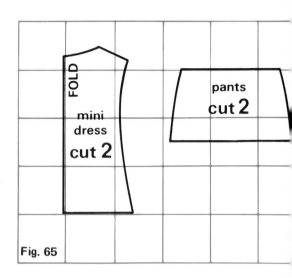

**Fig. 65**

back of the dress. Sew small hems on each side of the opening. Make a single turning round the neck on the right side and sew ric-rac braid over it. Turn the right sides inside again and sew the side seams. Turn inside out and press the seams. Make a single turning on the right side of the hem and sew ric-rac braid on top of it.

## Pants

With right sides inside, sew the side seams and make a narrow hem at the waist. Turn inside out and press. Make a narrow hem along the bottom edge and form legs by sewing the middle together with a few stitches.

**Fig. 66**

*Left above: basic knitted dolls.*

*Left below: twin boy and girl*

*Right: a knitted snowman*

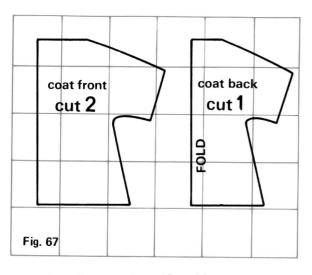

**Fig. 67**

## Coat for template 10 – 13
*You will need:*
felt or similar *for back:* 3¾ x 4½ in.
felt *for front:* two pieces, 3¾ x 2½ in.
matching thread
two very small buttons

Cut out the three pieces. Oversew the side and sleeve seams on the wrong side. Turn inside out and press well. Turn back the corners of the two fronts at the neck and catch down from the back with invisible stitches. Sew two buttons on the front and cut buttonhole slits to just fit the buttons.

## Dress with full skirt for templates 10 – 13
*You will need:*
fine cotton print *for bodice:* two pieces 2 x 2½ in.

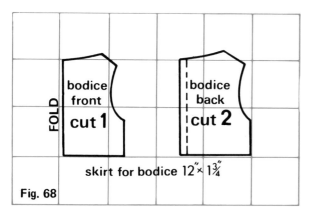

skirt for bodice 12″ x 1¾″

**Fig. 68**

60

fine cotton print *for skirt:* 1¾ x 12 in.
matching thread
¼ in. ribbon: 9 in.

Cut pieces as shown. It is helpful if the bottom edge of the skirt can be placed on the selvedge. Pin the bodice together with the right sides inside and sew the shoulder seams. Cut a 1 in. opening down the back of the bodice. Make very narrow turnings on the sides of the opening and the neck and sew with shell stitch.

Sew the side seams. Make narrow single turnings on the armholes and sew with shell stitch. Mark the middle of the back and the front at the waist. Sew the short sides of the skirt together. Mark the skirt in quarters. Gather along this edge and pull up the gathers.

Pin the skirt to the bodice matching the marks and draw up the gathers to fit the waist of the bodice. Sew them together with back-stitch. Turn inside out and press. Tie the ribbon round the waist with the bow in front.

## KNITTED DOLLS

### Basic knitted doll in three sizes
*You will need:*
oddments of double knitting or 4 ply wool
flesh coloured wool for face
pair No. 10 knitting needles
kapok or similar

Instructions are given for the largest doll with measurements for the two smaller ones in brackets. They are knitted in a single strip, starting with the feet in front, the legs, front of body, face, then the back of head, body, legs and feet. Arms are knitted separately then sewn on.

The colours can be varied as you wish, but for the purpose of the patterns, it is assumed you are using those shown in the pictures. Make sure that *all* joins of wool are made on the *same* side of the knitting.

### Front of legs
*With flesh coloured wool cast on 6 (5, 4) sts.
**1st row** Knit
**2nd row** K 1, knit into front and back of the next 4 (3, 2) sts, k 1, giving 10 (8, 6) sts on the needle.
Work in garter stitch for 3 (2, 1½) in.* Break wool.
Join red (blue, green) wool and knit 1½ (1, ¾) in.
Break off wool and leave the sts.

Repeat * to * for the second leg. Do not break off the wool.
Put both sets of stitches on to one needle, giving 20 (16, 12) sts.
Knit for 1½ (1, ¾) in. for the top of trousers.
Break off wool.

## Body
Change to wool for body — royal blue (purple, yellow) and knit for 3 (2, 1½) in. Break off wool.

## Head
Join on the flesh coloured wool and knit 2¼ (1¾, 1¼) in. for face.
Break off wool.
Join black wool and knit 2¾ (2¼, 1¾) in. for back of head. Break off black wool.
Repeat body, trousers and leg sections as given above, decreasing at the end of the foot to give it shape as in second row above.

## Arms
With flesh wool cast on 9 (8, 7) sts and knit one row.
**Next row**    K 1, knit into front and back of next 7 (6, 5) sts giving 16, (14, 12) sts.
Knit for 1 (1, 1½) in. Break off wool.
Join on royal blue (purple, yellow) for sleeve. Knit till arm measures 3 (2½, 2) in. from the beginning. Cast off. Knit a second arm to match.

## Making up
Fold the strip in half with the right sides inside and pin together so that the coloured stripes match. Oversew the edges with matching wool, starting from the neck at one side, then round the head, backstitching across the corners to give a rounded shape. Continue sewing the rest of the body, rounding off the corners of the feet and leaving the second side open for stuffing. Turn inside out and press the seams.

Stuff the head firmly and smoothly to make a good shape. To make the head more steady, fold a pipe cleaner in half and twist it. Pad it with a wrapping of stuffing and insert it in the doll so that half of it is in the head and half in the body. Stuff all round it to keep it in the centre of the neck. Run a thread through the neck where the colours join and draw up firmly. Fasten off securely. Stuff the legs smoothly using little pieces and easing into place with a blunted pencil or wooden skewer. Stuff the body and sew up the side seam. Oversew the arm seams on the wrong side leaving the top open. Turn inside out and stuff, keeping the stuffing thin at the top, and sew on at the shoulders. Cut features, buttons, belt and other decorations from scraps of felt and sew in place. Straight stitches of black wool worked across the forehead to join up with the back of the head will simulate hair.

## A knitted snowman

*You will need:*
    white double knitting or 4 ply wool: 1 ounce
    oddments of black and red wool
    pair No. 10 knitting needles
    scrap of red felt *for mouth*
    black felt *for eyes and buttons:* five ½ in. circles
    kapok or similar

With black wool cast on 6 sts.
**1st row**    Knit.
**Next row**    K 1, knit into front and back of the next 4 sts, k 1. (10 sts).
Knit till the work measures 1 in. Break off wool and leave sts.
Knit a second foot to match and put both sets of sts on to one needle (20 sts).
Break off black wool. Join on white wool and knit for 8 in.
Break off white wool and join black.
Knit 2 in.
Break off black wool and join white.
Knit 8 in.
Break off white wool, join on black wool and divide sts for feet.
Knit on 10 sts for nearly 1 in.
**Next row**    K 1, k 2 tog. 4 times. K 1 (6 sts).
Knit 1 row, and cast off.
Join wool to other 10 sts and finish off as before.

## Arms
With black wool cast on 7 sts.
**1st row**    Knit.
**Next row**    K 1, knit into front and back of next 5 sts, k 1 (12 sts).
Knit 2 rows, break off black wool. Join on white wool. Knit 2 in.
Cast off.
Knit second arm to match.

## Scarf
With red wool cast on 4 sts.
Knit 12 in. Cast off.

## Hat brim
With black wool cast on 40 sts.

**1st row**    Knit.
**Next row**    K 2, increase in next and every following 5th stitch to the last 2 sts. K 2.
Knit 1 row. Cast off.

## Making up

Make up as for the basic doll. Join hat brim seam and sew the narrower edge to the black part of the head. Cut a crescent in red felt for a mouth, and sew in place. Sew two of the black felt circles in place for eyes and the other three down the front for buttons. Tie his scarf round his neck. A black felt pipe shape can be sewn on to his mouth.

## Twin boy and girl

### Girl

*You will need:*
    flesh pink wool (double knitting or 4 ply): 1 ounce
    rose pink wool (double knitting or 4 ply): 1 ounce
    pair No. 10 knitting needles
    kapok
    dark brown wool: 8 in.
    embroidery silks

Cast on 8 sts in pale pink.
Knit 3 in.
Knit a second leg to match. Put both sets of sts on to one needle (16 sts).
Knit 1 in. Break off wool and join on rose pink.
Knit 2 in. finishing on the right side.
**Next row**    K 1, k 2 tog. 7 times, k 1.
Break off wool and join on pale pink wool.
**Next row**    K 1. Increase in each of next 7 sts by knitting into front and back of stitch. K 1.
Knit 4 in., finishing on the right side.
**Next row**    K 1, k 2 tog. 7 times, k 1. Break off wool and join on deep pink wool.
**Next row**    K 1, increase in each of next 7 sts, k 1. Knit 2 in. Break off wool and join on pale pink wool.
Knit 1 in.
Divide sts for legs and knit 3 in. on first one set of 8 sts and then on the other set.
Cast off.
**Arms**    Cast on 8 sts in pale pink wool.
**1st row**    Knit.
**Next row**    K 1, increase in each of next 6 sts, k 1 (14 sts).

*Left: Red Indian chief*

Knit ½ in. Break off wool and join deep pink wool.
Knit 2 in.
Cast off.
Repeat for second arm.
**Skirt**    Cast on 60 sts in deep pink wool.
Knit 2¼ in.
**Next row**    K 2 tog. all along the row (30 sts).
Knit 1 row.
Cast off.
**Bonnet**    Cast on 24 sts in deep pink wool.
Knit 2 in.
Cast off.
**Making up**    Make up as for basic doll.
    Embroider features and work loops of brown wool for hair on the forehead. Join the skirt seam and sew it on round the waist. Fold the bonnet strip in half and sew together the cast-off edge. Run a cord or ribbon through the bottom edge. Tie a ribbon round the waist.

### Boy

*You will need:*
    pale pink wool (4 ply or double knitting): 1 ounce
    medium blue wool (4 ply or double knitting): 1 ounce
    three No. 10 knitting needles
    kapok
    embroidery silks *for features*
    dark brown wool *for hair*

Cast on 8 sts in blue.
Knit 3 in. Break off wool and leave sts.
Knit a second leg to match and put both sets on to one needle (16 sts).
Knit 1 in. Break off wool and join on pale pink.
Knit 2 in. finishing on the right side.
Complete the neck decreasings and the head as for the girl.
Knit 2 in. Break off pink wool.
Join on blue wool and knit 1 in.
Divide for legs and knit 3 in. on each set of 8 sts.
**Arms**    Cast on 8 sts in pink. Complete the arms as for the girl using blue instead of the deep pink wool.
**Bib**    Cast on 12 sts in blue wool.
Knit 1½ in.
**Next row**    K 3, cast off 6, k 3.
Knit 4 in. on these last 3 sts. Cast off.
Join wool to other 3 sts and knit 4 in. Cast off.
**Making up**    Make up doll as for basic doll.
    Embroider the features. For hair, sew long and short stitches alternately all over the head. Join

bib on to the front of the trousers. Take straps over the shoulders, cross them over the back and sew to the waist of the trousers at the back.

## Red Indian Chief
*You will need:*
dark brown double knitting wool: 1 ounce
oatmeal colour wool
scraps of orange and blue wool
kapok
coloured beads
feathers
red, white and black felt *for features*
pair No. 10 knitting needles
crochet hook

Cast on 6 sts in oatmeal colour wool.
**1st row**    Knit.
K 1, increase in each of next 4 sts, k 1 (10 sts).
Knit till work measures ½ in.
Break off wool and join on dark brown wool.
Cast on 4 extra sts.
Knit for 4 in. Break off wool and leave sts.
Knit a second leg to match and put both sets of stitches on to one needle with the extra stitches at each end.
**Next row**    Cast off 4 sts. K to end.
**Next row**    Cast off 4 sts. K to end.
Knit 2 rows of brown.
Join orange and knit 2 rows. (Do not break off brown wool.)
Break off orange wool.
Knit 2 rows of brown.
Join blue wool and knit 2 rows. Break off blue wool.
Knit in brown till work from the cast off sts measures 4½ in. Break off brown wool.
Join oatmeal wool. Knit 5 in. for head. Change to brown wool and knit the back to the same measurements as the front and reversing colours. Do not cast on the 4 extra sts on the back half of legs.

## Arms
With oatmeal wool cast on 9 sts.
**1st row**    Knit.
**Next row**    K 1, increase in each of next 7 sts, k 1 (16 sts).
Knit ½ in.
Change to brown wool and knit 2½ in.
Cast off.
Knit a second arm to match.

## Headdress band
With brown wool cast on 96 sts.
Knit 3 rows.

Join on orange wool and knit 2 rows. Break off orange wool.
Knit 2 rows in brown wool.
Join on blue wool. Knit 2 rows. Break off blue wool.
Knit 3 rows in brown wool.
Cast off.
Cut about 48 one-inch lengths of brown wool to make a fringe down the sides of the trousers. Push the crochet hook through a stitch at the edge of the cast on sts, double a strand of wool over the hook. Pull the loop through the stitch, then pull the two ends of the wool through the loop so knotting it. Pull the two ends tight. Repeat this down each of the trouser flaps.

## Making up
Make up as for basic doll. Sew down the length of each flap so that no stuffing will get in. Sew rows of beads round the waist above the stripes, and round the sleeves. Sew beads in a V on the front finishing off in a medallion shape of beads. Push the feathers through the knitted band, keeping the longer feathers to the centre, which will be on the top of the head.

Cut two pointed ovals in white felt, and stick a small black felt circle in the middle. Cut a long thin shape in red felt for a mouth. Sew features in place. Sew the headdress on to the head, fairly low on the forehead and sloping across the face and over the shoulders, with the two ends hanging loosely down the back.

## A Witch
*You will need:*
black double knitting wool: 1 ounce
deep blue double knitting wool: 1 ounce
oyster or fawn wool: ½ ounce
black 4 ply wool *for cat, cloak and hat:* 2 ounces
piece of stick 8 in. long
scraps of black interlining
scraps of red and black felt for features
green Lurex thread
silver cord
two large green sequins
kapok
three No. 10 knitting needles
*For the cat, you will need in addition:*
two green sequins
½ pipe cleaner

*Right: a witch and her cat*

64

With black double knitting wool, cast on 6 sts.

**1st row**    Knit.

**Next row**    K 1, increase in each of next 4 sts, k 1 (10 sts).

Knit 4½ in. Break off wool and leave sts.

Knit a second leg and put both lots of sts on to one needle.

Knit 1½ in. Break off the black wool.

Join the blue wool. Knit 3 in. Break off the blue wool.

Join the oyster colour wool and knit 2 in. Break off the oyster colour wool.

Change to black wool and knit 3 in. for the head. Break off the black wool.

Join blue wool and complete the back to match the front.

## Arms

With oyster colour wool cast on 9 sts.

**1st row**    Knit.

**Next row**    K 1, increase in each of the next 7 sts, k 1. (16 sts)

Knit ½ in. Break off the oyster colour wool.

Join on blue wool and knit 3 in.

Cast off. Knit a second arm to match.

## Skirt

Cast on 50 sts in blue wool.

Knit 5½ in.

Cast off.

## Cloak

With the 4 ply black wool cast on 63 sts.

Knit 8 in.

**Next row**    K 2 tog. along the row.

Cast of tightly.

## Hat

With 4 ply black wool cast on 48 sts.

Knit 5 rows.

**Next row**    *K 6, k 2 tog*. Repeat * to * 5 times (42 sts).

Knit 7 rows.

**Next row**    *K 5, k 2 tog*. Repeat * to * 5 times (36 sts).

Knit 7 rows.

**Next row**    *K 4, k 2 tog*. Repeat * to * 5 times (30 sts).

Knit 7 rows.

**Next row**    *K 3, k 2 tog*. Repeat * to * 5 times (24 sts).

Knit 7 rows.

**Next row**    *K 2, k 2 tog*. Repeat * to * 5 times (18 sts).

Knit 7 rows.

**Next row**    *K 1, k 2 tog*. Repeat * to * 5 times (12 sts).

Knit 7 rows.

**Next row**    K 2 tog. along the row (6 sts).

Knit 1 row.

**Next row**    K 2 tog. 3 times (3 sts).

Knit 1 row.

**Next row**    Slip 1, k 2 tog., pass slip stitch over.

Fasten off.

**Brim**    Cast on 10 sts.

**1st row**    Increase in first stitch, k 7, k last 2 tog.

**2nd row**    Knit.

Repeat 1st and 2nd rows until work measures 6½ — 6¾ in., enough to fit round the edge of the hat.

**Making up**    Make up as for basic doll.

Join skirt seam and sew it on to the lowest row of blue knitting at the waist. Sew the cloak on with a few stitches at the neck.

Sew up the hat seam. Tack the crescent shape on the front of the hat and embroider over the outline in chain stitch with silver cord. Whip each stitch of the chain stitch to make a solid outline. Sew seam of hat brim. Fold the brim in half lengthwise and sew both edges to the edge of the hat.

## Features

Embroider slanting eyes in green Lurex thread and sew a big green sequin in the middle of each. Sew ragged looking straight stitches in black wool round the face for hair and one or two lines on forehead and each side of the mouth to make a bad tempered looking face. Cut a crescent shape in red felt and sew it on the face for a mouth with the ends pointing down for a cross looking mouth.

Stuff the crown of the hat and sew it on. For her broom cut a strip of black vilene into uneven notches and stick it in a roll round the end of a thin stick. Sew it under her arm.

## Cat

With black 4 ply wool cast on 7 sts.

**1st row**    Knit.

**Next row**    K 1, increase in each of next 5 sts, k 1 (12 sts).

Knit 1¼ in.

**Next row**    K 1, k 2 tog. 5 times, k 1 (7 sts).

Knit 1½ in.

**Next row**    K 1, increase in each of next 5 sts, k 1 (12 sts).

Knit 1¼ in.

**Next row**    K 1, k 2 tog. 5 times, k 1 (7 sts).

Cast off.

**Tail**    Cast on 5 sts.

Knit for 2 – 2½ in.
Cast off.

Fold the strip in half and oversew on the right side sewing across the corners of the head and pulling the stitches tight to make ears. Leave the bottom open. Sew the tail knitting round the pipe cleaner and sew it to the open end at the bottom.

Stuff the cat firmly. Sew a thread through the neck to pull the neck in tighter to give the head a good shape. Embroider green Lurex thread eyes and sew a green sequin in the centre of each. Sew the cat to the witch's shoulder.

# 2. Wire Dolls

Dolls made on wire frames are very versatile, are easily manipulated and can be made to take up a number of different positions, walking, running, jumping, climbing etc., because of their flexibility. Many kinds of wire are suitable for making them, but the main requirements are that it should be sufficiently flexible to allow it to be bent and twisted easily without the use of pliers and also that it is strong enough to hold a twist or bend without unfolding itself when pressure is released. Some plastic covered wires, especially those sold in garden shops have a softer wire as core and do gradually unwind, and are useless unless tied in some way. Before buying, test the wire by bending it into a V shape, which should hold its shape without any easing of the V.

Ordinary pipe cleaners are easy to use and can be twisted together to make any required length. The thicker one, pipe cleaner chenille which is used in many of the dolls described here is very good. In addition to the two above requirements it has a thick furry pile and in many cases needs no further padding before dressing the figure. It is very pleasant to handle and especially good for young children's use. The six figures shown here are frames made from a single length and show some of the positions which the dolls can be made to take up.

The running figure dressed in a jersey and shorts (see Fig. 69) shows that clothes do not impede the action of the doll. Small wire figures are quite sturdy on their own but the larger dolls do need to have legs and body straightened by having extra wire wound round them.

Some basic sizes are given, but these can be altered a little by adjusting the degree to which the wire is twisted – a smaller figure will result if the wire is twisted tighter. All the one-piece dolls are made in the same way, but there are no absolute rules and the right way is often just that which is found easiest for the individual.

## Basic doll
These are made from one single length of wire.

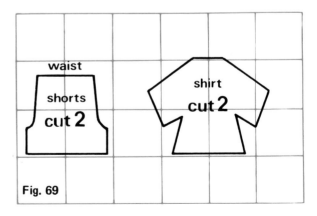

waist

shorts

cut 2

shirt

cut 2

**Fig. 69**

67

standing    walking    running    climbing    kneeling    crawling

*You will need:*
   30 in. wire (for a doll of 5½ – 6 in.)
     OR
   45 in. wire (for a doll of 8½ in.)
     OR
   60 in. wire (for a doll of 11 in.)
   polystyrene ball (available from most craft shops)
   clear adhesive
   felt tip pens or crayons
     OR
   nylon stocking or finger bandage, size 12
     PLUS
   scraps of felt or embroidery silks *for features*
   felt or wool *for hair*

Relative measures for the two bigger figures are given in brackets in the instructions.
   Begin by folding the length of wire in half.

## Head
Insert two fingers in the fold and twist twice making a loop for the head and a twist for the neck. Separate the wires (Fig. 70a).

## Arms
Bend the wire back 2½ (3½, 4½) in. from the neck and twist together, leaving not more than ½ in. at the neck for a shoulder, and forming a small loop for the hand. Make a second arm with the second piece of wire (Fig. 70b).

## Body
Bring the two wires together from the shoulder and twist together at waist level, making a triangle for the body from shoulders to waist (Fig. 70c).

## Legs
Use the remainder of each wire for the legs, doubling the wires back, twisting them together and forming loops for the feet. Twist remaining ends of wire round the waist of the figure (Fig. 70d).

## Hands
Felt hands or glove shapes can be cut out and sewn together in twos, pulled on to the arms

---

*Above: Some of the positions the wire figures can take up.*

*Below: two and three piece wire frames, felt covered wire frame, and clothed figure*

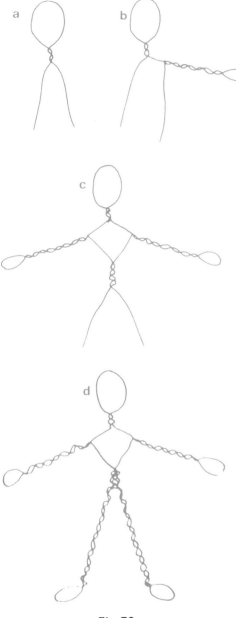

**Fig. 70**

*Basic wire dolls in three sizes, doll with a double head loop, and wire animals*

over the hand loops and sewn in position round the wrist.

## Feet
Felt feet or boot shapes can be cut in twos, pulled over the foot loops and sewn round the ankle.

## Heads
The head loop can be stuffed with a ball of wadding, or old nylon tights, or anything soft and covered with a piece of stretchy fabric like nylon or jersey or finger bandage.

Make a double head loop which is, of course, stronger. Allow an extra 3 or 4 in. on the wire according to the length of your original piece of wire and, having made the second head loop similar to the first and at right angles to it, pass the two remaining wires through each side of the first loop at the neck and twist them together for the neck. The loops will be free of each other at the top but can be tied together with a thread if wished.

The head loop can be made of a size to contain a polystyrene ball (polysphere). Run a line of clear adhesive round the loop inside, fit

69

the ball inside it and twist the neck wire so that the loop fits tightly over the ball.

Cut the head loop and shorten the wire to ½ (½, ¾) in. Bore a hole in a 1 (1½) in. polystyrene ball. Coat the wires with clear adhesive and push them up into the ball so that it rests on the shoulder twist.

## Features

These can be drawn on to the ball itself with coloured felt tip pens or crayons, or it can be covered with nylon stocking or finger bandage, sewn tightly round the neck and at the top of the head. Felt features can be sewn on or stuck on to it.

The frames can also be made with two or three separate pieces of wire and are quite successful but not so strong because the arm and leg wires are of single wires and not doubled and twisted.

### Two piece wire frame

*The amount of wire you will need:*
    for body and legs: 15 in.
    for arms: 7 in.

Fold the long wire in half. Form a head loop and twist the wires for the neck. Place the middle of the wire arms at the neck. Twist the body wire, enclosing the arm wire. Leave 4 in. untwisted for legs. Turn back the ends to form loops for hands and feet. Fold the left arm wire over to the right of the neck and the right arm wire over to the left to lock them into place.

### Three piece wire frame

*The amount of wire you will need:*
    for head and body: 10 in.
    for legs: 8 in.
    for arms: 6 in.

Fold the long wire in half. Form a head loop and twist twice for the neck. Insert arm wire and twist body wire to enclose it leaving 1½ in. of body wire untwisted. Fold the leg wire in half. Twist the remaining body wires round the top of each leg wire. Make loops for hands and feet.

### Felt covered dolls

Any of the wire frames can be strengthened by covering them with sewn strips of felt. This is particularly good if single core plastic covered wire has been used for making the frame, for it has neither the firmness nor the finish of the fluffy wire.

## Arms

Measure the length of the arm wires to the shoulder and cut each strip of felt this length and 1 in. wide.

## Legs

Measure the whole length of leg and cut 1 in. wide strips of felt to this length. If hands and feet are to be shaped and added separately then measure from wrist and ankle to the top of the limb. Cut two pieces of felt to the body measurements, measuring from neck to hips and from shoulder to shoulder so that the body pieces will cover the ends of the arm and leg strips.

### Felt covered wire with a polysphere head

The wire frame can be made in any of the given ways but, because the felt covers the frame, odd lengths of wire can be used by twisting them together to make the required lengths.

This one has been made with extra long legs for a fun doll.

*You will need:*
    wire *for body and legs:* 30 in.
    wire *for arms:* 11 in.
    wire *to reinforce body:* 14 in.
    1½ in. diameter polystyrene ball
    finger bandage, size 12, or nylon 6 in.
    flesh coloured felt *for body:* two pieces, 4¼ x 1½ in.
    flesh coloured felt *for arms:* two pieces, 4½ x ¾ in.
    flesh coloured felt *for legs:* two pieces, 9½ x 1 in.
    matching thread

Make the three piece frame as described above and wind the extra wire from top of legs, round the body to the neck and back to the legs. Turn the ends under.

Fold the arm strip of felt round the wire arm to cover the hand loop and oversew in place. Keep the seam to the inside of the arm, or oversew the folded edge to match. Repeat with the other arm and the legs.

Taper the long sides of each piece of body felt so that the shoulders are slightly wider than the hips. Pin them in place on each side of the frame. Trim off the top corners to fit the slope of the shoulder. If the head of the frame has been covered, tuck the ends down inside the neck of the felt and sew firmly to either side of the neck. Oversew all the other edges, enclosing the arm and leg felt and sewing them on both back and front. Hand and foot shapes can be added if wished. The doll is now ready to be dressed.

These wire shapes can be quite easily transformed into animals.

## A dog

Make a small frame as for a doll, turn the head at right angles to the body and the arms and legs at right angles on the opposite side of the body. It can be padded and covered with felt or fur fabric.

## Giraffe

For a long-necked animal such as this, allow extra wire and twist this into the length required for the neck and finish as for the doll, making the front legs longer than the back ones to give the correct slope to the back.

## A wire bodied clown

This clown is the 'dandy' of the circus. Although he joins in the antics of the other clowns, his beautiful, embroidered dress is never spoiled. He is dressed in white felt embroidered with many-coloured sequins and gold thread. He is about 15 in. tall from the tip of his hat to his toes.

*You will need:*
pipe cleaner chenille: 80 in.
3 in. diameter polystyrene ball
size 34 finger bandage, or nylon: 6 in.
white felt *for dress:* two pieces, 11 x 7 in.
white felt *for hat:* 5½ x 3 in.
white felt *for hat brim:* 8 x ¾ in.
flesh coloured felt *for hands:* four pieces, 2½ x 1¼ in.
black felt *for boots:* four pieces, 3½ x 1 in.
red felt *for mouth:* 1 x ½ in.
red felt *for nose:* ½ in. circle
orange felt *for cheeks:* two ½ in. circles
blue felt *for eyes:* two pieces, ¾ x ½ in.
coloured sequins or beads
gold Lurex thread
matching sewing thread
clear adhesive

Make up like the basic doll as described on page **70**, with the arms 5½ in. before twisting, and the legs 10 in. The figure can be strengthened by binding an extra 10 or 12 in. of wire round the body. Cut the head loop into two wires, bore a hole in the polysphere and push in the two wires firmly. Pull nylon stocking or finger bandage over the ball and tie firmly at the top and round the neck.

Cut out all the pieces for the clothes as shown above. When cutting the hands and feet reverse the pattern for two of the pieces and keep them in pairs with any pencil marks inside.

## Features

For the mouth, round off two of the corners on a long side to make a deep curve and cut out a crescent from the opposite long side. Round off

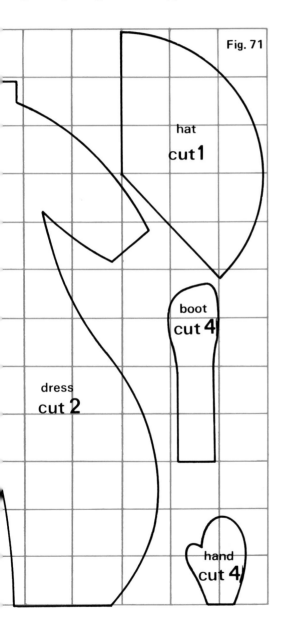

Fig. 71

hat
cut 1

boot
cut 4

dress
cut 2

hand
cut 4

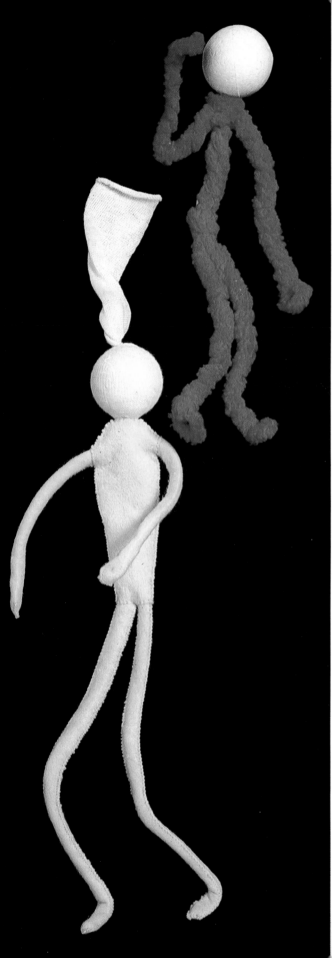

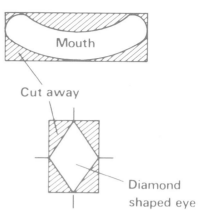

**Fig. 72**

the corners. For the eyes, find the middle points of each side of the blue rectangles and cut off the corners from point to point, making diamonds. Stick all the features in place starting with the nose and placing the other features accordingly.

Oversew the hands in pairs and sew on to the ends of the arm wires with thumbs inside. Oversew the boot seams, slide the foot loops into them with the longer line of foot on the inside and sew to the leg round the top. With gold Lurex thread sew a zig-zag pattern from top to toe, then back to the top again crossing the first lot of stitches to make a laced design.

## Dress

On a paper pattern of the dress front, draw a design in pencil, pin the paper to the felt front, and sew over the the design through paper and felt in a contrasting thread, using small running stitches. Tear away the paper without tearing out the stitches. Embroider over these running stitches and when completed pull them out carefully. Pin the embroidered front to the back on one shoulder seam and oversew this one seam. Fit the dress on to the doll and oversew the other shoulder seam. Oversew the side and inner leg seams.

## Hat

Pin the straight sides of the hat together and sew, cutting off any surplus. Pin to the head at

*Left: making a doll with a polysphere head*

*Right: a wire bodied clown and a clown with very big boots*

a slight tilt and sew neatly round the head. Place the brim with one long side slightly overlapping the hat edge, the rest of the brim over the face. Sew firmly to the hat. Turn up the other edge off the face to meet the join and sew in place on to the other stitches. Roll up the brim to cover the join. Oversew the small back seam.

## A pantaloon clown, juggling

*You will need:*
    pipe cleaner chenille: 60 in.
    1½ in. diameter polystyrene ball
    clear adhesive
    finger bandage, size 12: 4 in.
    cotton print *for dress:* 17 x 9 in.
    bright cotton print *for sleeves:* two pieces, 6 x 4½ in.

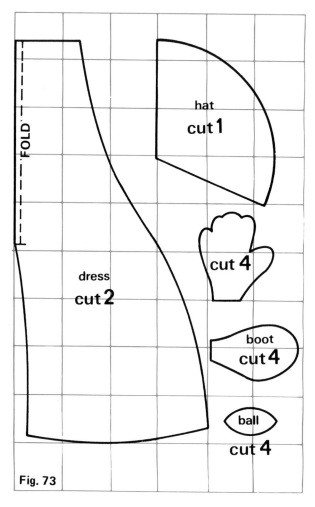

Fig. 73

white interlining or felt *for hat:* 2½ x 4½ in.
white interlining *for neck ruff:* 12 x 1½ in.
white interlining *for limbs ruffs:* four pieces, 12 x 1¼ in.
white felt *for gloves:* four pieces, 2 x 1½ in.
green felt *for shoes:* four pieces, 2½ x 1¼ in.
scraps of red, black and orange felt *for features and hat bobbles*
six pieces of coloured felt *for juggling balls:* 1 x 2 in.
matching sewing thread
kapok
fine fuse wire: 10 in.

Make the frame as described on page **70**.

Fold the cotton print in half and cut out the two dress shapes from the pattern. Cut two sleeves. Pink the edges of neck, sleeves and legs. Cut the five strips of interlining for the ruffs. Trace the hat pattern and cut out inside the pencil lines.

### Features

Cut a crescent shaped red felt mouth, a red circle for a nose, two orange or bright pink circles for cheeks and two black triangles for eyes. Stick all the features in place low down on the polystyrene ball to leave space over the brow for the hat.

Sew the side seams of sleeves, gather the top edge and sew on to the top of the wire arms. Gather up the pinked bottom edges tightly and sew to the wrist edges of the hands. Place the dress pieces together with the right sides inside and sew together the inside leg seams, and the outer seams, leaving them open at the top for 1 in. Turn inside out and pull on to the doll.

Make a narrow single turning on the side openings and pin the top of the gathered sleeve over them. Sew in place and sew up the side openings which remain. The sleeves and legs should be full and baggy. Gather up neck and leg fullness and fasten off securely. Fold the ruffs in half lengthwise and gather up along the crease. Pull the gathers up tightly and sew round neck, wrists and ankles — the wider ruff to be sewn round the neck. Cut two small circles in red felt and sew one above the other on the hat. Join the back seam and sew the hat to the head round the edge.

### Juggling balls

Cut four segments from the pattern from each of the six pieces of felt. Oversew the curved edges, leaving the last side open. Make up all six balls in this way. Make a knot in each end of the fuse wire. Wrap the knot in a ball of stuffing. Push this into one of the ball shapes so that the wire protrudes from the point where the segments join. Stuff firmly round wire. Sew up the last side, enclosing the wire. Repeat with the other end of wire.

Mark four equal spots on the wire. Wrap a ball of stuffing around it at the mark then wrap a felt ball round the padding so that the wire protrudes from the joining up points at each side of the ball. Sew up the opening to enclose the wire and padding.

Repeat with the other three balls. Sew the end balls to the palms of the hands using ladder stitch.

## Wire clown with very big boots
This is one of the knock-about comical clowns who always gets into trouble. His clothes look much too loose and too big for him. He is meant to look as if he is wearing someone else's bigger clothes and old top hat. The extra 12 in. of

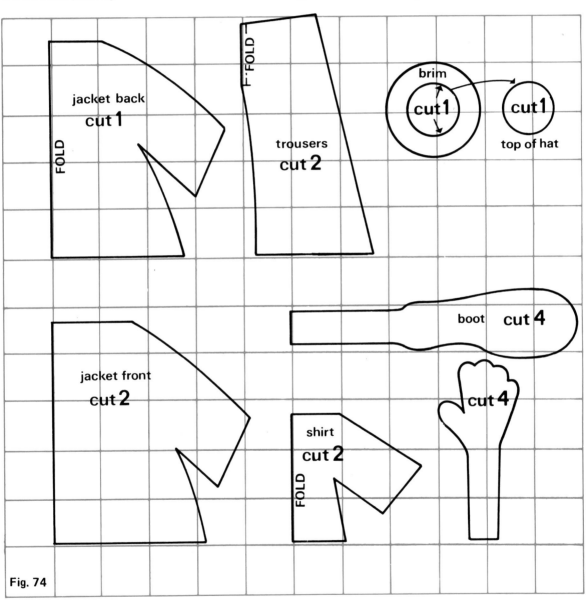

Fig. 74

*Juggling clown*

wire makes extra large foot loops, to fit 3 in. long boots.

*You will need:*
  wire: 72 in.
  1½ in. diameter polystyrene ball
  finger bandage, size 12: 4 in.
  clear adhesive
  bright cotton *for shirt:* two pieces, 2¾ x 5 in.
  thin orange felt *for trousers:* two pieces, 5 x 5¼ in.
  blue felt *for braces:* 5 x ½ in.
  woollen plaid *for coat back:* 4½ x 7 in.
  woollen plaid *for coat front:* two pieces, 4½ x 4 in.
  green felt *for gloves:* two pieces, 3½ x 1½ in.
  black felt *for boots:* four pieces, 6 x 1½ in.
  black felt *for hat brim:* 1¾ in. circle
  black felt *for hat crown:* $3\frac{1}{5}$ x 1½ in.
  black felt *for eyes:* four pieces, ½ x $\frac{1}{10}$ in.
  bright pink felt $\frac{2}{5}$ in. circle *for nose*
  red felt: $\frac{4}{5}$ x $\frac{2}{5}$ in. *for mouth*
  matching sewing thread

Make the frame as described for the 60 in. doll frame on page **70**.

## Features

Stick the pink felt circle in the middle of the face as a nose. Round off the corners of the red rectangle of felt to make an oval shape, then cut out a crescent from one of the long sides (see Fig. 72). Stick this in place under the nose. Stick crosses of black felt at either side of the nose as eyes.

## Clothes

Patterns are given for shirt, trousers, jacket back and front, gloves and boots. Cut out all pieces as indicated above, cutting gloves and boots in pairs and reversing the pattern for the second ones of each pair, so that any pencil marks can be kept on the wrong side.

Pin the glove pieces together in twos and oversew the edges down the arm and round the glove. Insert the wire hand loop into the glove and continue sewing the rest of the arm. Sew round the top to the arm.

To make the boots, pin one of the felt foot shapes under the wire foot loop and catch down round the edge. Pin the other boot shape on top and oversew the edges all round. Sew the top of it to the wire leg.

Place the two shirt pieces together with right sides inside and sew the side seams. Sew the top seams to within 1 in. of the neck. Turn inside out and press seams. Fit it on to the doll, sew the rest of the shoulder seams, turn in the neck edge and sew to the neck of the doll.

Pin the two trouser pieces together with right sides inside and sew the side seams and inner leg seams. Turn inside out and press seams. If fabric is used instead of felt, make hems at waist and legs. Fit trousers on to the doll. The waist will be very wide but this is meant to be so. Sew one end of the braces to the front of the trousers, cross it over one shoulder and sew the other end to the back of the waist. Catch it to the shoulder with a few stitches.

Oversew the side seams and shoulder seams of the coat on the wrong side. Turn under ½ in. down each front and catch down with small stitches. Oversew the edges of neck and sleeves and hem. Fit it on to the doll.

Draw a 1 in. circle in the middle of the hat brim circle and cut it out carefully, because this will be the broken top of the crown of the hat. Sew the long edge of the rectangle to the inner circle of the brim. Oversew the side edges of the rectangle together. Sew the smaller circle to the top of the crown for about ¼ of its circumference so that the rest of it stands up like a lid. Sew it to the head round the inner edge of the brim.

## A long-legged plaited wire doll

*You will need:*

coloured pipe cleaner chenille *for body and legs:* three 50 in. lengths
coloured pipe cleaner chenille *for arms:* three 20 in. lengths
coloured pipe cleaner chenille *to bind frame:* 6 in.
3 in. diameter polystyrene ball
clear adhesive
finger bandage, size 12: 6 in.
flesh coloured felt *for hands:* four pieces, 2½ x 1¾ in.
flesh coloured felt *for feet:* four pieces, 2½ x 1¼ in.
scraps of red and black felt *for features*

Fold the three long wires in half and tie round tightly with wire leaving the two ends of this wire twisted together. Closely plait the six wires for 6 in. to form the body and tie tightly. Divide the wires into threes, and closely plait each of them together for the legs and feet. Tie at the ankles. Plait together tightly the three wires for the arms and mark the middle of the plait. Push the arm plait through the body plait about 1 in. from the top and tie it firmly with the middle of the arms plait *in* the body plait. Turn back the ends of arms and legs, tucking in the sharp ends of wire and pushing them into the middle of the bunched wires.

Cut out four hands and four feet from flesh felt (Fig. 75). Oversew the hands and feet together, leaving the straight ends open. Push the hand wires into the hands so that the thumbs turn inwards. Push leg wires into feet so that the straight edges are together on the inside. Bore a hole in the polystyrene ball and, coating the neck wires with a little adhesive, push them firmly into the hole. The wires should be shortened if necessary to allow the ball to touch the top of the body plait.

Pull the finger bandage over the ball and tie it tightly on the top of the ball. Tie again round the neck, pulling it taut over the ball, pull the ends down over the shoulders and arms and sew firmly in place.

---

*Right: long-legged plaited wire doll*

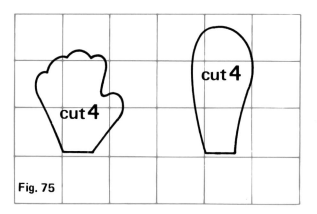

**Features**
Cut a crescent of red felt for a mouth and black circles for eyes and stick them in place. Two thin strips of black felt can be curved and stuck over the eyes for brows. Dress as you wish.

Fig. 75

# 3. Puppets

Puppets, like dolls, can range from the very simple to the very elaborate. Young children enjoy making them from easily obtained home 'rubbish'.
Here are some ideas:

empty cartons with features drawn on with crayons or stuck on with gummed paper,
cardboard picnic plates with the features drawn or stuck on, then fastened to a stick for holding,
paper bags with faces drawn on them, blown up or padded with a ball of newspaper or tissue paper and then tied on to a stick (fabric can be tied round them for a dress),
two sticks tied in a cross and 'dressed' in some fabric fastened round.

All of these are clothed, in effect, by the child's imagination to become soldiers, witches, princesses, goblins, dragons, etc. The often inarticulate child, himself too shy to take part in any kind of show, can become quite eloquent when putting words into his puppet's mouth, while he is safely anonymous and unseen behind a curtain or screen.

Puppets cut from card can have jointed limbs with strings attached to make simple marionettes. These card figures can be 'dressed' with stuck on clothes. Large wooden beads in various sizes, threaded in legs, arms, body and head, can be manipulated. Different sized rolls of corrugated card threaded together, dolls made from string, and many more things can make these simple puppets.

When sewing skills develop, then glove puppets and marionettes offer endless possibilities of representing everyday people like soldiers, policemen or nurses. Or story book and nursery rhyme characters, historical characters, people in national costume or from literature can be represented.

Heads can be sculpted, moulded or carved from a variety of craft materials.

Simple or elaborate stage sets can be created for the presentation of the puppets. Children's imaginations particularly can be stimulated greatly by either making characters to fit a particular story or play or, better still, by making up their own plays to fit figures of their own invention.

# CARD PUPPETS

## Basic card puppet

This small puppet can be made from card strips cut to size or from spatulas or lollipop sticks.

*You will need:*

pink manilla card *for head:* 1¾ in. circle
buff manilla card *for body:* 5 x 1¾ in.
buff manilla card *for neck:* 1 x ¾ in.
green manilla card *for arms:* two pieces, 3¾ x ¾ in.
blue manilla card *for legs:* two pieces, 6 x ¾ in.
six paper fasteners (the sort with a round metal head and two metal 'legs' which open out flat)
red, blue and black felt tip pens

Round off the corners of all the rectangles of card. Draw features with the felt tip pens on the pink card circle. Place the top half of the neck strip under the head. Mark the spot on the chin and on the neck piece and make small holes. Fasten the two together, face over neck, with a paper fastener through the holes. In the same way fasten arms and legs to the body and the top of the body to the lower half of the neck.

## The large puppet

This one has stiff arms and legs, jointed at shoulders and hips. It measures 34 in.

*You will need:*

pink manilla card *for head:* 7 in. circle
pink manilla card *for legs:* two pieces, 16 x 3 in.
pink manilla card *for hands:* two pieces, 2¼ x 3 in.
orange manilla card *for body:* 14 x 7½ in.
blue manilla card *for arms:* two pieces, 13 x 3 in.
black manilla card *for feet:* two pieces, 3 x 3 in.
five paper fasteners
adhesive
felt tip pens

Round off the corners of all the rectangles. Stick hands and feet in place and fasten all pieces together with paper fasteners. Features, clothes, etc., can be painted or drawn on the figure.

## A large puppet with jointed limbs

This puppet is more complex, and with strings attached to various joints of arms, legs, hands and feet will make a very successful marionette.

*You will need:*

pink manilla card *for head:* 7 in. circle
pink manilla card *for arms:* two pieces, 7½ x 3 in.
pink manilla card *for legs:* two pieces, 8½ x 3 in.
yellow manilla card *for arms:* two pieces, 7½ x 3 in.
red manilla card *for body:* 14½ x 7½ in.
blue manilla card *for legs:* two pieces, 8½ x 3 in.
black manilla card *for shoes:* two pieces, 4 x 3 in.
eleven paper fasteners
felt tip pens or paints

Fix shoes to lower legs (pink), lower legs to upper arms, and upper legs to the body. Fix lower arms (pink) to upper arms and these to the body. This

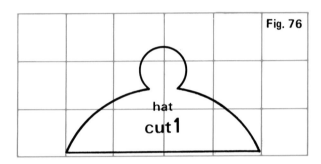

hat
**cut1**

**Fig. 76**

puppet also can have features and clothes drawn or painted on, or it can be dressed in the same way as the Covered Puppet.

## A covered puppet (not jointed)

This card puppet, covered with nylon felt in several colours, is similar in type to the straight limbed one already described, but smaller. The card shapes are covered with felt before fastening them together.

*You will need:*

manilla card (any colour) *for face:* 4 in. circle
manilla card *for body:* 8 x 4¾ in.
manilla card *for arms:* two pieces, 6¾ x 1¼ in.
manilla card *for legs:* two pieces, 8 x 1 in.
white felt *for face:* 4 in. circle

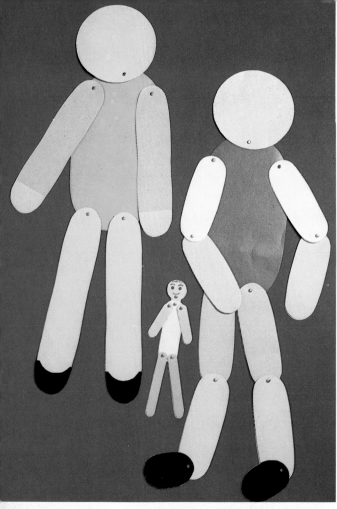

white felt *for hands:* two pieces, 1 x 1¼ in.
green felt *for body:* 8 x 4¾ in.
green felt *for sleeves:* two pieces, 6 x 1¼ in.
yellow felt *for legs:* two pieces, 7 x 1$\frac{3}{5}$ in.
black felt *for shoes:* two pieces, 1 x 1$\frac{3}{5}$ in.
purple felt *for hat:* 2 x 3¾ in.
five paper fasteners
adhesive
scraps of red and black felt *for features*

Cut out all the card pieces and round off the
corners of all the rectangles. Use the pattern to
cut the hat. Cut off a straight segment, measuring
1½ in. across the edge, from the side of the circle.

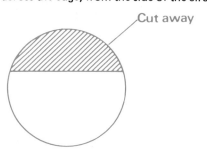

**Fig. 77**

Stick the remaining portion on to the card circle.
Butt together the edges of head and hat.

Cut and stick features in place. Stick the
body card on to the green felt, and then trim
off the felt corners. Stick the white felt rectangles to the bottom of the arms and the green
felt rectangles above them with the two felt
edges butted close together. Make up the legs in
the same way as the arms.

Trim off all the surplus felt from the card
edges. Fasten together with paper fasteners.

## Jointed puppet (felt covered)
He is a smaller version of the jointed card
puppet described above and can be used as a
marionette with strings on the joints if the parts
are fastened together loosely.

---

*Left above: basic card puppet, large card
puppet, and puppet with jointed limbs.*

*Left below: jointed and unjointed felt covered
puppets*

*Right: stick puppets — Scottish dancer, Dutch
girl, and Red Indian girl*

*You will need:*

manilla card *for head:* 4 in. circle

manilla card *for body:* 8 x 4¾ in.

manilla card *for arms:* four pieces, 3½ x 1¼ in.

manilla card *for legs:* four pieces, 4 x 1⅗ in.

manilla card *for feet:* two pieces, 1¾ x 1¼ in.

white nylon *for face:* 4 in. circle

white nylon *for lower arms:* two pieces, 3½ x 1¼ in.

deep pink felt *for upper arms:* two pieces, 3½ x 1¼ in.

deep pink felt *for upper body:* 4 x 4¾ in.

purple felt *for lower body:* 4 x 4¾ in.

purple felt *for upper legs:* two pieces, 4 x 1⅗ in.

green felt *for lower legs:* two pieces, 4 x 1⅗ in.

black felt *for boots:* two pieces, 1¾ x 1¼ in.

black felt *for hair:* two pieces, 3 x ¾ in.

eleven paper fasteners

adhesive

scraps of red and black felt *for features*

Cut out all the card pieces and round off all the corners from the rectangles. Stick the card circle to the white felt one and trim off the surplus felt. Cut the two pieces of black felt for hair to the head curve and cut the other long edges in notches for the hair. Stick it on round the top of the white felt head. Cut a crescent in red felt for a mouth and stick it in place, and two ½ in. circles in blue for eyes.

Mark the half way line across the body and stick deep pink above and purple felt below the

line, with the edges of the felt butted close together. Stick the appropriate felts on to arms and legs as indicated. Trim off all surplus felt from the card shapes, and fasten them together with the paper fasteners.

## STICK PUPPETS

### A girl

Use template A, Fig. 78, with the skirt shortened.

*You will need:*

flesh coloured felt *for face:* 3½ in. square

fawn felt *for back of head:* 3½ in. square

fawn felt *for curls:* four pieces, 1 in. square

scraps of black, blue and red felt *for features*

black embroidery silk

purple nylon felt *for dress:* two pieces, 7½ x 6½ in.

white nylon felt *for collar:* 3 x ½ in.

white nylon felt *for gloves:* four pieces, 1 x ¾ in.

white nylon felt *for buttons:* three ½ in. circles

matching thread

adhesive

kapok

12 in. stick or ½ in. diameter dowel rod

Trace round the head of the template from shoulder to shoulder on flesh felt for the face and on fawn felt for the back of the head. Trim off the corners of the squares for the hair to make them circular and cut each circle in a spiral from the edge to the centre (see Fig. 79). Pin the curls to the top of the head back.

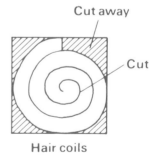

Hair coils

**Fig. 79**

### Features

Cut two ½ in. circles in blue felt and on the bottom curve of each stick a ¼ in. circle of black felt. Cut a crescent about ¾ in. long in red felt for a smiling mouth. Stick these in

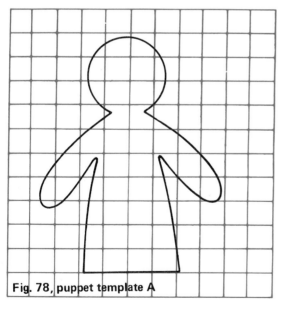

Fig. 78, puppet template A

82

place on the face. Embroider some stitches in black embroidery silk or thread for eyelashes and brows. Place face and head pieces together with right sides outside and oversew the curved edges together, sewing in the curls as well and leaving the neck edge open.

## Dress

Cut two dress shapes from the template tracing from neck edge to sleeve edge at the wrist, but not round the hand, then down to the shortened hem on each side. Trace the hand from the template four times for her gloves. Fold the white felt collar strip in half and cut away a corner of the folded edge to give curved edges to the front of the collar (see Fig. 80). Cut three white circles for buttons.

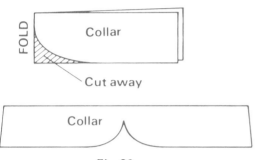

**Fig. 80**

Sew the collar on at the shoulders and the three buttons down the centre front. Sew a white glove piece on to the bottom of each sleeve on the back and front pieces. Sew the two dress pieces to front and back of head along the neck line.

Coat the top 1½ in. of dowel with adhesive and pad it with a little kapok. Push a little kapok into the top of the head, insert the padded stick and push more kapok all round it to keep it firmly in place. Pin the side seams of the dress together, matching the glove pieces and oversew the edges with matching thread.

## Red Indian girl

She is made from template A, Fig. 78, without separate hands.

*You will need:*
    chestnut felt *for face:* 3½ in. square
    black felt *for back of head:* 3½ in. square
    black felt *for forehead:* 2½ x ¾ in.
    brown felt *for jerkin:* two pieces, 7¾ x 4 in.
    orange felt *for headband:* 6 x ¼ in.
    orange felt *for feather:* two pieces, 1½ x ¾ in.

    blue felt *for skirt:* two pieces, 4¼ x 3 in.
    green felt *for neck fringe:* 3 x ¾ in.
    scraps of black, white and red felt *for features*
    dowel rod: 12 – 14 in.
    kapok
    matching thread
    colourless upholstery adhesive
    beads
    yellow embroidery silk
    black wool *for hair*
    3 in. of fuse wire

Trace round the template head from shoulder to shoulder once on chestnut coloured felt for the face and once on black felt for the back of the head. Trace round the top of the head on the black felt piece for the forehead, making it ¾ in. wide at the centre.

## Features

Cut two small almond shapes in white felt and stick a small circle of black felt in the centre of each. Cut a red felt crescent for the mouth. Stick these features in place with adhesive. Sew the black felt forehead piece in place on top of the chestnut felt face sewing along the straight edge only. Trim off the curved edge of chestnut felt behind it.

## Hair

Make two 3½ in. plaits with black wool or embroidery silk, binding the lower ends tightly with yellow embroidery silk. Sew the other ends in place one at each side of the hair line on the forehead.

## Dress

Draw a line across the template level with the hands and trace round the upper part of the template twice on to brown felt, for the front and back of the jerkin. Trace round the lower part of the template twice on blue felt for the skirt. Cut a strip of orange felt 4 x ¾ in. for the bottom front edge of the jerkin and a longer strip 6 x ¼ in. for the head band.

Sew a blue skirt piece to the bottom edge of a jerkin piece and on to this sew the short orange felt strip which will be cut into a fringe. Cover the double join by sewing on small coloured beads. Mark the centre of the chest and from each shoulder tack a contrasting guide thread to this centre point, making a V. Sew beads on this line, bugle beads if possible, with a row of small beads on the outside of it. Sew the face piece to the front of the jerkin along the neck line.

Sew the bottom edge of the jerkin back to

*Stick puppets — a snowman and Father Christmas*

Cut away

**Fig. 81**

### Head band

Lap the head band round the top of the head to cover the forehead join, and meeting in the centre back. Mark with a coloured stitch at the sides where it touches the side seams of the head. Embroider this middle strip. This one has a row of small beads along each edge with bugle beads in a zig-zag pattern in between.

### Feather

A felt feather can be made by cutting two feather shapes measuring 1½ x ¾ in. in coloured felt. Fold 3 in. of fuse wire with ends to the middle and catch this down the middle of one of the feather shapes. Place the other felt feather on top to cover the wire and sew the two together down the centre, sewing over the wire. Make oblique cuts down each side of the feather. Sew it on to the back of the head level with the forehead join. Pin the embroidered band round the head to cover the forehead join, and the tops of the plaits where they are sewn on to the head, and the sewn end of the feather. Cut the orange strip and the lower edge of the skirt in a fringe.

the second piece of blue skirt and sew the black head piece to the back jerkin along the neck line. Place the front and back dress together with the right sides outside and oversew all round the head from the neck join on one side to the other.

Coat the top 1½ in. of rod with adhesive and wrap a small pad of kapok or other stuffing round it. Push a small piece of stuffing into the top of the head and then insert the padded end of the rod. Push more small pieces of stuffing into the head all round the rod, keeping the rod in the centre of the neck and keeping the face smooth and even.

Pin the back and front of the dress together matching hands, under arms and skirt joins. Oversew the edges with matching thread, but leave the edges of the orange felt strip free. Cut the strip of green felt in a narrow crescent shape to fit the neck in front from shoulder to shoulder. Cut the curved edge in toothed notches and sew on over the neck join.

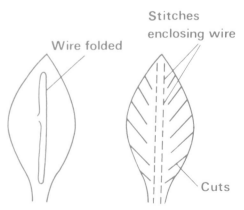

Wire folded

Stitches enclosing wire

Cuts

**Fig. 82**

84

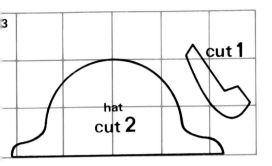

**3**

cut 1

hat
cut 2

## A Snowman
He is made from template A, Fig. 85, cut 3 in. longer.

*You will need:*
> white fluffy pile fabric *for body:* two pieces, 11 x 8½ in.
> thick black felt *for pipe:* 1¾ x ½ in.
> dowel rod: 12 in.
> black felt *for hat:* two pieces, 4½ x 2 in.
> scraps of black felt *for buttons and eyes:* five ½ in. circles
> red felt *for scarf:* two pieces, 4½ x ¾ in.
> red felt *for gloves:* four pieces, 1 x ¾ in.
> adhesive
> matching thread
> kapok

Trace twice round the template on the wrong side of the fluffy pile fabric, pressing down firmly on the edge of the template all the way because this fabric, being a type of jersey weave, stretches very easily and can lose its shape. Reverse the template for the second piece. Cut them outside the pencil lines.

Cut two circles for eyes and three for buttons from the scraps of black felt. Cut one pipe shape if the felt is thick, otherwise cut two and oversew them together all round. Stiff interlining of the same shape could be sewn between them if necessary. Sew eyes, buttons and pipe in position on one of the pieces for the body. Pin the two shapes together at the shoulders, with right sides inside and closely oversew the head seams only. Turn inside out.

Coat about 1½ in. of dowel rod with adhesive and pad with the stuffing, well covering the top. Push a small piece of stuffing into the top of the head, insert the padded rod, and make it firm by pushing small pieces of stuffing in all round it. Do not stuff it too hard. Pin arms and side seams together with right sides inside and oversew firmly. Double oversewing is a good locking stitch to use (see page 6 ). Turn it inside out.

Taper the strips of felt for the scarf, join the narrow ends and tie it round the neck, keeping it in place with one or two stitches. Oversew the curved edges of the gloves, slip over the hands and sew in place round the edge. Trace round the hat pattern twice on to black felt. Oversew together the curved edges. Fit it on to the head and sew it in place along the straight edge.

## Father Christmas
Made from template A, Fig. 78.

*You will need:*
> flesh coloured felt *for face:* 3½ in. square
> red fluffy pile fabric *for coat:* two pieces, 7½ in. square
> red fluffy pile fabric *for hood back:* 4 x 3½ in.
> red fluffy pile fabric *for hood front:* 3 x ¾ in.
> white fluffy pile fabric *for front trimming:* 7½ x ½ in.
> white fluffy pile fabric *for sleeve trimming:* two pieces 3½ x ¼ in.
> white fluffy pile fabric *for collar trimming:* 3 x ½ in.
> white fluffy pile fabric *for hood trimming:* 7½ x ½ in.
> scraps of black and pink felt *for features*
> white fluffy wool for moustache and eyebrows
> dowel rod: 12 – 13 in.
> adhesive
> kapok
> matching thread

Trace round the template head from shoulder to shoulder once on the flesh coloured felt and once on the wrong side of the red fluffy pile fabric for hood back. Press firmly on the edge of the template when tracing on a stretch material like the fluffy fabric because it pulls away from the template very easily and so the outline is distorted. Cut outside the traced lines.

### Features
Cut two small black circles for eyes and stick in place on the face. Fold 2 in. of fluffy white wool in half and sew in place for an eyebrow, leaving the ends free. Cut the loop and tease out the ends of wool. Repeat for the other eyebrow.

Cut six 2 in. strands of wool, and catch them down on the face in the middle of the strands for a moustache and beard. Trim the ends so that they are shorter on the cheeks and longer

85

on the chin. Tease out the ends to make them fluffy. Cut two small circles of pink felt and stick them on the cheeks.

### Hood front
Trace round the top curve of the template head on the wrong side of the hood front strip. Cut it out and sew it on to the forehead of the felt face.

### Coat
Trace twice round the template from the neck down on the wrong side of the fluffy fabric, reversing the template for the second piece. Sew the face to one piece on the neckline, and the hood to the neckline of the second piece, oversewing on the wrong side and using double oversewing. Sew a strip of white fluffy fabric down the centre of the coat front.

### Head
Pin back and front together at the shoulders with right sides inside. Oversew round the head only, using a close double oversewing stitch. Turn inside out. Insert the dowel rod as for the Girl puppet (see page **86**). Do not stuff fluffy pile fabric or other stretch materials too hard or the shape will be lost.

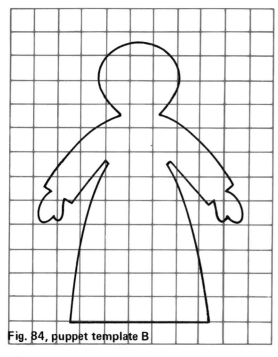

Fig. 84, puppet template B

### Coat
Pin side seams of coat together on one side with right sides inside and double oversew. Repeat on the second side. Turn the arms inside out, and press the seams as flat as possible.

### Trimming
Pin a strip of white fluffy fabric on the hood from the shoulder on one side across the forehead and down to the neck again so that all the joins are covered. Sew in place on both edges. Sew the collar in place on the front and a narrow strip on each cuff.

### Dutch girl
She is made from template B, Fig.84.

*You will need:*
flesh coloured felt *for face:* 3½ in. square.
flesh coloured felt *for hands:* four pieces, 1½ x 1 in.
light brown felt *for head:* 3½ in. square
blue and white cotton *for dress:* two pieces, 10 x 9 in.
white cotton *for apron:* 6 x 5 in.
white bias binding *for apron ties:* 16 in.
white interlining or stiff linen *for hat:* two pieces, 5½ x 4 in.
white interlining *for collar:* 3¼ x 1 in.
scraps of blue, black and red felt *for features*
yellow wool or knitting cotton *for hair*
matching thread
kapok
adhesive
dowel rod: 15 in.
black embroidery silk

Trace round the head of the template from shoulder to shoulder, once on flesh coloured felt and once on light brown felt. Cut outside the pencil lines. Cut two ½ in. circles in white with two smaller circles in blue for eyes. Cut off a small straight section from the bottom of each (see Fig. **85**). Cut a crescent shape in red

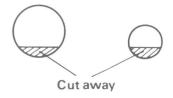

Cut away

**Fig. 85**

felt for a mouth. On the wrong side of the striped cotton, trace twice round the dress part

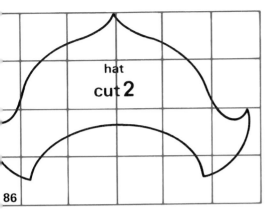

hat

cut **2**

86

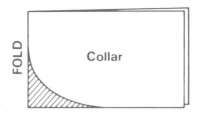

FOLD

Collar

**Fig. 87**

of the template, omitting the hands. Cut outside the pencil lines about ½ in. to allow for turnings.

Trace round the hand template four times on the flesh felt, reversing it for two of them. Allow ¼ in. extra length on the wrist when cutting out. Cut out just outside the pencil lines and keep them in pairs. Mark the waistline on the template. Trace the lower part of the dress on to the white fabric for an apron and cut it out. Trace the hat pattern twice and cut out just outside the lines. Trace and cut out the collar. Sew the flesh face and brown head pieces together on the right side, leaving the neck open. For eyes stick a blue circle on to each white circle on the straight edge. Stick all features in place. With black embroidery silk work five or six straight stitches above each eye for lashes. Insert the dowel rod as for the Girl puppet (see page 86 ).

## Dress

Place the two dress pieces together with right sides inside and sew the seams on the pencil lines with running stitch. Turn inside out and press the seams. Oversew the hands together on the right side. Turn in the ends of the sleeves, insert the wrist of the hand into the opening with thumbs pointing inwards and sew the sleeves on to them. Pull the dress up over the stick and pin the neck of the face piece and the back of the head over the dress neck and sew in place. Either sew a hem along the dress or trim with pinking shears.

## Apron

Either hem sides and bottom of apron or trim with pinking shears. Sew the binding along the top leaving two ends to tie at the back. Sew on to the waist of the dress. Fold the collar piece in half and trim as shown in Fig. **87**. Sew on to the front of the neck line.

## Hat

Sew the two hat pieces together with running stitch, starting at the bottom edge about 1 in. from the point and finishing 1 in. from the point at the other side. Trim off the surplus material especially at the points. Turn it inside out, taking great care in pulling out the three points and pressing the seam flat.

## Hair

Take 15 — 18 strands of wool 18 in. long and plait them together. Tie round the centre tightly in two places leaving 1 in. between the two ties. Cut through in between the ties. Sew the other ends one on each side of the face so that the cap will cover the sewing. Pin the cap in place and sew to the head all round the lower edge.

### Victorian Miss

Made from template B, Fig. **84**, shortened with separate legs.

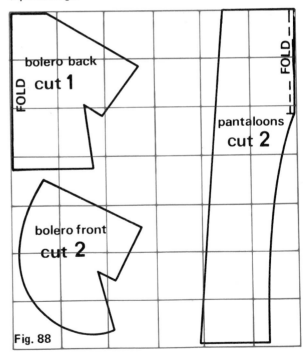

bolero back

FOLD

cut **1**

FOLD

pantaloons

cut **2**

bolero front

cut **2**

Fig. 88

87

*You will need:*
  flesh coloured felt *for face:* 3½ in. square
  flesh coloured felt *for hands:* four pieces, 1 x 1½ in.
  flesh coloured felt *for legs:* two pieces, 5¼ x 1 in.
  black felt *for shoes:* four pieces, ¾ x ¾ in.
  yellow felt *for head:* 3½ in. square
  cotton print *for dress:* two pieces, 8 x 8 in.
  blue felt *for bolero back:* 3¼ x 5 in.
  blue felt *for bolero front:* two pieces, 3¼ x 2½ in.
  white interfacing *for pantaloons:* two pieces, 7 x 3½ in.
  fringe trimming: 6 in.
  scrap of red felt *for mouth*
  braid trimming: 25 in.
  frilling or broderie Anglaise: 20 in.
  kapok
  black embroidery silk
  adhesive
  matching thread
  yellow wool *for hair:* about 4 yd
  dowel: 12 − 13 in.

Trace round the head of the template once on to flesh coloured felt for the face and once on to yellow felt for the back of the head. Trace round hands four times on to flesh coloured felt reversing the pattern for two of them. Cut out inside the pencil lines. Cut strips for the legs in flesh felt. On the template draw a line 7½ in. from the neck. Trace round the template above this line on to the wrong side of one piece of print, omitting the head and hands. Trace the pantaloon pattern on to the interlining and cut out two pieces for back and front. From the larger piece of blue felt cut the back of the bolero and cut two fronts from the two smaller pieces. Cut out four ¾ in. squares for the shoes. Trim off two corners on each to make a round toe. On two of the pieces only cut out a small square on the instep for the fronts (see Fig. 89). Cut a red felt crescent for a mouth.

## Head
Stick the red felt mouth in place on the face. Draw two curves for closed eyes and embroider each in black stem stitch with straight stitches under for lashes. Draw two curves above them for brows and sew in stem stitch. Oversew the face and back of the head together, leaving the

---

*Left: Victorian Miss and girl stick puppets*

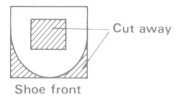

**Cut away**

Shoe front

**Fig. 89**

neck open. Insert rod as for Girl puppet (page 86).

## Legs
Fold the leg strip in half lengthwise and oversew the seams, cutting the corners off the bottom ½ in. to make a narrower end. Place a front and back shoe together and oversew one side. Fit it on to the foot and oversew the second side. Sew to the foot round the top and round the front opening. Repeat for second leg.

Sew both legs at the top to one of the pantaloon pieces so that the feet are 1½ in. below the bottom edge. Pin the other pantaloon piece underneath this and sew the seams. Turn inside out pushing the felt legs through the pantaloon legs. Sew fringe trimming on to the bottom of each leg.

Legs sewn to pantaloon

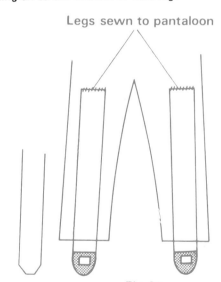

**Fig. 90**

## Dress
Place two dress pieces together with right sides inside and sew together on the pencil lines. Trim off surplus fabric close to the stitching. Turn inside out and press the seams. If using broderie Anglaise, gather it up to fit the hem and sew it on to the hem.

Pull the dress up over the stick and sew the neck edge of head over the neck of the dress. Sew braid over the join. Oversew the hands together in pairs, turn the edge of the sleeves, insert the wrist and sew the hands to the edge of the sleeves. Measure the legs against the length of the dress so that about 3 in. of leg shows below the dress and mark the rod where the top of the pantaloons reach. Put adhesive on the double edge of the pantaloon, stick it to the rod at the mark and tie around firmly with embroidery silk.

## Jacket

Oversew the side and shoulder seams of the jacket. Sew braid all round the edge and round the sleeves. Catch the edges of the braid together in the front with small stitches.

## Hair

Cut nine strands of yellow wool or knitting cotton 15 in. long. Sew the middle of them to the top of the face. Pin them together at each side of the face in a line with the mouth. Arrange into three plaits about 3 in. long at each side. Turn the ends up to the side of the face underneath the pinned strands and sew them to either side of the face, so that loops are formed.

## A Bride

Made from template B, Fig. **84**, shortened with separate legs.
*You will need:*
flesh coloured felt *for face:* 3½ in. square
flesh coloured felt *for hands:* 4 pieces, 1 x 1½ in.
brown felt *for head:* 3½ in. square
scraps of blue and red felt *for features*
white silk or satin *for dress:* two pieces, 8 x 9 in.
white net *for veil:* 11 in. circle
soft silver cord
beads
pearls
matching thread
kapok
brown wool *for hair*
dowel rod: 13 – 14 in.
brown, blue, pink and mauve embroidery silks
medium green felt: 3½ x 2½ in.
narrow silver ribbon

Trace round the head of the template once on flesh felt for the face and once on brown felt for the back of the head. Cut out inside the pencil lines. Trace the hand template four times on to flesh felt, reversing the template for two of them. Cut two ½ in. circles in blue felt for eyes and a red felt crescent for a mouth. Trace round the template on to the wrong side of one piece of silk, not drawing the head or hands. Trace an 11 in. circle on the net and cut out inside the tracing line.

## Head

Stick the features in place on the flesh felt face. With brown embroidery silk, make four straight stitches above each eye for lashes, and a gently curving arc above each for an eyebrow, using stem stitch. Oversew the face and the back of the head together leaving the neck open. Insert the rod as for the Girl puppet (page **86**).

## Dress

Cut off the surplus material ¾ in. outside the pencil lines on the traced piece of the dress. On the right side, mark the centre of the waist, and the centre of the hem. Mark with tacking thread points 1 in. to each side of the centre point on the hem. With contrasting cotton, tack from each shoulder to the centre waist and down to each of the hem points so that there is a graduated panel from shoulder to centre waist and from waist to hem. Sew crystal bugle beads on these guide lines. With soft silver cord make six tiny bows. Stitch one on at waist level and the other five down the middle of the front panel.

Place the dress pieces together with right sides inside and sew the seams using the pencil lines as a guide. Cut off the surplus material. Turn inside out and press the seams flat. Pull the dress up over the stick and sew the neck of the head to the neck of the dress. Sew small crystal beads over the front join. Oversew the hands together in pairs. Turn in the ends of the sleeves and sew a hand inside each, with thumbs turned inwards. Cut the bottom edge of the dress with pinking shears.

## Hair

Thread a darning needle with brown wool and join on at the side of the face. Make two or three small ½ in. loops close to the head and sew them to one side of the head seam. Sew a second lot of loops close to the first ones. Continue so until the loops cover the head seam from one side to the other. Continue over the rest of the head.

**Fig. 91**

## Veil

Fold the net circle almost in half and arrange the folded edge with a little fulness over the top of the head. Catch it down to the head in several places. Arrange some pearls or silver beads across the net and sew them in place.

## Bouquet

From the green felt cut one circle 2 in. in diameter and one 1¼ in. in diameter. From the larger one cut out a segment (see Fig. 92). Mark

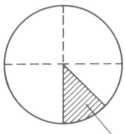

Cut away

**Fig. 92**

twelve equal spaces round the rest of the edge. Sew soft silver cord in a zig-zag round the edge between the marked points. Trim off the surplus felt between the cord to give a scalloped edge. Oversew the two straight edges to make a cone. With double-coloured embroidery silk work small loops over the smaller circle. Sew it on to the cone with straight stitches of green embroidery silk to simulate leaves. Sew loops of narrow silver ribbon to the point of the cone and sew both hands to the back of the posy.

Cut away

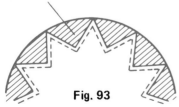

**Fig. 93**

## Scottish dancer

The body is made from template A, the hands from template B. The legs are made separately.

*You will need:*

flesh coloured felt *for face:* 3½ in. square
flesh coloured felt *for hands:* 4 pieces, 1 x ¾ in.
flesh coloured felt *for legs:* 2 pieces, 6½ x 1½ in.
brown felt *for head:* 3½ in. square
white interlining or felt *for blouse:* two pieces, 7 x 3½ in.
plaid cotton *for kilt:* 14 x 3 in.
plaid cotton *for sash:* 14 x ¾ in.
plaid cotton *for bonnet:* 5 in. circle
plaid cotton *for band:* 8 x ¾ in.
plaid cotton *for socks:* two pieces, 4½ x 2 in.
scraps of red, white and brown felt *for features*
black felt *for shoes:* two pieces, 2 x 1 in.
black felt *for belt:* 6 x ¼ in.
white lace *for jabot:* 2½ x 2 in.
silver cord
small feathers
two small fancy buttons
kapok
adhesive
matching thread
black embroidery silk
dowel rod: 12 – 13 in.

Trace round the head of the template once on to flesh felt for the face and once on brown felt for the back of the head. Trace four hands from template B reversing the pattern for two of them and keeping them in pairs. Cut the leg strips. Cut everything out inside the pencil lines.

## Features

Cut two ½ in. circles in white felt for eyes and stick a small brown circle in the middle of each one. Cut a red felt crescent for a mouth. Stick the features in place on the flesh felt face. With black embroidery silk work stem stitch round the top of the eye circle and an arc above each eye for brows. Oversew the face to the back of the head leaving the neck open. Insert dowel rod as for the Girl puppet (page 86).

## Clothes

For the blouse trace twice round the top part of the template above the waist line, except the head, on white interlining or felt. If fabric is used then cut out ¼ in. outside the lines to allow for turnings, and sew up on the wrong side.

Cut kilt (if possible with one long edge on the selvedge) sash, socks and head band from the plaid fabric and trace the 5 in. circle for the bonnet. Cut two rectangles in black felt for the shoes, fold them in half and cut off the corners of the fold to form round toes. Cut the strip for belt in black felt.

Sew the blouse seams, and press them. Sew the neck edge of head on to the blouse neck. Oversew the two hand pieces and sew the wrist inside each sleeve end with the thumbs pointing inwards. Fold the leg strips in half longways and oversew the seams. Make a single turning on the short end of the sock pieces, wrap round one end of the legs and seam together down the back. Sew a rectangle of silver cord on the front of the shoes for a buckle and oversew one side seam. Fit shoe on to a sock covered leg and sew up the second seam, sewing the shoe to the leg along the top edge. Sew both legs to the middle of the front edge of the blouse.

If the kilt has no selvedge on one long side, then make a narrow hem and sew it. Pin pleats along the whole length and press in place very firmly with a hot iron and a damp cloth. Pin the top edge to the edge of the blouse with the join at the back, and sew in place. Sew the black felt strip for a belt over the join.

To make the bonnet — pleat round the edge of the circle to fit the head, about 2¾ in. in diameter. Sew the band in place round the pleated edge. Trim the feathers to 1 in. and fasten in an upright position on the band. Sew a decorative button over the quill. Sew the bonnet slantwise on to the head with the feather over one eyebrow.

Fold the lace not quite in half and gather

Gathering line

FOLD

Jabot

**Fig. 94**

*Left: bride stick puppet.*

*Right: jester stick puppet*

about ¼ in. down from the fold. Draw up the gathers and sew in front on the neck edge as a jabot.

Fringe ¾ in. at each end of the scarf piece and arrange diagonally across the front of the puppet and under one arm with the two ends crossed and hanging loose over one shoulder — one end in front and one behind. Fasten it in place with a decorative button.

### Jester puppet

Patterns are given for face, hat, eye, mouth, collar, tunic and under-tunic.

Four complete heads are mounted on a dowel rod and are then dressed as one unit. The pictured puppet has two flesh pink faces and orange hats, and two greyish beige faces with yellow hats. Felt is used throughout for heads and dress.

*For each head you will need:*

flesh or grey felt *for face:* two pieces, 3½ x 3 in.

orange or yellow felt *for hat:* two pieces, $1\frac{2}{5}$ x 3 in.

red felt *for mouth:* two pieces, 1 x ½ in.

white felt *for eyes:* two pieces, 1 x ½ in.

blue felt *for eyes:* two pieces, 1 x ½ in.

a gold coloured bead

kapok

adhesive

black, pink and green embroidery silks

matching sewing thread

brown thread

*To assemble the jester, you will need:*

$\frac{3}{8}$ in. dowel rod: 14 in.

fawn felt: 5 x $1\frac{2}{5}$ in.

orange felt *for collar:* four pieces, 2 x ¾ in.

orange felt *for tunic:* four pieces, 4 x 1½ in.

orange felt *for under-tunic:* four pieces, 3¼ x 1¾ in.

yellow felt *for tunic:* four pieces, 4 x 1½ in.

yellow felt *for under-tunic:* four pieces, 3¼ x 1¾ in.

Trace and cut two of all the pieces as shown above for the head, reversing the pattern for all second pieces so that pencil marks can be on the wrong side. Sew a hat to the top of each face so that the point projects over the nose, and press the seam flat.

### Features

Cut two blue circles for eyes small enough to leave a rim of white when they are stuck on to the white felt circles. Cut the mouth shape in red felt. Stick eye and mouth in place with upholstery adhesive. Embroider a line in green stem stitch all round the white felt eye and a line of stem stitch in black round the outer half of the blue eye. Mark a curving eyebrow and a cheek curve with tacking cotton and embroider over it in black stem stitch for the eyebrow and in pink for the cheek. With dark brown sewing thread embroider stem stitch lines on the mouth to indicate lips. Complete the other faces to match.

### Heads

The half faces (eight of them) are now to be sewn together on their straight edges, in a zig-zag line and then these seams sewn to the strip of fawn felt which will cover the top of the dowel rod. So, pin the half faces together in twos with the right sides outside, pinning carefully at hat and mouth to match up. Lay the faces in a pile, with the straight edges together and in alternate colours of face, if two colours have been used, with a flesh pink one on top of the pile.

Leave the first straight edge of the top pink face free. Pin the second edge of the first pink face to the first edge (next to it) of the grey face. Repeat this process, leaving the second edge of the last grey face free. Now three sets of edges are pinned together and the two outside edges are free. Oversew these three pinned seams, taking care to match the joins of hat and face. This oversewing will be on the wrong side.

Measure four equal sections lengthwise on the 5 in. strip of felt and mark down the divisions

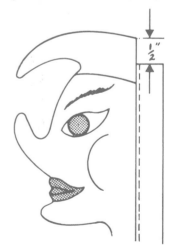

**Fig. 95**

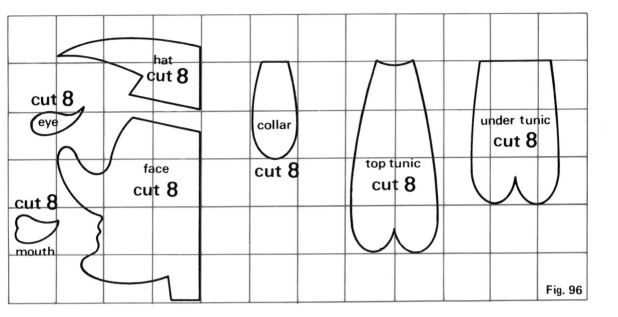

cut 8 (eye)

cut 8 (mouth)

hat cut 8

face cut 8

collar cut 8

top tunic cut 8

under tunic cut 8

Fig. 96

with contrasting running stitches. On the face seams mark points ½ in. from the top of the hat seam. Pin each face seam, from the right side on to a line of tacking on the strip of felt, pinning the edge to the marked point ½ in. from the top of the hat. Sew them firmly in place using backstitch. Pin the two outside face edges to the edges of the felt strip and oversew them together. Oversew the top ½ in. of hat edges together on this last seam.

Place the felt strip with the faces sewn on to it round the top of the dowel rod with the top of the felt strip level with the top of the rod so that the hats project ½ in. above the top of the rod. Sew the strip firmly in place.

Now join up the faces. Pin together where the hat and face are joined, and at the mouth. Start oversewing from the top along the top curve of the hat, round the point and about ½ in. along the under curve. Push small pieces of stuffing very carefully into the point of the hat with a blunted orange stick, to make it firm and smooth. Continue sewing the rest of the hat pushing in more stuffing as you go. Sew down to the inner curve of the nose, and now stuff the top of the head. Sew round the nose to half of the outside curve, and stuff that.

Continue doing a little oversewing and then stuffing. Do *not* oversew completely before stuffing otherwise the stitches will be torn away and spoiled. Complete sewing and stuffing the other three heads in the same way. Sew a small

pearl or gold bead on to the point of each hat.

## Dress

Cut out the pieces as described in the beginning for the dress, so that there are in all eight pieces, four of each colour, for tunic, under-tunic and collar. Pin together the side seams as far as the start of the scallop curve of both lots of tunic pieces, pinning alternate colours together. Oversew all the seams so that each tunic forms a circle. Turn inside out and press the seams flat, without stretching the felt.

Pin the scalloped edge of the tunic over the top edge of the under-tunic so that the V of the scallop is just covering the under-tunic, placing an orange scallop over a yellow one.

Keep the seams of both tunics in line. Sew them together on the wrong side along the straight edge of the under-tunic with invisible stitches, not letting any show through on the right side. Turn inside out. Pull it up over the dowel rod and pin to the jester's neck as low as possible, leaving room for the collar to be sewn on above it. Sew the tunic in place. Pin the collar pieces together in alternate colours and oversew the seams for about ½ in. from the narrow end, and leaving the two ends open. Press the seams flat. Place the collar round the neck and pin in position so that the colours alternate with those on the tunic. Sew it in place with invisible stitches.

95

# 4. Dolls from Fairy Stories and Nursery Rhymes

## The Gingerbread Boy

He is developed from a Kewpie doll and is cut from template 12 (page **24**).

*You will need:*

biscuit coloured felt *for body:* 10 x 16 in.
two black felt ('currants') *for eyes:* ½ in. circles
fawn felt oval ('sultana') *for nose*
red felt semicircle ('cherry') *for mouth*
white felt crescent ('icing') *for collar:* to fit neck
green felt strip ('angelica') *for belt:*
brown felt ('chocolate icing') *for trouser stripes:* four strips
brown felt ('chocolate drops') *for buttons:* four circles
brown felt ('chocolate coconut') *for hair:* four or five strips
matching thread
kapok
adhesive

Trace round the template twice on to the biscuit coloured felt, reversing the template the second time. Cut inside or outside the pencil lines.

Sew or stick the trimmings and features on to one of the biscuit coloured shapes for the front of the doll. Place the two shapes together with right sides outside and oversew with matching thread. Sew from one armhole round the arm to the neck, and stuff the arm. Continue oversewing round the head and then stuffing the head, then continue with the second arm and so on. Stuff the rest of the body firmly but not too hard and sew up the rest of the seam. The doll should be soft and flat rather than hard and round.

## Baby Bunting

A Kewpie doll made from template 3 (page 15).

*You will need:*

white fluffy pile fabric *for body:* two pieces, 12 x 10 in.

flesh coloured felt *for face:* 3½ in. square
card circle: 2 in. diameter
kapok
white sewing thread
embroidery silk
scraps of black, white and red felt *for features*

Place the template on the wrong side of one piece of the fluffy pile fabric and trace round it with a very sharp pencil. Press down firmly all round the edge of the template when drawing as this type of fabric stretches easily and if it moves during drawing the shape will be spoiled. This will be the front of the doll. The other piece of fabric will be left untraced.

Trace round the head of the template on to the flesh felt and cut it out, cutting inside the pencil lines, so that it is slightly smaller than the doll shape. Pin the felt shape in place on the wrong side of the traced fluffy fabric face and sew round the edge just inside the pencil line and not letting the stitches show on the right side. Turn it over and place the card circle in the centre of the fluffy fabric face on the right side and mark the edge of the circle with coloured running stitches. Cut out the circle of

**Fig. 97**

white fluffy fabric so marked by the tacking, exposing the circle of flesh felt which will now be the face. Turn in a very narrow single turn-

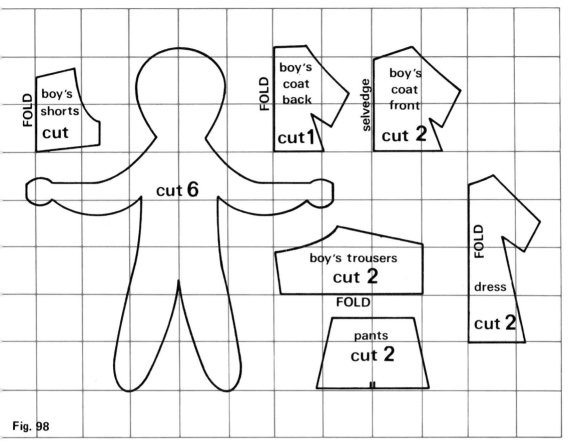

**Fig. 98**

ing on the edge of the fluffy fabric and sew it to the pink felt, keeping the stitches as invisible as possible.

Pin and then tack the two pieces of doll together with the fluffy (right side) inside and machine stitch them together on the pencil line leaving one side open for stuffing. Cut off surplus fabric about ¼ in. outside the stitching. If hand sewing is preferred either backstitch closely all round the pencil line leaving an opening at one side for stuffing, then trimming off surplus to within $\frac{1}{8}$ in. of the stitching, or tack the pieces together *inside* the pencil outline and cut out the shape $\frac{1}{8}$ in. outside the pencil line.

Sew the pieces together with double oversewing stitch (see page 6). Snip carefully into all the corners and snip V's out of the curved edges of head, hands and feet to make the seams lie flat. Turn the doll inside out and press out the seams.

Stuff the doll lightly so that it is not too hard and sew up the side opening with ladder stitch (see page 8), pulling the thread tight so that

the edges are drawn close together. Either embroider or sew felt features to the pink. felt face and embroider a few stitches in brown for hair.

**Ring - a - ring - o' - roses**

Ring - a - ring - o' - roses,
A pocket full of posies,
A-tishoo, a-tishoo,
We all fall down
*Old rhyme*

Three boys and three girls are dancing with clasped hands in a ring. All of them are cut from the same template, Fig. 98. All are made up in the same way, then dressed individually. The back views are important.

*To make all the basic dolls, you will need:*
natural muslin or pale pink poplin 15 x 39 in. or 30 x 20 in. (that is, 15 x 6½ in. for each doll)

97

scraps of coloured felt *for features*
pieces of patterned cotton fabric and felt *for clothes*
embroidery silks
wool *for hair*
adhesive
short lengths of ribbon

Cut out 12 body pieces for the 6 dolls and make them up as for the basic doll (page 97).

### First boy
*You will need:*
yellow felt *for coat back:* 2 x 3 in.
yellow felt *for coat fronts:* two pieces, 2 x 1¾ in.
brown felt *for shorts:* two pieces, 1½ x 2½ in.
brown wool *for hair*
matching thread
brown and pink sewing thread *for features*

Embroider a pink oval mouth in thread and stem stitch and two pink seed stitches for a nose, and two stem stitch circles in brown thread for eyes. (Ordinary embroidery silks are too thick for the features of these small dolls.) Hair is loops of brown wool caught down with small stitches in brown thread. (Again, the wool is too thick to do the actual sewing.) Work from along the crown of the head all round the hair line.

Cut out jacket and shorts as described above. Oversew the side seams and shoulder seams of the jacket on the wrong side. Turn them inside out and press the seams flat. Sew the leg seams of the shorts on the wrong side. Pin the front and back seams matching the leg seams, and oversew them. Turn inside out and press the seams flat. Fit the clothes on to the doll.

### Second boy
*You will need:*
dark pink felt *for trousers:* two pieces, 3 x 2½ in.
mauve felt *for jacket:* one piece, 2 x 3 in. and two pieces, 2 x 1¾ in.
brown embroidery silk *for hair*
pink and blue thread *for features*
matching thread

Embroider the features. The mouth is a crescent of stem stitch, and the nose two seed stitches. The eyes are circles of blue chain stitch with a fly stitch in brown above each one for brows.

Using double brown embroidery silk sew from the top of the head down the parting (which should be faintly pencilled) with long and short stitches to make a hair line on the forehead and round the back of the head (see Fig. 99).

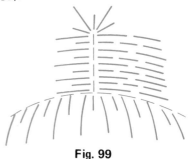

**Fig. 99**

Make up the trousers in the same way as the shorts for the first boy doll and complete the jacket in the same way also. Fit them on to the doll.

### Third boy
*You will need:*
green felt *for shorts:* two pieces, 1½ x 2½ in.
turquoise felt *for jacket:* one piece, 2 x 3 in. and two pieces, 2 x 1¾ in.
brown felt *for hair:* 2 in. square
pink and black embroidery silks *for features*
matching thread

Embroider the features. — a crescent of pink chain stitch for the mouth and circle shapes cut straight across the bottom in black sewing thread for eyes. Use chain stitch.

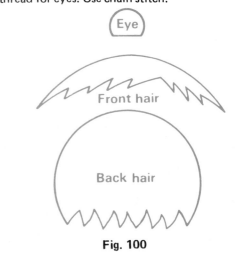

**Fig. 100**

---

*Right: Ring-a-ring-o'-roses*

98

Cut two pieces in brown felt for front and back of the head. Trace round the top of the head template. The front should be a crescent about ½ in. deep, and the back a crescent about 1½ in. deep. Cut the lower edges in notches, pin them in place round the top of the head and oversew them together. Sew to the face and head round the notched edges.

Make up shorts and jacket as for the first boy doll.

## First girl

*You will need:*

> blue cotton print *for dress:* two pieces, 3½ x 3 in.
> blue cotton print *for pants:* two pieces, 1¾ x 2 in.
> brown wool *for hair*
> blue ribbon: 8 in.
> pink, blue and brown sewing thread *for features*

Embroider the features — a circle in pink chain stitch for a mouth, smaller circles in blue thread for eyes, crescents of brown stem stitch for brows and straight stitches for lashes.

For the hair, cut strands of wool 6 in. long. Lay them over the head from shoulder to shoulder and backstitch down over the middle of the head from the forehead to the nape of the neck for a parting. Catch the strands down to the head in several places. Trim evenly to the required length and finish off with a bow at the back.

Cut out the two dress pieces, with the selvedge at the hem if possible, and the two pants pieces. Sew the side seams of the pants on the wrong side. Make a small hem at the waist and draw it up to fit. Turn it inside out and press the seams. Oversew the bottom edge with a few stitches in the middle to form legs. Fit them on to the doll. Sew the side seams and one shoulder seam of the dress on the wrong side. Sew small turnings on sleeves and neck, or pink the edges with pinking shears. Turn inside out and press the seams.

Fit the dress on to the doll. Make a single turning on the front edge of the shoulder and sew to the back edge. Tie a ribbon round the waist.

## Second girl

*You will need:*

> red cotton *for dress:* two pieces, 3½ x 3 in.
> red cotton *for pants:* two pieces, 1¾ x 2 in.
> white narrow braid: 8 in.
> blonde wool or silk: *for hair*

red ribbon: 4 in.
> pink, blue and black thread *for features*

Embroider the features — two fly stitches close together for the mouth and two seed stitches for the nose. Black circles in black stem stitch with blue satin stitch circles in the middle of them for eyes, and black stem stitch arcs above them.

Cut strands of wool 7½ in. long and sew to the head as for the first girl doll. Gather the strands loosely to each side and catch down in a bunch at each side. Tie with a bow of ribbon, Plait the wool firmly and sew round the ends of the plaits or tie with another bow.

Make up the pants and dress as for the first girl doll. Trim with braid round the neck, down the front and round the waist.

## Third girl

*You will need:*

> blue and pink print *for dress:* two pieces, 3½ x 3 in.
> blue and pink print *for pants:* two pieces, 1¾ x 2 in.
> white ribbon: 18 in.
> gold silk lustre embroidery silk *for hair*
> pink, blue and black sewing thread *for features*

Embroider the features — a crescent for a mouth in pink chain stitch, with two seed stitches for the nose. The eyes are two satin stitches in blue thread with black crescents in chain stitch above, finished with black straight stitches for lashes.

Make the hair as for the second girl doll, using gold lustre embroidery silk. Gather in bunches at ear level, sew round the bunch catching it down to the side seam of the face, and finish off with little bows.

Make up the pants and dress as for the first girl doll. Trim the neck with white ribbon, tying it in front. Tie a sash round the waist with a bow at the back.

## Grouping the dolls

Place the dolls in line, alternating boys and girls and mixing clothes colours effectively. Sew the tips of the hands together. Sew the last two together so that they face into the ring. They will stand up.

### Tweedledum and Tweedledee

The two fat little brothers from 'Alice Through The Looking Glass'.

Each of them requires the same materials, the only difference being colours of trousers, cap

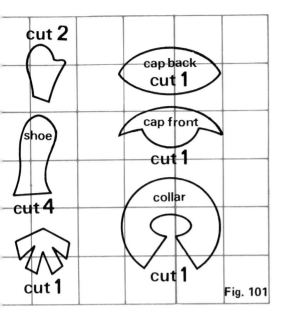

cut 2

cap back
cut 1

cap front
cut 1

shoe

collar

cut 4

cut 1

cut 1

Fig. 101

upholstery adhesive
matching thread
coloured felt for button

## Features

Cut two circles, ½ in. diameter in black felt for eyes and one ¼ in. circle for a nose. Cut a crescent shape in red felt for a smiling mouth. (For contrast, Tweedledee could have an oval $\frac{3}{5}$ x ½ in. for a surprised looking mouth.) Stick these in place on the face circle with upholstery adhesive. Pin the front and the back of the head together with two small circles of wadding between and the right sides outside. Oversew the

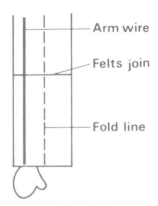

Arm wire

Felts join

Fold line

Fig. 102

and buttons. They are both made up in the same way. Directions are given for Tweedle-dum.

## For Tweedledum

*You will need:*

a round flat cheese box 4½ in. diameter, ½ in. deep

flesh coloured felt *for face:* two 2½ in. circles

flesh coloured felt *for hands:* two pieces, 1 x ½ in.

flesh coloured felt *for arms:* two pieces, 1½ x 1 in.

royal blue felt *for coat:* circle 4½ in. diameter cut into semicircles

royal blue felt *for sleeves:* two pieces, 1½ x 1 in.

royal blue felt *for gusset:* 7½ x ½ in.

yellow felt *for trousers:* circle 4½ in. diameter cut into semicircles

yellow felt *for legs:* two pieces, 4½ x 1 in.

yellow felt *for gusset:* 7½ x ½ in.

green felt *for cap:* 2 in. square

black felt *for shoes:* 3 x 1 in.

black felt *for belt:* two pieces, 5 x ¼ in.

black felt *for bow:* 1 in. square

scraps of black and red felt *for features*

white felt *for collar:* 2 in. square

wadding: two 4¼ in. circles, 4 in. circle, 3¾ in. circle, two 2¼ in. circles

pipe cleaners or pipe cleaner chenille
*for arms:* 8½ in.
*for legs:* 12 in.

edge. Place a royal blue sleeve and a flesh felt arm together and oversew one short seam. Press out flat. Cut two hand shapes from flesh felt and sew one on to the end of the flesh felt arm with thumb to the inside. Repeat for the other arm. Bend over ¼ in. at each end of the arm wire, fold the arm felt round it and oversew the seam, matching the colours where they join and enclosing the wire. Repeat with the second arm keeping the thumbs on the same side. The seam will be under the arm.

## Legs

Fold back 1 in. at each end of the leg wire and twist into a loop. Fold the leg felt round the wire, leaving the loop free. Oversew the seam. Repeat with the other leg.

## Front Body

Oversew the straight edges of a blue and a yellow semicircle together and press out flat. Find the middle of the yellow arc and pin a leg each side of this point on the wrong side. Find the centre of the blue arc and pin an arm about 1 in. each side of it, again on the wrong side.

101

Pin the blue gusset strip all round the blue arc with right sides inside. Oversew them together, sewing in the arms firmly. Repeat with the yellow gusset round the yellow arc, sewing in the legs firmly. Trim off any surplus felt on the gusset ends and sew the edges together. On the wrong side of this front body place three circles of wadding, the smallest circle next to the felt and the biggest one on top, tucking it under the leg and arm wires so that they rest on the wadding and not on the felt.

Fit the cheese box on top of this with the gusset fitting snugly round the side of it. Place the remaining wadding on top of the box and the second felt circle over it, matching the colour joins. Oversew all the way round. Sew about ¾ in. of the head to the body. Hold the head upright and take a stitch in it and a stitch in the body. Do this all the way round taking stitches first in the head and then in the body, keeping the head as upright as possible all the time. Pull the stitches tight. If the head is a little shaky, take another row of stitches all round.

## Shoes
Cut four shoe pieces from the pattern in black felt and sew them in pairs. Oversew down one edge and round the toes. Insert the foot loop and continue sewing the second side.

## Belt
Cut a strip of black felt 10 x ¼ in. and sew it round the middle over the colour join.

## Collar
Place the collar pattern on white felt or interlining and cut one. Fasten it round the neck with the opening in front.

## Bow
Cut a bow from the pattern in coloured felt and sew it in front of the collar opening.

## Buttons
Cut two ¾ in. circles in contrasting felt and sew or stick them on the front of the coat.

## Cap
Cut one back and one front in green felt from the pattern and oversew the curved edges together. Catch it down at the sides and back of the head.

## Tweedledee
Make up Tweedledee in the same way. You could vary the features by giving him a surprised-looking mouth made from a red oval of felt $\frac{3}{5}$ x ½ in. Dress him in red trousers and buttons, black bow and orange cap.

## Humpty Dumpty
Templates are given for body, hands, boots, bow, jacket front and hair.

*You will need:*
flesh felt *for head:* two pieces, 4¼ x 6½ in.
flesh felt *for hands:* four pieces, 1¾ x 1½ in.
yellow felt *for boots:* four pieces, 2 x 1¼ in.
orange felt *for bow:* 2½ x 2 in.
red felt *for jacket back:* 6½ x 4½ in.
red felt *for jacket fronts:* two pieces, 3½ x 4¼ in.
red felt *for sleeves:* two pieces, 3 x 1½ in.
blue felt *for trousers front:* 6½ x 4½ in.
blue felt *for trouser legs:* two pieces, 4 x 2 in.
blue felt *for eyes:* two ½ in. circles
black felt *for legs:* two pieces, 5½ x ¾ in.
black felt *for brows:* 1 in. square
white felt *for collar back:* 6½ x ½ in.
white felt *for collar front:* 6½ x 1 in.
white felt *for eyes:* two 1 in. circles
brown felt *for hair back:* 3 x 5½ in.
brown felt *for hair front:* 3 x 5½ in.
four pipe cleaners
kapok
matching thread
red, pink and black embroidery silk
adhesive

Cut out all the pieces listed above. Cut the template in half across the middle. Trace and cut two flesh coloured felt shapes for the head from the narrower part of the pattern. Cut one blue felt and one red felt shape from the bottom half of the pattern for jacket back and trousers front. Cut two jacket fronts in red felt reversing the template for the second one and marking with coloured cotton the two corners which will be in the centre because the curved sides are slightly different.

Cut four hands in flesh felt, reversing the pattern for two of them, and keeping them in pairs with pencil lines inside. Cut four boots from yellow felt as for the hands. Cut two jacket sleeves in red and two trouser legs in blue. Cut the collar strips in white felt, the narrower piece for the back. Fold the wider

---

*Right: Tweedledum and Tweedledee, Baby Bunting, Red Riding Hood, and the Gingerbread Boy*

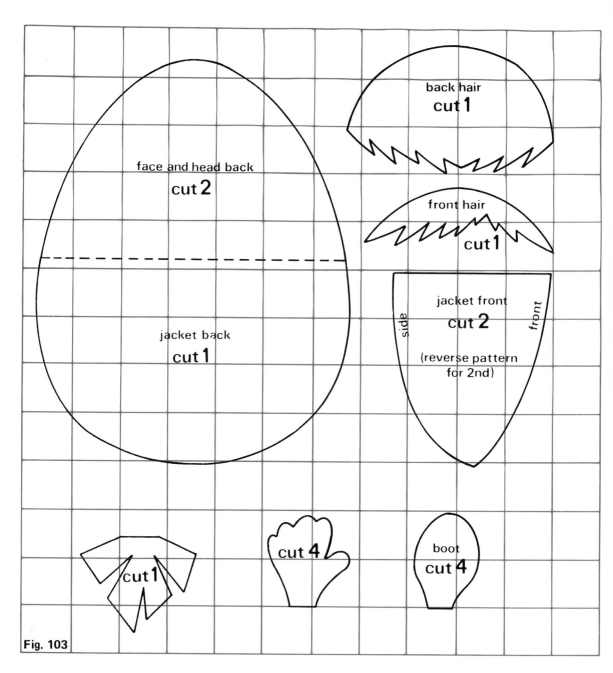

face and head back
cut 2

back hair
cut 1

front hair
cut 1

jacket front
cut 2

side

front

(reverse pattern for 2nd)

jacket back
cut 1

cut 1

cut 4

boot
cut 4

Fig. 103

strip in half and cut a curved corner from the folded edge (see Fig. 87). Trim off the bottom edges, to make it the same width as the back collar. Cut a single bow in orange felt.

## Features
Cut two 1 in. circles in white felt and two ½ in. ones in blue. Cut off small segments from the

bottom of each circle. For brows, cut the brown square in half diagonally and cut a small triangle from the middle of each diagonal line (see Fig. 105). Stick the blue circles on to the white circles and stick them in place on the pink felt face. Stick the black felt eyebrows over them. Embroider a pink curve for the nose in stem stitch and a curve for the mouth in red

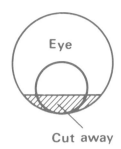

Eye

Cut away

Fig. 104

chain stitch. Embroider a line of black stem stitch round the eyes with small straight stitches for lashes above.

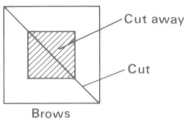

Cut away

Cut

Brows

Fig. 105

## To make up

Sew the blue trouser front to the face along the straight edges, and the red jacket back to the piece for the back of the head. Press the seams flat. Pin the hair pieces in place on back and front. Sew the front jacket pieces in place along the top of the trouser join.

Cut pipe cleaners about 1 in. longer than the sleeve pieces, turn the ends under, lay them along the sleeve felt and sew the seams, enclosing them. Sew two hand pieces together, insert the pipe cleaner end into the hand and sew it to the sleeve with the wrist inside the cuff. Pin each arm in place on the sides about ½ in. below the middle join. Make up the black felt legs and boots in the same way, but join the boots over the black legs. Oversew the seams of the blue trouser legs and pull them over the black legs, with the seam at the back. Pin them in place.

Pin the back and front pieces together, matching the seams. Oversew the seams, starting at the bottom and working along one side and over the top of the head. Leave open the right side of the jacket. Stuff firmly and smoothly, but not too hard. Sew up the opening. Join the two collar pieces together and sew in place over the middle join. Sew the bow in the middle.

## Jack and the Giant

Both dolls are made on cardboard tubes of

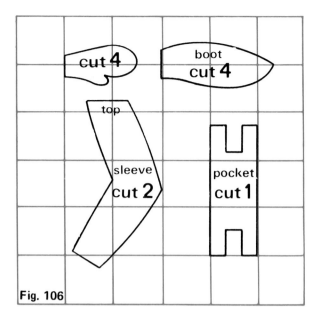

Fig. 106

different sizes. Patterns are given for hands, feet, dagger, sleeves, pocket.

### Jack

*You will need:*
    tube 9 x 1¾ in. diameter
    flesh felt *for face:* 5½ x 2 in.
    flesh felt *for hands:* four pieces, 1½ x 1 in.
    green felt *for jerkin:* 5½ x 3 in.
    fawn felt *for legs:* 5½ x 4 in.
    fawn felt  1¾ in. diameter circle
    white felt *for sleeves:* two pieces, 4½ x 3 in.
    yellow felt *for hair:* 2 x $\frac{2}{5}$ in. and 4¼ x 1 in.
    yellow felt 1¾ in. diameter circle
    yellow felt *for collar:* 5½ x ¾ in.
    orange felt *for belt:* 5¾ x ¼ in.
    orange felt *for pocket:* 2½ x 1 in.
    brown felt *for feet:* four pieces, 2½ x 1 in.
    brown felt *for eyes:* two ½ in. circles
    brown felt: 1¾ in. diameter circle
    red felt *for mouth:* ¾ x ½ in.
    matching thread
    kapok
    adhesive
    cocktail stick sword

Cut out all pieces as shown. Fit the face piece round the top of the tube and oversew the edges together at the back. Sew the leg piece similarly round the bottom of the tube, then the jerkin.

All seams must be at the back, and the jerkin edges should slightly overlap the face and leg

105

*Humpty Dumpty*

pieces. Sew the jerkin to them round the edges. Sew the collar round the neck join.

Cut both hair pieces in a fringe along one long side on each. Sew the narrower piece to the top edge of front of the face and the wider piece along the back and sides, the edges slightly overlapping the front fringe. Sew the yellow circle to the top edge.

For the mouth, round off the corners of the red felt and cut a small curve from the top long edge, leaving a crescent shape for the mouth (see Fig. 107). Stick it in place, with the eyes in the place above.

Mouth

**Fig. 107**

Oversew the hands together in twos. Oversew the sleeves together in twos leaving top and bottom edges open. Sew the hands inside the sleeve edges. Push a little kapok into the sleeve,

106

just enough to round it a little and then sew the arm on at the shoulder.

Fold the pocket in half and oversew the edges. Slip the belt strip inside the handles and sew them to the belt. Sew the belt round the join of the jerkin and trousers so that the pocket is at the side front.

Sew feet together in twos. Pin in place on the brown circle and sew the circle, including feet, round the bottom edge of tube.

Sew a small cocktail sword in the hand. Cut out a small dagger in felt or cut down a cocktail stick sword and stick in the belt opposite the pocket.

## The Giant

He is made on a much larger postal tube measuring 21 x $2\frac{1}{5}$ in., such as the type used for maps.

*You will need:*
  cardboard tube
  fawn felt *for face:* 7 x 4 in.
  fawn felt *for hands:* four pieces, 2½ x 2 in.
  fawn felt *for feet:* four pieces, 3½ x 2 in.
  fawn felt: $2\frac{1}{5}$ in. diameter circle
  chestnut felt *for jerkin:* 7 x 9 in.
  chestnut felt *for sleeves:* two pieces, 7 x 4 in.
  green felt *for trousers:* 7 x 9 in.
  grey felt *for collar:* 7 x 1 in.
  yellow felt *for pocket:* 1½ x 2½ in.
  yellow felt *for strap:* 9 x $\frac{2}{5}$ in.
  red felt *for mouth:* 2 x ¾ in.
  white felt *for teeth:* 1¼ x $\frac{3}{10}$ in.
  black felt *for eyes:* 1¼ x ¼ in.
  black felt *for club:* two pieces, 4½ x ½ in.
  black felt: $2\frac{1}{5}$ in. circle
  fur or wool *for hair:* 2½ in. circle
  wire *for club:* 16 in.
  pipe cleaner chenille *for arms:* 35 in.
  kapok
  black embroidery silk
  matching thread

Cut out all the above pieces. Sew the face felt round the top of the tube. If it is too wide it can be trimmed off or lapped over and sewn. Seam to be at the back. Sew the top circle in place. Sew the green felt round the bottom part of the tube.

Measure up 1 in. from one short end of the jerkin piece and cut along the edge in 1 in.

*Right: Jack and the giant*

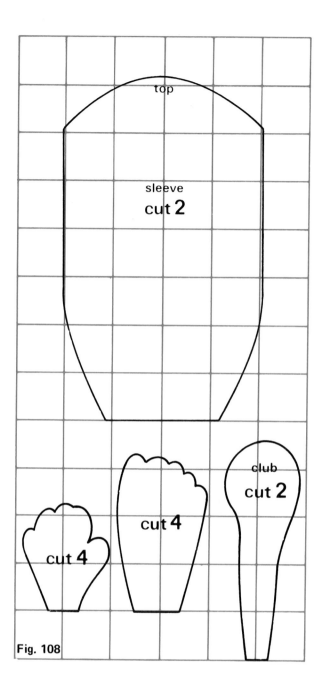

top

sleeve

cut 2

club

cut 2

cut 4

cut 4

**Fig. 108**

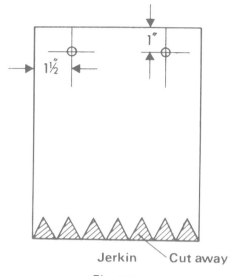

Jerkin        Cut away

**Fig. 109**

the holes in the jerkin, from the back. Fit the jerkin on to the tube with the wire loop at the back of the tube and the points of the jerkin bottom edge just covering the trousers. Oversew the jerkin down the back seam, and catch down between the points to the trousers, and along the top edge to the face. Oversew the side seams of the sleeves, fit them on to the wire arms and sew them on to the jerkin at the shoulder over the holes. Oversew the hands together in pairs, pull them over the wire hand loops and sew to the wire. Sew the collar round the neck to hide the join.

Cut curves on each long side of the red felt rectangle for the mouth, making a deeper curve at the top, and cut a slit along the middle. Cut one edge of the white felt into jagged uneven points for teeth (see Fig. **110**), fit the straight

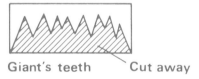

Giant's teeth       Cut away

**Fig. 110**

edge of it into the slit in the mouth so that the teeth project over the bottom lip. Stick it in place. Cut the black felt for eyes into long thin crescents, stick a small white felt triangle in the middle of each and stick them on the face. Sew a circle of fur or fur fabric over the top of the head for hair.

Fold the wire for the club in half. Keep the fold of wire for the handle and twist the ends

points. Measure down 1 in. from the other short side and 1½ in. in from each side and cut two small holes (see Fig. **109**).

Find the centre point of the arms wire and mark 1½ in. each side of it. Bend back the ends of the wire to these points and twist leaving loops for the hand. Push the wire arms through

108

into a knob. Oversew the edges of half of the belt pieces for the club and fit in the wire. Pad it round with kapok where necessary, but do not make it too heavy. Sew up the second side. Attach the club to one hand, sewing fingers and thumb round the handle. Bend the arm back over top of head.

To make the pocket, fold the rectangle into an envelope shape, cut off the points on the flap, sew up the sides, catch the flap down at the sides and sew the strap to the corners. Fit it on over the shoulder and catch down to the jerkin inside the flap.

Sew the feet in pairs. Pin in place on the fawn circle and sew circle, including the feet, round the bottom of the tube.

## Miss Muffet and the Spider
The doll for Miss Muffet is made from template 1 (page 21) in natural muslin or poplin, using a 12 in. square of fabric.

*You will need:*
 pink and blue embroidery silks *for features*
 black sewing thread
 kapok
 blonde or yellow wool *for hair*
 cotton print *for dress bodice:* two pieces, 3 x 6 in.
 cotton print *for skirt:* 4½ x 18 in.
 narrow broderie Anglaise or similar: 1¼ yd
 silk or muslin *for pants:* two pieces, 3 in. square
 silk or muslin *for sash:* 18 x 1 in.
 silk or muslin *for hat:* 6 in. circle
 narrow pink ribbon: 6 in.
 black felt *for shoes:* four pieces, 1 x 1¼ in.
 matching thread

Make up the doll from directions for the basic doll on page 21. Sew across the tops of the legs to enable the doll to sit.

## Features
With pink embroidery silk sew a circle $\frac{2}{5}$ in. diameter in stem stitch for her mouth. Embroider two circles in blue silk for eyes. With black sewing thread embroider a straight line

**Fig. 111**

$\frac{2}{5}$ in. long in stem stitch immediately under and touching the eyes (see Fig. 111). Embroider a ¾ in. circle on this line. Sew five or six straight stitches along the top curve for lashes.

## Hair
With blonde wool sew loops along the hair line from one cheek, across the forehead and down to the other cheek.

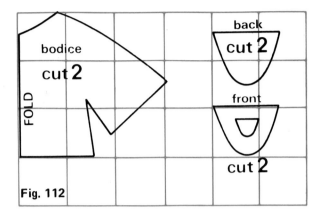

**Fig. 112**

## Clothes
Cut out the pieces as indicated above, allowing extra on the bodice for turnings.

Slightly slant the sides of the pants pieces to be narrower at the waist. Sew the side seams and a narrow hem at the top. Turn inside out and press. Make a narrow hem at the bottom and sew in the middle with a few oversewing stitches to make the legs. Fit on the doll.

Sew the side seams of the dress bodice together on the wrong side. Sew the back seam of the skirt on the wrong side. Press all the seams flat. Gather up one long side of the skirt to fit the bodice waist. Make a single turning on the waist of the bodice and sew the gathered skirt on to it evenly, with the seam at centre back. Fit the dress on to the doll.

Make small single turnings on the front shoulder seams and sew them to the backs of shoulders. Sew broderie Anglaise or a frill on to the hem. Make frills of the same material for the elbow length sleeves and neck and sew them in place.

For the mob cap make a single turning all round the edge of the hat circle. Sew on to it the broderie Anglaise and gather up along the edge to fit the head. It should be a floppy hat, not fitting snugly to the head. Sew the hat in place on the head, letting the wool curls show

...ll round the front. Finish off in the front with a ribbon bow.

With pinking shears cut the length of sash ¼ in. wide and tie around the waist with a big bow at the back.

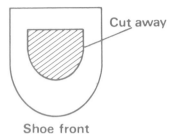

Fig. 113

Cut crescents out of two of the shoe shapes or fronts. Oversew together the curved edges of one front and one back for each shoe. Fit them on to the feet and sew in place round the tops.

## Spider

*You will need:*
   black nylon felt *for body:* two pieces, 3½ x 2½ in.
   black nylon felt *for legs:* eight pieces, 5½ x ½ in.
   eight pipe cleaners
   white felt *for eyes:* two ½ in. circles
   blue felt *for eyes:* two ¼ in. circles
   red embroidery silk *for mouth*
   black thread
   kapok

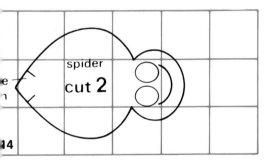

Cut two body shapes from black felt. Trace round the template with a white pencil or tailor's chalk.

*Left: Miss Muffet and the spider*

Cut eight strips of felt to size. Turn over ½ in. at the end of the pipe cleaner, place it on a felt strip and oversew the edges of the felt strip to enclose the pipe cleaner. Repeat for the other seven legs. Sew four on each side of one of the body pieces.

Place the two body pieces together with right sides outside and oversew the edges starting near the back end (tail) and leaving an opening there for stuffing. Stuff the head quite firmly. Stuff the body and sew up the opening.

Embroider a smiling crescent for mouth in red silk, and sew the circles of blue felt on the white felt circles and sew in place for eyes.

Bend the legs so that the spider stands.

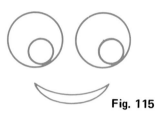

Fig. 115

## Jack and Jill

These twin boy and girl dolls can be made from a strip of stockinette or made from a white pair of children's socks.

If using stockinette, follow the directions for the basic dolls using template 8, (see page 20).

### Sock dolls
*You will need:*
   white pair of children's socks
   embroidery silks or coloured felt
   wool
   white thread

The socks need not be new, but the back of the heel must be strong, with no holes or darns, because this will be the doll's face. Cut off the toe at the instep, and cut it in half lengthwise for the arms. Fold the sock so that the back of the heel is uppermost. Cut up the middle of the welt of the sock to make the legs. Turn it inside out and sew the legs with backstitch as shown. Turn inside out again.

Stuff the legs and sew across the top of the legs. Stuff the body and tie firmly round the neck. Stuff the head. Gather up the cut ends and sew to the back of the head. Sew the seams of the arms with backstitch. Turn inside out, stuff, and sew at the shoulders.

Either embroider the features or cut out shapes in coloured felt and sew in place. Sew on wool loops for hair, or lay wool in strands

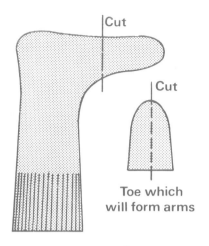

Cut

Cut

Toe which
will form arms

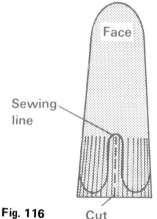

Face

Sewing
line

**Fig. 116**

Cut

yellow felt *for hat:* 3½ x 3 in.
three press studs, size 000
adhesive
matching thread
scraps of red, brown and pink felt *for features*
black embroidery silk

Using a red felt rectangle, $\frac{9}{10}$ x $\frac{2}{5}$, cut one long side into a curve by rounding off the lower corners. Mark the middle point of the other long side and cut out a small crescent shape each side of it (see Fig. 117.) to make a mouth.

Mouth

**Fig. 117**

Stick in place. Cut two brown felt circles ½ in. in diameter and stick in place *for eyes.* Sew an arc above each eye with black silk in stem stitch, with three straight stitches at the top of each eye for lashes. Cut two pink felt circles for rosy cheeks and stick on.

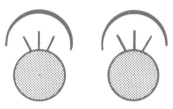

**Fig. 118**

For the hair, sew 1 in. loops of brown wool all round the head at eye level. Cut loops and trim ends level.

Patterns are given for the dress yoke, the pants, the back, front and sleeve of the blouse and for the shoes. The yokes are double so fold the fabric in half and cut out the pattern twice. Cut all other pieces as indicated above.

Place the two pieces for the pants together with right sides inside and sew the side and inner leg seams. Make a narrow hem at the top. Make a single turning on the legs and sew in shell stitch (see page 8). Turn inside out and press.

Sew the side and shoulder seams of the blouse and the sleeve seams. Pink the bottom edges of sleeves. Gather the top curve of each sleeve, draw up the gathers to fit the armhole and sew in place. Gather the bottom edge and draw up the fullness to fit the arm. Fasten off. Make a narrow turning on the neck and sew a press stud at the back.

To make socks, turn the finger bandage inside

across the head and sew down the centre. Tie in bunches at the sides of the face. Your doll is now ready to be dressed.

### Jill
A stockinette doll made from template 8 (see page 20).

*You will need:*
 cotton print *for dress yoke:* four pieces, 3 x 2 in.
 cotton print *for dress skirt:* 15 x 4 in.
 cotton print *for pants:* two pieces, 4 x 2½ in.
 white cotton *for blouse front:* 4 x 3½ in.
 white cotton *for blouse back:* two pieces, 3½ x 2¼ in.
 white cotton *for sleeves:* two pieces, 4½ x 1½ in.
 narrow finger bandage, size 12: two 4 in. lengths
 black felt *for shoes:* two pieces, 1¾ x 1¼ in..

112

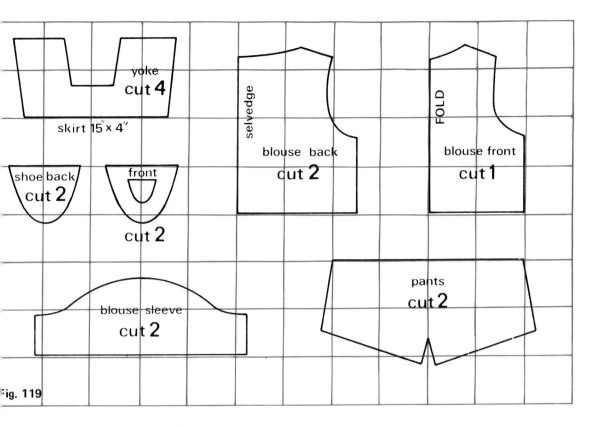

yoke
cut 4

skirt 15" x 4"

selvedge

blouse back
cut 2

FOLD

blouse front
cut 1

shoe back
cut 2

front
cut 2

blouse sleeve
cut 2

pants
cut 2

Fig. 119

out, pull it up over the leg till one cut end is level with the bottom of the foot. Sew all round the leg 2 in. from the toe. Pull the bandage down over the line of stitching to the toe. Gather up both lots of raw edges and sew under the toe.

Cut two shoes from each pattern and keep in pairs, marking left and right foot. Cut a shield shape out of one of each for fronts. Place a front and back shoe together and oversew the curved edges together. Fit on the foot and sew on round the top.

Pin the pieces for the dress yoke together with right sides inside and sew seams, leaving the bottom long edges open. Snip into the corners and turn inside out. Pink one long edge of the skirt with pinking shears. Sew the short edges together on the wrong side. Turn inside out and press the seam.

Mark the quarters of the long side. Gather this edge and pull up the gathers a little. Pin the skirt seam to the middle of one yoke edge and the opposite halfway mark to the middle of the other yoke. Draw up the gathers to fit the yokes allowing 1 in. at each side for under arms. Fasten off securely. Pin the rest of the

skirt to the yokes, pinning the gathers with more fullness in the yokes than under the arms. Sew to the yokes. Make turnings under the arms and sew. Sew a press stud to each shoulder. Fold the hat felt in half along the 3 in. side and oversew the two seams. Fit the cap on to the head to come over the ears, and sew round the sides and back of head, leaving the front unsewn.

### Jack
Also made in stockinette from template 8.
Patterns are given for overalls, shirt, hair, shoes.

*You will need:*
 green felt *for overall legs:* two pieces, 5 x 3½ in.
 green felt *for overall bib:* two pieces, 2¼ x 2½ in.
 green felt *for overall pockets:* two pieces 1 in. square
 white cotton *for shirt back:* 7 x 3½ in.
 white cotton *for shirt fronts:* two pieces, 3¾ x 3½ in.
 brown felt *for hair back:* 2¾ x 3½ in.
 brown felt *for hair front:* 3 x ½ in.

113

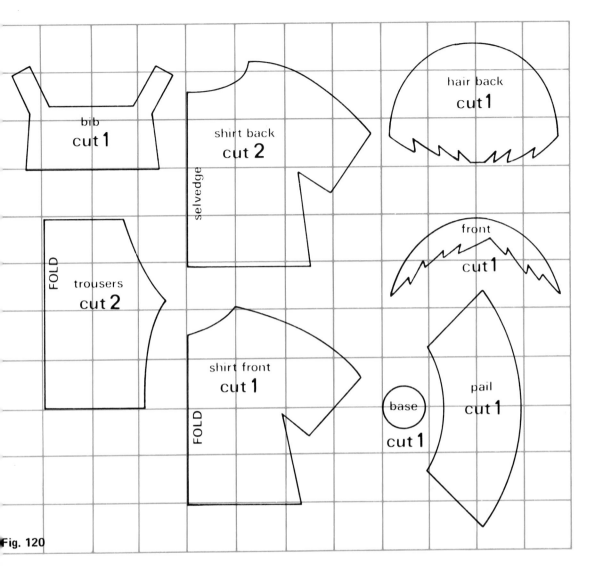

**bib** cut **1**

**shirt back** cut **2**

**hair back** cut **1**

selvedge

**trousers** cut **2**

FOLD

**front** cut **1**

**shirt front** cut **1**

FOLD

**base** cut **1**

**pail** cut **1**

**Fig. 120**

scraps of red, brown and pink felt *for features*
black felt *for shoes:* two pieces, 1¾ x 1¼ in.
finger bandage *for socks:* two 4 in. lengths
red felt *for pail:* 5 x 2 in.
red felt *for pail base:* ¾ in. circle
adhesive
black embroidery silk
matching thread
kapok

Cut a 1 x ½ in. rectangle of red felt in a cres-

*Left: Jack and Jill*

cent and stick in place for mouth. All the other
features are the same as Jill's. Cut the hair in
brown felt from the pattern. Pin in place and
sew closely over the top and all round front and
back edges.

Cut out all pieces for the clothes as shown.

Sew side and shoulder seams of the shirt on
the wrong side. Turn inside out and press the
seams. Hem the sleeve edges. Make single turnings at the neck and down one straight edge at
the back. Draw up neck to fit the doll and sew
in place at the back of the neck.

Oversew the leg seams of the overalls on the
wrong side. Pin front and back seams matching
up the leg seams and oversew on the wrong

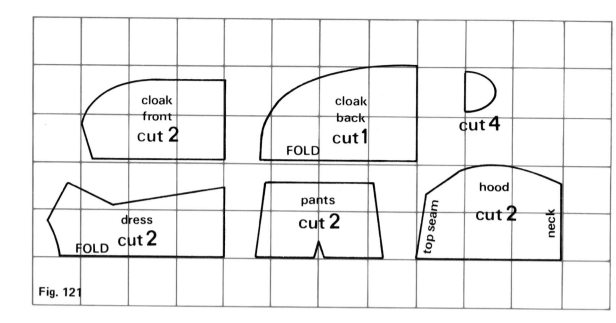

cloak front cut **2**

cloak back cut **1** FOLD

cut **4**

dress FOLD cut **2**

pants cut **2**

hood cut **2** top seam neck

Fig. 121

side. Turn inside out and press the seams flat. Mark the middle of the long edge of the bib and pin the mark to the front seam at waist of trousers. Pin the rest of the bib and sew in place on the wrong side. Sew second side to match. Turn out and press seam. Sew a pocket on to each leg. Fit the overalls on the doll and sew the shoulder seams of the bib.

Finish socks and shoes as for Jill.

### Pail

Cut one pail shape from the pattern in red felt. The handle is a strip of red felt and the base is a circle. Sew the narrow curve of the pail to the circle. Trim off any excess from the side of the pail. Sew the side seam. Fold the strip for the handle in half lengthwise and oversew both long sides. Sew to each side of the pail. Either sew a hand of each doll to the pail, or to Jack's only. A pattern can be embroidered round the top of the pail if desired.

### Red Riding Hood

This is a small 7 in. doll made from template 11 (page 23) in flesh coloured felt.

*You will need:*
scrap of red felt *for mouth*
adhesive
red felt *for cloak back:* 3 x 4 in.
red felt *for cloak front:* two pieces, 3 x 2 in.

red felt *for hood:* two pieces, 3 x 2 in.
brown and blue thread *for features*
wool *for hair*
blue felt *for dress:* two pieces, 2 x 2¾ in.
blue felt *for pants:* two pieces, 1½ x 2½ in.
black felt *for shoes:* four pieces, ½ x 1 in.
matching thread

### Features

Cut a small crescent shape in red felt and stick in place for her mouth. With brown thread sew two small rings in stem stitch and work blue thread satin stitch circles in the centres. Finish off with two arcs in brown stem stitch above them and a few straight stitches for lashes.

### Hair

Sew small rings of wool in clusters all round the hair line from cheek to cheek.

### Clothes

Cut out all pieces as shown above.

Oversew the side and inner leg seams of the pants. Turn inside out and press seams flat. Fit them on to the doll.

Sew the side seams and one shoulder seam of the dress. Turn inside out and press seams. Fit the dress on to the doll, and sew the front shoulder to the back one.

To make the cape sew the side seams from hem to neckline. Turn and press seams. Sew the curved seam of the hood, leaving the front and neck seams open. Pin the seam of the hood to

116

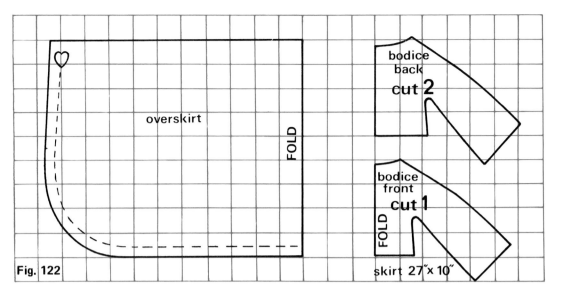

**Fig. 122**   overskirt   FOLD   bodice back cut 2   bodice front cut 1   FOLD   skirt 27″x 10″

the middle of the cape neck at the back. Pin round the rest of the neck and sew. Press the seam. Fit it on to the doll and fasten with a bow.

Oversew the curved edges of the shoes in pairs. Fit them on to the doll and sew to the leg round the top of the shoe.

## The Queen of Hearts
She is made in natural coloured muslin from template 5.

*You will need:*
    felt tip pens or coloured embroidery silks *for features*
    wool *for hair*
    interlining *for underskirt:* 28 x 8 in.
    red satin *for skirt:* 27 x 10 in.
    red satin *for bodice:* 13 x 2 in.
    white silk *for overskirt:* 9 x 20 in.
    red felt: 6 x 9 in.
    gold or silver cord
    matching sewing thread
    gilt card  7½ x ¾ in.

## Features
Felt tip pens can be used quite successfully on some types of muslin, but before using them test them on a small, separate piece of the same fabric for running or blurring. If you wish, you can embroider the features like those of the doll in the picture. Work in chain and stem stitch in coloured embroidery silks.

## Hair
Cut lengths of wool long enough to stretch from just below the shoulder on one side, over the top of the head, to the other shoulder. Lay the strands across the head and sew down the centre with backstitch. Catch the strands down in several places over the head, gathering the ends of wool into the nape of the neck. Twist them into a coil, tucking in the ends and sewing securely.

Cut out all the pieces as shown above.

### Underskirt
Sew together the two short sides of the rectangle of interlining. Gather one long side and draw it up tightly to fit the doll's waist. Fasten off securely.

### Skirt
Sew up the short seams on the red satin, sewing on the wrong side. Turn inside out and press the seam. Make 1 in. hem along one side for the hem at the bottom. With tacking cotton mark this hem into twelve equal sections. Couch down silver or gold cord along the sewn line of the hem, making a small loop at each mark and

**Fig. 123**   Stitches

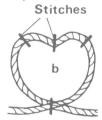

a     b

117

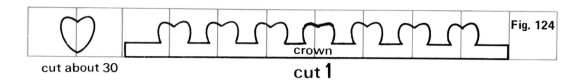

cut about 30        **cut 1**        **Fig. 124**

catching the loop down at three points to make a heart shape (see Fig. 123). Continue in this way all round the hem. Gather the other side of the skirt and draw up the gathers to fit the waist, fastening off securely.

## Overskirt

Make a narrow hem all round the curved edge, leaving the straight edge (waist) unsewn. Cut small hearts from the red felt, and sew them at close intervals all round the hemmed edge — about ten on each curved front and ten along the back. Gather the straight edge to fit the waist over the red skirt so that the two front edges of the overskirt meet in the front, edge to edge. Sew firmly in place round the waist.

## Bodice

Sew side, shoulder and sleeve seams. Make hems on the sleeve edges. Finish off the hems on the right side with couched down gold cord to match the hem. Make a single turning on the neck and couch cord on to it. Make a single turning on the back opening. Fit the bodice on to the doll, pin the back opening together and pin in place round the waist. Sew up the opening and round the waist.

## Crown

Cut the crown from the gilt card, using the pattern. Overlap the two ends and stick them together. Press firmly in place on the head over the brows.

### Knave of Hearts

He is made from a 12 in. square of natural muslin using template 9, page 27.

*You will need:*
blue felt *for eyes:* two ¼ in. circles
blue felt *for tabard:* two pieces, 4½ x 3½ in.
white felt *for eyes:* two ½ in. circles
red felt *for mouth*
red felt *for trousers:* two pieces, 4 x 3½ in.
red felt *for hearts:* two 1½ in. squares
adhesive
yellow felt *for hair front:* 2 x ¾ in.
yellow felt *for hair sides:* 4 x 1 in.

yellow felt *for hair top:* 3¼ x 2 in.
black embroidery thread
black felt *for shoes:* four pieces, 1½ x 1 in.
white silk *for sleeves:* two pieces, 4 x 5 in.
silver cord about 30 in.
silver Lurex thread
matching sewing thread

## Features

Stick the blue circle onto the white circles. Cut an oval red felt mouth and stick it in place to give him a surprised look. Stick the eyes in place (see Fig. 125). Embroider two crescents in

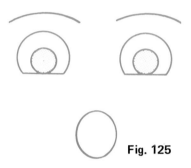

**Fig. 125**

black chain stitch for brows. Cut one long edge of felt for the front of the head into a fringe and sew it across the forehead. Cut the second strip in a fringe and sew round the head from cheek to cheek. Cut a fringe on all edges of the third strip and sew it on to the head, the long edge from side to side to cover the top of the front and side pieces.

## Clothes

Cut out all the pieces as shown above, reversing the templates for two of the shoe pieces and keeping them in pairs.

Seam together the two narrow sides of each piece of white silk. Turn inside out and press. Make single narrow turnings on one long side and sew with running stitch. Fit on to the arm and draw up the gathers to fit the wrist. Fasten off securely. Make a single turning at the top, gather and draw up to fit the top of the arm. Sew on to the shoulder. Repeat with the other sleeve.

Oversew the leg seams of the trousers. Pin

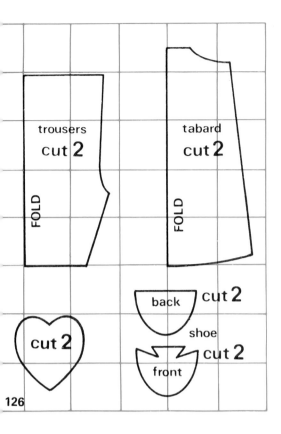

trousers
cut 2

FOLD

tabard
cut 2

FOLD

back cut 2

shoe

cut 2

front

cut 2

126

The Queen and Knave of Hearts

together the front and back seams, matching the leg seams and oversew. Turn inside out and press seams flat. Sew silver cord ¼ in. from the bottom of each leg. Fit on to the doll and sew on at the waist.

Cut out two hearts in red felt from the template and sew one in the middle of each tabard piece for back and front. Couch silver cord all round the heart, finishing off with a small bow. Couch down silver cord ¼ in. from the sides and bottom of each tabard side taking the cord 1½ in. up each side. Oversew one shoulder seam, fit the tabard on to the doll and sew second shoulder seam. Fasten the sides with a silver cord bar.

To make the front of the shoes snip V's out of the top points to make a 'tongue' in the middle edge (see Fig. 127). Under the tongue, on the toe, embroider a rectangle with silver Lurex

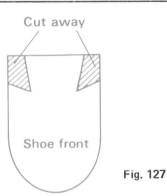

Cut away

Shoe front

Fig. 127

thread to simulate a buckle. Oversew the curved edges of a back and front shoe piece together, fit it on to the foot and sew in place round the top edge except for the tongue.

119

# 5. Dolls of All Shapes

All of the dolls described in this chapter are made up from geometrical shapes, and young children especially enjoy piecing them together in different ways. It is fun to start off by making them in paper. Some packets of coloured gummed paper can be a good stand-by for rainy days in the holidays.

The amounts needed to make each doll are given in the colours used in the illustrated dolls for easy recognition, but they can of course be made in any colours and any style, and with imagination and experiment many interesting ones will evolve. Arms, for instance, can be placed in many different positions (pointing up, out or down). These dolls can also be made in double felt with a pipe cleaner or wire enclosed in the sewing, so that the body, as well as the legs, can be bent into many different positions.

The finished dolls are much stronger and more durable if the main parts of body, arms and legs are made from nylon felt which does not tear and is very easy to sew.

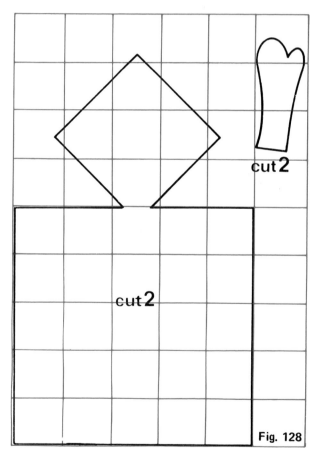

cut 2

cut 2

**Fig. 128**

## Square Sam

As his name implies, all of him except arms and legs is derived from squares — his head, body and trimmings. The pattern or template is cut with head and body in one, and is very easily made. Head and body squares can be cut separately and different colours used for each of them.

*You will need:*
  green nylon felt *for body and head:* 16 x 5 in.
  red nylon felt *for legs, arms and pockets:* 5 x 6 in.
  yellow felt *for hair:* 2 in. square
  scraps of black, white and pink felt *for features and trimmings*
  three pipe cleaners
  adhesive
  round elastic: 12 in.
  wadding or interlining: 8 x 5 in.
  matching sewing thread

Cut out two body pieces from the green felt, and from the red felt cut two strips 2 x 5 in. for legs. Fold each leg strip in half lengthwise and taper the edges so that the leg narrows towards the bottom. Turn in the ends of a pipe cleaner to make it fit the length of felt and with the felt doubled over it oversew the edges enclosing the pipe cleaner. Make a second leg. Pin both legs in place on one of the body pieces.

Cut another felt strip 5 x 1 in. and cut this across in half for the arms. Cut them from the pattern and pin them in place on the same body piece.

Fold the elastic in half, tie the ends in a big knot and sew to the top corner of the head, inside. From one corner of the yellow felt, cut a 1½ in. square, leaving a right-angled strip (see Fig. 129). Cut the two long edges of this in a fringe, making slanting cuts at the corner, and pin it in place on the head on te same body piece for hair.

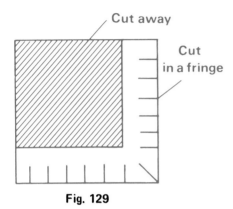

Fig. 129

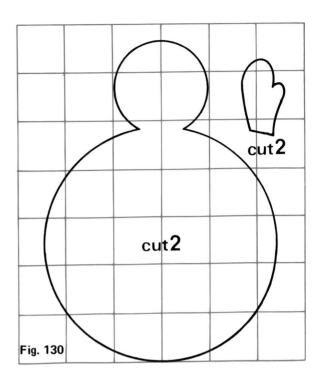

Fig. 130

Use the second body piece for the front decoration. Cut two 1 in. and two ½ in. squares in the remaining strip of red felt for pockets and pin the two bigger ones below the two smaller ones. Two ½ in. squares of white felt with a ¼ in. square of black felt in the corner of each are the eyes, with a ½ in. pink square for a mouth and a $\frac{1}{8}$ in. square for a nose. Three small squares of green felt make his tie. These front decorations can be sewn or stuck on.

Pin the underlining or wadding in place on the wrong side of the front piece and catch in place on the corners with small invisible stitches. Fold the ends of the third pipe cleaner to the middle and sew it to the interlining at the neck with half in the head and half in the body. This will prevent the head from flopping over. Pin both body pieces together with the right sides outside and oversew all the edges using a stab stitch to sew in the arms, legs and hair. He can be hung up on the elastic loop from his head.

## Circle Cis

Cis' body is a 5 in. circle and her head a 2 in. circle which overlaps the body circle, so both can be cut together in one piece, or separately if different colours are used for head and body.

All her trimmings are cut from circles too. Her legs are narrower than Sam's, and not shaped.

*You will need:*
red nylon felt *for body:* two pieces, 5 x 7 in.
yellow nylon felt *for legs:* two pieces, 4 x 1 in.
yellow nylon felt *for hands:* two pieces, 1½ x ¾ in.
orange nylon felt *for mouth:* ½ in. circle
orange nylon felt *for hair:* nine $\frac{2}{5}$ in. circles
orange nylon felt *for buttons:* three $\frac{2}{5}$ in. circles
black nylon felt *for eyes:* two $\frac{2}{5}$ in. circles
pink nylon felt *for buttons:* two $\frac{2}{5}$ in. circles
white nylon felt *for nose:* ¼ in. circle
embroidered ribbon with circle design *for belt*
red thread
round elastic: 12 in.
interlining or wadding: 5 x 7 in.
three pipe cleaners
adhesive

Cut all the pieces shown above.

Tie a big knot in the doubled elastic and sew the knot at the top of one body piece. On to the same body piece, pin the arms, legs and hair circles. On the other body piece pin the em-

121

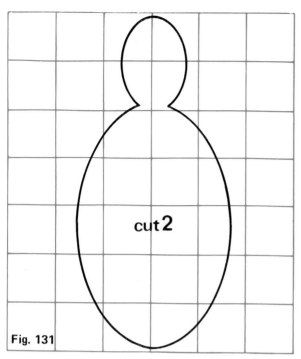

**Fig. 131**

cut 2

interlining: 3½ x 7 in.
round elastic: 12 in.
purple sewing thread
pipe cleaner
adhesive

Cut out all the pieces as indicated above. Curve the ends of the pieces for arms and legs. Cut the eyes and buttons from rectangles of the given measurements, rounding off the corners. The legs and arms are in single felt, but can be cut double if wished. Cut the yellow felt in a fringe along one long side for the hair. Stitch the knotted double elastic to the top of one head piece. Pin arms, legs and hair to the same body piece; the yellow fringed felt will pin quite easily round the curve of the top of the oval and the fringe will fan out and separate a little. Stick all features and decorations on to the second body piece. The yellow bow tie is two joined ovals cut out in one piece. Complete the making up as for Sam.

## Tear-drop Tom

Tom's mouth, arms, legs and collar are not made tear-shaped but the rest of him is.

*You will need:*
  black nylon felt *for body:* two pieces, 7 x 4 in.
  green nylon felt *for arms:* two pieces, 3½ x ¾ in.
  green nylon felt *for legs:* four pieces, 3¾ x ¾ in.
  scraps of turquoise felt *for eyes*
  scrap of pink felt *for nose:*
  scrap of red felt *for mouth*
  scrap of yellow felt *for collar*
  interlining: 7 x 4 in.
  pale green nylon felt *for buttons*
  elastic: 12 in.
  three pipe cleaners
  adhesive
  matching thread

Cut out all the pieces as indicated. Round off the corners of hands and feet. Draw a rectangle $\frac{3}{5}$ x $\frac{3}{10}$ in. and draw a tear shape in it like the body shape. Cut this out and use as a pattern to cut out the twelve buttons, eyes and nose. Cut

broidery belt and sew it in place, and either sew or stick on the features and buttons. Pin the interlining or wadding on to the other side of this front body piece and catch down in 3 or 4 places with invisible stitches. Twist the pipe cleaner and insert in the neck. Place the two pieces together with right sides outside and oversew all round.

## Oval Oswald

He is made from one oval 3½ x 5½ in. for the body, and one 1½ x 2 in. for the head. The two overlap at the neck.

*You will need:*
  purple nylon felt *for body:* two pieces, 3½ x 7 in.
  pink nylon felt *for legs:* two pieces, 3½ x 1 in.
  pink nylon felt *for arms:* two pieces, 2½ x $\frac{3}{5}$ in.
  yellow nylon felt *for hair:* 2 x ¾ in.
  yellow nylon felt scrap *for bow*
  green nylon felt *for buttons:* six pieces, $\frac{2}{5}$ x $\frac{4}{5}$ in.
  orange nylon felt *for eyes:* two pieces, $\frac{2}{5}$ x $\frac{3}{5}$ in.
  bright pink nylon *for mouth:* ¾ x ¼ in.

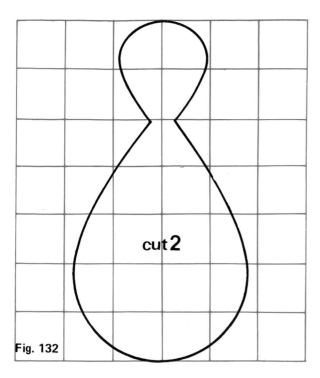

cut 2

Fig. 132

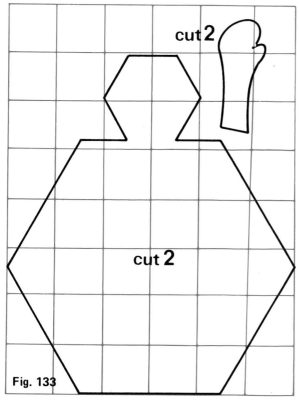

cut 2

cut 2

cut 2

Fig. 133

a crescent in red felt for the mouth and a crescent in yellow to fit the neck for a collar. Join the leg felt pieces in twos, starting at the top and continuing round the foot, inserting the pipe cleaner folded to fit it, and sewing up the second side. Stick on features and trimmings with upholstery adhesive. Make up as for Sam (page 120).

## Hexagon Hetty

Arms and legs are parts of Hetty which cannot be cut as hexagons, but otherwise even her hat is part of a hexagon.

*You will need:*

yellow nylon felt *for body:* two pieces, 6 x 7 in.
red nylon felt *for legs:* two pieces, 4 x 1 in.
red nylon felt *for arms:* two pieces, 2½ x ¾ in.
red nylon felt *for mouth:* ½ x ¼ in.
blue nylon felt *for trimming:* two pieces, 6 x $\frac{3}{10}$ in.
blue nylon felt *for bow:* 1 x $\frac{3}{10}$ in.
black nylon felt *for eyes:* two ½ in. squares
black nylon felt *for nose:* ½ in. square
orange nylon felt *for hat:* 2½ x 1 in.
three pipe cleaners
interlining: 6 x 7 in.
round elastic: 12 in.
adhesive
matching thread

Cut out all the pieces as indicated. The mouth is a hexagon with two sides longer than the others. The two strips of trimming are longer hexagons also — these are made by cutting out small V's opposite each other all along the

**Fig. 134**

strips. The bow similarly has the corners cut off the rectangle and a V cut out of the middle of each side opposite one another. The hat is cut from half a hexagon with the long side cut in a curve for a brim. Fold the leg felts in half lengthwise and cut off the corners at the bottom of each to make a pointed foot. Make up as for other geometric dolls.

## Rectangle Reg

His body is a rectangle measuring 4½ x 2 in. placed upright. On top for a head is placed a

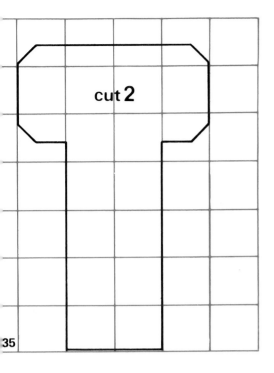

cut 2

35

rectangle 4 x 2 in. The two are cut as one pattern. The corners of the head have been trimmed off.

*You will need:*
green nylon felt *for body:* two pieces, 6½ x 4 in.
red nylon felt *for legs:* four pieces, 4½ x 1 in.
red nylon felt *for arms:* two pieces, 3¾ x ¾ in.
deep pink nylon felt *for mouth:* 1 x ¼ in.
deep pink nylon felt *for nose:* $\frac{1}{5}$ x $\frac{3}{5}$ in.
pale green nylon felt *for eyes:* two pieces, ¾ x ½ in.
black nylon felt *for eyes:* two pieces, $\frac{2}{5}$ x $\frac{1}{5}$ in.
yellow nylon felt *for buttons:* six pieces, ½ x $\frac{1}{5}$ in.
interlining: 6½ x 4 in.
green and red thread
two pipe cleaners
round elastic: 12 in.
adhesive

Cut out pieces as shown above.

Trim off the corners of the leg pieces to make pointed feet. Turn under the ends of the pipe cleaners to fit the legs. Sew leg pieces together in twos to enclose the pipe cleaners. Make up as for the other geometric dolls.

## TRIANGULAR DOLLS

The following dolls are made from equilateral triangles. The bodies have 6 in. sides and the heads 2½ in. sides.

### Triangle Tubby
A small and a large triangle overlapping, cut in one piece.

*You will need:*
green nylon felt *for body:* two pieces, 7¾ x 6 in.
orange or red nylon felt *for feet and arms:* four pieces, 2 x 1 in.
yellow nylon felt *for hair:* 4½ x ¾ in.
white nylon felt *for tie:* 1¼ x ¾ in.
red nylon felt *for mouth:* ½ x $\frac{2}{5}$ in.
blue nylon felt *for eyes:* two pieces, ½ x $\frac{2}{5}$ in.
scrap of black felt *for eyebrows*
three pipe cleaners
interlining: 7¾ x 6 in.
elastic: 12 in.
adhesive
matching thread

Cut out all pieces as indicated. On the strip of yellow felt mark one side in ¾ in. lengths. On the other side make the first mark $\frac{3}{8}$ in. and divide the rest in ¾ in. lengths. Cut across the strip in diagonal cuts from marks on one side to marks on the other to get ten triangles in all — four for hair and six for trimming (see Fig. 136). Stick all features and trimmings in place on one body piece. Place the feet one on each side of the bottom point of the triangle, and the hands at the two top points. For hair, stick a triangle over each point at the top and the other two pointing up between them. Make up as for the other geometric dolls.

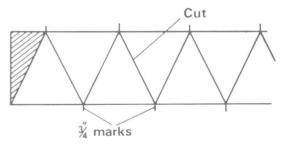

Cut

¾ marks

**Fig. 136**

### Triangle Tessie
She wears a white party dress. Her body triangle is the other way up from Tubby's.

125

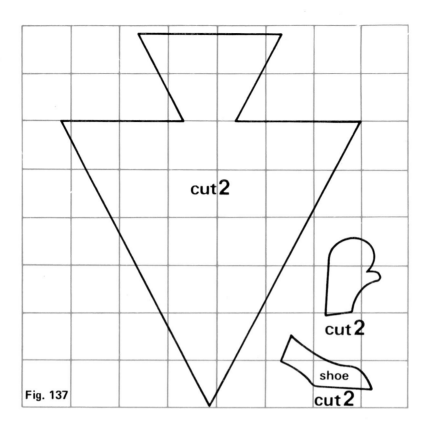

cut 2

cut 2

shoe
cut 2

Fig. 137

*You will need:*
  white nylon felt *for body:* two pieces, 7¼ x 6 in.
  red nylon felt *for legs:* four pieces, 4½ x ¾ in.
  red nylon felt *for arms:* two pieces, 3½ x ¾ in.
  yellow nylon felt *for hair:* 3¼ x 2½ in.
  scraps for trimming
  red felt *for mouth*
  green felt *for eyes*
  red and black embroidery silk
  white thread
  three pipe cleaners
  adhesive
  interlining: 7¼ x 6 in.

Cut out all the pieces as shown. Taper the leg pieces from ¾ in. at the top to ¼ in. at the bottom. Taper the two arm pieces similarly. For hair, mark lines $\frac{3}{8}$ in. in from the edge on two sides and cut the edges into points (see Fig. 138). Make the top two cuts shallower or the corner will be too weak. Stick features in place.

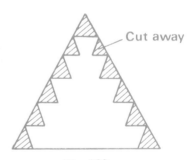

Cut away

Fig. 138

Make two fly stitches in black silk over the eyes, two straight stitches for the nose and a much bigger fly stitch in red silk at the neck for a tie. Cut small yellow triangles and stick them on to the dress. Make up as for other geometric dolls.

---

*Right: Hexagon Hetty, Triangle Tilda, Triangle Tubby, and Triangle Tessy*

126

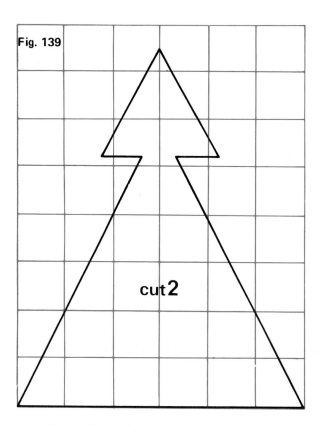

Fig. 139

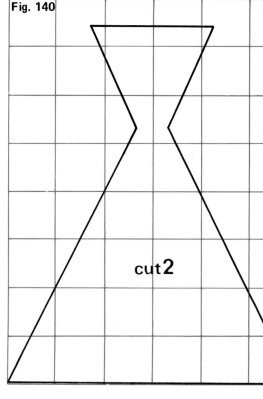

Fig. 140

## Triangle Tilda

She looks rather angry, but if her eyes are arranged differently she can look happier. The large triangle is again on a 6 in. base and the smaller one a 2½ in. line, but the points of the triangles overlap each other by a good ½ in. to give a stronger neck.

*You will need:*
deep pink nylon felt  two pieces, 6 x 7¼ in.
blue nylon felt *for legs:* four pieces, 4 x ¾ in.
blue nylon felt *for arms:* two pieces, 4 x ¾ in.
blue nylon felt *for trim:* 6 x ½ in.
green nylon felt *for hat:* two pieces, 3 x 1 in.
scraps of black felt *for eyes*
white felt *for collar:* ¾ x ¼ in.
yellow felt: four $\frac{2}{5}$ triangles
interlining: 6 x 7¼ in.
adhesive
blue and pink thread
three pipe cleaners
round elastic: 12 in.

Cut out all pieces as above. Shape felt pieces for the arms to taper to the top and round them at the bottom for hands. Taper leg pieces slightly

at top. Mark the blue strip for trimming into ¾ in. spaces along one long side and cut in triangles. Cut the two pieces for the hat into triangles measuring 2¾ in. on the long side and 1 in. in height. Complete the making up as for the other geometric dolls, and oversew together the short sides of the hat and sewing the long sides to the back and front of the head.

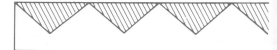

Fig. 141

## MAKING FACES ON SHAPES

These faces are all worked on various geometric shapes and all can be dangled from an elastic. Besides making amusing toys they are a pleasant way of practising making varied expressions which can be used on more conventional dolls. Both embroidery and felts, and sometimes both are used.

*Right: geometric faces*

128

Before cutting any shapes for features experiment with various shapes in paper, using crayons or coloured gummed paper and later felt shapes. The results of this practising need not be wasted but can be strung up for mobiles to interest a child.

*For each face you will need:*
padding (interlining, wadding or kapok)
adhesive
matching sewing thread
round elastic: 12 in.

## Circle 1

*Additional requirements:*
scraps of red, pink, black and white felt *for features*
green felt: two 3½ in. diameter circles
black embroidery silk

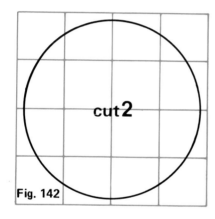

cut 2

Fig. 142

Cut out the circles of felt from the template and four circles of interlining — two 3 in. and the two 2 in. in diameter.

Cut a long thin crescent in red felt for a mouth, and a ½ in. circle in pink felt for a nose. A circle ¾ in. in diameter cut in half will make two eyes and two small ¼ in. circles in black felt, cut straight across the bottom to fit on the straight side of the semicircle will make the eyes. Stick the nose and then the mouth in place. Stick the straight edge of the small black pieces of felt for eyes to the straight edges of the bigger ones and stick them in position. Embroider straight stitches in black embroidery silk all round the curve of the eyes.

Place the padding on the felt circle with the two big circles in the middle and the smaller ones to each side. Pin the face piece on top. Knot the elastic ends together and sew them on at the top

of the face inside the felt. Oversew the felt circles together round the edges.

## Circle 2

*Additional requirements:*
pink felt: two 3½ in. circles
white felt: *for eyes:* two 1 in. circles
blue felt: *for eyes:* two ½ in. circles
scraps of dark pink, and flesh coloured felt *for mouth and nose*
black embroidery silk

Cut the two pink circles to size from Fig. 142. Stick the blue circles on the white circles for eyes. Cut a crescent in pink felt for a mouth, and a narrow pear shape in flesh felt for the nose. Stick all the features in place on a pink circle, taking care to place the eyes at the same angle or the expression will be peculiar.

With black embroidery silk work rows of chain stitch close to the edge of the white circles and an arc across each eye for an eyebrow. Finish off as Circle 1, using the same amount of padding.

## Oval 1

*Additional requirements:*
pale blue felt: two pieces, 4½ x 3¼ in.
black felt *for moustache:* 1¾ x ½ in.
black felt *for eyes:* two $\frac{2}{5}$ in. circles
white felt *for eyes:* two ¾ in. circles
pink felt *for nose:* $\frac{2}{5}$ in. circle
black embroidery silk

Cut the blue felt rectangles to the shape shown in Fig. 143 Cut two pieces of wadding or interlining, 4 x 2¾ in., and two pieces, 3½ x 2¼ in. to the same shape as the felt.

Stick a black felt circle on the edge of a white circle for eyes and cut a moustache from the pattern in black felt. Stick all the features in place on one blue oval, keeping the widest part of the oval from side to side to make a fat face, and embroidering arcs of stem stitch over each eye for a brow. Complete as for Circle 1.

## Oval 2

*Additional requirements:*
purple felt: two pieces, 4½ x 3¼ in.
white felt *for eyes:* two pieces, $1\frac{1}{5}$ x $\frac{3}{5}$ in.
green felt *for eyes:* two pieces, 1 x $\frac{2}{5}$ in.
red felt *for mouth:* 1 x ½ in.
yellow felt *for eyebrows*

Cut two pieces of wadding, 4 x 2¼ in., and two

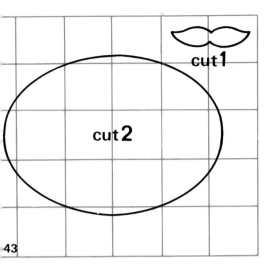

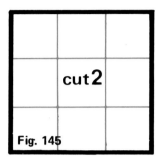

cut1

cut2

cut2

Fig. 145

43

white felt *for eyes:* two 1 in. circles
¾ in. flat brown buttons *for eyes*
½ in. pink pearl button *for nose*
¼ in. red or dark pink button *for mouth*
black embroidery silk

pieces, 3½ x 2¼ in., and cut to the shape shown in Fig. 143 Cut the felt from the template also. On this face have the narrowest part of the oval from side to side to make a long face.

Cut the red felt into a triangle shape with a curved top for the mouth. Round off the corners of the white felt to make two ovals. Trim one side of the green felt to fit the long curve of a white felt oval and the other side almost straight with a slight curve (see Fig. 144).

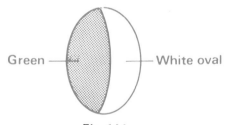

Green ——— ——— White oval

**Fig. 144**

Stick the green shapes on to the white ovals for eyes, keeping the green shapes on the same side in both eyes. Cut two crescent shapes from the yellow felt for eyebrows. Stick the features in place starting with the mouth. Complete as other geometric faces.

## Square 1
In this one, buttons are used to make the main features.

*Additional requirements:*
   orange felt: two pieces, 3 in. square

Sew a pink pearl button in the middle of the purple felt square, slightly in the bottom half of the square, for a nose. For the mouth, sew a crescent of black chain stitch under the pink button and sew a red button in the middle of the crescent. For eyes, sew a brown button to the centre of a white felt circle to show a rim of white, and sew in place with an arc of black stem stitch above each one. Complete as for the other geometric faces.

## Square 2
The features are sewn diagonally on this square so that it can be suspended from one corner. As for Square 1, buttons are used for features.

*Additional requirements:*
   green felt: two 3 in. squares
   white felt: two 1 x $\frac{4}{5}$ in. ovals
   $\frac{3}{5}$ in. red button *for mouth*
   $\frac{2}{5}$ in. pink pearl button *for nose*
   ½ in. fancy grey pearl buttons *for eyes*
   black, yellow and red embroidery silks

Sew a pink pearl button in the centre of a green square for the nose, and the red button halfway between it and a corner for the mouth. Sew the grey pearl buttons in the lower half of the white felt ovals and sew in place for eyes. Embroider two star shapes in red silk on the cheeks, some long yellow straight stitches in the top corner for hair and black buttonhole stitch round the top curve of the white felt eyes. Complete the making up as for the other geometric faces, using two 2½ in. and two 2 in. squares of wadding.

131

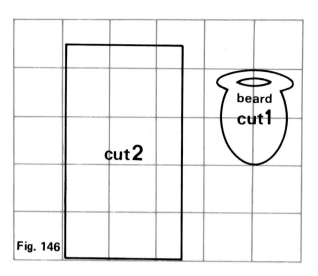

**Fig. 146**

## Oblong 1

*Additional requirements:*
 yellow felt: two pieces, 4½ x 2½ in.
 red felt *for hat:* 2½ x 1¼ in.
 red felt scrap *for mouth*
 white felt *for eyes:* two $\frac{3}{5}$ in. circles
 black felt *for eyes:* two $\frac{3}{10}$ in. circles
 black felt *for brows:* 1 in. circle cut in half
 black felt *for moustache and beard:* 2 x
  1½ in.
 black felt *for hat brim:* 2¾ x ¼ in.
 black embroidery silk

Cut out pieces as above and turn the yellow felt on its side to make a long face with the short edges at top and bottom. Cut one long edge of the red felt for the hat into a curve from the corners (see Fig. **147**) and stick or sew it on to a

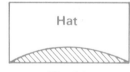

**Fig. 147**

short edge of the yellow felt. Stick a strip of wadding along it for trimming. Cut a small thin oval with pointed ends for a mouth and stick it in place about 2¾ in. from the top edge. Stick the moustache and beard over it so that the mouth shows through the slit. Trim off the tops of the white circles in a flat curve, and stick a black circle to each flatter edge. Stick them in place on the face with the two semicircles for brows above them. Embroider curving lines of black stem stitch over the eyes. Complete as

132

others, using two pieces of wadding 4 x 2 in. and two pieces, 3½ x 1½ in. for padding.

## Oblong 2

This face has features along the long side to make a fat face. It is made wider by sewing a straight gusset all round between the two rectangles. This can be stuffed with kapok or a similar material.

*Additional requirements:*
 green felt: two pieces, 4½ x 2½ in.
 green felt strip: 14 x $\frac{3}{5}$ in.
 white felt *for eyes:* two pieces, 1 x ½ in.
 blue felt *for eyes:* two ½ in. circles
 pale pink felt *for cheeks:* two ½ in. circles
 rose pink felt *for mouth:* $1\frac{1}{5}$ x ½ in.
 black embroidery silk

Cut two leaf shapes in white felt and stick a blue circle in the centre of each one for eyes. Cut one long edge of rose pink felt in a semi-circular curve. Mark the centre of the top edge and cut as shown in Fig. **148**. Stick this mouth in

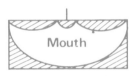

**Fig. 148**

place with the lower curve about ½ in. from the bottom long side of the oblong. Stick a pink circle on each side of it for cheeks. Embroider black straight stitches along the top of the white eye and two curving brows in stem stitch above it and two french knots above the mouth for a nose. Mark points along the straight strip at 2½, 4½ and 2½ in. and pin these points to the corners of one oblong. Oversew the edges.

Sew the knot of the double elastic through the centre point of the gusset at the top. Cut four pieces of wadding 4¼ x 2¼ in. and place in the box shape made by the gusset. If the wadding is too thin, then before pinning on the second oblong, cut more layers of wadding to fill out the shape. Alternatively, stuff with kapok. Pin the second oblong on top, taking care to pin the marked points on the gusset to the appropriate corners of the oblong. Oversew the edges.

## Diamond 1

*Additional requirements:*
 pale pink felt: two pieces, 6 x 3½ in.

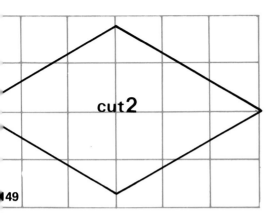

cut 2

**149**

brown felt *for hair:* 2¼ x ½ in. and 1¾ x ½ in.
white felt *for eyes:* two pieces, ¾ x ½ in.
blue felt *for eyes:* two ⅖ in. circles
rose pink felt *for mouth:* ¾ x ⅖ in.
black, white and pink embroidery silk

Cut the diamond shapes in pink felt, using Fig.
**149** For a mouth cut a semicircular curve on one
long side of the rose pink felt, mark the middle
point of the top and cut out a small crescent each
side of the mark. Stick this in place with its
bottom curve about ¾ in. from the bottom wide
angle of the diamond. Round the bottom curve
of the mouth sew a row of rose pink stem stitch
with two seed stitches above it for a nose. Cut
two leaf shapes from white felt, and stick a blue
felt circle in the centre of each. Stick them in
place on the face. Sew a few satin stitches in
white in the centre of the blue eye circles.
Embroider all round the white eyes with stem
stitch in black, extending the top lines in a curve
at each side. Embroider stem stitch curves above
for brows. Cut the straight edges of the brown
felt, on one side each, into curves and scallops for
hair and stick one on each side of the top wide
angle of the diamond. Complete as for other
geometric faces, using two pieces of wadding, 5½
x 3 in., and two pieces, 5 x 2½ in., for padding
Cut into diamond shapes as the felt.

## Diamond 2
*Additional requirements:*
   dark pink felt: two pieces, 6 x 3½ in.
   white felt *for eyes:* two pieces, 1 x ¾ in.
   black felt *for eyes:* two ½ in. circles
   black felt *for moustache:* ¾ x ½ in.
   pink felt *for nose:* ½ x ⅖ in.
   black embroidery silk

Cut out diamond shapes as for Diamond 1.
Round off the corners of the white felt to make
two ovals. Cut off a section of the black eye
circles to fit the smaller curve of the white ovals
and stick in place. Taper the short sides of the
brown felt for the moustache and slightly curve
the longer side (see Fig. **150**). Cut this longer

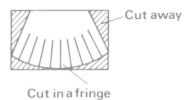

Cut away

Cut in a fringe

**Fig. 150**

side in a fringe. Stick all the features in place.
Above each eye, with double black embroidery
silk work two long fly stitches close together.
Complete as for Diamond 1.

## Triangle 1: A clown
*Additional requirements:*
   white felt: two pieces, 4 x 4 in.
   red felt *for mouth:* 1 x ½ in.
   pink felt *for cheeks:* two ½ in. circles
   orange felt *for nose:* ¼ in. circle
   blue felt *for eyes:* two ½ in. squares
   black felt *for brows:* two pieces, 1 x ½ in.
   red embroidery silk

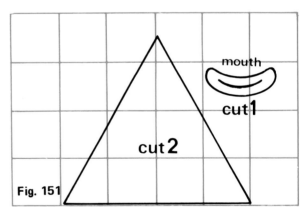

mouth

cut 1

cut 2

**Fig. 151**

Use Fig. **151** to cut the white felt to shape. Cut a
mouth in red felt from the pattern. From each
blue eyepiece cut a small square from each corner
to make a cross (see Fig. **152**). Mark the centre
point on each of the black felt rectangles for
brows. Also mark the middle points of one long
side and of both short sides. Join the bottom

133

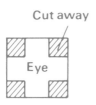

Cut away

Eye

**Fig. 152**

corners to the centre point of the rectangle and cut. Join the middle point of the short sides to the middle point of the long side and cut. This will give a chevron shape. Wind red embroidery

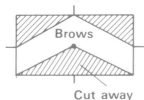

Brows

Cut away

**Fig. 153**

silk round a pencil with thread laid along it about ten times. Slide off the loops on the thread and tie the thread round them tightly. Cut the loops to make a small pompon. Make another. Stick all the features in place, sewing the pompons on just below the top point of the triangle. Cut two 3½ in. and two 3 in. squares of wadding into triangles to fit and complete as for other geometric faces.

## Triangle 2: A witch
*Additional requirements:*
    black felt: two pieces, 4 in. square
    scraps of green, red and pink felt *for features*
    grey embroidery silk

Cut the triangles as for Triangle 1. Cut a long thin pear shape in pink felt for a nose and stick it in the centre of the triangle with the thin end pointing down. Cut a long thin crescent in red felt for her mouth and stick it in place with the curve pointing downwards to give a disagreeable look. Cut two thin ovals in green felt for eyes and stick them on, slanting them upwards a little. Embroider three or four small straight stitches above the nose to make a frown and straight stitches each side of the mouth. Embroider hair each side in ragged straight stitches and a row of uneven stitches above the eyes to represent hair appearing below her steeple hat, which is of course only the top of the triangle. Cut two 3½ in. and two 3 in. squares of wadding into triangles to fit. Complete as for other geometric faces.

134

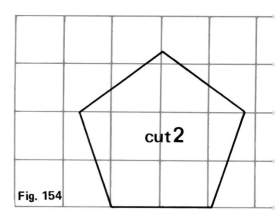

cut 2

**Fig. 154**

## Pentagon: A weeping baby
*Additional requirements:*
    pale flesh pink felt: two pieces, 3 in. square
    black, rose and yellow embroidery silks

Place the template on the felt and cut out two pieces. Make one of the straight sides the base of the face. Work two little straight stitches in pink silk in the lower half of the shape (all baby features are in the lower half of the face), and a down curving arc in pink chain stitch for a sad little mouth. The eyes are arcs of chain stitch in black with straight stitches underneath for lashes and the tears are single detached chain stitches in black. The hair is loops of yellow embroidery silk sewn in a curve round the top angle of the pentagon. Use two 3 in. squares of wadding and cut in similar shapes — two of them ½ in. smaller and two ¼ in. smaller than the felt. Complete as for other geometric shapes.

## Hexagon 1: A hound
*Additional requirements:*
    green felt: two pieces, 4½ in. square
    pink felt *for mouth:* $1\frac{3}{5}$ x $1\frac{2}{5}$ in.
    black felt *for nose:* ¾ x $\frac{3}{5}$ in. oval
    black felt *for eyes:* 1 x ½ in.
    flesh coloured felt *for eyes:* two pieces, 1 x
        ½ in.
    yellow felt *for brows:* $1\frac{4}{5}$ x $1\frac{1}{10}$ in.
    black embroidery silk

Cut two shapes in green felt from the pattern. Round off the corners of the pink felt to make an oval shape and stick in the lower half of the face shape over a straight edge. Stick the black felt nose near to the top of this oval. Round off the corners of the black rectangle for

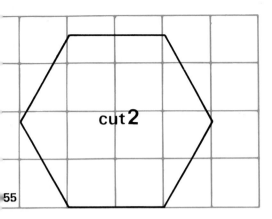

cut 2

55

to the angles on the face and oversew the edges. Pad the inside with stuffing or with four or five pieces of hexagonal wadding, fractionally smaller than the felt hexagons. Pin strip to the second side, matching points and angles exactly and sew.

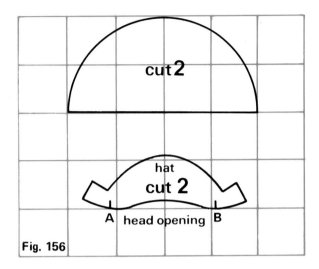

cut 2

hat
cut 2

A head opening B

**Fig. 156**

eyes and cut this in half. Cut a slight inward curve on one long side of each flesh piece to fit the curve of the mouth oval and stick these in place so that the corners touch on the mouth edge above the nose. Round off the corners of the yellow felt rectangle and cut it in half. Stick the straight edge of each to the straight edge of the flesh felt and butt them up against the straight edge of the black felt. Embroider three straight stitches in an arrow shape in between the brows. Using two 4½ in. squares of wadding, complete as for the other geometric faces.

### Hexagon 2: A Chinese man

This face, because of its box-like shape with the gussetted sides can quite easily be stuffed with kapok or a similar material.

*Additional requirements:*
  bright yellow felt: two 4½ in. squares
  bright yellow felt: 12 x ¾ in.
  white felt *for eyes:* two pieces, 1 x ½ in.
  black felt *for eyes:* two pieces, $\frac{2}{5}$ x $\frac{3}{10}$ in.
  black embroidery silk

Cut two felt shapes from the same pattern as the hound. Cut two almond shaped white felt eyes and in the centre of each stick an oval black felt pupil. Mark the position of the mouth and embroider it in two rows of black chain stitch tapering to each corner and finishing in 2½ in. loops of embroidery silk for a moustache. Stick the eyes in place slanting up towards the outside of the face. Embroider black stem stitch closely all round and two slanting brows also in black stem stitch. Mark the strip in 2 in. points. Sew elastic in the middle between two of these points, and keep this as the top of the face. Match these points

## Semicircle: A schoolgirl

*Additional requirements:*
  orange felt: 4 in. circle
  white felt *for eyes:* two pieces, ½ x $\frac{2}{5}$ in.
  blue felt scraps *for eyes*
  pink felt scraps *for nose*
  black felt *for hat:* two pieces, 3 x 1 in.
  black, red, yellow and white embroidery silk
  brown wool *for hair*

Cut a 3½ in. and a 3 in. circle of wadding in half. Cut the orange felt in half also. Round off the corners of the white felt to make two ovals. Cut two small ovals in blue felt and stick them in a corner of each of the white ovals (see Fig. **157**).

Eye

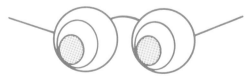

Spectacles  **Fig. 157**

135

Cut a small ¼ in. circle in pink felt for a nose. Stick nose and eyes on to one of the orange felt semicircles, the straight line of the semicircle at the bottom. Embroider a crescent in red chain stitch for her mouth and two circles $\frac{3}{5}$ in. in diameter in black stem stitch round the eyes for spectacles (see Fig. 157). Straight lines in stem stitch to each side of the face and a small curve between the rings completes the spectacles. Make two small plaits 3 in. long with 12 strands of wool (use less if the wool is thick) and sew them one on either side of the face just above the spectacle arms. Place the two semicircles together with the wadding in between and oversew

the edges together. Cut two hat shapes in black felt. With yellow silk embroider a star motif in the front for a badge, and on each side parallel with the brim embroider a line of white chain stitch and a line of red chain stitch at each side of it. Knot the elastic and sew it at the top of one hat piece. Pin the two hat pieces together and oversew from point A in the diagram round the small piece of brim, over the crown to point B. Fit the hat on to the head and sew round the edge to the front and back of the head. With brown wool sew some irregular straight stitches at the sides of the face from the edge of the hat to the plaits.

# 6. Games with Dolls

## NINEPINS OR SKITTLES

The nine pins are all cut from the same pattern. Two shaped pieces are joined and stuffed and mounted on a stiff base to make them stand firmly. The pattern when traced on to thin card is easy to use because it can be placed on fabric or felt and the outline traced round it, and it can be used many times.

*For each ninepin you will need:*
    felt: 6½ x 8½
    felt scraps *for features and trimming*
    thick card: 1⅘ in. diameter circle
    kapok or similar stuffing
    embroidery silks
    matching sewing thread

Cut two ninepin shapes and two circles from the felt. Place the template on the felt and trace round it twice, reversing it to trace the second one. Use a very sharply pointed pencil, using a white pencil or tailor's chalk on dark colours. Cut out the body shapes just inside the pencil lines to avoid grubby seams, but cut *outside* the lines for the base felt circles to allow for the thickness of the card base.

One piece of the body felt is embroidered for a front view. Faces can be happy, sad, comical, grotesque, etc. It is a good plan to trace the shape on to thin paper and draw features etc., on to it and so plan the trimmings before using the felt shapes. Much experimenting can be done on paper but not on felt which retains marks and pin holes, and any mistakes are difficult to rectify. Felt features can be stuck or sewn on with matching thread. Young or inexperienced needlewomen find it helpful if the small pieces of felt for features etc. are lightly stuck in place with a small dab of upholstery adhesive, so making the actual sewing easier.

The joining stitch used is oversewing. When the front piece is ready with face and trimmings finished, place the two pieces together with the right sides outside and oversew the curved sides and head leaving the base open. Oversew the two felt circles together half way round, (pencil marks on the inside). Insert the card circle and complete the oversewing to enclose the card. Stuff the body, with small pieces of stuffing, smoothly and firmly, but not too hard. Place

*Right: ninepins*

the base circle in position and pin, then oversew its edges to the bottom edges of the skittle, pushing in more stuffing if necessary.

## The balls

Cover small, light rubber balls 1½ in. in diameter with brightly coloured felt segments. Trace round the pattern of the segment four times and cut out the pieces. Oversew the pieces together leaving the last two sides open. Insert the ball and oversew the last two sides to enclose it.

## Some ninepins to make

### A clown

This one has lime green felt for the body and

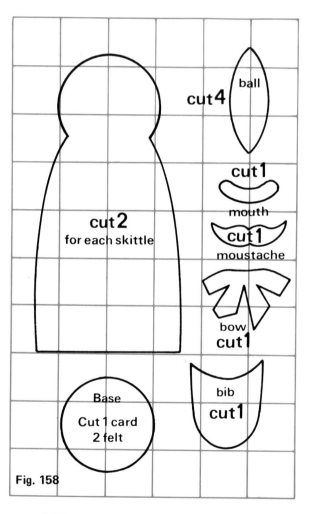

cut 4
ball

cut 1

cut 2
for each skittle

cut 1
mouth

cut 1
moustache

bow
cut 1

Base
Cut 1 card
2 felt

bib
cut 1

Fig. 158

138

base. He has black felt crosses for eyes and a large red circle for a nose. His mouth is in red felt, cut from the pattern. He has two round pink spots on his cheeks. There are three big yellow circles with fringed edges as pompons on the front of his dress, and he wears a strip of narrow white ric-rac braid at his neck for a ruffle.

### The dog face

This ninepin has a yellow felt body and base with a red collar holding his identity disc round his neck. His black felt round nose and mouth are embroidered in black stem stitch on a beige coloured felt circle, and his square blue eyes with black semicircle pupils have semicircles of pink felt above them for eyelids.

### The blue boy

He has a pale green collar and three big white and yellow buttons on his blue felt body. His black felt eyes, pink felt nose, mouth and cheeks are all circles, and his eyebrows are in black stem stitch.

### The girl in pink

She has two white felt semicircles with two smaller blue semicircles on them for her eyes and a round pink felt nose. Her eyelashes are embroidered black straight stitches, her eyebrows are in stem stitch and her mouth in dark red chain stitch. She wears a blue bow at her neck cut from felt.

### The crying baby

He is made up in flesh pink felt and has embroidered features all worked in stem stitch. He has closed eyes with straight stitch lashes, and tears falling on his cheeks, and a pink nose and mouth. His yellow felt bib, cut from the pattern, has a red felt cat on it.

### The city gent

He is made in bright red felt and has black felt eyes on white ovals. His fine moustache is cut from the pattern in black felt, and his collar and tie are in white and black felt respectively.

### The green goblin

He has eyes of black and white felt, an embroidered chain stitch mouth, a nose in pink, and eyebrows in black stem stitch. An orange scarf and yellow buttons all in felt complete him.

### The schoolboy

He looks very mischievous and is made in beige

felt with eyes of black and white felt in crescent shapes. His mouth and nose are pink chain stitch, and eyebrows black stem stitch. A semicircle of brown felt, cut to fit the curve of his head, has the straight edge notched to look like untidy hair. Collar and buttons are in white and black felt respectively. He wears a bow cut from the pattern.

## A demure lady

She is made of pale blue felt and her features are entirely in embroidery. Her closed eyes are of black stem stitch with straight stitch lashes and stem stitch eyebrows. She has a pink stem stitch smiling mouth and straight stitch star shapes on her cheeks. A string of red beads is sewn on to her neck, and six gold sequins are sewn down the front of her dress for buttons.

Now you are ready for a game.

## DRESS A DOLL

These felt covered ply wood or cardboard dolls will stand up with their feet set in a groove cut in a block of balsa wood. They are dressed for front view only, their dresses, coats, pyjamas, etc., hooking on to their shoulders. Once you have made a basic pattern of their measurements you can make as many kinds of clothes as you want, and in fact become model dress designers. The templates for the boy's and girl's clothes measurements only differ in that the boy's template has a slightly thicker waistline than the girl's.

The boy is made from thin three-ply wood, and the girl from a thick cardboard. Directions are given for making them in both ways. Both cut-out shapes are covered with flesh felt in front and brown felt backs. The dolls when cut measure 11¼ in. from head to toe and 5¼ in. from hand to hand. Larger dolls can be made adding ¼ in. in width for each additional 1 in. in height.

## The boy

*You will need:*
a piece of 3-ply wood: 11¾ x 5½ in.
flesh coloured felt: 11½ x 5¾ in.
brown felt: 11½ x 5¾ in.
brown felt *for hair*
scraps of red, white and black felt *for features*
black embroidery silk
fret saw
sandpaper

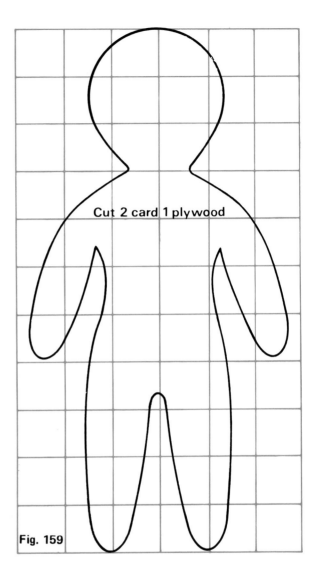

Cut 2 card 1 plywood

**Fig. 159**

adhesive
vest or stockinette fabric: 5¼ x 3½ in.

Trace round the template on to the wood and cut out the shape with a fret saw. Mark one side of the doll with a cross and make this the front of the doll. Smooth the rough edges by rubbing with a medium coarse sandpaper. Place the wooden cut out doll on to the flesh felt with the side marked with the cross downwards resting on the felt, and trace round the outline on to the felt. Trace with a very sharply pointed pencil to get a clear outline. Reverse the template on to the brown felt so that the side with the cross is uppermost. Use a white pencil or

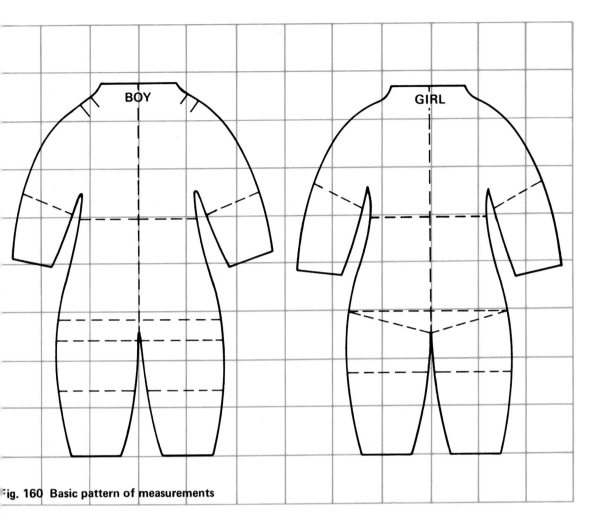

**Fig. 160 Basic pattern of measurements**

tailor's chalk on the dark coloured felt. Cut out the felt shapes, cutting $\frac{1}{8}$ in. outside the pencil outline all the way round — this is to allow for the thickness of the wood.

Place the wooden cut-out doll between the two pieces of felt with the pencil lines on the inside and the pink felt on the side of the doll with the cross marked on it. Starting at the right side of the neck with matching sewing thread, oversew all round the head. Sewing this first will anchor the doll firmly because of the neck being narrower.

Continue sewing the rest of the body, being careful not to stretch the felt, and matching the hands and feet of back and front. Cut circles of

white felt and smaller circles of blue felt to go on top of them for eyes. Cut out a red felt crescent for a mouth and stick all the features in place. Embroider two wide fly stitches in black embroidery silk for eyebrows.

Cut out the hair in brown felt and sew this in place over the forehead.

His singlet and shorts are cut in one piece from stockinette or vest material, allowing $\frac{1}{8}$ in. turnings on the sides only. Tack single turnings

*Left: boy dress a doll*

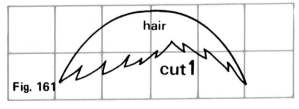

Fig. 161

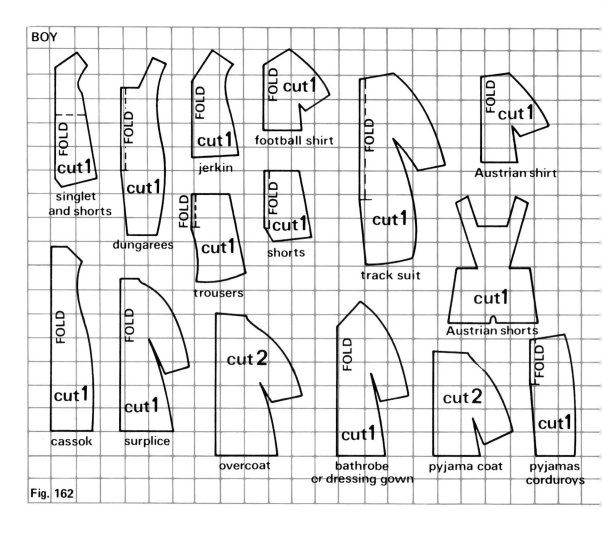

BOY

FOLD cut1
singlet
and shorts

FOLD cut1

FOLD cut1
jerkin

dungarees cut1

FOLD cut1

FOLD cut1
football shirt

FOLD cut1
shorts

trousers cut1

FOLD cut1

cut1
track suit

FOLD cut1
Austrian shirt

cut1
Austrian shorts

FOLD cut1
cassok

FOLD cut1
surplice

cut2
overcoat

FOLD cut1
bathrobe
or dressing gown

cut2
pyjama coat

FOLD cut1
pyjamas
corduroys

Fig. 162

on the sides and oversew to the sides of the doll. Sew to the doll round the neck, arms and legs. A line of blue chain stitch can be embroidered across the middle for a waist band.

## Girl

*You will need:*
  thick cardboard: two pieces, 11¼ x 5½ in.
  flesh coloured felt: 11½ x 5¾ in.
  brown felt: 11½ x 5¾ in.
  scraps of blue, white and red felt *for features*
  yellow or brown wool *for hair*
  vest or stockinette fabric: 5½ x 3¾ in.
  pink and black embroidery silk
  adhesive

Trace round the template twice on to the thick

card and cut out the shapes. Mark one of them with a cross on the pencilled side to be the front of the doll. Stick the two card shapes together to make a firmer figure. Place the shape on the flesh felt with the cross side down and trace round it. Reverse the template on to the brown felt and trace on it. Cut out $\frac{1}{8}$ in. outside the pencil lines to allow for the thickness of the card. Make up the doll. Cut out and stick on features as for boy.

Embroider straight stitches in black for eyelashes. Cut about ten strands of wool long enough to go over the head from shoulder to shoulder and oversew them in a bunch to the top of the head. Gather them in bunches at each side of the face or arrange as you wish. If you intend to give the doll plaits, the strands of wool could be cut longer.

142

Cut a one piece vest and pants from the template allowing an extra $\frac{1}{8}$ in. for turnings on the sides only. Sew on as for the boy, sewing top and legs in blanket stitch with pink silk.

Now both dolls are ready to try on their clothes.

## Clothes

To make a basic template for the dolls' clothes, trace round the doll template on to thin manilla card (more durable than a paper pattern) leaving out the head, feet and hands, so that the pattern will cover the doll from neck to ankles and wrists, and can be adjusted to any required length for hem, and can be sleeved or sleeveless.

Mark the traced side with a cross and make it the right side. Cut out the shape allowing $\frac{1}{8}$ in. extra on the outside edges of arms and body On the reverse side of the template for the

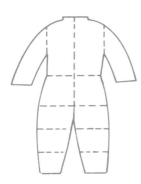

**Fig. 163**

clothes, draw lines marking waist, hips, just below the tops of the legs, knees, calf, elbows and shoulder (see Fig. **163**). Draw a line down the middle from the neck to the legs.

*For all the clothes, you will need:*
  a variety of suitable fabrics (e.g. leather or plastic vinyl fabric, fur fabric etc.)
  a variety of trimmings
  sewing thread
  buttons
  pipe cleaners
  fusible (iron on) interlining
  adhesive

The following clothes have been devised for the boy.

## Dungarees

On a piece of paper trace the shape of the pattern (Fig. 162). Cut a rectangle of interlining 8 x 4 in. Iron the interlining on to the back of the fabric shape and trim away the surplus. The interlining will prevent any kind of fabric from fraying.

Cut two 2 in. lengths of pipe cleaner. Turn over the ends as small as possible to enclose the sharp ends and fold the resulting piece in half. Stick one on the wrong side of the dungarees on each of the shoulders, to form a hook. (Each dress or item of dress has these pipe cleaner hooks which will hold the garment on to the doll's shoulders.)

### Leather top and slacks

The top is traced on to the wrong side of the leather or leatherette. Place the top right side down with the trousers overlapping (use Fig. **160** to test for the right position). Cut a rectangle of fusible interlining to cover both. Place on top on the clothes and iron well. Stick on the pipe cleaner hooks at shoulders.

### Football outfit

The waist of the shorts should overlap the shirt on the right side, the legs being thigh length. Cut a shield shape in interlining and iron on the left side of chest. Iron on interlining to wrong side of both garments, tested for size with the template, and stick on hooks.

### Track suit

This is cut wider than the body and legs and arms, to give a gathered up effect at the neck, wrists and ankles. Use a suitable fluffy pile fabric similar to that used for dressing gowns. Allow a good ½ in. extra on outside of arms, body and legs. Run a gathering thread along neck, wrists and ankles and draw up to fit the template measurements. Trace the doll outline on to the interlining and tack the cut out track suit to this, fitting the sides to the pencilled outline. Only iron the outside edges of the suit to the interlining, to leave the middle free to show fullness. Sew on hooks.

### Austrian or Swiss outfit

Cut the top as for the football shirt, to just below the waist with elbow length sleeves. The sides of the bib on the shorts are cut into the waist to make a narrower bib. Place shorts, right side down and the shirt on top, matching shoulders and sides. Iron on the interlining over the two. Use upholstery adhesive to stick braces and edges of bib to shirt. Sew on hooks.

### Choir boy

Cut surplice and cassock from the pattern and stick the two together at neck edge and with just a dab at waist level sides. Iron interlining to cassock. Stick a small frill at the neck and embroider a line of black chain stitch along the middle of the frill. Sew on hooks.

## Overcoat

Cut in two pieces for right and left sides, allowing an extra ¼ in. on each front edge for lap over. Place the two pieces together so that the left front laps over the right, checking the width with clothes template, Fig. 160. Iron on the interlining over both pieces, ironing down well the edges of the lap-over front. Sew on buttons in front. Sew on hooks at shoulders.

## Pyjamas

Lay trousers over the jacket, check size with template and iron on the interlining. Sew on hooks.

## Bath robe

Cut two ½ in. strips to tie over for a belt. Lap the belt slightly over on to the wrong side at each side. Iron on the interlining to the back of the robe. Tie the belt pieces in front and if necessary sew at the sides. Sew on pipe cleaner hooks.

## Corduroy trousers

Cut them out using the same pattern as for the pyjama trousers. Iron on interlining and trim off any threads at the edges. Sew on hooks.

For the girl choose from the following:

## Mini dress

Cut out from the pattern, Fig. 164 Iron on interlining, and sew on hooks.

## Party dress

This has a frilly skirt.

Cut the bodice from the pattern. The skirt is almost a semicircle. Cut a ¼ in. wide strip of white felt for a belt. Tack the waist of the bodice to the waist of the skirt, keeping the edges together. Trace the outline of the doll on to interlining and tack the sides of the full skirt to the side lines of the interlining skirt. Iron only the sides and waist of the skirt and the whole of the bodice. This will allow the skirt to hang free. Add hooks.

## Kaftan

The sides from the hips down are straight instead of curved in to give more width at the hem. The sleeves are wrist length. Sew a length of decorative braid down the front, across the neck and on the sleeves. Iron on interlining and sew hooks.

*Left: girl dress a doll*

*Jack-in-the-box*

## Fur trimmed coat

Cut the coat from the pattern and iron on the interlining and then stick strips of fur or fur fabric down the front and round the neck and wrists. Use colourless upholstery adhesive. Iron on interlining and add hooks.

## Leather coat

Cut in two pieces allowing an extra ¼ in. each side of the centre line for the wrap. Take care to cut a left and a right side piece. Trace the outline from the template on to the interlining and wrap the fronts over each other to fit this width. Iron on the interlining, pressing well down on each edge of the wrap, and sew on buttons through both thicknesses. Sew on hooks.

## Nightdress

Gather at the neck, sleeves and round the waist, drawing it up to fit the measurements on the template, Fig. 160. Finish the gathers with a line of chain stitch in coloured embroidery thread. Trace the shape of the template on to the interlining and iron only the neck, sides of sleeve

145

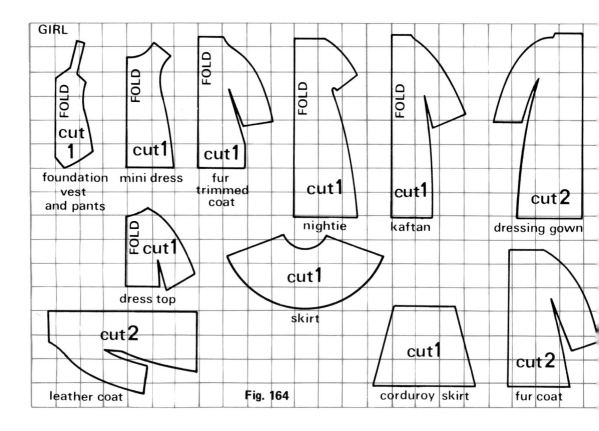

GIRL

cut 1 — foundation vest and pants

cut 1 — mini dress

cut 1 — fur trimmed coat

cut 1 — nightie

cut 1 — kaftan

cut 2 — dressing gown

cut 1 — dress top

cut 1 — skirt

cut 2 — leather coat

cut 1 — corduroy skirt

cut 2 — fur coat

Fig. 164

and sides of skirt, leaving the centre gathered parts free. Sew on hooks.

## Dressing gown
Allow ¼ in. extra each side for the front wrap. Trace the template outline on to the interlining and fit the gown on to it lapping the fronts over. Sew on a decorative button at the neck and finish as others.

## Fur coat
Allow ¼ in. extra on each side of the centre line for the wrap. Take care to cut a left and a right hand side, and cut from the back of the fur, sliding the point of the scissors through the pile and cutting to avoid the actual fur. Trace the outline on to the interlining and fit the coat pieces on to it, wrapping the front right side over the left. Press down well on the fronts. Sew on buttons and hooks.

## Corduroy skirt
Iron on the interlining and trim the edges of threads. Sew on the hooks to the sides of the waist.

## A JACK-IN-THE-BOX

You will need:
ply wood *for box base:* 5 in. square
black felt *for box base:* 5½ in. square
scrap of black felt *for features*
natural felt *for box base:* 5½ in. square
natural felt *for box sides and top:* five $5\frac{1}{8}$ in. squares
wire spring, 1½ in. extending to 4½ − 5 in.
thick cardboard five 5 in. squares
pink felt *for box sides and top:* five $5\frac{1}{8}$ in. squares
unbleached calico: 12 in. square
gummed linen tape: 2 in.
embroidery silks
matching thread
2 in. diameter polystyrene ball
fluffy pile fabric: 8½ in. square
scraps of red felt *for features*
ginger or orange wool *for hair*
scraps of suitable fabric *for clothes*
scrap of white felt *for hands*

## Base

Find the exact centre of the square of wood, and bore a small hole. Mark the centre of the square of natural coloured felt. Thread one end of the spring through the hole in the felt square and then through the hole in the wood so that one complete coil is underneath the base. Seal this firmly in place with the gummed tape.

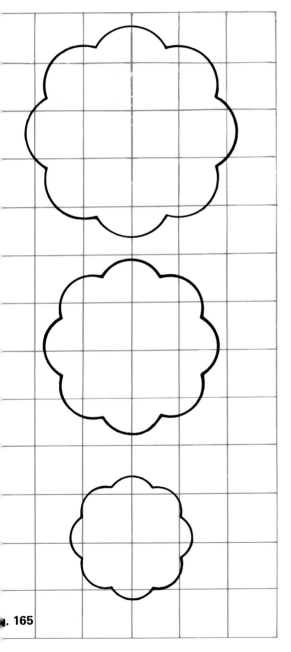

Place the black felt square on the under side of the base and oversew to the edges of the natural coloured square so that the wood base is enclosed. (If necessary, to hold the end of the spring more securely, an extra piece of thick card 5 in. square can be placed on the underside of the board and both card and board sewn in between the two felt squares. In this case, cut the two felt squares bigger making them $5\frac{3}{16}$ in. square.)

## Lid and sides

Embroider each outside piece of pink felt with a design of your choice. Patterns are given for the pictured one, three concentric circles with curved segmented edges are outlined in simple stitches — chain, detached chain, chain stitch whipped and threaded, stem stitch, straight stitch and fly stitch.

## Front and two sides

In sewing up, place a plain lining piece of felt and an embroidered outside piece together with right sides outside and oversew the edges together round three sides. Insert a card through the open end and oversew the fourth side so as to encase the card completely. Complete the two other sides similarly.

## Back of box and lid

The joining up of these two parts of the box will form a hinge, so it needs to be reinforced. Cut two lengths of a firmly woven strong material, such as unbleached calico, 6 x 12 in. Fold each piece in half and place a card on it with one edge to the fold, slightly away from the fold to allow for the thickness of the card. Trace with a pencil round the other three sides (see Fig. 166). Sew or machine stitch just outside

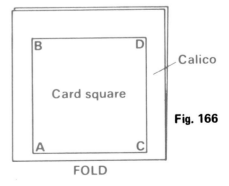

Fig. 166

the lines A-B and C-D, leaving B-D open. Cut off the surplus fabric outside the stitching, leaving B-D uncut. Turn inside out. Insert a card and sew along the line B-D close to the edge of the card. Repeat this with the remaining card.

Now place the two calico covered cards end to end so that the surplus fabric on each card is between them and lying flat on either side (see Fig. 167). Sew together with firm stab stitch

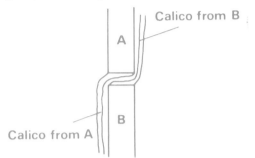

**Fig. 167**

through both lots of material between the cards. Hem down the remaining material on to each card.

Place the two embroidered felt squares together with right sides outside and oversew one lot of edges. Press out flat. Oversew the two lining pieces of felt together on one lot of edges and press flat. Place lining and embroidered pieces together with right sides outside, taking care that the two seams already sewn are exactly together. Oversew two short sides and one long side. Insert the joined cards into the long felt pocket, stretching the felt very gently if necessary so that the join in the felt exactly covers the join in the cards, or the hinge will not work.

Oversew the remaining edges together. Stab stitch through the two joined seams in the middle to fasten the felt and card sections together at the hinge. Sew the other three covered cards to these joined ones to make a hollow box with a lid but no base.

## The Jack

Stretch the piece of fluffy fabric over the ball tightly, and mark the gathers at the base by pencilling round them. Gather along these marks with strong thread, place the ball in the circle so made and draw up the gathers as

---

*Left: tube dolls — Mandarin, Father Christmas, and a monk*

*Guardsman and Red Indian chief tube dolls*

---

tightly as possible and fasten off securely making the surface of the ball firm and free from wrinkles.

### Features

Cut four narrow ¾ in. black felt strips for eyes. Cut a 1 in. circle from red felt for a nose and a

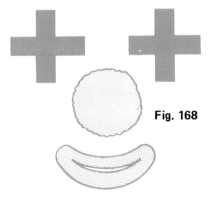

**Fig. 168**

149

curved smiling mouth from a 1 x ½ in. rectangle
of red felt. Gather round the edge of the nose
circle, place a ball of stuffing in the middle and
draw up the gathers to make a ball. Fasten off
securely and sew it on to the side of the head.
Sew the mouth shape underneath and on each
side the eyes in the form of crosses.

## Hair

With orange wool, embroider four or five tufts
of hair on the top of the head. Make maltese
tassels for these tufts. To do this, thread
a large-eyed needle with two strands of wool
and use it double. Draw the needle through a
small piece of the head at the top centre and
leave about 1 in. ends. Take another small
stitch in the same place but at right angles to
the first stitch and over the other threads. Pull
through gently, pulling the 1 in. tuft of threads
upright so that they are encircled and held
upright when the threads are pulled tight. Snip
off to 1 in. in length (see Fig. 169). Trim off the
surplus head covering at the neck leaving about
¾ in.

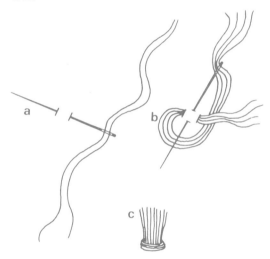

**Fig. 169**

## To complete the Jack-in-the-box

Cut two dress pieces for back and front from a
piece of brightly coloured fabric, cutting it long
enough to cover the spring when extended.
Seam up the side and shoulder seams on the
wrong side and turn inside out. Cut four hand
shapes from white felt. Sew them together in
twos for each hand and sew them on the inside of
the sleeve ends. Sew the neck of the dress to the
neck of the doll as near to the head as possible.
Turn the dress back over the head. Stuff the cut

150

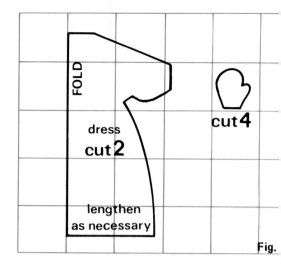

**Fig.**

ends of head material at the neck into the top of
the spring and sew it firmly in place to the top
coils of the spring. Pull the dress down to cover
the spring.

Cut a length of interlining 16 — 20 in. long
and 1 — 1½ in. wide for a ruffle. Cut each long
edge with the pinking shears. Gather it along
the middle and pull up the gathers to fit round
the neck. Sew it in place.

Place the open box over the base so that the
open lid and hinge is behind Jack's face. Oversew
the base firmly to the box.

Sew a decorative button to the middle front
edge of the box, near the top. Sew a loop of
round elastic to the lid of the box opposite the
button, tying the ends in a little fringe to hold
when opening it.

## TUBE DOLLS

All of the dolls in this following section have
been dressed on to cardboard tubes. The kind
used here had kitchen foil on them and so are
mostly the same diameter. The measurements
for dressing the dolls are, of course, applicable
to these particular tubes. Postal tubes used for
maps and documents are good and can be cut
to the desired size with a fine saw. The cardboard should be firm and fairly heavy so that
the figures will stand. Any size of tube can be
used but sizes for dressing and covering them
must be adjusted to these particular sizes. The
determining measurement is that of the
diameter of the tube, which governs the sizes of
the covering. Measure round the tube with a
piece of thread or fine string to get this width.

If fabric other than felt is used then add ¼ – ½ in. extra for turnings.

Amusing and comical tube families can be made and of course their tube 'pets' by adding pipe cleaner legs to the tube used horizontally. Men from the moon or Mars would give wonderful opportunities for flights of fancy.

## A Monk

*You will need:*
tube 11 in. long, diameter 1¾ in.
green nylon felt *for body:* 12 x 6 in.
black nylon felt *for hair:* 3½ x 1 in.
black nylon felt: two 1¾ in. circles
black nylon felt *for feet:* two pieces, 2 x 1¼ in.
orange felt *for nose:* 2 x 1¼ in.
white felt *for eyes:* two pieces, ¾ x 1¾ in.
pink felt *for mouth:* 1¾ x ¾ in.
blue felt *for eyes:* two pieces, $\frac{4}{5}$ x ½ in.
black embroidery silk
matching thread
white cord

Cut a strip 6 x 1 in. off the narrow end of the green felt for arms. Fit the rest of the green felt round the tube and sew down the seam at the back. Cut the two circles from the black felt and sew one on to the green felt at one end of the tube.

## Features
Trim off the corners of the pink felt rectangle to make an oval for the mouth. Sew it on to the front of the tube so that the top of the narrower end of it is 4 in. from the top of the tube.

Roll the orange felt along the long side and sew the edge to the roll so that it makes a small roll 2 in. long for a nose. Sew it in place above the mouth with the seam downwards, using ladder stitch. Hold the nose at right angles to the body and take a stitch in the nose and a stitch in the body, pulling the stitches taut. Continue all round the nose in this way. Fasten off securely.

To make the eyes, trim off the corners of the two white felt rectangles to make oval shapes. Cut two fat leaf-shaped pieces from the blue felt, measuring ¾ x ½ in. and sew them in place in the bottom left side of the white ovals (see Fig. 171). Sew the eyes in place on each side of the nose. Embroider five straight stitches in black silk at the top of each eye to make

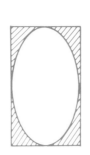

**Fig. 171**

eyelashes and two arcs in chain stitch above them for brows.

## Hair
Cut a strip of black felt 3½ x 1 in. and cut one long side into a fringe. Sew it in place to the top circle leaving the face clear.

## Arms
Cut the 1 in. strip of green felt in half along its length, in a slightly diagonal line (see Fig. 172). Trim each wide end into a curve and snip up for fingers. Sew in place on each side of the tube, lower down than the mouth.

**Fig. 172**

## Feet
Using the pattern, Fig. 173a, cut the black felt into feet shapes. Pin them in position on the front bottom edge of the green felt with the long sides together in the middle. Sew them to the green felt. Place the black felt circle on top of

151

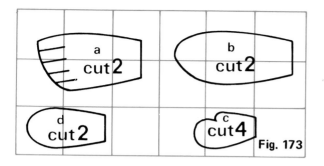

a cut 2

b cut 2

d cut 2

c cut 4

**Fig. 173**

## Hair

Sew loops of the wool along the top of the tube on the flesh felt over the eyes and cut into a fringe of hair.

## Arms

Cut the strip of felt for the arms in half lengthwise and trim each one as shown in the diagram. Sew in place on each shoulder.

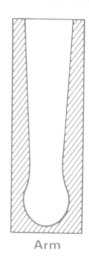

**Fig. 174**

Arm

## Hood

Fold the felt in half and sew down one of the seams from the fold. Fit it over the back of the tube with the seam at the back, pin it in place on each side of the face and sew round the neck of the robe. Sew the second strip of fur round the face edge. Cut the black felt rectangles for feet as in the pattern, Fig. 173b Pin them in place on the bottom edge of the tube and sew to the edge of the red felt. Sew the black felt circle to the bottom edge of the robe.

them and sew it all round to the edge of the green felt tube.

Tie a cord around his waist.

## Father Christmas

*You will need:*
tube 11½ in. long, $2\frac{1}{10}$ in. diameter
flesh coloured felt *for face:* 2½ x $7\frac{1}{5}$ in.
flesh coloured felt $2\frac{1}{10}$ in. diameter circle
red nylon felt *for coat:* 9 x $7\frac{1}{5}$ in.
red nylon felt *for hood:* 8 x 2½ in.
red nylon felt *for arms:* ¾ x 4½ in.
black nylon felt *for circle:* $2\frac{1}{10}$ in. diameter
black nylon felt *for feet:* two pieces, 2 x 1 in.
black nylon felt *for eyes:* two $\frac{2}{5}$ in. circles
white felt *for eyes:* two pieces, ½ x $\frac{3}{5}$ in. ovals
white fur fabric *for front:* 9 x ¾ in.
white fur fabric *for hood:* 8 x ½ in.
white fluffy wool *for moustache and hair*
matching thread

Cut out all pieces as shown above. Fit the flesh coloured felt round the top of the tube and sew the edges together down the back. Sew the flesh felt circle on to the top of this at the end of the tube. Fit the big piece of red nylon felt round the tube with the join at the front so that the bottom edge is level with the bottom of the tube, and the top of it just covers the edge of the face. Sew down the front and catch it down round the flesh coloured felt. Sew the wider strip of fur fabric down the front to cover the join.

## Features

Cut two ovals in white felt and sew small black felt circles at the bottom of them. Sew them in place on the face. Twist the wool round a finger about ten times, cut the ends, tie them tightly in the middle and sew to the middle of the face for a moustache.

## Red Indian Chief

*You will need:*
tube 12 in. long, $1\frac{3}{5}$ in. diameter
chestnut felt *for face:* $5\frac{1}{5}$ x 2¼ in.
chestnut felt *for arms:* 5¼ x 2½ in.
black felt *for hair:* 3 x 1 in.
black felt: two $1\frac{3}{5}$ in. diameter circles
black felt *for feet:* two pieces, 1½ x 1 in.
black felt *for eyes:* two $\frac{3}{10}$ in. circles
red felt *for neck band:* 5½ x ¼ in.
red felt *for head band:* 5½ x ¼ in.
red felt *for tail piece:* 4 x ½ in.
white felt *for eyes:* two pieces, ¾ x ½ in.

152

coloured felt *for feathers:* several pieces, 1 x ¼ in.

thin brown leather or similar: 10¼ x 5$\frac{1}{5}$ in.

turquoise beads: about 48 long ones and 36 small round ones

matching thread

Cut out all the pieces as indicated.

Sew the chestnut felt round the top of the tube, and sew it down the back.

## Hair
Cut the strip of black felt for hair into a fringe along one side and sew it in place to the felt along the top of the tube. Leave the face free. Sew a black felt circle to the top of the tube, to face and hair.

## Features
For the eyes, cut two leaf shapes in white felt and stick a circle of black felt in the centre of each. Sew them in place on the face. Cut a small crescent shape in red felt for the mouth and sew in place with the corners pointing down.

## Dress
Fit the piece of leather round the tube so that the bottom edge fits to the bottom of the tube, the top slightly overlapping the face, with the join at the back. Sew down the back with strong thread. Sew a row of small beads round the tube 5 in. from the bottom and above it a row of long beads sewn on the slant. From shoulder to shoulder on the chest sew a semi-circle of long beads and underneath, in front, two daisy shapes of long beads with a small one in the centre. Slightly stretch the felt neck band round the neck to cover the join of dress and face and sew it in place.

## To complete the figure
Cut the two arm strips to shape (see Fig. **175**) and sew them on at the shoulders. Trim each piece of felt for the feet into shape as shown in Fig. 173b. Pin them in place at the bottom of the tube with the longer sides together in the middle, and sew them to the leather edge. Sew the black felt circle on to the bottom edge of the tube.

## Headdress
Cut out about 25 feather shapes from various coloured felts and sew 14 of them on to the head band. Lurex thread can be used, or small beads sewn on to decorate the right side of the band. Stretch it slightly to fit tight round the

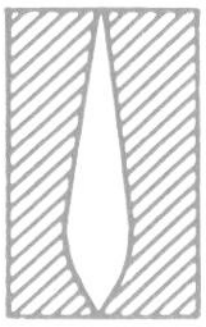

Feather

**Fig. 176**

**Fig. 175**

head at the top of the tube and catch down with small stitches round the head. Sew the remaining 'feathers' to the tail piece and sew one end to the join of the head band, so that it hangs down the back.

## A Guardsman

*You will need:*

a tube 12 in. long, 1½ in. diameter

flesh coloured felt *for face:* 3¾ x 5$\frac{1}{5}$ in.

flesh coloured felt *for hands:* four pieces, ¾ x ½ in.

red felt *for coat:* 4½ x 5$\frac{3}{8}$ in.

red felt *for arms:* two pieces, 4½ x ¾ in.

red felt *for stripes:* two pieces, 4 x ¼ in.

blue felt *for trousers:* 4 x 5$\frac{1}{5}$ in.

black felt *for bearskin:* 3¼ x 5$\frac{1}{5}$ in.

black felt *for boots:* four pieces, 2 x 1 in.

black felt *for moustache:* 1½ x ¼ in.

black felt *for eyes:* two ¼ in. diameter circles

black felt: two 1½ in. circles

brown felt *for hair:* 2 x 1½ in.

white felt *for eyes:* two ½ in. circles

white felt *for belt:* 5$\frac{3}{8}$ x $\frac{3}{8}$ in.

gold Lurex thread

ten gold sequins

kapok

matching thread

Fit the flesh coloured felt round the tube at the top and sew the seam down the back. Sew a black felt circle over the top of the tube.

## Bearskin
The rounded top is made by cutting the top

153

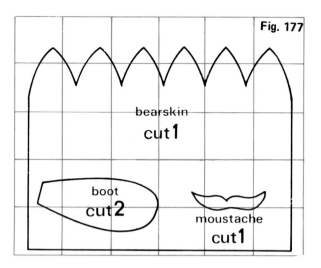

**Fig. 177**

bearskin
cut **1**

boot
cut **2**

moustache
cut **1**

1¼ in. of the felt rectangle into curved points as in the pattern. Oversew the curved sides together and sew the points together at the top, so that there is no hole. Turn it inside out and stuff the resulting dome shape very firmly with kapok.

On the right side oversew the back seam a little way and then fit the bearskin in place on the top of the tube pulling it down carefully over the flesh felt. The bottom of the dome padding rests on the felt circle, the rest of the bearskin covers top of face. If the top does not feel firm enough, then remove it and push in some more padding. Replace it and continue oversewing the back seam keeping the bearskin pulled down firmly over the flesh felt face.

When ½ in. from the bottom of the seam, fit the brown hair semicircle on to the back of the head so that the straight edge will fit just underneath the lower edge of the bearskin when completed.

Sew the hair in place. Finish sewing the bearskin seam. Sew the edge of it to the face and hair with invisible stitches.

## Trousers

Fold the blue felt in quarters and tack with contrasting thread down the ¼ and ¾ lines. Stitch the red stripes down these lines, stitching them over the guiding tackings. Fit the trousers round the lower end of the tube, and sew, keeping the seam at the back.

## Coat

Fit the red felt on to the middle of the tube to overlap the trousers a little and a bigger overlap

on to the face. The join should be at the front and the straight edges should lap over, the left over the right. Fasten them together by sewing on gold sequins in twos. Sew a chain stitch in gold Lurex thread about ¼ in. from the edge at the neck to fasten it to the face. Catch it down lightly at the bottom edge to the trousers. Place the strip of white felt round the middle, overlap it in the front and sew together with gold Lurex thread to form a buckle.

## Arms

Trim the arm felt pieces to a curve which tapers to ½ in. width at the shoulder. Join the hand pieces in twos, oversewing the edges, and sew them to the ends of the arms. Sew the arms in place on the shoulder.

## Features

Sew a small black circle on to each of the white circles and sew them in place just underneath the bearskin. Cut out the moustache in black felt from the pattern and sew it on to the face, sewing only in the middle so that the ends are free.

## Boots

Cut two boot shapes from the pattern and two slightly wider. Cut two card shapes in the smaller size. Place the card between a small and a bigger boot shape and oversew the edges starting with the heel. Push in some stuffing to make the toes rounder. Pin boots in place on the bottom of the tube and sew to the blue felt.

Sew a black circle over the end of the tube to complete the guardsman.

## A Mandarin

*You will need:*
    tube 12 in. long, 1½ in. diameter
    black felt *for hat:* one 2¼ in. circle, one 2½ in. circle
    black felt *for hat band:* $5\frac{1}{3}$ x ¼ in.
    black felt *for collar:* 5¼ x $\frac{3}{8}$ in.
    black felt *for front band:* 9 x ½ in.
    black felt *for feet:* two pieces, 1½ x ¾ in.
    black felt: two circles 1½ in. diameter
    black felt *for eyes:* two $\frac{1}{5}$ in. circles
    scrap of black felt *for moustache*
    flesh coloured felt *for face:* $5\frac{1}{5}$ x 2¼ in.
    flesh coloured felt *for hands:* four pieces, 1 x ¾ in.
    scrap of white felt *for eyes*
    orange felt: ¾ in. diameter circle
    silk or satin *for robe:* 5½ x 10 in.

silk or satin *for sleeves:* two pieces, 6 x 4½ in.
scrap of fusible interlining
black embroidery silk
black sewing thread
strand of gold Lurex thread

Cut out the pieces as shown above.

Fit the flesh coloured felt on to the end of the tube and sew the seam down the back. Sew a black felt circle on to the end of the tube.

## Hat

Pin the two black felt circles together, easing the fullness of the bigger one to the smaller one. Oversew them together three quarters of the way, then pad in between them very firmly with stuffing, making the bigger circle rounder to raise it up. Complete the oversewing. Sew the padded circles to the end of the tube, keeping the larger circle on the top. Pin the hat band in place round the edge of the padded top and sew them together. Sew the other edge of the band to the flesh felt. Sew the circle of orange felt in the centre with gold Lurex thread, to simulate a mandarin's button.

## Robe

Tack single turnings on both short sides and on one long side of the silk and fit it on to the bottom end of the tube, with the long turned-in edge overlapping the raw edge down the front, and the other short edge on to the flesh felt. Sew up the middle seam and round the neck. Place the long black felt strip down the centre front to cover the join, and sew down each side of it. Pin the neck band round the top of the robe to cover the neck join and sew it in place to the face and to the robe.

## Arms

Cut hand pieces from the pattern, Fig. 173c, and oversew in twos, leaving the straight edges open.

Fold the 6 x 4½ in. piece of silk in half with the right side inside so that it measures 3 x 4½ in. Sew it together along one short side and along the long side. Turn it inside out. Tack together the other edge with the single turning inside, pinning one hand inside at the folded edge (see Fig. 178). Sew the hand in place on both sides of the sleeve and sew up the rest of the sleeve. Pin point A to the shoulder immediately under the collar and pin seam A — B down the tube parallel with the centre strip. Sew firmly to the robe. Repeat with the other sleeve. Bend sleeves towards the front and catch down each side of the centre so that the hands seem to be folded over one another.

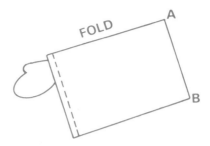

**Fig. 178**

## Feet

Cut two shapes in black felt from the pattern and two smaller shapes in fusible interlining. Iron on the interlining to the middle of the feet leaving a margin of black showing all round. Another way is to cut the smaller shapes from white felt and sew them in place on the black felt feet. Sew the feet in place on the tube at the bottom of the robe and sew a black circle to the edge of the tube.

## Features

Make a 7 in. long cord of black embroidery silk, or crochet a strip and sew the middle of it to the lower part of the face. Cut a small crescent shape from black felt and sew over the same place for a moustache. Cut two almond shapes in white felt and sew a small black circle in the centre of each. Sew the eyes in a slanting position above the moustache. Embroider fine crescents above the eyes in chain stitch worked in sewing thread. Make a 6 in. plait with three strands of embroidery cotton and sew on to the back of the cap.

## A Japanese Girl

*You will need:*
   tube 12 in. long, 1½ in. diameter
   flesh coloured felt *for face:* $5\frac{1}{5}$ x 3 in.
   flesh coloured felt *for hands:* four pieces, 1 x ¾ in.
   black felt *for feet:* two pieces, 1¾ x ¾ in.
   black felt: two 1½ in. diameter circles
   black felt *for eyes:* two 1½ in. circles
   white interlining *for feet:* two pieces, 1¾ x ¾ in.
   red felt scrap *for mouth*
   printed fabric *for kimono:* 10 x 6 in.
   printed fabric *for sleeves:* two pieces, 4½ x 6 in.
   binding: 14 x ½ in.
   silk *for sash:* 7 x 2 in.
   silk *for bow:* 4¾ x 4 in.

black wool for hair
pearls or beads
fine wire: 10 in.
matching thread

Make the face, dress and sleeves as for the Mandarin. Pin on the binding, starting at the waistline, up to the shoulder, round the back of the neck and back to the waist leaving the V of the kimono showing in front, then continue the binding down the front to cover the join of the kimono.

Make a single turning on both long sides of the sash strip. Fold it into two lengthwise tucks. Place around the waist and pin in position. Place a thin piece of padding lengthwise on the strip for the bow and fold the two edges on top to make a padded strip 2 in. wide. Tuck one end under the sash. Bring the fold over and

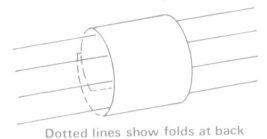

Dotted lines show folds at back

**Fig. 179**

tuck the other end under. Pull the sash tight and sew the ends together. Pull the sash through the bow so that the join of the sash is concealed in the bow.

Sew the feet and the circle as for the Mandarin.

Cut a mouth in red felt and sew on the face. Sew on two small black circles for eyes. Round them embroider slanting almond shaped eyes in black sewing thread, and work curving eyebrows similarly in chain stitch. Sew coils of black wool on top of the tube for her hair. Fold the two ends of a length of wire to the middle. Thread pearls or beads on one loop and twist the end over. Slide the other loop through the coils of wool, thread pearls to match the first side, twist the loop and push the end through into the wool.

## A Crusader King
*You will need:*
tube 12 in. long, $1\frac{3}{5}$ in. diameter

*Left: a Crusader king with his page, and a Japanese girl*

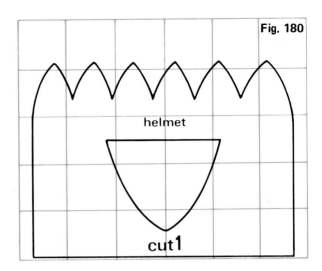

**Fig. 180**

helmet

**cut 1**

flesh coloured felt *for face:* 5¼ x 3 in.
flesh coloured felt: $1\frac{3}{5}$ in. diameter circle
grey felt *for helmet:* 5¼ x 4 in.
grey felt *for trousers:* 4½ x 5¼ in.
grey felt *for feet:* two pieces, 2¼ x 1 in.
grey felt: $1\frac{3}{5}$ in. diameter circle
grey felt *for arms:* two pieces, 5 x ¾ in.
white felt *for surcoat:* 5¼ x 5 in.
white felt *for eyes:* two pieces, $\frac{7}{10}$ x $\frac{2}{5}$ in.
black felt *for beard:* 1¾ x ¼ in.
scrap of black felt *for moustache*
red felt *for cross:* 4 x 2 in.
scrap of red felt *for mouth*
blue felt *for eyes:* two $\frac{1}{3}$ in. circles
blue felt *for sword belt:* 5¼ x ¼ in.
gold felt *for crown:* 5¼ x 1 in.
kapok
gold thread or soft cord
gold Lurex thread
matching thread

Cut out all pieces as shown above.

Sew the flesh coloured felt face on to the top of the tube with the seam down the back and sew the flesh coloured circle to the top of the tube.

Cut out the helmet from the pattern. Oversew the curved edges together, making a close join at the top. Turn inside out and press the seams flat. Stuff the domed shaped top very firmly, to make a good rounded shape. Place it on the head and pull it down gently over the flesh felt so that the stuffing and the dome are resting on the sewn in circle at the top. If not firm enough, then remove and push in more stuffing. Replace and pull down over the flesh felt keeping the seam at the back.

157

Cut out a shield shaped piece of the helmet in the front, pinning the pattern centre front and taking care not to cut the flesh felt. Complete the sewing of the helmet seam. Sew the edges of the cut out shield shape to the face.

Cut a crescent shaped mouth in red felt and sew on the face. Above it and curving over the mouth sew a smaller crescent shape in black felt for a moustache. Stick the small blue felt circles on to the almond shaped white felt eyes and stick them in place. Cut the narrow strip of black felt for the beard into a fringe along one long side and sew it under the mouth in a curve.

Sew the grey felt trousers in place at the bottom end of the tube. Cut a red felt cross measuring 4 x 2 in. with the arms ½ in. wide

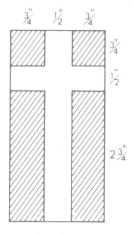

**Fig. 181**

and sew it on to the middle of the piece of white felt. Sew this in place on the middle of the tube with the seam at the back. Sew it to the grey felt above and below it.

Couch down two rows of gold cord at top and bottom edges of the surcoat. From the grey felt pieces cut elongated feet as in the pattern

and sew them to the bottom of the tube. Sew a circle on to the bottom edge. Shape the arms and sew on at each shoulder. Cut out the crown in gold coloured felt and sew it on round the head and face just above the eyes, and below the edge of the helmet. Use gold Lurex thread and a long chain stitch for the sewing. The two ends of the sword belt are sewn on to the right hip so that the belt hangs loosely over the left hip.

## The King's Page
*You will need:*
   small tube 7½ in. long, 1½ in. diameter
   flesh coloured felt *for face:* $5\frac{1}{5}$ x 1¾ in.
   yellow felt *for hair:* 4 x $1\frac{1}{5}$ in.
   yellow felt *for fringe:* $1\frac{1}{5}$ x $\frac{3}{10}$ in.
   yellow felt 1½ in. diameter circle
   orange felt *for body and legs:* $5\frac{1}{5}$ x $5\frac{3}{5}$ in.
   orange felt *for arms:* 3 x ½ in.
   red felt *for tabard:* two pieces, 3 x 2¼ in.
   black felt *for feet:* two pieces, 1½ x ½ in.
   black felt 1½ in. diameter circle
   scrap of brown felt *for eyes*
   scrap of red felt *for mouth*
   soft gold cord: 30 in.
   matching thread

Cut out all pieces as indicated.

Sew the flesh felt round the top of the tube, with the seam at the back. Cut out and sew on a crescent shaped red felt mouth, and two small brown felt circles for eyes.

Cut both pieces of yellow felt into a fringe on one long side of each. Sew the narrow piece to the top of the face and the wider piece round the sides and the back of the head.

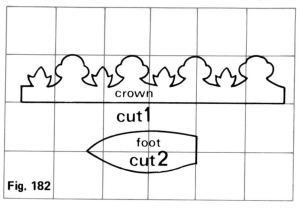

crown

cut 1

foot

cut 2

**Fig. 182**

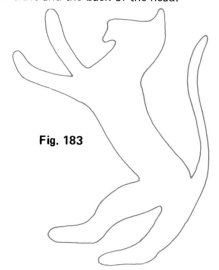

**Fig. 183**

Sew a circle round the top of the tube. Fit the orange felt on to the rest of the tube and sew the seam down the back. Sew it to the face. Cut two slim pointed feet in black felt, like the King's but slightly smaller, and sew in place on the bottom edge of the tube and sew a circle over the tube opening.

Embroider a symbol on the tabard; this one has a leopard rampant on the front and a crown in a shield on the back. Work them in couched gold cord. Sew the top edges of the tabard to the front and back of the doll just below the edge of the neckline. Cut the arms to shape and sew in between the edges of the tabard.

## A Clown

*You will need:*
  tube 9 in. long x $1\frac{3}{5}$ in. diameter
  white felt *for face:* $5\frac{1}{5}$ x 2½ in.
  pink felt *for dress:* two 7 in. squares
  purple felt *for hat:* 5½ x 3 in.

black felt *for eyes:* two pieces, ½ x $\frac{3}{5}$ in.
black felt *for feet:* two pieces, 2½ x 1¼ in.
black felt $1\frac{3}{5}$ in. diameter circle
flesh coloured felt *for hands:* four pieces, 1 x ¾ in.
red felt *for mouth:* 1½ x ¾ in.
red felt *for nose:* 1 in. circle
white fluffy wool
matching thread
selection of coloured sequins

Cut out all pieces as shown.

Sew the white felt rectangle round the top of the tube, with the seam at the back. Run a gathering thread all round the edge of the red felt circle, draw up the gathers, place a small ball of stuffing in the centre, draw up the edges more tightly and sew it to the middle of the face.

### Features

Cut the mouth shape from the pattern and sew under the nose. Make the two oval eyes by

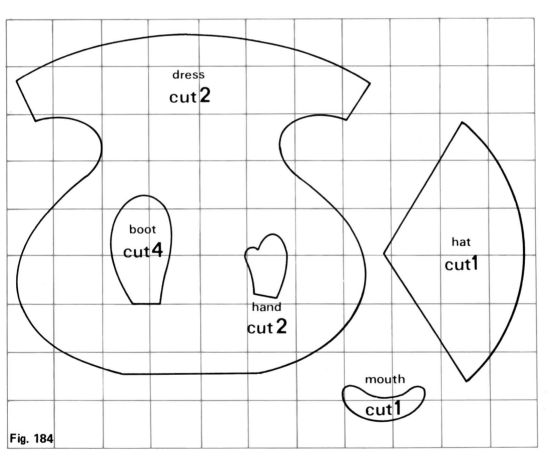

dress
cut 2

boot
cut 4

hand
cut 2

hat
cut 1

mouth
cut 1

Fig. 184

trimming off the corners of the rectangles and sew them in place.

## Dress

Embroider the back and front of the dress. Sequins have been used for the doll in the picture to give a sparkle as well as colour. On the front they are sewn in flower motifs and on the back in lines radiating from the neck.

Cut four hand shapes in flesh felt; sew them together in twos. Pin them at the ends of the arms, with one thumb pointing up and one pointing down.

Pin the centre front of the dress to the middle of the white felt neck, and the centre back of dress to middle of the neck back. Pin each piece in place round the neck to meet at the shoulder. The neck edge should slightly overlap the white felt. Pin the centre front and back of dress to the middle of the bottom of the tube, and pin it round the tube to meet at the sides. Pin the arms and sides of the dress together. Sew to the white felt and oversew the other edges, sewing the bottom of the dress to the edge of the tube. Sew the feet in place on the front edge at the bottom and sew a black felt circle on to it round the edge.

## Hat

Cut a thread of wool and lay it along a thick pencil. Wind the wool about twenty times round the pencil and thread of wool. Slip the loops off the pencil and tie round them tightly with the thread. Sew the bobble in the centre of the hat piece. Cut and trim the loops to make a fluffy ball. Oversew the straight edges of the hat together, place it slightly aslant on the head with the bobble in front and sew round the edge to the head.

## A Tumbler Boy and Girl

Sit them on a cloth-covered sloping surface and they will tumble head over heels to the bottom of the slope and come to rest again either sitting down or standing on their heads.

### Girl

*You will need:*
a tube 2 in. long, $1\frac{2}{5}$ in. diameter

*Left above: tube clown.*

*Left below: tumblers*

flesh coloured felt *for head:* $4\frac{3}{5}$ x 2 in.
flesh coloured felt two $1\frac{2}{5}$ in. circles
flesh coloured felt *for hands:* two pieces, 1 x
$\frac{3}{4}$ in.
chestnut felt *for hair:* 1½ x 3½ in.
chestnut felt *for fringe:* $\frac{2}{5}$ x $1\frac{1}{5}$ in.
chestnut felt: two $1\frac{2}{5}$ in. circles
card: two $1\frac{2}{5}$ in. circles
red felt *for body:* 8½ x 6½ in.
blue felt *for eyes:* two $\frac{2}{5}$ in. circles
red felt *for mouth:* ¾ x ½ in.
yellow felt *for buttons:* three ½ in. circles
marble or round pebble
adhesive
matching thread

Cut out all the pieces as shown, cutting round the
dotted line to form a skirt. Fit the flesh
felt round the tube and sew the seam down the
back. Oversew two flesh coloured felt circles
together half way, insert a card circle and complete the sewing enclosing the card completely.
Sew the circle to the edge of the felt at one end
of the tube. Cut one long side of the hair strip
into a fringe and sew on round the other edge
of the tube. Cut the narrower piece into a
fringe and sew along the front edge.
  Sew two chestnut coloured felt circles together round the second card circle. Put a
marble into the tube and sew the chestnut
coloured circle round the edge to close the
tube. Mark the middle point of the back of
neck opening of the body piece. Push the
bottom end of the tube through the neck opening and pin the marked point to the back seam
of the tube as near to the bottom of the tube as
possible. Pin the rest of the neck opening round
the tube and sew very firmly in place. Fold the
sleeve ends in half and pin a hand inside it with
the thumb next to the fold. Stretch the middle
portion of the back flap right across the bottom
of the tube and pin it to the front of the dress.
Pin the rest across evenly from wrist to wrist,
(not on the front sleeve edge which slopes away
to the waist but rather like a yoke in a slightly
curving line from one side to the other).
  Oversew the ends of the sleeves, sewing the
hands in between the ends with stab stitch —
putting the needle in at right angles from the
front, and back at right angles through the hand
only. Sew the back edge to the front with
herringbone stitch, and sew in the second hand
to match the first.
  Cut red felt in a crescent shape for a mouth
and stick or sew it in position. Place the eyes
and the buttons in position likewise.

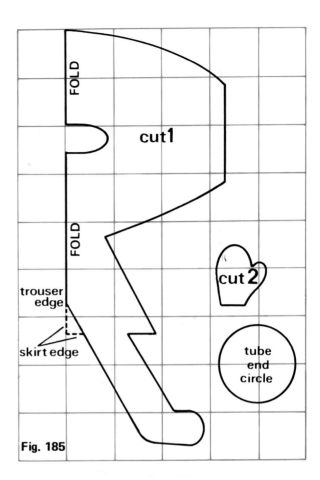

**Fig. 185**

FOLD

cut1

FOLD

trouser edge

skirt edge

cut 2

tube end circle

## Boy
*You will need:*
  tube 2½ in. long, $1\frac{2}{5}$ in. diameter
  flesh coloured felt *for head:* $4\frac{3}{5}$ x 2½ in.
  flesh coloured felt: two $1\frac{2}{5}$ in. circles
  flesh coloured felt *for hands:* two pieces, 1 x
  ¾ in.
  brown felt *for hair back:* 3½ x 1¾ in.
  brown felt: two $1\frac{2}{5}$ in. circles
  card: two $1\frac{2}{5}$ in. circles
  card two $1\frac{2}{5}$ in. circles
  blue felt *for body:* 8½ x 6½ in.
  black felt *for eyes:* two $\frac{2}{5}$ in. circles
  red felt *for mouth:* ¾ x ½ in.
  green felt *for buttons:* three ½ in. circles
  one marble or round pebble
  adhesive
  matching thread

Make up exactly as for the girl tumbler, using
the above colour variations and cutting round the
solid line.

# 7. Novelty Dolls

## A HUMPTY DUMPTY FAMILY

This is a jolly little family consisting of Dad, Mum, a boy and his sister and their baby. All are made on firm bases and can sit on a wall like their namesake or on chairs round a table.

### Dad

*You will need:*
  orange felt *for front:* 6 x $4\frac{3}{5}$ in.
  orange felt *for legs:* two pieces, 5 x ¾ in.
  orange felt *for arms:* two pieces, 2½ x ¾ in.
  black felt *for back:* 6 x $4\frac{3}{5}$ in.

black felt *for feet:* four pieces, 1 x ¾ in.
black felt two $3\frac{1}{10}$ in. diameter circles
black felt *for hair:* 4½ x 2½ in.
three pipe cleaners
white felt *for collar:* 4½ x 1 in.
kapok
felt or fabric *for tie:* 2½ x ¾ in.
adhesive
flesh coloured felt *for hands:* four pieces, 1 x ¾ in.
matching thread
card: 3 in. diameter circle

Trace round the template once on orange felt

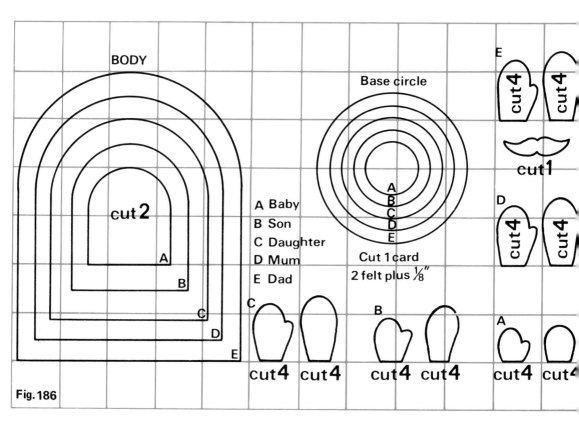

BODY

cut 2

A Baby
B Son
C Daughter
D Mum
E Dad

Base circle

A
B
C
D
E

Cut 1 card
2 felt plus $\frac{1}{8}$″

E  cut 4  cut 4

cut 1

D  cut 4  cut 4

C  cut 4  cut 4

B  cut 4  cut 4

A  cut 4  cut 4

Fig. 186

162

for the front and once on to black felt for the back, and cut out the pieces.

Cut two ½ in. black felt circles for eyes, a red felt crescent for a mouth. Cut a black felt moustache from the pattern, and stick them all in position on the rounded top of the shape for the front.

For hair, trace round the top of the template on to the black felt using a light coloured pencil, and cut it out. Trim the underneath of the curve to simulate a hair line with parting (see Fig. 187).

**Fig. 187**

Fold the white felt collar strip in half and trim it to shape as in Fig. 188 with pinking shears. Trim the tie piece to measure ½ in. at the top and widening to the bottom. Cut off the corners with pinking shears.

**Fig. 188**

Cut the four hand shapes in flesh felt and the four foot shapes in black. Cut a 3 in. card circle and trace round it twice on to the black felt. Cut out the circles outside the lines. Cut two of the pipe cleaners to measure 5¾ in. and from the third one cut two pieces for the arms measuring 3¼ in. Turn back the ends of all of them so that they measure a little less than the strips of felt plus hand or foot length.

Pin the trimmed hair shape in place at the top of the front piece and sew at the sides and across the top edge. Sew the tie in place in the middle of the collar V.

Oversew the hands together in pairs, leaving the wrist open. Fold the arm felt in half lengthwise enclosing the pipe cleaner. Oversew the seams to ½ in. from the end. Insert the projecting end of pipe cleaner into the hand, pulling the wrist inside the sleeve end. Finish the sewing.

Complete the second arm to match. Pin an arm on each side of the front shape, just under the collar, with thumbs pointing towards the

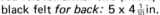

*Right: a Humpty Dumpty family*

face. Pin the front and back pieces of the body together and oversew from the bottom to the hair line, sewing in the arm very firmly. Complete the other side. With black thread sew the top of body, including back, front and hair piece in the oversewing. Sew the leg pieces in same way as the arms, but sewing the boot top over the leg.

Place the two felt circles together and oversew half way round. Insert the card circle and complete the sewing. Sew the tops of the legs to the circle, overlapping the edge by about ¼ in. Stuff the body firmly, pushing small pieces of stuffing into the top seams to prevent puckering. Pin the circle round the bottom edge of the doll so that the legs are at centre front and the leg join inside. Oversew the edges together all round.

## Mum

*You will need:*
  card: 2½ in. diameter circle
  red felt *for front:* 5 x $4\frac{1}{10}$ in.
  red felt *for legs:* two pieces, 4 x ¾ in.
  red felt *for arms:* two pieces, 2¼ x ¾ in.
  black felt *for back:* 5 x $4\frac{1}{10}$ in.

black felt: two 2 $\frac{3}{5}$ in. diameter circles
black felt *for hair:* 3¾ x 2 in.
black felt *for feet:* four pieces, 1 x ¾ in.
flesh coloured felt *for hands:* four pieces, 1 x
  ¾ in.
scraps of brown and pink felt *for features*
white fabric *for apron:* 3¼ x 2 in.
white fabric *for apron tie:* 4 x ¼ in.
three pipe cleaners
kapok
adhesive
matching thread

Cut out all pieces as indicated above.

Trace round the top of the template on the black felt for hair and shape the bottom in two shallow curves up to the centre. Cut two ½ in. circles in brown felt for eyes and a bright pink felt crescent for her mouth and stick these features in place on the top part of the red felt front.

With pinking shears cut all round the apron piece, tapering the sides to be narrower at the top. Sew in place. Pink the edges of the waist tie and sew on. Pin the black hair piece on to the front curve.

Complete the rest of the doll as for Dad.

## Daughter
*You will need:*
card: 2 in. diameter circle
pink felt *for front:* 4 x 3$\frac{2}{5}$ in.
pink felt *for arms:* two pieces, 2¼ x ¾ in.
pink felt *for legs:* two pieces, 4 x ¾ in.
pink felt *for hands:* four pieces, 1 x ½ in.
black felt *for back:* 4 x 3$\frac{2}{5}$ in.
black felt: two 2$\frac{1}{10}$ in. diameter circles
black felt *for hair:* 8 x ½ in.
black felt *for feet:* four pieces, 1 x ¾ in.
scraps of black and red felt *for features*
fabric *for dress:* 10 x 1½ in.
narrow ribbon: 9 in.
three pipe cleaners
kapok
adhesive
sewing thread
strand of black embroidery silk

Cut out all pieces as shown above.
Fold the hair strip in half and mark this point for the centre parting. Shape it in a shallow curve at each side for about half the length and then widen it to the ends. Cut two blue felt circles for eyes, and a red oval for the mouth and stick them all in place on the top half of the pink front. Sew three or four straight stitches for

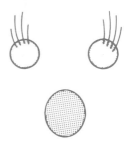

**Fig. 189**

eyelashes. Pin the hair in place, allowing the longer ends to hang free.

Pink the long edges of the dress fabric and gather along one side. Complete the doll as for Dad and Mum above. Sew the gathered dress round the waist. Sew ribbon bows at each side of the face.

## Son
*You will need:*
card: 1½ in. diameter circle
yellow felt *for front:* 3 x 2½ in.
yellow felt *for arms:* two pieces, 2 x ¾ in.
yellow felt *for legs:* two pieces, 3½ x ¾ in.
black felt *for back:* 3 x 2½ in.
black felt two 1$\frac{5}{8}$ in. diameter circles
black felt *for shoes:* four pieces, 1 x ½ in.
black felt *for hair:* 2 x 1 in.
black felt *for belt:* 2½ x $\frac{1}{8}$ in.
flesh coloured felt *for hands:* four pieces, 1 x
  ½ in.
scraps of pink and brown felt *for features*
two pipe cleaners
kapok
matching thread
strand of black silk
adhesive

Cut out all pieces as shown above.

Trace round the top of the template on to the black felt for the hair. Trim off the lower edge into a ragged notched line, ½ in. at its widest point. Cut two small brown felt circles for eyes and a red felt crescent for a mouth and stick these features in place like the others. Pin the hair in place.

Sew the belt across the middle about ¼ in. below the mouth. Embroider a line in black down the middle of the front from just under the belt to the bottom to simulate shorts. Complete the making as the others.

## Baby
*You will need:*
card: 1½ in. diameter circle

flesh coloured felt *for front:* 2 x 1$\frac{9}{10}$ in.

flesh coloured felt *for legs:* two pieces, 2½ x ¾ in.

flesh coloured felt *for arms:* two pieces, 1¼ x ¾ in.

flesh coloured felt *for hands:* four pieces, ¾ x ½ in.

black felt *for back:* 2 x 1$\frac{9}{10}$ in.

black felt *for shoes:* four pieces, ¾ x ½ in.

black felt: two 1$\frac{1}{8}$ in. diameter circles

scraps of blue and pink felt *for features*

white fluffy pile fabric *for cap:* two 1¼ x ¾ in. semicircles

white fluffy pile fabric *for coat:* 1$\frac{9}{10}$ x ½ in.

fluffy wool *for bobble:* 18 in.

adhesive

kapok

two pipe cleaners

matching thread

Cut out all pieces as indicated.

Trace twice round the top of the template on to the wrong side of the fluffy fabric. Cut $\frac{1}{8}$ in. outside the traced line. Make up the doll in the same way as the rest of the family.

With right sides inside sew together the two cap pieces across the top curve. Turn inside out and press the seam flat. Sew on to the head along its bottom edge. Make a bobble for the top by winding wool round a thread laid along a pencil. Push the loops off, tie tightly with the thread and sew to the top of the cap. Cut the loops and trim into a ball. Sew the strip of fluffy fabric along the bottom edge.

## HUMPTY DUMPTY CLOWNS

This set of dolls is made in the same way as the Humpty Dumpty Family. All of them are different in looks, although the same template is used for each.

### Clown 1

*You will need:*

green felt *for front:* 5½ x 4$\frac{1}{5}$ in.

green felt *for legs:* two pieces, 4½ x ¾ in.

green felt *for arms:* three pieces, 3¾ x ¾ in.

black felt *for back:* 5½ x 4$\frac{1}{5}$ in.

black felt *for boots:* four pieces, 2 x 1½ in.

black felt: two 2$\frac{5}{8}$ in. diameter circles

white felt *for face:* 3½ x 3¼ in. oval

white felt *for gloves:* four pieces, 2 x 1½ in.

red felt *for mouth:* 2 x 1 in.

yellow felt *for eyes:* two pieces, 1 x 1½ in.

emerald green felt *for nose:* 1¼ x ½ in.

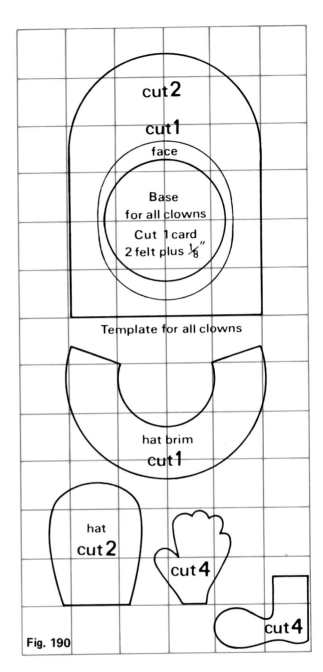

cut 2

cut 1

face

Base
for all clowns

Cut 1 card
2 felt plus $\frac{1}{8}$"

Template for all clowns

hat brim

cut 1

hat

cut 2

cut 4

cut 4

**Fig. 190**

orange felt *for hair:* one piece, 3½ x 1, and one piece, 1½ x 1 in.

pink felt *for hat brim:* 4$\frac{1}{5}$ x 3 in.

blue felt *for hat crown:* two pieces, 2½ x 2 in.

card: 2½ in. diameter circle

adhesive

three pipe cleaners

165

matching thread
kapok

Templates are given for body shape, boots, gloves and hat. Cut out all the pieces to size as given above. Reverse the template when cutting two of the four glove pieces and keep them in pairs with pencil marks inside. Round off the corners of the white felt rectangle to make an oval face. Mark the middle point on each side of the yellow rectangles, and cut off the corners from these points to make diamond shapes for the eyes. Stick a small

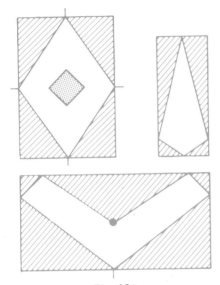

**Fig. 191**

square of black felt in the centre of each. For the nose, mark the middle points on the two short sides of the green felt and cut as in the diagram. The mouth shape is made by marking the centre of the rectangle, and the middle of the bottom edge. Cut off small points from the top two corners giving two small slanting lines. Join the top points of these small lines to the centre of the rectangle and the two lower points of the lines to the middle of the bottom edge. Join these and cut along the resulting lines (see Fig. 191). This will give a chevron shape for the mouth.

Stick all these features in place on the oval white face and stick or sew the oval itself on to the top rounder part of the green front.

---

*Left: Humpty Dumpty clowns*

Cut one long side of each orange hair piece in a fringe. Mark a space at the top of the front, slightly off centre, for the hat, about 1½ in. in length, and pin the fringed felt at each side of this, the shorter piece on the side where the hat is tilted. Stretch the uncut edge of fringe round the curve of the front and this will cause the fringe to fan out and show that it is cut.

Fold the arm pieces lengthwise and oversew them to enclose a pipe cleaner, which should be cut long enough to extend into the glove. Sew the completed glove over the green felt wrist. Pin an arm at either side of the front, about 1 in. from the bottom corners. Pin the black felt back to the front, and oversew all round, including the arms and the hair in the sewing.

Sew the leg felts in the same way, again extending the pipe cleaner to fit into the boot. Oversew the boot edges together and push a little stuffing into the toes to make them rounder. Sew the boots on over the leg ends.

Oversew the black circles together half way, insert the card circle and complete the sewing. Sew the tops of the legs to the circle so that the feet point outwards away from each other.

Stuff the body firmly and smoothly. Pin the centre edge of the front to the space between the legs on the circle, and oversew all round. Sew together the curved edges of the two hat pieces and stuff, not too hard. Sew in position all round its edge to the space between the hair pieces. Pin the pink brim piece round the crown, with the smaller circle downwards on to the head. Oversew the straight edges together while it is round the crown. Pin it in place with the seam at the back and sew it to the head, not to the crown, round its lower edge.

## Clown 2
*You will need:*
royal blue felt *for front:* 5½ x 4 $\frac{1}{5}$ in.
black felt *for back:* 5½ x 4 $\frac{1}{5}$ in.
black felt: two 2 $\frac{5}{8}$ in. circles
black felt *for boots:* four pieces, 2 x 1½ in.
flesh felt *for hands:* four pieces, 2 x 1½ in.
turquoise felt *for arms:* two pieces, 2¼ x ¾ in.
turquoise felt *for legs:* two pieces, 4½ x ¾ in.
white felt *for eyes:* two pieces, 2 x 1 $\frac{2}{5}$ in.
pale blue felt *for eyes:* two ¾ in. circles
orange felt *for brows:* two pieces, 1½ x 1¼ in.
red felt *for nose:* $\frac{3}{5}$ in. circle
red felt *for mouth:* 3 x 1½ in.
yellow felt *for mouth:* 3¼ x 1¾ in.
black embroidery silk

matching thread
kapok
three pipe cleaners
yellow weaving cotton or yarn: 2 yd.
narrow white ricrac braid: 5½ in.
adhesive
card: 2½ in. diameter circle

Templates are given for body, hands, boots, eyes, brows, mouth.

Cut out all the pieces as shown. Reverse the pattern for two of the boots and two of the hands and keep them in pairs. Any pencil lines should be on the inside. To make the mouth, first cut the pattern in red felt. Pin this on to the piece of yellow felt and cut it $\frac{1}{8}$ in. wider all round. Cut a curved slit in the red mouth which widens in the middle. Stick the nose in position in the centre of the face. Stick the two white eye surrounds in place with the blue circles in the lower middle. Stick the eyebrows above and slightly over-lapping the white eyes. Stick the yellow mouth in place with the red mouth on top of it.

With black embroidery silk work a cross on each eye across the middle of each blue eye in back stitch. Extend the lines on to the white surrounds. Sew ricrac braid across the bottom of the front, underneath the mouth, curving up to each side.

Mark the middle of the top curve of the back

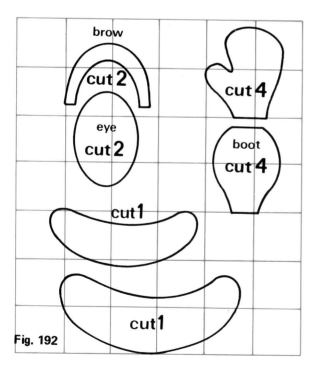

Fig. 192

168

and a point 1 in. each side of the middle. Cut the weaving cotton into 24 in. lengths, and cut each length into eight pieces. Fold these pieces together in a bunch and sew on to the back curve at the marked points (see Fig. 193).

Complete the making up as for Clown 1. Trim off the three tufts of hair to ¾ — 1 in. lengths.

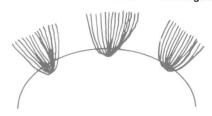

Fig. 193

## Clown 3

*You will need:*
yellow felt *for front:* 5½ x $4\frac{1}{5}$ in.
yellow felt *for arms:* two pieces, 2½ x ¾ in.
yellow felt *for legs:* two pieces, 4¼ x ¾ in.
black felt *for back:* 5½ x $4\frac{1}{5}$ in.
black felt: two $2\frac{5}{8}$ in. diameter circles
black felt *for boots:* four pieces, 1¾ x ¼ in.
black felt *for hair:* 2½ x 1½ in.
black felt *for eyes:* 1¼ x $\frac{4}{5}$ in.
turquoise felt *for gloves:* four pieces, 1¾ x 1½ in.
turquoise felt *for button:* 1¼, and ¾ in. circles
white felt *for mouth:* 2¼ x 1½ in.
red felt *for mouth:* 2 x 1¼ in.
pink felt *for nose:* ¾ in. circle
pink felt *for buttons:* several 1 in. and ½ in. circles
kapok
adhesive
three pipe cleaners
matching thread
card: 2½ in. diameter circle

Cut out all the pieces. Reverse the pattern for two boots and two gloves, keepng them in pairs with pencil marks inside. For the eyes, cut the rectangle of black felt into four strips 1¼ in. long and $\frac{1}{5}$ in. wide. Cut the mouth in red felt from the pattern, pin it on to the white felt and cut the white felt $\frac{1}{8}$ in. wider all round. Stick all the features in place on to the yellow felt front. Place the felt buttons on top of one another in their sizes and alternate colours and stitch them through the centres to the space under the mouth, leaving the edges free. Snip the edges. Cut the black felt for hair in a crescent shape on one long side and cut this curve in a fringe. Cut the piece into three lengths to make three

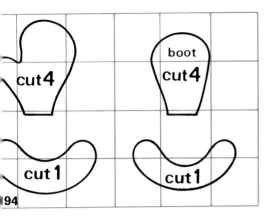

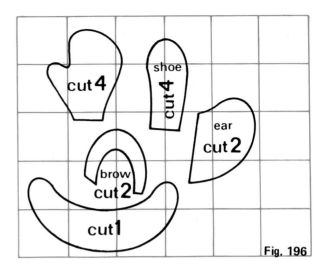

**Fig. 196**

tufts of hair. Sew these in place at the top and sides of the back. Complete making up as for Clown 1.

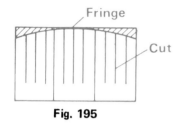

Fringe

Cut

**Fig. 195**

## Clown 4

*You will need:*
   blue felt *for front:* 5½ x 4⅕ in.
   black felt *for back:* 5½ x 4⅕ in.
   black felt *for arms:* two pieces, 2¼ x ¾ in.
   black felt *for legs:* two pieces, 4¼ x ¾ in.
   black felt two 2⅝ in. diameter circles.
   black felt *for eyes:* two ⅖ in. circles
   yellow felt *for feet:* four pieces, 2 x 1 in.
   yellow felt *for hair:* 4 x 1½ in.
   orange felt *for mouth:* 2¾ x 1½ in.
   orange felt *for brows:* 1¼ x 1 in.
   red felt *for ears:* four pieces, 1 x 1¾ in.
   red felt *for nose:* ½ in. and 1 in. circles
   white felt *for gloves:* four pieces, 2 x 1½ in.
   kapok
   three pipe cleaners
   adhesive
   matching thread
   white fluffy wool: 16 in.
   card: 2½ in. diameter circle

Cut out all pieces as shown above. Stick the small nose circle in the centre of the larger one and stick both to the front shape just above the centre with the smaller one underneath. Stick the other features in place. Oversew the curved edges

of the ears and pin in position on each side level with the nose.

Cut one long edge of the yellow rectangle for the hair in a crescent shape, tapering to ½ in. at each side. Cut this curved edge into a fringe and pin the straight edge of it round the curve of the front shape.

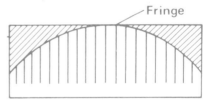

Fringe

**Fig. 197**

Lay a short strand of white wool along a pencil and wind the rest of the wool round it. Push off the loops and tie the thread tightly round them. Sew the bobble on to the front edge under the mouth. Cut the loops and trim the strands into a ball.

Complete the making up as for Clown 1.

## Clown 5

*You will need:*
   pink felt *for front:* 5½ x 4⅕ in.
   pink felt *for arms:* two pieces, 2¼ x ¾ in.
   black felt *for back:* 5½ x 4⅕ in.
   black felt *for hat:* two pieces, 4½ x 1½ in.
   black felt *for feet:* four pieces, 2 x ¾ in.
   black felt: two 2⅝ in. circles
   black felt *for eyes:* two ⅗ in. circles
   white felt *for hands:* four pieces, 2 x ½ in.
   white felt *for eyes:* two pieces, 1½ in. square
   green felt *for nose:* 2 x 1 in.

169

*Wooden spoon cook and plaited nylon and wool dolls*

green scrap *for leaf:* 1 x ¼ in.
red felt *for mouth:* 3 x 1 in.
orange felt *for flower:* two 1½ in. circles
striped fabric *for trousers:* two pieces, 5 x 3½ in.
card: 2½ in. diameter circle
three pipe cleaners
green pipe cleaner 3½ in. long
matching thread
kapok
adhesive
fluffy white wool: 24 in.

Cut out all pieces as shown above. Stick the features in place on the pink felt front. Cut the white wool into twelve 2 in. pieces. Fold six strands in half and sew on the side of the face level with the top curve of the eyes. Sew the other six strands on the opposite side. Cut the ends about ¾ in. long and fluff them out into a fuzz.

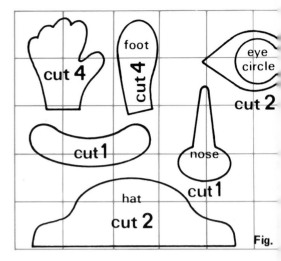

Make up the striped trouser legs. Sew the side seams, gather the tops and sew round the top of the pipe cleaners for the legs. Sew this end to the felt covered card circle. Pink the other edges and sew round the pipe cleaner to the top of the boots. Complete the making up as for Clown 1.

Place the two flower circles together and cut all round the edges in points. Coat one end of the piece of green pipe cleaner with adhesive and stick it in between the flower shapes. Cut a single leaf shape from the scrap of green felt left from the nose shape and stick it on to the pipe cleaner. Sew the pipe cleaner to one of the hat shapes, to stick out at an angle. Place the other hat shape on top and oversew all round the curved edges, leaving enough open on the lower edge to fit over the head. Sew it on to the head round the edge of the brim.

## SPOON DOLLS

### A Wooden Spoon Victorian Cook
*You will need:*
  a wooden spoon
  red, blue and black felt tip pens or scraps of felt
    *for features*
  checked or striped cotton *for dress:* 13 x 6½ in.
  checked or striped cotton *for sleeves:* two
    pieces, 3 in. square

*Right: pyjama cord dolls and a small cord doll in a green dress*

white muslin *for apron:* 5 x 4 in.
white muslin *for mob cap:* 5 x 4 in.
pipe cleaner chenille *for arms:* 16 in.
brown wool *for hair:* 20 in.
white tape *for belt:* 8 in.
adhesive
embroidery silk
matching thread

The bowl of the spoon used for the pictured doll measures 3 x 2 in., the handle 7 in. The rounded back of the bowl is the doll's face.

Find the middle of the piece of wire and place at the neck. Twist the two ends once tightly round the neck (top of the handle). Double the ends back and twist together for arms, leaving small loops at each end for hands.

Cut out all the pieces as shown above. Pink one short side on each of the sleeve pieces. Sew the side seams and gather the pinked edge. Turn inside out. Pink all the edges of the piece of dress fabric. Fold it in four and cut down 1¾ in. on the double fold for armholes. Sew the sleeves into these cut edges with the sleeve seam underneath. Gather with embroidery silk along the top edge of the dress about ½ in. from the top edge. Draw up the gathers, fit it on to the doll and tie the thread at the back.

Pink all the edges of the white apron. Cut off a one inch square from each of the top two corners to make a bib front. Cut two lengths of

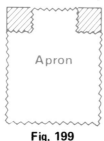

*Apron*

**Fig. 199**

tape to $\frac{1}{8}$ in. wide. Sew the ends to the corners of the bib, cross them over the back and sew to the corners of the apron. Tie the two remaining ends round the waist.

From the scraps of felt cut two small blue circles for eyes, two pink circles for cheeks and a red felt crescent for a mouth. Stick all of these in place on the bottom half of the outside of the bowl of the spoon. Round off the corners of the muslin for the cap with pinking shears, and make an oval shape. Gather all round it about ½ in. from the edge and draw it up to fit round the top of the bowl. Stick loops of wool on each side of the bowl for hair and pull the cap over to cover the ends.

172

# CORD AND PLAITED DOLLS

## Pyjama cord doll
*You will need:*
four woollen pyjama cords 42 in. long
flesh felt *for face and head:* two 3½ in. circles
kapok or wadding
scraps of brown, red and pink felt *for features*
adhesive
matching sewing thread

Three of the cords are used for the body and legs, and the fourth will be cut in half for head and arms. Tie the three cords together tightly in the middle so that the ends are even. Cut the fourth cord into two equal pieces. Untie all the knots at the ends of the cords. Take one of the half pieces for the head. Cut this piece in half again and tie the two pieces together tightly in

Head

Body

**Fig. 200**

the middle. Loop the head cords and body cords round each other with the tied parts touching and tie the head cords together and the body cords together above and below the looped part. Tie knots at each end of the arm cords to match each other and fray out the ends. Mark the middle point of the arm cords.

Plait the six body cords once, place the arm cords across the plait so that the middle point is on the plait. Continue with the plaiting enclosing the arm cords, till the body plait measures 6 in. Divide the cords into threes for the legs and plait each set along the whole length. Bind the ends tightly with matching wool or embroidery silk and leave the fringed ends for feet.

### Features
Cut a crescent in red felt for a mouth, cut two ½ in. brown felt circles for eyes, two the same size in pink for cheeks, and two brown felt

crescents for eyebrows. Stick all features in place on one of the flesh coloured felt circles.

Unravel the head cords for hair. Spread the strands out in a fan shape on the other flesh coloured felt circle. Pin the strands in place round the edge of the circle. Pin the face felt circle on top of this with right sides outside and the pyjama cord between the circles and pin at top and bottom and round one side only.

Push some stuffing into the pinned half to make a smooth shape, not too fat. Oversew the edges of this half. Continue sewing over the top of the head, including the wool strands in the sewing. Push in more padding in the other half, keeping the face smooth, and complete the sewing. press seams. Sew braid or cord to trouser

## Dressing the doll

The picture shows a pyjama cord doll dressed, of course, in a pyjama outfit of trousers and over-blouse or tunic. Back and front of each are the same, so two shapes are cut from each pattern. The material used here is nylon felt which is quite stiff. The doll has not been padded at all, so a fairly stiff fabric is necessary to give it some support and shape. A thinner softer fabric could be used over an inner suit made' of interlining, similar in texture to the nylon felt, or fusible interlining could be ironed on to the back of the chosen fabric to stiffen it and prevent fraying.

*You will need:*
    felt *for trousers:* two pieces, 11 x 9 in.
    felt *for tunic:* two pieces, 11 x 8 in.
    matching thread
    soft gold cord (or other decorative braid)

## Trousers

Place the two pieces together with right sides inside. Oversew the seams. Turn inside out and press seams. Sew braid or cord to trouser edges, turn inside out and sew inner leg seams. Turn inside out. Sew on to the doll at the waist.

If using fabric place the two pieces together with right sides inside. Sew the outside seams together with running stitch. Turn. Sew on the braid. Turn inside out, and sew the inner leg seams. Turn inside out. Make a hem at waist and sew on to the doll's waist.

## Tunic

On one piece cut a neck opening down for 2½ in. Place the two pieces together with right sides inside and oversew one of the side seams and under arm seams. Turn to the right side and sew braid on to the bottom of the tunic and to

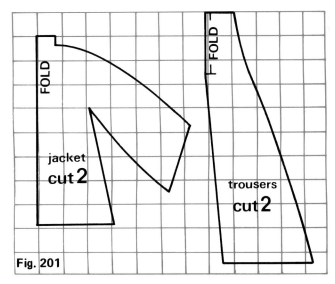

Fig. 201

the edge of the sewn sleeve using a zig-zag pattern. Oversew the other side and under arm seams in the same way. Sew braid on the right side of the second sleeve. Oversew the top seams of the sleeves on the wrong side. Turn the tunic inside out. Sew braid round the neck and the opening. Sew a bow to the doll's hair in front.

### A cord doll
*You will need:*
    piping cord: 36 in.

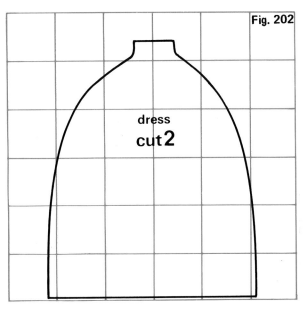

Fig. 202

dress
cut 2

173

A *Two-faced clown*

1½ in. diameter polystyrene ball
size 12 circular finger bandage: 8 in.
narrow ribbon: 12 in.
nylon felt *for dress:* two pieces, 5½ x 4½ in.
contrast felt *for pocket:* 1 in. square
felt *for trimming:* one piece, 4½ x ¼ in. and
   one 1¼ x $\frac{3}{8}$ in.
matching thread
blue, red, black felt tip pens

Cut off 10 in. of piping cord for arms. Tie a tight knot in each end of it, and also in each end of the remaining cord. These knots are for hands and feet. Tie the two cords together in the middle with a strong thread.

Pull the finger bandage over the polystyrene ball. Gather the ends and sew them down over the tied cords. Bind firmly round the neck. Pull the bandage tightly to the top of the head and bind it firmly at the top. Cut the end of bandage left at the top lengthwise into three equal

parts and plait them. Tie a bow at the end of the plait and one at the top of the head.

Draw the features with the felt tip pens. Cut the two pieces of felt into the dress shape. Leave about ¾ in. in the centre of the top edge. Stick on the contrasting felt square for a pocket, the long strip across the hem and the shorter strip at the neck join.

Pin the cord arms at the shoulder of one dress piece, pin the back piece to it and oversew all round the edges, enclosing the arms and sewing very firmly to the neck.

## Plaited nylon doll

*You will need:*
   9 old nylon stocking legs
   flesh felt *for face:* two 3½ in. circles
   red felt *for mouth:* 1 x ¾ in.
   blue felt *for eyes:* two ¾ in. circles
   two $\frac{2}{5}$ in. blue sequins
   black and red embroidery silk
   orange nylon felt *for dress:* two pieces, 8 in.
      square
   6 green sequins
   8 small beads
   narrow green ribbon: 12 in.
   matching thread
   adhesive
   kapok

For arms, tie three nylon stockings or tights legs together at the toes and plait together tightly for 12 in. (unstretched). Tie the end of the plait tightly. Cut off the surplus nylon at each end to make a ¾ in. frill for hands.

### Body

Tie together six nylon legs at the toes, about 3 in. away, and plait together tightly for about 3½ in. Tie tightly, leaving about 2½ in. unplaited and tie again. Plait together for three twists. Lay the arm plaits across with the middle of it on the body plait and continue body plaiting, enclosing the arms plait, till 4½ in. is plaited.

Divide into two lots of three and plait three nylons together tightly for the legs for 9 in. Tie round tightly and cut off the ends to leave a 1 in. frill for feet.

### Face

On one of the flesh felt circles for the face stick the features. Cut a deep crescent shape in red felt for a mouth and sew or stick it in place. Place a sequin low down on a blue circle for an eye, bringing the needle through the sequin from the back. Thread a small bead on the needle, and put the needle back through the hole in the sequin, so securing it. Embroider six straight stitches radiating from the eye at the top and two arcs of stem stitch in black embroidery silk, above the eyes. Embroider two star shapes in red silk on the cheeks.

Pin the two felt circles together enclosing the unplaited portion of the nylons with the top plait exactly in the middle at the top, between the eyes, and the bottom immediately under the mouth. Pin in place and then oversew the edges all round sewing in the plaits as well. Cut off the actual toe part of the nylons, and cut the remainder into a fringe for hair. Tie a ribbon bow on top of the head.

## Dress

Mark the middle 1 in. off the top edges of the pieces of nylon felt, and cut from there to the bottom corners in a curving line from the top. Sew six sequins down the front of one piece, using small beads to hold the sequins (as for the eyes). Pin the two pieces together. The top inch on each side of the neck will enclose the plait and 1 in. down at each side the arms. Pin the back of the dress on to the front to match these points and oversew the seams, sewing the arms and neck firmly.

## Plaited wool doll

Any kind of wool can be used to make these dolls, even odd ½ ounces of mixed colours can make a very attractive rainbow doll.

The doll can be made from 4-ply wool, using 108 strands, 15 in. long for the body and 42 strands, 10 in. long for the arms. (Any number of strands may be used, but should be divisible by three.)

The doll in the picture, however, wearing a Scots plaid dress, is made from double knitting wool, using 90 strands, 20 in. long for body and head and 36 strands, 15 in. long for arms.

*You will need:*
wool (see above)
flesh coloured felt *for face:* two 2¼ in. circles
flesh coloured felt *for hands:* four pieces, 1¼ x 1 in.
black felt *for shoes:* four pieces, 1½ x 1¼ in.
black felt *for lashes:* two pieces, $\frac{2}{5}$ x $\frac{1}{5}$ in.
red felt *for mouth:* ¼ in. circle
narrow ribbon: 15 in.
plaid fabric *for dress:* 6½ x 11 in.
kapok

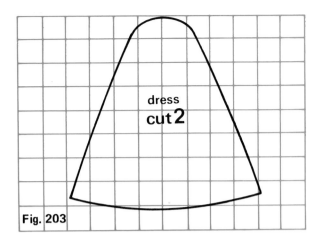

**Fig. 203**

matching thread
adhesive

Cut the wool into the required number of strands for body and for arms by winding the wool round a piece of firm cardboard cut to the length you intend the strands to be and snipping the ends of the wool. This length of strand makes a doll 12 in. long with 4 in. long hair.

## Arms

Tie the strands together tightly near one end and plait them very firmly, again tying them tightly at the end.

## Body

Tie the strands together 6 in. from one end. This will make the face and hair. Divide into equal thirds, plait once, then lay the arms plait across the body plait so that the middle point of it is actually on the body. Continue with the body plait till it measures 3½ in. Divide the strands in two equal parts for the legs and plait each part firmly to the end testing them for equal length before tying them.

## Features

Stick the red felt mouth in place near the edge of the flesh felt circle. Cut one long side of each strip of black felt into a fringe and stick on the face in curves for eyelashes.

## Face

Bunch the remaining strands of wool together and pin a felt circle cut from the pattern to them with the bottom of the circle pinned to the plait. Pin the face on to the other side of it and oversew the edges, leaving a small hole at

175

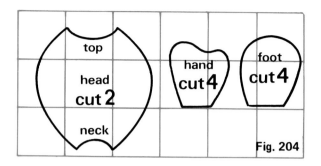

**Fig. 204**

the top for the wool ends which make hair. Pin a ribbon bow to the wool at the forehead.

If the face is not firm, push in a little stuffing each side of the wool before sewing the edges.

## Hands and feet

Cut four hands in flesh felt and sew them together in pairs, keeping pencil lines to the inside. Leave the wrist open. Push the ends of the arm plaits into the hands and sew to the plait round the wrist. Cut out the four shoes in black felt and sew to the legs in similar fashion.

## Dress

Pink one long edge of the fabric and sew together the short sides. Fold it in quarters and mark and cut a small slit down from the neck on the ¼ and ¾ points for the arms. Oversew the edges of the slits. Make a narrow turning at the neck and draw it up to fit the neck. Fit the dress on the doll, and fasten off the neck gathers firmly.

## OTHER NOVELTY DOLLS

### A two-faced clown

This fellow has no back view, but has two different front views. The shapes used to make each half are identical, but they are different in colour and features. Both have white gloves and black boots.

### First side

He has a white face, a blue body with orange sleeves, green trousers and a pink hat.

*You will need:*
  white felt *for face:* 5 x 4 in.
  white felt *for gloves:* two pieces, 2¼ x 1¾ in.
  blue felt *for body:* 5 x 3½ in.
  orange felt *for sleeves:* two pieces, 3 x 2¼ in.
  green felt *for trousers:* two pieces, 5¼ x 2 in.
  black felt *for boots:* two pieces, 2 x 1 in.
  black felt *for eyes:* four pieces, $1\frac{1}{10}$ x $\frac{1}{5}$ in.

black felt *for brows:* two pieces, 1 x ½ in.
pink felt *for hat:* 3 x 2 in.
pink felt *for hat brim:* 3 x ¾ in.
orange felt *for mouth:* 2¼ x 1 in.
red felt *for nose:* 1 in. circle
pale blue felt *for eyes:* two ¾ in. circles
yellow fluffy fabric *for buttons:* three ¾ in. circles
wadding
adhesive
matching thread

Cut out all the pieces as above, reversing the template for any second pieces when two shapes are needed, so that any pencil marks can be kept on the wrong side. Stick the features on to the white face, placing the nose on first, slightly nearer the lower half. Stick the buttons on the front.

Cut the wadding shapes for each piece from the appropriate patterns for head, body, arms, hands, legs, boots and hat.

### Second side

This has a white face too, but with a red body, yellow sleeves and blue trousers. His hat is turquoise.

*You will need:*
  white felt *for face:* 5 x 4 in.
  white felt *for gloves:* two pieces, 2¼ x 1¾ in.
  red felt *for body:* 5 x 3½ in.
  red felt *for mouth:* 1½ x ¾ in.
  red felt *for nose:* 1 in. circle
  yellow felt *for sleeves:* two pieces, 3 x 2¼ in.
  blue felt *for trousers:* two pieces, 5¼ x 2 in.
  white fluffy fabric *for buttons:* three 1 in. circles
  black felt *for boots:* two pieces, 2 x 1 in.
  black felt *for brows:* two pieces, 1 x ¾ in.
  turquoise felt *for hat:* 3 x 2 in.
  turquoise felt *for hat brim:* 3 x ¾ in.
  turquoise felt *for eyes:* two $\frac{3}{10}$ in. circles
  pink felt *for cheeks:* two ¾ in. circles
  purple felt *for eyes:* two pieces, 1 x $\frac{3}{5}$ in.

Cut out all the pieces as for the first side.

### Main body frame
*You will need:*
  pipe cleaner chenille *for head wire:* 10 in. length
  pipe cleaner chenille *for arms:* two 6 in. lengths
  pipe cleaner chenille *for legs:* two 16 in. lengths
  (total amount of wire 54 in.)

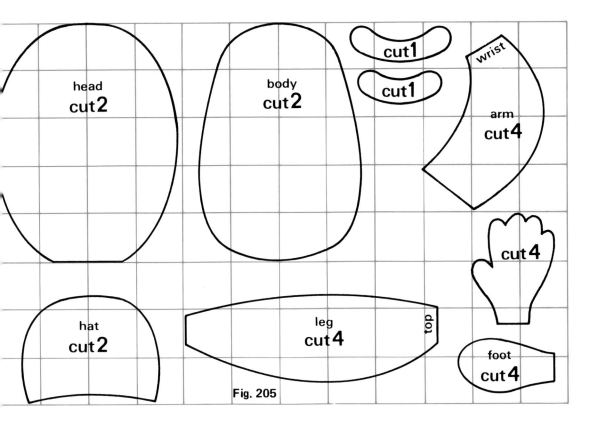

head
cut 2

body
cut 2

cut 1

cut 1

wrist

arm
cut 4

cut 4

hat
cut 2

leg
cut 4

top

foot
cut 4

Fig. 205

Cut the length of wire into the required lengths.

Assemble the pieces for both clowns side by side and in making up the body and limbs take one piece from each clown, taking care to reverse the second arm and leg so that they are kept in pairs.

Fold the wires for legs and arms in half and twist them together.

Place the wadding for a boot one piece on each side of the end of a leg wire and pin a boot felt from each clown on to it. Oversew the curved sides of the boot to enclose the wadding and wire. Place a piece of leg wadding each side of the wire above the boot and pin a leg felt from each clown on each side. Oversew the edges sewing in the top of the boot on each side. Make up the other leg, reversing the boot and leg felts to make a pair.

Make up the hands and arms in the same way, doing first one and then the other to make a pair. Fold and twist the head wire, forming into a small ring.

Place the wadding on one face piece with the wire on top of the wadding so that half of the wire twist projects at the bottom. Place the other wadding and then the second face piece on top and oversew all edges.

Oversew the curved edges of the hat pieces, enclosing the wadding and sew the bottom edges to both sides of the top of the head. Place the brim edge to edge with the bottom edge of the hat, and backstitch it into place. Fold back the other edge of the brim and sew it on to the hat edge. Fold the brims back against the hat and oversew the two side seams of the brim.

Lay one piece of wadding on to one body piece. Pin arms, legs and head in position on to it. Place the other wadding and the second body piece on top, pin them together securely and oversew all the seams, sewing both sides of the head and limbs.

### A Clown from felt circles

His body, arms and legs are made from circles of nylon felt cut in different sizes, strung together on elastic. He can also be made from larger circles of fabric in many gay colours, gathered round the edge and drawn up tightly and pressed out into a circle, the padded circles

177

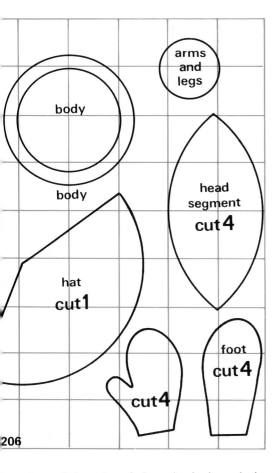

body

body

hat
**cut 1**

arms
and
legs

head
segment
**cut 4**

foot
**cut 4**

**cut 4**

so formed then threaded on elastic through the centres for body and limbs.

If you use ordinary felt, you will need more circles to make a doll of the same size.

*You will need:*
    nylon felt *for body:* ten 3 in. circles and twenty-two 2 in. circles
    nylon felt *for arms:* forty 1 in. circles
    nylon felt *for legs:* sixty 1 in. circles
    felt or fluffy pile fabric *for face:* 4½ x 9 in.
    white felt *for hands:* four pieces, 2½ x 1½ in.
    white felt *for hat:* 5 x 2½ in.
    black felt *for feet:* four pieces, 2½ x 1¼ in.
    black felt *for eyes:* two ½ in. circles
    red felt *for nose:* ¾ in. circle
    orange felt *for mouth:* 1½ x 1 in.
    3 in. diameter polystyrene ball
    white interlining *for ruffles at neck:* 30 x 1 in.

---

*Left: clown from felt circles and matchbox dangle dolls*

    white interlining *for ruffles at wrists and ankles:* four pieces, 24 x 1 in.
    round elastic: 48 in.
    red wool *for hat bobbles:* 36 in.
    matching thread

Cut out all the pieces as shown. Cut the elastic into equal lengths and thread these through large eyed needles. Knot both ends of elastic together. On one of the pieces of elastic, for one leg and one side of the body, thread the following:

    thirty of the 1 in. circles for the leg
    eight of the 2 in. circles, threaded slightly off-centre, for the body
    ten 3 in. circles, threaded slightly off-centre, for the body
    fourteen 2 in. circles threaded slightly off-centre, for·the body

On the second elastic thread the remaining thirty 1 in. circles through their centres, then thread through the body circles slightly off-centre on the opposite side of centre so that the pieces of elastic are running parallel through the body circles on each side of the centres. The

**Fig. 207**

circles should not be packed together too tightly — the legs and body should each measure about 6 in.

Knot the two lots of elastic together at the top of the body then separate them again for the arms. Thread twenty arm circles on each elastic. Make a knot at the ends and cut off remainder.

## Head

Cut four segments in white fabric for the head covering, and oversew them along the curved edges on the wrong side. Use a double oversewing stitch (see page 6). Leave the last side

179

open. Turn it inside out and press the seams. Place the polystyrene ball inside and sew up the last edges with ladder stitch (see page 7) and pull the edges together firmly. Instead of using a polystyrene ball, the ball cover can be stuffed firmly with kapok or a similar material.

## Features

To make the mouth, round off the corners on one long side of the orange felt and cut a crescent shape from the opposite side. Sew the red circle for the nose in place, the mouth underneath and the two black felt eye circles each side. Sew hand and foot pieces together in pairs and sew them at right angles to the last circle on arms and legs, over the elastic knot. Use ladder stitch for sewing them. Sew the head very firmly to the top body circle over the knot.

## Ruffles

With strong white thread, sew along the middle of the strip with running stitch. Draw the gathers up as close as possible, place round the wrist where it joins the circle and sew it in place. Complete the other three for the wrist and ankles in similar fashion, using the longer one for the neck.

## Hat

Lay a 6 in. thread of wool along a pencil and wind the remaining length of wool round both. Slide the loops off the pencil, tie the thread round them tightly and sew the bobble to the centre of the hat. Cut the loops and trim the ends to make a ball. Knot the remaining elastic, doubled, to the top of the head. Pin the hat round it, and oversew the straight edges together so that the elastic loops come through the top point of the hat. Press the seam flat and pin the hat to the head so that the bobble is at centre front. Sew it round the edge to the head.

## Matchbox Dangle Dolls

Small matchboxes can be used to make these dolls, but are rather fiddling to do, and if larger match boxes are not available, simple boxes can be made to any size from medium thick card. Decide on the size and measure length, width and thickness, to find the size of card required. The length of the piece of card will be two widths plus two thicknesses one way and one length plus two thicknesses the other way. Directions given here are for making a box which is 3½ in. long, 2½ in. wide and ½ in. thick, so the piece of card for making it measures 6 x 4½ in.

Mark out the shape as in the diagram and cut away the shaded parts with a cardboard cutting

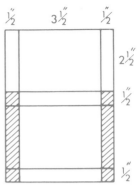

**Fig. 208**

knife. Cut lightly part way through the lines (score). Bend the card away from the cuts and stick the edges together with adhesive tape. The edges should butt up against each other and not overlap or the corners will not be square.

Fabric for covering the resulting box should be cut ⅛ in. bigger all round to allow for the thickness of the card. Both of these dolls are made on the same size box, 3½ x 2½ x ½ in., so the same materials are needed for both.

*You will need (for one box):*
  a matchbox or card (see above)
  felt to cover box: 4¼ x 6¼ in.
  felt *for arms:* two pieces, 2¼ x 1 in.
  felt *for legs:* two pieces, 4½ x ¾ in.
  felt *for hands:* two pieces, 1 x ¾ in.
  felt *for feet:* two pieces, 1 x ¾ in.
  felt *for hair:* 2½ x 1 in.
  felt *for mouth:* 1¾ x ½ in.
  felt *for nose:* $\frac{2}{5}$ in. circle
  felt *for eyes:* two $\frac{7}{10}$ in. circles and two ½ in.
    circles
  pipe cleaner *for arms:* two 3¼ in. lengths
  pipe cleaner *for legs:* two 5¼ in. lengths
  matching thread
  adhesive
  black embroidery silk
  round elastic: 12 in.

Cut out two hands and two feet from the pattern. The pipe cleaners are cut longer than the pieces of felt, so that the ends can be turned over. They should then be slightly shorter than the felt strips. Lay the pipe cleaner along the appropriate felt strip and oversew the edges to enclose it. When nearly to the end of the seam, pin on the hand or foot to one side of the narrow end, and sew it in with the end seam. Finish sewing the seam.

All sewing is done on the right side, and all pencil lines should be kept on the inside.

Fold short lines AC along lines BC and sew the edges. Fold along CC and oversew the fold to give a sharper edge. Fold along BB and oversew the fold. Fold along CD and oversew both folds.

Oversewing the folds gives a sharper outline, but keep checking measurements before and during sewing or the cover may not fit well when finished.

At (•) in the diagram sew round elastic from the wrong side to the right side and then back to the wrong side again and knot both ends firmly. Find point (•) by drawing diagonal lines from corner to corner on the wrong side.

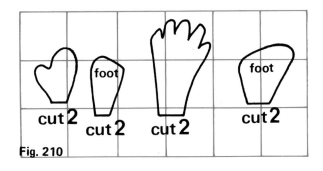

Fig. 210

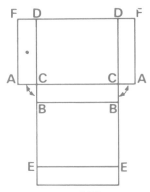

Fig. 209

Pin edges AF to BE and oversew leaving a flap ½ in. wide along EE (see Fig. 209). Pin the legs into the seam on the side opposite the elastic with the straighter sides of the feet on the inside, together. Sew the legs in with the seam, using stab stitch, but oversewing the rest of the seam.

Slide the box into the felt shape, oversew the remaining seam and the fold too.

Sew an arm on at each side from the back seam to the front seam about 1 in. from the bottom. Cut one side of the felt strip for hair in a fringe, roll it and sew on in a tuft with the elastic loop through the centre of it. Cut a crescent in the red felt for a mouth and stick it in place. Stick the big eye circles in place with the smaller one stuck in the middle or slightly to one side on the edge. Embroider a curve of black stem stitch above each eye. Stick a small felt bow between the mouth and the bottom of the box.

### Violet dangler doll

This doll has its features placed along the length of the box to make a fat face. The short arms are single with no pipe cleaner stiffening. The feet are cut from the pattern. The bobble is made of soft white wool, made like the bobble on the tube clown's hat (see page 160), but with the wool wound round about thirty times to make a bigger one. Sew the elastic through the long side of the box and sew the bobble just in front of it. Trim the bobble ends to a round ball.

# 8. A Nativity

A group of seven dolls of different kinds makes up the Nativity scene, the centre of the group being Mary with the Baby in the manager with Joseph watching with her. On one side are the shepherds, one of whom is a boy with a lamb and in contrast on the other side, the three kings, richly dressed, with their gifts.

## Mary

She is a stockinette doll made from the basic template No. 8. She is made up in the same way as the doll on page 20.

*You will need:*
   dark blue linen *for dress:* two pieces, 9 x 8 in.
   white bias binding *for headdress:* 6 in.
   pale blue soft cotton *for cloak:* 18 x 9 in.
   matching thread
   press stud
   red felt *for mouth:* 1 x ½ in.
   black sewing thread *for eyes*

## Features

Cut a deep crescent from the red felt for a mouth and sew it in place. The eyes are closed and are two curves embroidered in fine cotton thread chain stitch with straight stitches radiating from the lower edge, and two arcs of chain stitch above them for brows.

## Dress

Cut two pieces from the pattern, as back and front are alike. Sew the side and shoulder seams. Make small hems on sleeve edges and the bottom of the dress. Cut down from the neck on the back of the dress for 2 in. for an opening. Sew turnings on the opening and round the neck. Fasten it at the back with a press stud.

## Cloak or veil

Make a single fold along one long side of the pale blue cotton and iron it in place. Cut the other long side into a semicircle so that the bottom of it is about 1 in. above the bottom of

the dress. Cut the curved edge with pinking shears. Stretch the white bias binding over the brow of the doll, low on the forehead. Sew the ends in place on the back of the head, low down and catch down the edge of the binding away from the face. Arrange the blue veil over the doll so that the white edging of the bias is just visible. Catch the veil in place from the inside, on each side of the chin and on top of the head.

## Baby

*You will need:*
   2 or 3 pipe cleaners
   stuffing
   muslin: 5 in. square

Fold a pipe cleaner in half and twist a small loop for a head. Twist the pipe cleaner leaving the ends for legs. Put a small ball of stuffing into the head loop, twist the other pipe cleaners round to keep a ball shape and round the body to give some shape, the ends forming arms. Wrap the muslin round the head and body and fasten in place.

## Joseph

He is a wire figure made from pipe cleaner chenille or any firm and workable wire, with a polystyrene ball as a head, and felt hands and feet.

*You will need:*
   wire for head, body and legs: 64 in.
   wire *for arms:* 26 in.
   wire *for extra binds:* two 24 in. lengths
   1½ in. diameter polystyrene ball
   fluffy pile fabric or wadding *for head padding:*
      6 x 3 in.
   dark brown nylon stocking *for face covering*
   dark flesh coloured felt *for hands:* four
      pieces, 1¾ x 1 in.
   black felt *for shoes:* four pieces, 2½ x 1 in.
   scraps of black and red felt *for features*

matching thread
adhesive
coarse calico or linen type fabric *for gown:*
    two pieces, 10½ x 6½ in.
striped cotton or jersey *for coat:* two pieces,
    10 x 9 in.
muslin *for headdress:* 6 in. square
black wool: 12 in.

Make the doll's frame following the directions
given for the basic doll in Chapter 2 (see page
70).

## Hands
Cut out four hands from the pattern (Fig. 211),
reversing the pattern for two of them. Oversew
them in pairs, pull them over the wire hand loops
and sew round their top edges to the wire arms.

## Boots
Cut out four and sew together in pairs. Pull
them over the foot loops and sew the tops of
them to the leg wire.

## Head
Trace round the head padding pattern on to the
wrong side of the fluffy pile fabric and cut out.

*Above: Nativity group*
*Below: Mary, Joseph and Baby*

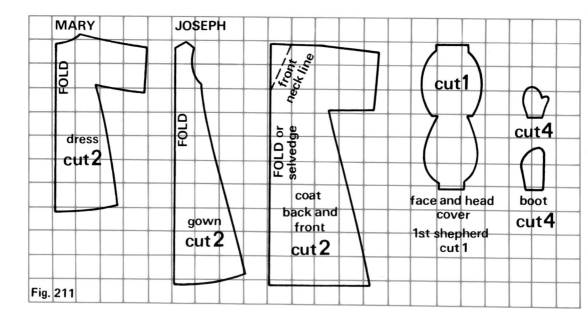

MARY  JOSEPH

FOLD

dress
cut 2

FOLD

gown
cut 2

FOLD or selvedge

front neck line

coat
back and
front
cut 2

cut 1

face and head
cover
1st shepherd
cut 1

cut 4

boot
cut 4

Fig. 211

Pin it over the head to keep the face smooth. Sew the side seams and sew round the neck. Cover it with one or two layers of nylon stocking, keeping the fullness to the back of the head, and the face smooth.

## Features

Cut a small crescent from red felt and two ¼ in. black felt circles for eyes and stick in position.

## Clothes

Cut out the pieces from the patterns as above, allowing extra ¼ in. for turnings.

Sew the side seams of the robe and make a hem at the bottom. Fit the robe on to the doll. Make a single turning on the front shoulder pieces and sew them on to the back shoulders. Make a single turning on the neck and sew it to the doll's neck, over the cut ends of the nylon.

Cut one of the two coat pieces in half from neck to hem for the open fronts. Sew the side seams, under arm and upper arm seams. No hems are necessary if jersey fabric has been used, but if fabric is likely to fray, then make hems on neck, sleeves and bottom.

Cut off two corners from the veil square to make a semicircular shape. Fold under about 1½ in. of the straight edge and arrange this side over the head. Slip a rubber band over the head to hold it in place. Pull the gathers round evenly and sew a cord round the head over the rubber band.

## Shepherd

His basic shape is made in exactly the same way, as Joseph's and his clothes are cut from the same pattern.

*For his clothes, you will need:*
  unbleached calico or linen type fabric *for gown:* two pieces, 10½ x 6½ in.
  grey and black jersey *for coat:* two pieces, 10 x 9 in.
  muslin *for headdress:* 6 in. square
  four or five pipe cleaners *for crook*
  brown felt *for crook:* 12 x ¾ in.

Make the clothes in exactly the same way as Joseph's.

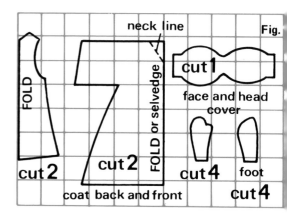

neck line  Fig.

FOLD

FOLD or selvedge

cut 2

cut 2

coat back and front

cut 1

face and head cover

cut 4

foot
cut 4

184

## Crook

Twist the pipe cleaners together to make a 12½ in. strip. Turn back the two ends to make it just less than 12 in. Lay it along the felt strip, fold the felt over it and oversew the long edges together, enclosing the wire. Turn the top over the form the crook.

## The shepherd boy

He is made in the same way as Joseph and the Shepherd, but, as he is a smaller figure, less wire is needed.

*You will need:*
wire *for head, body and legs:* 36 in.
wire *for arms:* 16 in.
wire *for extra bind:* two 16 in. lengths
1 in. polystyrene ball
fluffy pile fabric or wadding: 4 x 1½ in.
dark nylon stocking
dark flesh coloured felt *for hands:* four pieces, 1½ x ¾ in.
dark flesh coloured felt *for feet:* four pieces, 2½ x 1 in.
scraps of red and black felt *for features*
adhesive
matching thread
unbleached calico *for gown:* two pieces, 6 x 4 in.
striped cotton *for coat:* two pieces, 5½ x 7 in.
black or dark brown wool *for hair*

five or six white pipe cleaners *for lamb*
fluffy pile fabric 6 in. square

Make up the basic shape and the clothes as for Joseph, using the smaller version of the pattern, Fig. 212.
Sew small wool loops close together all over his head for hair. They can either be left as loops or can be cut evenly.

## Lamb

With two pipe cleaners make a doll shape, making the head loop extra big so that it can be pinched into shape for ears. Turn the head up at right angles to the body and the arms and legs down the opposite way. Bind the pipe cleaner chenille or more pipe cleaners round the head and body to shape it.

## First King

Measurements given here are for a cardboard tube which is 12 in. long with a diameter of $1\frac{3}{5}$ in. This diameter measurement is the one which determines the width of the pieces used for the dressing.(see page 150).

*You will need:*
tube 12 x $1\frac{3}{5}$ in. diameter
dark flesh coloured felt *for face:* 3 x $5\frac{1}{5}$ in.
dark flesh coloured felt *for hands:* four pieces, 1½ x 1 in.

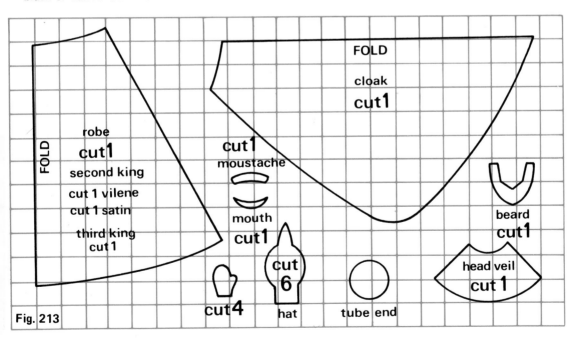

Fig. 213

robe
cut 1
second king
cut 1 vilene
cut 1 satin
third king
cut 1

FOLD
cloak
cut 1

cut 1
moustache
mouth
cut 1

beard
cut 1

head veil
cut 1

cut 4

cut 6
hat

tube end

dark flesh coloured felt: $1\frac{3}{5}$ in. diameter circle
white interlining or stiff cotton *for robe:* 15 x 10½ in.
green satin *for cloak:* 15 x 16½ in.
gold cord: 42 in.
blue felt *for hat:* six pieces, 2 x 2½ in.
yellow satin *for hat band:* 8 x 2½ in.
chiffon or voile *for veil:* 2½ x 6 in.
brown felt *for beard:* 1¾ in. square
brown felt *for moustache:* 1 x ½ in.
brown felt *for eyes:* two ¼ in. circles
white felt *for eyes:* two pieces, $\frac{7}{10}$ x $\frac{3}{10}$ in.
red felt *for mouth:* 1 x ¼ in.
pearls
strip of wadding
gold fringe
kapok
matching thread
adhesive

Trace round all the pattern pieces on to the wrong side of all the fabrics. Reverse the pattern for two of the hands and keep them in pairs. Cut out all the pieces as shown.

*Left above: shepherd and shepherd boy*
*Left below: first king*
*Right below: second king*

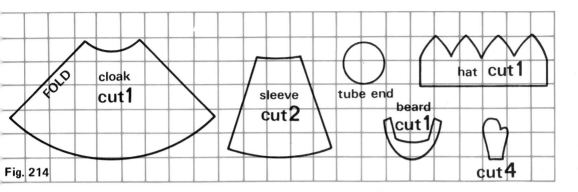

Fig. 214

## Face

Spread adhesive thinly round the top of the tube and again 2¾ in. down from the top. Pin the flesh coloured felt round the top of the tube and sew up the seam at the back. Sew the circle on at the top, oversewing the edges.

## Robe

Fit the narrow part of the robe round the bottom edge of the face felt and pin in place. Stand the tube on a level surface and check that the bottom edges of skirt and tube are both level so that it will stand without tilting. Sew it to the face felt and down the back seam.

## Hat

Join the six hat pieces together along the curved edges by oversewing them. Turn it inside out and press out the seams to make a good curved dome shape. Stuff the curved part very firmly without straining the stitches, pushing little pieces of stuffing gently into the seams to keep a good shape. Fit it on to the head and sew it on all round the edge. Lay a small roll of wadding along the yellow satin strip, in the middle, and fold the two long edges over it. Sew the top edge down. Wind a string of pearls or shiny beads in slanting rows round the satin roll and sew them in place at intervals. Fasten it securely at the ends. Sew the smaller curve of the hat veil along the inside edge of the hat and over this join sew the satin roll with invisible stitches.

## Features

Cut the mouth from red felt and the moustache from brown felt and stick in place. Cut the lower pointed edge of the beard into a fringe and stick to the face so that the beard fits round the mouth curve. For eyes, cut two small circles in brown felt and stick them in the centre of two small almond shapes in white felt. Stick the eyes in place. Embroider the eyebrows or draw with felt tip pens.

## Cloak

Make a very narrow single turning on the *right* side all round the curve of the cloak. Couch down gold cord or similar trimming all round the front and back edges to cover the single turning. Pin the centre back of the cloak neck to the back of the tube, pin round the rest of it and sew in place.

## Sleeves and hands

Sew the hands together in pairs. Make narrow single turnings on one long edge of the sleeve. Fold it in half with the right side inside and sew together the two short edges. Run a gathering stitch along the other long side and draw up the gathers. Place the felt hand inside with its straight edge level with the gathered edge and the thumb towards the fold of the sleeve. Sew the gathered edges together including the hand in the sewing. Turn inside out and pull the gathers in place evenly. It should now look as though the hand is protruding from a full gathered sleeve.

Keeping the other two edges (with turning inside) together, pleat them three times reducing the width to about 1 in. Sew the pleated edge, with the seam at the bottom and the thumb pointing up, to the shoulder of the cloak, taking the stitches right through to the interlining robe to hold it in place more securely. Complete the other sleeve to match.

## Second King

He is also made on a tube.

*You will need:*
   tube: $12 \times \frac{3}{5}$ in.
   brown felt *for face:* $3 \times 5\frac{1}{5}$ in.

187

brown felt *for hands:* four pieces, 1½ x 1 in.
brown felt: 1⅗ in. diameter circle
green felt *for hat:* 5¼ x 1¾ in.
stiff gold cord: 16 in.
soft gold cord: 3 yd.
15 amp fuse wire: 18 in.
orange silk or felt *for hat:* 7 x 3½ in.
orange silk or felt *for sleeves:* two pieces, 4 x 4½ in.
orange silk or chiffon *for cloak:* 14 x 8 in.
interlining or stiff cotton *for robe:* 15 x 10½ in.
red satin *for robe:* 16 x 11 in.
black felt *for beard:* 1½ x 2 in.
black felt *for eyes:* two ¼ in. circles
white felt *for eyes:* two pieces, ⅗ x ⅖ in.
red felt *for mouth:* ¾ x ½ in.
sequins
a jewel
kapok
sewing thread
adhesive

Cut out all pieces as shown. Round off the corners of the white rectangles for eyes, to make an almond shape and stick a black circle in the centre of each. Cut the lower edge of the beard in a fringe. Reverse the pattern when cutting two of the hands and keep them in pairs. Cut the red felt in a crescent shape for the mouth.

## Face
Stick and sew the felt in place as for the first king. Sew on the top circle.

## Hat
Cut the stiff gold cord and the fuse wire into four equal lengths. Insert the fuse wire through the cord, allowing it to protrude at the ends and winding these round the cord to prevent it unravelling. Sew one end of each cord to the wrong side of each hat point. Oversew the curved sides of hat together in twos on the wrong side. Turn it inside out and press the seams flat. Oversew the remaining hat seam and press it out flat. Stuff firmly the rounded dome part of the hat with kapok or similar, and sew it over the top edge of the tube. Make three or four pleats along the length of the orange silk or felt, making the centre of it, for the back of the head 2 in. wide and tapering at each end for

**Fig. 216**

the front to ½ in. or less. The length of the finished band should be sufficient to go round the back of the head, low on the neck, and just meet in the front, over the forehead. Stretch it round the head and sew it in place invisibly round the bottom edge. Fasten the two ends very firmly. Sew on a jewel or ornament at the front to cover the join. Couch soft gold cord in points along the edge of the green top of the hat and finish off by winding the cord two or three times round the edge of the green and couching it down.

## Features
Stick the mouth in place with the beard about ⅛ in. below. Stick the two eyes in position above and draw in thick eyebrows.

### Wired cords

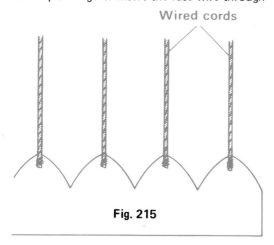

**Fig. 215**

## Robe

Place the neck edges of the interlining and red satin together and pin side seams and bottom edges. The satin should be slightly wider — about $\frac{1}{8}$ in. at the side and $\frac{1}{2}$ in. at the bottom. Turn the side of the satin over on to the interlining and tack in place. Snip the bottom edge

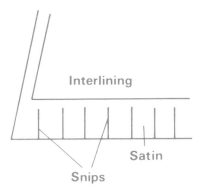

**Fig. 217**

of the satin almost to the edge of the interlining. Turn this cut satin edge over on to the interlining and tack it. Sew both edges down with herringbone stitch, taking care to keep the stitches from showing on the right side. Mark the centre front of the neck of the satin and pin it in place round the edge of the brown felt head. Make sure that the bottom edge of tube and dress are level when standing. Pin the back edge, lapping the hemmed side over the other. Sew round the neck and down the back seam. The doll should now be able to stand on this stiffened robe.

## Sleeves

Oversew the hands in pairs. Fold the sleeve in half and pin a hand at the bottom at the folded edge with the thumb towards the fold. Stab stitch the hand in place. Leave the rest of the cuff open. Join the seam and sew the sleeve in place at the shoulder, with the sleeve pointing forwards and not down. Repeat with the other sleeve. If silk is used for the sleeves, then sew seams on the wrong side and turn inside out. Sew soft gold cord round the cuff and form into little tassels at the seam.

## Cloak

Sew the soft gold cord round the edge of the cloak. Gather the neck edge a little and sew it in place from just in front of the shoulder, along the back to the other side. Sew sequins or an embroidered strip round the neck to cover the join.

## Third King

He is a figure made of wire and can be made to kneel.

*You will need:*
  pipe cleaner chenille *for head, body and legs:* 64 in.
  pipe cleaner chenille *for arms:* 26 in.
  pipe cleaner chenille *for extra bind:* 16 in.
  pipe cleaner chenille *to reinforce legs:* two 24 in. lengths
  1½ in. diameter polystyrene ball
  fluffy pile fabric *for head padding:* 6 x 3 in.
  brownish nylon stocking *for head cover:* two pieces, 6 in. square
  black felt *for moustache and beard:* 1 x 1¾ in.
  black felt *for eyes:* two ¼ in. circles
  white felt *for eyes:* two pieces, $\frac{3}{5}$ x $\frac{3}{10}$ in.
  red felt *for mouth:* ¾ x ¼ in.

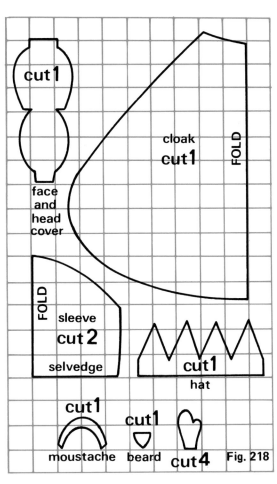

**Fig. 218**

189

*Third king*

---

The wire frame is the basic one for which directions are given in Chapter 2 (see page 70). Twist the head circle to fit tightly over the polystyrene ball. Wind the extra wire round the body and legs tightly to strengthen them.

## Head

One half of the head covering is slightly bigger than the other. Pin this on to half the head, pulling it in place to stretch it over the ball, and to lap over the wire ring, with the straight-sided edge at the neck. Stretch the other half over the ball pinning it at the neck first and then to the first piece, overlapping the edge of it. Sew firmly all round. Keep it quite taut and un-wrinkled. Stretch the nylon pieces over the head, seaming it down the back. Gather up the fullness at the top of the head and sew in place. Sew the lower part to the neck.

## Hat

Oversew the points in twos on the wrong side, turn inside out and press flat. Cut the gold cord into six 3 in. lengths. Cut the fuse wire a little longer. Insert it through the cord till an end of wire protrudes at each end. Twist the ends round the cord to prevent fraying. Repeat for the other five pieces. Mark six equal spaces round the edge of the hat. Fold the cords in half. Place the end of the cord to the edge of the hat at A and sew it in place. Sew the other

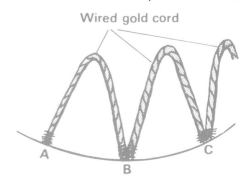

**Wired gold cord**

**Fig. 219**

flesh coloured felt *for hands:* four pieces, 1 x 1½ in.
blue silk *for robe:* 16½ x 11 in.
rose pink silk *for cloak:* 17 x 12 in.
rose pink silk *for sleeves:* two pieces, 7 x 5 in.
white fluffy pile fabric *for cloak trimming:* 42 x ½ in.
white fluffy pile fabric *for sleeves:* two pieces, 16 x ½ in.
white fluffy pile fabric *for hat:* 5⅖ x 2 in.
stiff gold cord *for crown:* 18 in.
15 amp fuse wire *for crown:* 21 in.
gold embroidery *for crown:* 7 x ¾ in.
gold lace: 3 x ½ in.
pink tinsel cord: 16 in.
adhesive
matching thread

The robe is cut from the same pattern as the first king's. The cloak is slightly shorter. In cutting the sleeves, if possible, place the top edge, the one opposite the curved side, to the selvedge. Cut out all the pieces as shown. Keep the hands in pairs.

end of cord to the next mark, B, on the hat edge, so that the folded wire points up in an inverted V. Sew the second wire in the same way, sewing first on the mark B and then on to mark C. Continue with the other four wires so that the second end of the last wire will be sewn on to point A on the hat edge, so completing the circle. Sew the hat to the head. Cover the join with more cord wound round or with suitable sparkling embroidery.

## Features
Cut a crescent of red felt for a mouth and stick it in place fairly low on the face. Stick the drooping moustache in place over the mouth, and drooping down the chin. Stick the beard on to the chin. The eyes are small circles of black felt stuck in the centre of two almond shaped white felt pieces. Stick them in place.

## Robe
Make a small dart in each shoulder of the robe. Under the darts, cut out a small oval for an armhole and neaten the edge. Make a single turning on the bottom edge on the right side and sew a decorative cord along the edge of it. Pin the robe in place round the neck with the opening at the back. Sew round the neck and down the back seam.

Oversew the hands in pairs, leaving the straight edge open. Push the wire hand loops inside them and sew them to the wires with thumbs pointing up.

## Cloak
Make a very narrow single turning on the right side all round the curved edge and tack it with small stitches in matching thread. Sew the strip of white fluffy fabric all the way round the edge over the turning, taking the stitches through the turning only and not letting them show through. The top edge of the trimming need not be stitched. Sew a narrow single turning on the neck edge on the wrong side. Cut two small ovals for armholes 1 in. for the neck edge and 1½ in. in from the front edge. Neaten the edges with a small hem or oversew them. Sew the sleeve seam. Make a very narrow turning on the curved edge on the right side and sew trimmings over these turnings to match the cloak edge. Pin the sleeves to the cloak over the armholes with the seam at the top. Sew them in place.

Sew the cloak on to the doll round the neck. Sew gold lace or sequin embroidery over the join.

## Gifts
*You will need:*
gold top from a wine or spirits bottle
small box covered with gold paper
felt covered shape
pearls, beads, sequins
adhesive

The first King carries gold — a curved gold top from a wine bottle with sequins glued on to it. The second King's frankincense is in a gold casket, made from a small box covered with gold paper. A jewel and pearls is stuck on to it. The kneeling King bears myrrh in a jewelled container made up in felt covered shapes with sequins and pearls stuck on.

191